ALONE

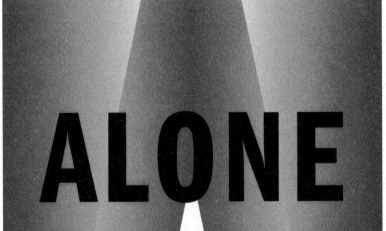

ALONE

BOOK THREE OF THE GENERATIONS TRILOGY

SCOTT SIGLER

DEL REY

NEW YORK

Copyright © 2016 by Scott Sigler

Published in the United States by Del Rey, an imprint of Random House, a division of Penguin Random House LLC, New York.

DEL REY and the HOUSE colophon are registered trademarks of Penguin Random House LLC.

Library of Congress Cataloging-in-Publication Data
Name: Sigler, Scott, author.
Title: Alone / Scott Sigler.
Description: First Edition. | New York : Del Rey, [2017] | Series: The generations trilogy ; 3
Identifiers: LCCN 2016033771 (print) | LCCN 2016040149 (ebook) | ISBN 9780553393194 (hardback) | ISBN 9780553393200 (ebook)
Subjects: | GSAFD: Science fiction.
Classification: LCC PS3619.I4725 A792 2017 (print) | LCC PS3619.I4725 (ebook) | DDC 813/.6—dc23
LC record available at lccn.loc.gov/2016033771

Printed in the United States of America on acid-free paper

randomhousebooks.com

2 4 6 8 9 7 5 3 1

First Edition

Book design by Caroline Cunningham

For Shannon. The world is a bit darker without you in it.

I miss you.

THE BIRTHDAY CHILDREN

Italics=deceased

EM'S GROUP	
◎	B. Aramovsky
○	K. Bello, M. Savage
◑	*K. O'Malley*
✪	*J. Yong*
✿	T. Spingate
⊕	

BISHOP'S GROUP	
◎	
○	R. Cabral, M. D'souza, *J. Harris,* O. Ingolfsson, Y. Johnson, E. Okereke
◑	G. Borjigin, Q. Opkick
✪	Y. Bawden, R. Bishop, *U. Coyotl, T. El-Saffani, T. El-Saffani,* Q. Farrar, *S. Latu, W. Visca*
✿	*G. Beckett,* X. Gaston
⊕	K. Smith

XOLOTL KIDS

◎	B. Walezak
◯	D. Abbink, G. Abrams, W. Alves, R. Andreasson, R. Ansel, A. Aucciello, K. Baardwijk, M. Bardsley, S. Bohner, R. Broz, V. Buffone, H. Chowdhury, A. Csonka, *D. Doyle,* L. Esser, K. Grosser, N. Harman, M. Hoffman, P. Howland, E. Jahoda, K. Jepson, W. Kysely, *E. Lestrange,* U. Marshall, L. Maus, D. McBride, G. Mehmet, R. Pecora, *I. Perreault,* A. Poole, F. Pope, J. Queen, Y. Raske, J. Rigby, T. Romagnoli, D. Roth, M. Savona, A. Schoettmer, I. Sharman, V. Sherazi, E. Simonis, G. Snider, D. Szwarc, Z. Taylor, A. Tittensor, J. Tosetti, I. Tosto, M. Traverso, P. Van Kane, G. Vincent, L. Wieck, *J. York*
◑	*J. Abrantes, T. Aeschelman,* L. Bariso, H. Bemba, N. Derrickson, T. Schuster
✪	V. Abdul, O. Afoyalan, *E. Argyris,* T. Arkema, H. Blaha, C. Boesch, U. Brankovich, K. Brown, P. Bruhn, *W. Cadotte, B. Cody,* I. Darzi, P. Değirmenci, *N. Derrickson,* A. Dreesens, I. Fields, D. Giroux, N. Holub, H. Horn, D. Hornick, P. Horvat, C. Hrabe, M. Krejci, *S. Kysely,* E. Loncar, S. Marija, F. Metharom, V. Metharom, *R. Mohammed,* V. Muller, S. Myska, J. Olson, C. Pokorny, S. Radic, I. Resnik, S. Schovajsa, *J. Thorn,* C. Tosi, A. Uzun, *M. Vendi,* Q. Wakefield, S. Xanth
✿	M. Cathcart, C. Kalle, A. Nevins, N. Peura, B. Zubiri
⊕	L. Pokano, F. Yilmaz

SHUTTLE KIDS

A. Aaltink, P. Abbink, V. Agim, J. Aiolfi, Z. Akinyi, C. Albert, A. Almog,
E. Aloísio, A. Amsel, M. Andrews, Í. Angerona, H. Anima, A. Antónia,
I. Antonizius, C. Anxo, A. Apollodoros, K. Armbruster, J. Asta,
S. Attar, B. Babirye, J. Bartram, K. Benson, V. Bernhard, G. Bjarne,
M. Blanco, X. Bobbi, S. Bohumír, K. Bousaid, O. Boyce, V. Breindel,
B. Bureau, A. Carlota, O. Charmchi, T. Chinwe, T. Church, T. Cindi,
K. Costello, H. Dalibor, C. Danailov, A. Danica, B. Danielle,
X. De Campo, P. De Felippis, R. De Witte, F. Doretea, R. Dykstra,
S. Eadburg, F. Eccleston, H. Einarsson, K. El-Amin, C. Eld, D. Érica,
V. Erikanos, D. Esparza, F. Estera, H. Fabian, C. Fehér, M. Ferrari,
V. Filipov, S. Fortunato, S. Frank, H. Gerben, C. Gilbert, P. Glietezzia,
W. Golanz, D. Grieve, I. Hachilinski, E. Haig, D. Hallman, B. Hanley,
H. Harald, N. Hasenkamp, A. Heimirsson, E. Hinog, L. Höfler,
A. Hornik, A. Hovanesian, L. Iakovu, N. Adoha, T. Iona, I. Jonkheer,
P. Ivanov, M. Jäger, S. Jeffers, A. Jelena, T. Jolánka, J. Joris, C. Júlia,
E. Jurre, T. Juvenal, F. Kamala, A. Kay, K. Klavdiya, E. Kowalcyzk,
M. Lagunov, R. Lan, N. Leary, M. Leblanc, J. Lei, A. Livia, É. Llorenç,
B. Lunete, L. Lyudmyla, A. Machado, S. Machán, N. Malley,
X. Merckx, S. Metharom, Z. Min, H. Min-Jun, C. Miron, S. Morgan,
C. Nauer, M. Nicolson, J. Nikole, N. Nilsson, K. Nogah, T. Oberto,
S. Ochoa, O. Oliver, A. Oluwatoyin, N. Ophelia, Y. Pajari, G. Pandev,
C. Pavia, L. Peak, N. Pemphero, N. Poindexter, A. Potenza,
C. Quintana, J. Rhee, J. Royston, Z. Salut, H. Salvay, W. Scarpa,
K. Schlusser, H. Schwenke, D. Shemaiah, A. Shepherd, K. Siet,
A. Sigurosson, E. Skye, A. Sniegowski, P. Spini, G. Stabile, N. Taalay,
E. Tabitha, J. Tawfeek, M. Tesar, S. Uidhir, E. Vaccaro, S. Van Der
Beek, O. Vanev, B. Vasilyev, Y. Vibius, L. Vincent, C. Wasylyna,
D. Weekes, R. Williams, S. Winona, K. Yancy, C. Yazhu, Y. Yeriyahu,
J. Zénaïde, B. Zheng, J. Zinat, T. Zola, P. Zuleika

PART I

HOME AND HEARTH

ONE

A stabbing pain jolts me awake.

My neck . . . the needle, the *snake* . . .

No, not a stab. A poke . . . a poke of cold metal. I lift my head, look around. My silver bracelet. I wear it over the sleeve of my black coveralls, its wide ring circling my right forearm just below my elbow—I must have rolled over in my sleep, laid my neck on the long point that extends from the flat ring down to just behind the back of my wrist.

I'm cold. I'm wet. It's raining again. Correction: it's raining *still*. I was sleeping on the tiny metal deck of a spider cockpit, other people crammed in around me. My thigh is numb—I rolled over onto the combat knife I always have strapped to my leg.

So tired. As uncomfortable as I am, I just want to go back to sleep.

A boy's voice: "Em, wake up."

Victor Muller, part of my spider's three-person crew.

"D'souza spotted them," he says. "She's coming."

That wakes me up for real. If Maria is coming, maybe it's time to fight.

Finally.

I sit up. Muscles, cramped and stiff. My cold skin feels like it's made of half-dry clay. Our black coveralls are good at keeping us warm, but in the jungle the dampness always finds a way in.

Ten days of this. Ten days of hiding, without fire or heat, without a hot meal, eating prepackaged food and raw jungle plants. Ten days since I bathed—I want a shower almost as much as I want to catch the Belligerents. I want to lie on my couch, Bishop's arms around me as I watch the jungle from afar, not from within it.

I miss him. I miss his eyes, his hair and his smile. I miss the very smell of him. If we're able to force our enemy to battle— and that is a very big *if*—I might be hurt in the fighting. Possibly even killed. Before I left, he told me he loves me.

Did I tell him the same thing?

I think I did. Yes, I must have.

You would have told O'Malley, and you know it.

Well, hello, Annoying Little Voice. How nice of you to show up now.

Annoying Little Voice always wants me to second-guess my-self, to doubt my decisions. It always seems to think things would be better *now* if they'd gone a different way *then*. If I'd made different choices. If I'd had stronger self-control. I hate that damn voice.

Wiping the last of the sleep from my eyes, I reach up and grab the armored ridge that surrounds the cockpit. I stand, slowly, careful to not jostle the branches that hide our position.

The twin moons of Omeyocan—one bluish, one maroon— shine through sparse cloud cover. In the daytime, this jungle is bright with yellow leaves, brown tree trunks and long blue vine stems. At night, everything is a blue-purple shade of gray. The plants gleam with wetness.

Spingate still insists on calling our machines "pentapods," but no one listens to her about that. To us, they are *spiders*. Five-legged, yes, but spiders all the same. The machines are meant for a two-person crew: driver and cannon operator. We use them with crews of three, adding one person who can fire with whatever weapon they have at hand. Three makes for close quarters. The cockpit is open-air. No glowing holograms here—all the controls are manual, built to last a thousand years, to take a real beating and keep on working. A waist-high, horseshoe-shaped armored ridge surrounds the cockpit, protects us from bullets and musket balls. The ends of the horseshoe blend into the cockpit's rear wall, which comes up to my sternum. If I stand straight, I can rest my arms on the spider's sloping back and fire my bracelet at whatever is behind us.

We've repainted the spiders to cover up centuries of superficial damage. Each one has black numbers on the sides (ours is 05), while most of the shell is dark yellow with jagged stripes of brown and blue—the colors of the jungle. When the machines work correctly, they blend in well. Of course, they're all a couple of centuries old, so they don't work correctly all that much. Parts often clatter and gears frequently grind, making unmistakable noise. We do our best to fix those problems when they come up.

There are two legs in front, two on the sides—one each below where the armored ridge blends into the back wall—and one leg in the rear. The three-jointed legs all end in hard, sharp points, which can slice right through any enemy unfortunate enough to be in our way.

I ride in the cockpit's right side. Yoshiko Bawden, the driver, is on my left, in the middle. She's a tall, muscular circle-star who thinks it's funny to make fake burp sounds. When she's not being crude, though, she is a fierce warrior. She's always kept her black hair shaved down. Before we began this campaign, she had some of her fellow circle-stars tattoo the word KILLER on the right side of her head. She has a pitchfork strapped across her back and a bracelet on her right arm over her coveralls. She used to use an axe, like Bishop does, but she prefers the pitchfork for jungle fighting. I have known her almost since I first woke up. I'm so grateful to have her as part of my crew.

"Little" Victor Muller is on Bawden's left, where he mans the beam-cannon. He's not little anymore, though. When the circle-star came out of his coffin, I was a bit taller than he was. Now my eyes come up to his chin. He's added muscle as well. He's not as thick as Bishop, probably never will be. Victor has the same wiry frame my friend Coyotl had—long, lean, athletic. Victor wears a bracelet on his right arm. In his hands, he holds a spear. Not *my* spear, of course, but one that looks close to it. A repeating rifle is slung over his back, black barrel and the black loop lever that lets him reload it with a flick of his hand gleaming from a recent cleaning and oiling. Victor has become one of our best warriors, almost as skilled as Farrar, Bishop and Bawden, who are all fully grown.

I am brave enough to fight, but I'm not stupid—I want people in my crew who can protect me. I'd rather have Bishop instead of Victor, of course, but right now it's more important to our people that Bishop remains back in Uchmal.

The lower half of our spider is buried in the jungle floor, the upper half covered in branches and vines. Sometimes you hunt your enemy—but only if you can find them. When you can't, your best bet is to set a trap and hope your enemy falls into it.

It looks like they finally have.

A light rustling from the jungle in front of us. I see what looks like a thick, yellowish snake rise from the underbrush and move toward us. The furry snake ends in wicked, hooked pincers that can snap together so hard they'll damn near cut a person in two.

A few meters away, the full animal rises up from the underbrush. A year ago, the sight of this predator would have scared me half to death. Now? It only scares me a quarter of the way.

When I first saw these creatures, I didn't have the memories or words to describe them. It's still hard. Different people have remembered different things at different times, filling my head with images of animals that Matilda only read about in books. The heavy body of a bear. The thick trunk of an elephant. Below where the trunk connects to the head is a piranha's dagger-toothed mouth. Claws of a tiger. All of it covered in brown-striped yellow fur. Heavy plates of mottled yellow bone on its chest. Three beady black eyes in a line on each side of the head, which is also plated in yellow bone.

On the back of this beast, on a saddle made of tough leather, sits Maria D'souza, a fellow "empty."

She took to calling the big predators *hurukans*. We're not sure where that word comes from, but as soon as any of us heard it, we agreed it was the perfect name.

"Hail, Em," Maria says. *"Guthana, Yalani."*

Maria greets me first in English, then in the Springer language. She always wants the Springer fighters in her squad to know I am in charge—*Yalani* means "leader."

"Hail, Maria," I say. "You've found them?"

She nods. "The Belligerents are coming from the east, closing in on the cornfield. I have the Creepers circling behind them to cut off any escape. Barkah and his infantry battalion are positioned to the north as a reserve, per your orders."

Cornfield sounds a bit grand for our sickly crop, but we have invested countless hours getting it to grow.

"How many Belligerents?" I ask.

"Maybe a hundred," Maria says. "All on foot. No cavalry of any kind."

"Excellent. Where do you want us?"

Maria points north.

"Straight ahead, *Yalani*. My squad will attack from the southwest. When you strike, we'll be on your left flank."

Atop the 650-kilo hurukan she calls Fenrir, Maria is a striking figure. She wears cloth strips of yellow, green and blue, just like the Springer warriors. Vine juice and dirt cover her brown skin, helping her blend into the jungle. She has a half-dozen knives strapped to her body and a repeating rifle slung across her back. When the violence began months ago, I offered her one of our precious bracelets. She declined. She chooses to use the same weapon as the Springers in her cavalry squads.

The snake-wolves are the top predators of this world. As far as we can tell, they kill and eat everything they see. That included the Springers. Then came Maria, who somehow learned how to not only capture the beasts, but *tame* them as well. She's trained others to do the same.

Mounted atop her monster, Maria D'souza has become a death goddess of the jungle. She has killed more enemy soldiers than anyone. Except for Farrar, of course, but that's why we used him as bait.

We used to think Barkah controlled all the Springers on Omeyocan. We were wrong. There are four main tribes that we know of. Barkah's tribe, the Malbinti, claims the areas around Uchmal. The Khochin are far to the south of our city. The Podakra are just a day's ride to the west. The largest tribe of all, the Galanak, fill the jungle to the northeast.

"Belligerents" is what we've come to call the Springers that attack us at every turn. We haven't taken any alive yet, but based on the clothing of those we killed in battle they have members from all four known tribes, *including* the Malbinti. Barkah doesn't know why some of his people joined them.

The Belligerents don't have uniforms, but they do have one unifying element. In addition to the jungle rags of blue, yellow and green, they all wear at least one bit of red.

Red—the same color as the robes Aramovsky wore, as the robes in the carvings on the Observatory.

In the past few months, the Belligerents have been burning our crops, attacking us when we go outside the walls. Whatever their reasons, the Belligerents are aggressive and trying to kill my people.

I can't allow that to continue.

"Get into position," I say to Maria. "We attack immediately."

Maria and Fenrir vanish into the jungle with barely a sound. How something that big can move so quietly, I have no idea.

"Finally," Bawden says. "Those bug-eyed bastards can't escape this time."

I give her a short glance. Bawden was close with J. York, a circle boy who was killed by Belligerents a few months ago. Bawden wants revenge. Too many of my people want revenge.

"Our allies are also *bug-eyed bastards*," I say. "Do you forget that? Or do you want to cuss at the people who are fighting on our side?"

Bawden answers with only a belch, which makes Victor laugh.

I'll never understand circle-stars.

"Clear away the brush," I say. "We go now."

Victor and Bawden toss aside our cover of branches. My spear is held by a bracket mounted on the cockpit's rear wall. I yank the spear free, then raise it high and circle it in the air—the signal for my platoon to move out. Branches rustle around us as two other spider crews clear them away and prepare to leave. A dozen young circle-stars silently rise up from hidden places in the underbrush. They wear black coveralls, like me, but are wrapped in vines, their faces and hair smeared with dark mud. They make ready to march, make ready to fight.

Including me, my platoon has twenty-one humans: nine on spiderback, twelve on foot. Maria's squad—"D'souza's Demons"—has three snake-wolves and their riders, along with eighteen Springers on foot. Squad Two—called "the Creepers" and led by Lahfah, Barkah's mate—has the same numbers as D'souza's Demons. That means we'll attack with a combination of sixty-three troops, three spiders and six snake-wolves. We're slightly outnumbered, but technology is on our side. And in reserve, we have two hundred Springers led by Barkah himself. I almost feel sorry for the Belligerents we're about to attack.

Almost.

"Bawden, lead us out."

She does. Our spider rises up, the cockpit now four meters above the jungle floor. Mud drips down from the dented yellow shell and the black *05* painted on either side.

We march to battle.

The Belligerents like to hit and run. They never fight in the open. When they started attacking our people, our crops, Barkah's patrols and his new city of Schechak, we would ride our spiders out from Uchmal to fight them. But as fast as the spiders are, by the time we reached the conflict the Belligerents had already melted into the jungle, leaving bodies and carnage behind.

Just over a year ago, Aramovsky led our people to war with Barkah's father, the former Springer king. The battle was brief but bloody. Barkah and I brought our two peoples together. We made peace. While some hatred and distrust remained between our two races, we worked hard to coexist, to learn from each other so that both cultures could flourish and grow.

Other than a few scuffles, there was little trouble.

But six months ago, that started to change.

Barkah's people started to confront us. Verbally at first, then arguments turned to fistfights. Then knife fights. My people—and Barkah's—started getting hurt. Barkah and I both punished the aggressors, trying to set an example that hate would not be tolerated.

It's not just the Springers who are changing. My people have grown steadily angrier. More vocal about making Uchmal "human-only," about driving *all* Springers out of the jungle around our city. Whenever I hear this talk, I shut it down—as do Bishop, Borjigin and many others—but these hateful feelings are gaining momentum.

We initially blamed our own increased hostility on the stress and anxiety caused by three starships closing in on Omeyocan. The first of those will reach orbit any day now, Spingate tells me. We don't know what these aliens want. We don't know where they came from. We have to assume they're coming to kill us, bringing death just as our *Xolotl* brought death to the Springers.

Now, however, I don't think the approaching starships are the reason for these troubles. As a people, our attitudes have shifted too far, too fast—and the presence of those ships wouldn't explain why the Springers have become more violent. I'm at a loss to explain what is happening to all of us.

Before the Birthday Children arrived, all Springers lived underground. It was the only way they survived the endless attacks of roaming spiders, machines still following commands given to them centuries ago. Since Barkah and I made peace—and since I stopped the spiders from ravaging the countryside—most of his tribe now lives in Schechak, the first aboveground city his species has had in at least two hundred years.

As more Springers move into that city, they have abandoned the underground villages and endless tunnels surrounding Uchmal. The Belligerents have made good use of these hidey-holes. Once the terrorists are out of sight, it's nearly impossible to find them again.

That's why we had to stay hidden for days, suffering through the pouring rain, freezing our butts off—so we could catch them aboveground. We have to hit them with force before they can slither beneath the surface like the worms they are.

It frustrates me to no end that we spend so much time trying to defeat the Belligerents. Three alien ships are coming to Omeyocan, which means the beings already on this planet should be working together to create a common defense. But instead, we fight among ourselves. Diplomacy is complicated; fighting is simple. I guiltily admit to myself that part of me—a *big* part—is excited this battle has come. Maybe we can eliminate our enemy, then Barkah and I can concentrate our energies on the larger threat yet to come.

The Annoying Little Voice creeps up again: *It's too late for that. If you were a better leader, you'd have unified everyone already.* I smile to myself as I put that voice in its place, lock it into the shadowy back room of my mind—something I seem to be able to do only when it's time to fight.

Bawden guides our spider through the jungle. Behind us are two more spiders and a dozen tireless young circle-stars armed with bracelets, rifles and their handheld weapon of choice. Somewhere off to my left, D'souza's Demons are moving in as well.

I smell smoke: our corn crop, burning.

The Belligerents have eluded me for months, but now they've taken the bait.

We have them.

I rotate my right hand sharply left, then right, the hard twitch that activates my bracelet. I feel a vibration as the weapon powers up. The white stone at the base of its long point starts to glow with a soft light.

"Bawden, keep moving forward, quietly," I say. "Victor, get ready, see if we can take out their lookouts before they sound a warning."

I didn't think the corn crop was enough bait by itself, so I ordered Farrar to build a small outpost right in the middle of the field. The presence of the outpost means that the Belligerents have to bring a larger force if they want to destroy it. But the outpost isn't the real bait—Farrar is.

Among Barkah's tribe and the Belligerents both, Farrar has come to be known as *meh ahn nahak.* Loosely translated, it means "the digger of graves." Many jungle battles result in hand-to-hand combat, where Farrar is deadly with his preferred weapon—a long-handled shovel sharpened to a razor's edge. He's almost as big as Bishop, and his skin is nearly as black as that of the Grownups. Even from a distance, Farrar is an instantly recognizable figure. I had hoped his presence might be too much for our enemy to resist.

That meant, though, putting him and his squad of five young circle-stars in significant danger. This is war, and those are the chances a leader has to take to catch an enemy that refuses to stand and fight. Now that the trap has been sprung, all Farrar and his squad have to do is hunker down and survive the next few minutes.

Our spider quietly steps through the underbrush, a stalking

predator worthy of its namesake. Victor rolls out his neck, loosening up for the coming battle. He unslings his rifle, raises the stock to his shoulder and scans the jungle. His bracelet is a more powerful weapon, but he can fire eight rifle rounds in the time it takes the bracelet to recharge for a second shot.

The rifles are made in Schechak's new factories. At first, the Springers used muskets against us. Muskets have to be reloaded after every shot, while the more accurate rifles can fire ten times before reloading. Victor is probably our best marksman, although Maria is close—she can hit a bull's-eye from fifty meters away while the hurukan beneath her tears through the jungle at a full gallop.

Me? I'll stick with the bracelet. Rifles kick too much. They hurt my shoulder.

"Coming up on the clearing," Bawden says.

I raise my spear, point it right, then left, telling the trailing spiders to fan out. Spider 04 goes right, 02 goes left.

The crescent-shaped clearing. The same place where Aramovsky led my people against the Springers. That battle created too many corpses on both sides for us to completely forgive each other. That's why I chose the clearing as a site to grow crops. I hoped that if we could turn a place of death into a cradle of life, the memories of that battle might fade a bit faster. It seemed to work for those first six months. Now the Belligerents constantly attack our crops. They don't want the field of death to grow over—*hate* is the only crop they want to harvest.

Filtering through the jungle, I hear the unmistakable sounds of war. Rifle fire, echoing musket reports, the telltale hiss of bracelet beams lashing out.

The battle has begun.

"Bawden," I say, "take us to full speed!"

I grip the armored ridge with one hand. We lurch forward,

the need for silence forgotten. I duck down to avoid the branches and snagging vines that slap against the metal shell. The two flanking spiders will match our speed. We'll pull ahead of our foot soldiers, but I don't have a choice—if we don't close quickly, the Belligerents could either escape or overrun Farrar and his squad.

Through the dark jungle, I see the bright glow of flames. Our spider bursts from the trees and into the clearing. Our carefully tended field of corn is a sea of writhing orange.

We've surprised several Belligerents. At the sight of our powerful machines, they flee, flames silhouetting their graceful movements. Strong legs launch the Springers in powerful leaps, long tails trailing behind to balance out their thick bodies. Firelight reflects off their three eyes. Wide toad-mouths bark out what might be commands, might be screams of panic.

Victor slings his rifle and grasps the cannon controls. I wish we didn't have to use this horrible weapon, but the Belligerents are destroying our crops, attacking us, *killing* us.

I duck down, so that only my head and shoulders are above the protective ridge. I straighten my bracelet arm, find a target, and give the order.

"Fire!"

I flick my fingers forward. A beam of white light lances out from my bracelet's long point, ripping toward the closest Belligerent—I miss.

Victor does not. The cannon's beam is larger than mine, glows so bright it seems to dim the flames. The beam hits a leaping Springer, blasting the living creature into a hundred bits of smoking meat and bone.

Beam-cannon fire lashes out from my left and right, tearing up thick chunks of dirt. Flaming corn spins away in pinwheeling clouds of sparks.

I hear the terrified, pain-filled screams of our enemy.

But I also hear muskets boom and rifles crack, see cones of flame flicking from the dark, there one second, then gone the next. One of those cones flares up just to my right: I pivot in place, as Bishop showed me, squaring my shoulders toward the target. At first I see nothing but smoke and flame, then movement, a hopping Springer silhouetted against burning corn.

I fire.

White light catches the Springer in midair. Over the roar of the flames and the bursts of weapons fire, I hear it shriek in the split second before it is torn in half.

This is not the first time I've killed.

It won't be the last.

The few Belligerents we can see realize they are cut off from the jungle. They scatter along the edge of the flames, rushing to my left. Big mistake. I hear the growling howls of snake-wolves, then D'souza's Demons rip from the darkness and into the flickering light. She stands in her saddle, rifle tight to her shoulder, her knees bending in time with her mount's galloping stride. She fires: I see a Springer go down.

Her mount overruns a fleeing Belligerent. The snake trunk snaps forward. Pincers slam shut on the poor creature, bony points punching through cloth and flesh. The trunk curls up, raising the Springer high before whipping it down so fast that bones shatter on impact.

Bawden slows our spider. We stop at the edge of the blazing corn crop. I see narrow paths through the flames. The Belligerents cleared space before they set the fires, giving themselves a way to escape where our cavalry could not follow. Smart. But this time, we are smarter.

Far off to my right, I hear rifle fire and hurukan roars echoing over the flames.

"Lahfah's Creepers," Victor says. "The Belligerents must have fled and run right into them."

Bawden unslings her rifle, sights down the barrel and slowly turns left, then right, looking for a target.

"Bastards," she says. "I hope they all die. Em, some of them could be hiding in the flames. Let me go into those paths and root them out."

I don't want any more death if it can be avoided.

"Stay in the spider," I say. "If we see any Belligerents, try to capture them. A prisoner is more valuable than a corpse."

From the north, we hear distant rifle cracks. That's Barkah's battalion. The Belligerents fled in all directions, and in all directions we were waiting for them.

Our corn burns. There's no putting out this fire. It would have been better to catch the Belligerents before they set this blaze, but the large crop was part of the bait. When you want something bad enough in life, you have to make sacrifices to get it.

"Movement," Victor says as he swings the cannon to bear.

I look, see a Springer hop out from the fire. Its jungle rags are smoldering; its three yellow eyes are wide with fear. Its skin is mostly red—it is so young the purple coloration that marks a teenager has barely begun to set in. A child soldier. But a strip of red cloth tied around each arm tells me this "child" is our enemy.

"Hold your fire," I snap at Victor. To the Springer, I shout: "*Gaintox!*"

I know very little of the Springer language, but I made sure I learned their word for "surrender."

The Springer panics, rushes back into the burning cornfield, instantly vanishing behind shimmering flames.

"*I'll kill it,*" Bawden shouts as she leaps over the ledge.

I instinctively reach out to grab her, to stop her, but my fingers clutch only empty air.

Victor tilts the spider cannon up, a reaction to keep from accidentally shooting the circle-star woman who hits the ground running. In an instant, he's over the ridge and chasing her, rifle slung, both hands on his spear.

The circle-stars move so fast I feel like I'm in slow motion. Spear in one hand, I swing over the rail, then descend the built-in ladder rungs. Circle-stars can leap out of the cockpit and not kill themselves, but I'm not engineered for war like they are.

I hear shouts from the other spider crews, and from the circle-star infantry behind me that is finally reaching the clearing, yet there is no time to wait.

What is Bawden doing? She's never disobeyed an order before. This isn't like her at all.

I rush into the flames after my people. The narrow path twists and turns through the tall burning corn—I'm instantly lost in a maze of fire. Heat bakes my face and hands, stings my eyes.

Through the shimmering haze, I see Bawden in a small open space where the fire has mostly burned down. She's smiling, pitchfork in hand as she and the yellow-eyed Springer child soldier circle each other, each step kicking up fresh ash. The Belligerent holds a hatchet in its two-fingered hand. Bawden is at least twice as large as her terrified foe.

From another path, two more Belligerents rush in, the rags tied around their bodies smoldering with small flames. They hold muskets tipped with long bayonets—the sharp metal shimmers with reflected firelight. The hammers of their muskets are not cocked back; the weapons are empty. The Springers are either out of ammo or haven't had time to reload.

I aim my bracelet, but don't shoot. My eyes are watering and the heat makes everything shimmer madly—I might hit Bawden. I sprint toward her.

Outnumbered three to one, Bawden attacks. She roars, jabs

with the pitchfork. The young Springer flinches in terror, turns away—the sharp pitchfork tines plunge into its back. Before she can pull it free, the second Springer's bayonet pierces her shoulder. Bawden screams in pain, but grabs the musket barrel—she and her foe struggle for the weapon.

Just as I enter the small space, the third Springer comes straight at me, long hopping steps closing the distance. I raise my arm and flick my fingers. A beam of white light shoots out . . .

. . . and *misses*.

The Springer ducked down and to the left.

The bracelet needs a moment to recharge, something the Springer seems to know.

"*Yalani, nahnaw,*" it growls: *Kill their leader.*

It recognizes me.

My enemy lunges forward, bayonet point driving at my belly. I sidestep, sweeping the spear in front of me, knocking the musket aside.

Everything happens so fast. I have a moment to strike, but I hesitate and that moment vanishes. The Springer's wide mouth curls into a very humanlike, hateful snarl.

Bawden screams again. A snap-glance: the second Springer's bayonet is buried in her thigh.

We are all so close together, two humans and three Springers, walled in by a circle of flame, locked in a fight to the death.

The burning corn seems to blast apart—Victor bursts into view, startling all of us. Flaming cinders and sparks cling to his black coveralls. A vision of fire and rage, he steps forward and thrusts his spear—the blade punches deep into the guts of Bawden's attacker. Without a pause he yanks the weapon free and stabs it home again.

A flicker of movement in the corner of my eye is the only

warning I get, but it is enough. My attacker thrusts again, driving the bayonet at my face. I flinch and turn: the point slashes my cheek.

Then Victor is there, closing the short distance with two fast steps. The Belligerent turns to face him, but three eyes take in Victor's bracelet point, aimed right at the wide mouth.

"*Gaintox,*" Victor says, loud but calm. His stare is steel. His arm and fist are rock-still.

The Springer tosses the musket aside, then kneels in the ash.

The small child soldier, the red-skinned one, lies still, eyes wide open and unmoving. It's dead. The third rolls in the dirt, hands on its belly, thick fingers smeared with blue blood. I wish I couldn't hear its wail of pain and fear, but there is no shutting that out.

The fires are fading fast. Tall young corn quickly becomes ankle-high embers.

I hear no more gunfire.

This fight is over.

TWO

Morning dawns on Omeyocan. Blurds buzz through air that smells of wetness and mud.

My spider marches on.

Victor drives. Bawden lies on the small deck at our feet, asleep. We stabilized her wounds. Her injuries are bad, but not life-threatening—she'll be all right once we get her into Smith's medical coffins.

We have a guest crammed into the cockpit with us: none other than Barkah, the Springer king. He's on my left, pressed in between me and Bawden. I smell the burned-toast scent that has become so common I almost never notice it unless I'm very near a member of his species.

Gone are the jungle-colored rags he wore when we first met. His orange jacket is smooth and wrinkle-free, dotted with intricate patterns of colored glass. I think the orange clashes with his reddish-purple skin, but we've found that Springers' taste in fashion is far different from ours.

Barkah lost his middle eye in our fight with Matilda and her Grownups. He wears a patch over it: orange, made from the same fabric as his coat. The two eyes that remain are a pretty shade of emerald green.

An intricate copper plate hangs from his thick neck. The Springer equivalent of a crown, it marks him as royalty. The polished metal gleams in the reddish morning sun. *Everything* about Barkah now seems polished. He is so different from when I first met him in the jungle.

This road, too, is different from when I first saw it. It was a footpath through the trees and vines, so narrow you felt leaves brush against you on both sides. Now it is wide, cleared of plants. The surface is an uneven mishmash of dirt, stone, gravel and flat bits of broken buildings. While it is a far cry from the highways of Matilda's memories, this is the greatest road Omeyocan's jungle has seen in at least two centuries.

Trees rise up on either side, as do the shattered, vine-covered buildings of the once-massive Springer city. The ruins are vast. No matter how much progress we make, they will be here for centuries to come.

My spider marches in a long column made up of the two other spiders in my platoon, our circle-star infantry, D'souza's snake-wolves, and Farrar's squad, which has a place of honor directly behind Barkah and me. A few of Farrar's circle-stars suffered wounds when the Belligerents attacked, but our trap closed so quickly that they didn't have to fight for long.

Shockingly, we didn't lose a single person. Luck? Superior tactics? Superior weapons? I don't really care which, I'm just happy that we don't have to dig yet another grave.

Barkah's foot soldiers march with us as well, two long lines that flank the fifteen Belligerents who survived the battle. Each prisoner wears one of those telltale strips of red cloth some-where on its body. Most of the prisoners are wounded.

I glance at Victor. His face and hands are dotted with burns. Our coveralls are flameproof—another legacy left by the Grownups—but there was no protection for his exposed skin. Some of the dirty-blond hair on the right side of his head is gone, replaced by a red and black burn. It looks painful. If it is, Victor shows no sign.

He fought flawlessly. Fast and efficient, no wasted movement. He killed one Springer, yes, but took a prisoner, as I requested. Not only can he fight, he follows orders. Unlike Bawden. She ignored my commands, almost got herself killed, almost got *me* killed. It's just not like her.

I'll let Bishop figure out what to do about her actions. He's in charge of our "military," what little of it there is.

Bishop. I haven't seen him in over a week. I can't wait to see him again.

Victor notices me looking his way.

He smiles. "You were amazing, Em."

I laugh. "Me? You should have seen yourself."

"You were in danger," he says. "I'd do anything to protect you. Anything."

To protect me, Bawden . . . everyone, probably. Victor is a circle-star, born to defend us all.

"Are you excited to see Zubiri?" I ask. "It's been ten days since you two were together."

He shrugs, looks forward. "I suppose. She's nice, but I think I enjoyed being in the jungle with you more."

Maybe he's still excited from the battle. I've seen the way Victor and Zubiri adore each other. Once the thrill of the fight has worn off, I know he'll be ready to spend some time with her.

But the love lives of my people aren't important at the moment. We fought, we won, and now I need to focus on bigger issues.

I turn to Barkah. "I'll ask you again—what's going to happen to the captured Belligerents?"

He snorts, indicating his disgust. The Springers have some very humanlike mannerisms. Or is it that we humans have Springer-like mannerisms?

"They traitors," he says. *"They earn punish."*

A Springer's wide mouth and thick throat can make more sounds than we can. Chirps and clicks, growls and glassy tones, as well as most of the noises that go into our human words. When Barkah addresses a crowd, his words boom with volume and power. But when he speaks one-on-one, his voice sounds coarse, like spilled gravel.

Barkah has learned English at a frightening pace. Even though he doesn't have all the words right and has trouble forming sentences, he can carry on full conversations. His grammar is off, but I understand his tone—when he says the word "punish," he's *excited*.

"If you kill them, we won't know if there are more," I say. "Or where they're hiding."

Barkah laughs, a sound that always reminds me of a boot heel grinding broken glass against stone.

"What they know, I know. They talk." He frowns, knowing he missed a word. He glances at me. *"They* will *talk."*

We ride on in silence.

Barkah has changed. A year ago he tricked me. His friendship was a ruse, a way for him to kill his father and become king. I knew then to never trust Barkah. I still don't, but he's proven to be a good leader for his people. He led them above-

ground. He ordered this new city to be built. When he negoti-
ated with me about human-Springer relations, he was always
firm, but fair.

Then the fighting between our peoples flared up again.

Since the Belligerents started attacking, I feel like Barkah has
become . . . *meaner.* I suspect the biggest reason we haven't
taken prisoners so far is because his troops are merciless. Maybe
even cruel.

I don't know what is going to happen to these captured Belligerents. Nothing good, I am sure. I want to take them back
with me, put them in the Observatory's prison cells. There, at
least, they would be fed and we could heal their wounds.

But that choice isn't mine to make.

I've already tried to pressure Barkah into turning the prisoners over to us. That made him angry. *Very* angry. Right now our
two species are cooperating. At least the ones under his control
are. If he was to turn his people against us, join with the remaining Belligerents—or even other tribes—and attack Uchmal?
We'd be outnumbered at least a thousand to one.

I don't dare risk our uneasy truce. When it comes to the
Springers, what Barkah wants, Barkah gets.

We are entering the small Springer city. Barkah hops up on
the spider's back, waves Lahfah forward to join us. He is the
king and, even though she lives in Uchmal with us, she is his
queen—he wants his people in the city to see the royal couple
arrive together.

A hurukan trots up beside us, Lahfah atop it. Even though we
fought together, she's been deep in the jungle with her platoon
and hasn't talked to me in days. When our eyes meet, she lets out
an oh-so-familiar bellowing laugh that sounds like the tinkling
of broken glass.

I killed a living, thinking being only a few hours ago. We buried eighty-three enemy bodies. One of my own almost died. Those things hang heavy on my heart, to be sure, but to lay eyes on my friend makes me all smiles.

"*Hem,*" Lahfah says. She is as delighted to see me as I am to see her. "*Face good?*"

"I am fine. Thank you for asking, Lahfah."

Lahfah has trouble understanding the difference between the words *you* and *face*. They seem to mean the same thing to her.

She tried to greet me in my language. I try to do the same for her.

"*Nin yawap tallik ginj?*"

Lahfah screams with delight. Looks like I said it right for once. How about that? It's only taken me a year to learn how to say the equivalent of "Do you feel well?" Barkah can converse with any of my people, while the best I can do is manage a few pleasantries with his.

Barkah barks a single, harsh syllable. Lahfah stops laughing. She's obeying his command, but doesn't look the least bit upset at his tone. She's used to it. In that way, their relationship reminds me of the way Spingate treats Gaston.

Part of what makes Barkah an effective leader is knowing what looks impressive. Coming into the city after a successful battle, with prisoners in tow, riding side by side with the human leader on a human war machine? For Springers, it's hard to get more impressive than that.

That's why he insisted my troops ride with him into Schechak. He's the king, but not *everyone's* king. The Belligerents are proof of that. Some of his own subjects are among the Belligerent dead and captured.

The wide road we're on runs through Schechak and then straight on to Uchmal. Such a contrast between the two cities.

Uchmal's vine-covered walls rise high, an intimidating message of strength and accomplishment. In comparison, the Springer city seems like little more than an overpopulated frontier town.

Some of Schechak's six-sided buildings are new, made from rocks and chunks of ancient buildings mortared together with concrete and even dried mud. Most buildings, though, are repaired ruins. Every building is topped with a pointed, six-sided thatch roof woven from the blue stems of jungle vines. The smaller buildings are houses or shops. Larger buildings have brick smokestacks rising up from the sides. These are the Springers' new factories, where they weave fabric, cut cloth, forge metal, hammer out tools and weapons or process food.

A year ago, the land that is now Schechak was nothing more than ancient ruins. Springers continue to migrate here from all across Omeyocan. Borjigin tells me that Schechak's current population is already over five thousand. In another year, how many Springers will live here, only a short march from our own city gate?

The wide road leads through the city. Springers are gathered on either side, packed in deep. They cheer, a crazy yell that sounds a bit too much like Matilda's memories of croaking toads. Springers lean from the windows of the six-sided brown buildings. Many sit on the blue roofs. All welcome their victorious king back from battle. Music blares, several instruments and several songs all fighting against each other for dominance.

Whenever I visit Schechak, vendors are hawking everything you can think of. This time is no exception. Fabric, clothes, furniture, food, polished glass, raw metal . . . it's all for sale. I see vendors in the crowd waving beautiful woven tapestries and detailed paintings, wood and stone carvings so lovely they take my breath away. I've traded for many pieces of Springer art that decorate my house. Maybe my people will learn how to make art, but if so that will be many years in the future. For now, the Birthday Children have more than enough real work to keep us busy.

Barkah plays to the crowd. Instead of waving at his people, which humans would do, he tilts his head up in a quick jerky motion. It always makes me think he's having trouble swallowing something.

A flash of movement overhead makes me flinch. A rock, but not thrown my way. It crashes into the head of a marching Belligerent prisoner, makes the already wounded Springer stumble. More rocks fly out, as do rotten fruit, garbage, sticks and clumps of dirt, hitting and splattering the prisoners.

I wait for the Springer guards on either side to stop the assault. They don't. I look to Barkah, knowing he won't let this shameful act continue.

He doesn't say anything. He stares straight ahead, thrusting his chin up and out at his loving subjects.

"Your *Highness,*" I say, and this time it's my tone that carries the meaning, "I remind you, again, that I want to talk to these prisoners. Will any of them still be alive when I come back in a few days?"

Barkah looks at me. His green eyes are piercing, intelligent, calculating.

"*Some will live,*" he says.

At the city center, the road bends slightly left. When we make that turn, I see a wooden framework, so new some of the lumber sparkles with fresh sap. It's like a small building without sides. No . . . it's a *stage.*

At the center of that stage, two thick poles stick up, joined together by a long crossbeam. From the crossbeam hangs six ropes, each ending in a noose.

Matilda's memories flash, define what I see, and I'm horrified: I am looking at a gallows.

I grab the shoulder of Barkah's fancy orange coat.

"You're going to *execute* them?"

Barkah looks at me, then at my hand. I'm suddenly aware that we're surrounded by thousands of his people. Three spiders, a few snake-wolves and a dozen circle-stars are a dangerous force, but in the middle of the Springer city we would be overwhelmed in seconds.

I let go of his coat, smooth out the fresh wrinkles. I smile warmly at him for the benefit of his watching people.

"Execute," I say quietly. "Prisoners . . . *nahnaw*?"

He looks forward.

"Some will live," he says again.

I feel a chill inside. It stuns me that I once thought of Barkah as my friend, that we were like-minded individuals. I sought peace—he sought only power. He used me then. He uses me now. He will hang some of the prisoners, make an example of them, show his people what happens if they cross his will.

"You can't kill them," I say. "They surrendered."

His two good eyes blink slowly. His chin juts out, brings cheers from his subjects.

"Not your laws," he says. *"Not your culture."*

He's being pleasant enough, but his message is clear. Unless I want to start a war, there is nothing I can do. Does respecting another culture mean standing by idly while prisoners are tortured and murdered?

"Barkah, we're leaving," I say. "We have to return to Uchmal. Victor, stop and lower."

Victor stops the spider. The machine lowers until the metal belly clangs against the broken road. Maybe Barkah thought I would drop him off on his gallows, so his people could see how the humans serve him so well, but now they can watch him get out and walk.

I know the Springer king well enough to see he's not pleased with me. He hops down the street to the gallows as his subjects croak their approval.

"Victor," I say, "take us home."

THREE

The Birthday Children march home.

Three five-legged machines, yellow and brown, ridden by teenagers in dirty black coveralls. Six snake-wolves—massive, tawny predators ridden by humans and Springers clothed only in strips of fabric that help them fade into the foliage. On foot, some two dozen rifle-carrying Springers, also wearing jungle rags. Finally, guarding our rear, young humans wearing black coveralls and wrapped in vines, rifles slung over their shoulders. Some of them carry farm tools they use in battle. That strange tradition was born from our initial lack of weapons, yet has persisted long after we were able to arm everyone with spears and knives.

Most of the Springers who fought with us stayed in Schechak. The ones still with us are mostly from D'souza's units, but a few dozen of Barkah's soldiers live inside Uchmal's circular walls, side by side with humans.

In total, our city houses about two hundred Springers. Most are civilians, teenage purples and young reds, studying math, science, medicine and engineering. We also have a handful of purple-blue adults as well as a few pure-blue elderly, who teach us about native plants and animals, the seasons and how to survive them, the places that are rich in metals and minerals, Springer culture and history . . . all the knowledge of Omeyocan passed down from generation to generation over the centuries.

Uchmal's vine-covered walls loom before us, much taller than the trees of the jungle ruins. We filled in the holes that Barkah's people used to crawl under the walls. We rebuilt the Water Gate that blocks anyone from entering the city via the river flowing in from the jungle. Our gates are always closed, always locked from the inside. Hundreds of thousands of Springers live in the jungle ruins around us—we can be friendly, yes, but we also have to be careful.

The most important repair, though, was to several ancient tower cannons. Borjigin and his engineers have fixed four of them so far. These weapons possess terrifying power. As our bracelets are to Springer muskets, the tower cannons are to our bracelets. If the Belligerents—or any other Springer tribe, for that matter, *including* Barkah's—ever try to assault our city, the tower cannons will blast them to bits.

Even from outside the walls, I see the massive Observatory rising up from the city center. It is the biggest building in Uchmal. I wonder if it might be the biggest building in all of existence, the biggest that has ever been. It is so tall its shadow stretches beyond the wall and into the jungle.

The road ends at the East Gate. Towers, built into the wall, rise up on either side. One tower flashes with a gleam of reddish light—the morning sun reflecting off a long, silver tower cannon.

"We should be close enough," Victor says. "Try using the jewel?"

I sigh. "Jewels haven't worked in a while."

"I could try, if you like," he says. "Can I do that for you?"

He's got that look on his face again—so eager to do something for me.

I pull out a communication jewel from one of my many pockets and hand it over. He nestles it into his ear and taps it twice.

"This is Victor Muller, calling to the East Gate, over?" He waits. I see him squint, trying to listen. "Sorry, can't understand you. Say again?"

We found the jewels in an Observatory storeroom. They don't have much range, but from this distance we used to be able to communicate jewel-to-jewel with someone at the gate. Lately, the devices haven't been working that well. No one knows why.

The East Gate is the same one we went through the first time we left Uchmal to see what the jungle held in store for us. As we approach, the massive metal doors slowly swing outward. They are oiled now and open smoothly, without the piercing metal screeches they once made.

Barkah had thousands of Springers waiting to welcome him home. We have only five humans—two halves, along with three circles.

Borjigin is one of the halves. In the past year, he's grown taller and even more handsome. He spends most of his time outside, fixing things, which has tanned his skin and sun-bleached the long black hair he wears in a knot atop his head. In one hand he holds his messageboard, the little flat computer he's never without.

He is one of many who have put away their tough black coveralls in favor of actual clothes. He wears blue pants and a long-sleeved orange shirt. The shirt's color is so close to that of Barkah's jacket I assume both garments were made in the same place. Borjigin wears the same shoes as I do, though, as almost everyone does—tough black boots left for us by the Grownups.

Standing with him is Tina Schuster, one of our three young halves. She also holds a messageboard, but wears something very new for my people—a dress. The white cloth fits her nicely, ripples in the same slight breeze that caresses her long blond curls.

Dresses seem so strange. So impractical. Tina is all arms and legs, still growing into her body, but the dress looks pretty on her. I wonder how I would look in one. Would I like it?

More importantly, would Bishop?

As Victor drives our spider through the gate, he points to his ear and shouts down at Borjigin.

"When are you going to fix these stupid jewels?"

Borjigin frowns. "As soon as we figure out what's wrong with them. It's not just the jewels"—he holds up the messageboard—"these won't connect with the Observatory computer unless we're right next to the building. We're working on it." He glances up and down the column entering the city, a worried look on his face. "Where's Bawden?"

I point toward my feet, where Bawden lies hidden behind the spider's thick metal ridge.

"She's down here, wounded but stable."

Borjigin touches his cheek, mimicking where the bayonet point sliced me.

"That's a nasty cut," he says.

My fingertips trace the spot, draw forth a slight sting. I'd forgotten about the wound. Maybe I'm so used to being hurt by now that I don't think anything of it.

"Doc Smith is waiting at the Observatory, ready to tend to the wounded," Borjigin says. "What other casualties do we have?"

I shrug. "Other than Bawden, just a few minor wounds."

Borjigin smiles in amazement, both pleased and surprised.

"*No one* died? Did the Belligerents run away or something?"

"They tried," Victor says before I can answer. "But Em's plan worked perfectly! Fifteen Springers captured, another eighty-three killed. They burned the corn crop, though."

Borjigin shakes his head. Schuster taps something on her messageboard, perhaps a little too hard. The engineers have worked tirelessly on our food and water supply. Not a week seems to go by without the Belligerents destroying something we need for survival. Perhaps now, after our victory, that will change.

Food is our biggest long-term problem. While we *can* eat native Omeyocan plants and animals, they don't give us the nutrition we need. If that was all there was for us to eat, we wouldn't starve right away, but eventually we *would* starve. Most of our diet comes from prepackaged food the Grownups sent down centuries ago. Those stores were poisoned by the mold, but vine-root juice kills the mold and neutralizes the toxin. There is enough packaged food to last us years. If we don't find another solution, we'll be in trouble when that supply runs out.

The Observatory held several chambers full of carefully preserved seeds from our "home" system—wherever that is—but no instructions on how to make the plants survive Omeyocan's animal and insect pests, or flourish among this alien water, soil and air. The gears have been working hard to turn those seeds into crops. We've had little success so far. The cornfield was the closest we've come to an actual harvest, so of course Borjigin and Schuster are angry.

I really like Borjigin. He has a brilliant mind for managing this city, and when it comes to working with machines he is the best on this planet. He's everything a half should be—but he's not *my* half. I would give anything for O'Malley to be here waiting for me instead.

Today, like every day of my life, I miss that boy with all my heart.

"I'll take Bawden straight to Doc Smith," I say. "You close the gate and make sure everyone gets food, water and rest, all right?"

Borjigin nods. "Oh, and Bishop called an all-hands meeting. Everyone is to report to the Grand Hall in an hour."

Maybe Bishop wants a group debriefing or something. I'll worry about that later. Right now I need to get my friend to the hospital.

"Victor," I say, "take us to the Observatory."

"Yes, ma'am."

The spider quickly speeds up. Pointy metal feet *clack-clack-clack* against the street's flat stones.

Our city has changed so much. We've cleared away vines and repaired buildings. Ziggurats rise up on both sides of the wide street, as do square and rectangular structures. Borjigin tells us this place was made to hold three million people. Perhaps even more. We'll never clear away *all* the plant growth—that would take forever—but the areas that we use have been restored to their original grandeur.

So much progress. We have a long way to go and the work will never end, at least not in our lifetimes, but I am so proud of what we've accomplished.

We pass the Spider Nest, the huge ship that originally brought the spiders and the construction machines down from the *Xolotl*. We cleared away the vines that hid the ship's silver hull. It will never fly again—too many holes and the engines have long since rusted to junk—but now it gleams and shimmers with reflected sunlight.

As our spider races by, I see machines going in and out of the Nest: a truck carrying a load of excavated dirt and rocks; a spider wobbling madly on two damaged legs; a long four-legged machine that we use to cut down trees and bring back logs.

We pass a side street that Kalle, the gear primarily responsible for our food research, has turned into a garden to grow experimental crops. She has dozens of small plots like this spread across the city. This one holds turnips, I think. Like the corn, these plants don't look good. The leaves are shriveling, turning brown. Stems sag slightly, as if the plants can never quite get enough water.

The best-looking part of this small plot is Kalle's "scarecrow." It's a pressure suit from the shuttle that would supposedly let people go outside—into the blackness of *space*, if you can believe it—and fix problems on the shuttle's hull. The pressure suit is tied to a cross. It's supposed to scare away blurds that like to nibble the plants. Judging from the chewed up leaves, I don't think it works very well.

We approach the open space where Huan Chowdhury works. He's our budding archaeologist. Uchmal was built upon the ruins of a destroyed Springer city, which itself was built on top of yet another city built by yet another race of aliens—the Vellen—who appear to be gone for good. Digging through the layers can tell us about those that came before us.

Huan started his work by going down the open shaft in the Observatory's Control Room, where O'Malley and so many others died. That shaft is surrounded by a red metal wall. We've come to call it "the Well," because it looks like one. Huan studied the layers of the shaft for a few days, even found a natural tunnel complex at the bottom, but said it felt "too spooky" down there and refused to explore any further. He asked me if we could knock down a small building instead, so he could excavate below the foundation and continue his research. I approved—he's been digging in this spot ever since.

Huan's job is to learn all he can, see if he can identify why at least three races came to this very spot and at least three more are on the way. We have many mysteries to solve, but right now that is the most pressing one.

He sees our spider. He waves as we pass by. Victor and I wave back. Huan has brown skin and a bright smile. He's *always* smiling.

I am so proud of him. He isn't a gear, like Spingate and the other scientists, and he isn't a half, like Borjigin and the other city managers. Huan is a circle—like me. He was bred to know nothing, to do what he was told. He was bred to be a slave. And yet here he is, doing an important job, quickly becoming our expert on the subject. Whenever one of my people goes beyond the duties expected of their caste, I know there is hope for our future.

Unlike the jungle roads, Uchmal's ancient streets are straight and smooth. We named the big east-west road Yong Boulevard, after the first of us to die on the *Xolotl*. The north-south road is named Latu Way. Both roads lead to one place: the Observatory.

Even after over a year of living in this city, I'm still stunned by the size of this towering ziggurat. Many of us live inside. It has thousands of rooms, as well as our hospital, storerooms, prison and the all-important Control Room. The thirty-layered Observatory offers more space than we could ever need. Borjigin tells me it could house two hundred thousand people with ease, a city within a city. The Observatory is so large that we haven't fully explored it—to this day, we're still finding new rooms and the interesting things left inside of them.

Wide streets surround the Observatory. We've cleared them of plants. Borjigin insisted on that, saying that a fire could spread across the vines that cover almost everything in this city. He wanted to make sure such a blaze wouldn't reach the Observatory. Flames couldn't really hurt the building, of course—it's a mountain of stone—but the project gave the shuttle kids something to do. It took them over a month to complete the work. I have to admit, it does look very nice to see the vine-covered Observatory surrounded by neat, clean streets.

Our shuttle sits in the wide plaza just south of the Observatory. Gaston and Opkick have spent countless hours working on the shuttle's computer, trying to see if there's any history in the system's memory. So far, nothing. They discovered the shuttle has a name, though—*Ximbal*, which apparently means "to journey" in some ancient language. It's unlikely *Ximbal* will ever move from this spot, because we used the last of the fuel in its tanks to get it here. Unless we learn how to make more, *Ximbal* will never fly again.

Most of our people are on the plaza, working. Many wear black coveralls, but more than a few wear colorful clothes: shirts, pants, jackets and dresses made by the Springer factories. I see a spider—number 01, Bishop's spider—sitting idle, along with a few small wheeled vehicles and a hulking, beat-up black truck we've nicknamed Big Pig. The truck's front end kind of resembles a pig's snout. Big Pig's flatbed is surrounded by thick metal walls, and each of its black wheels is taller than I am.

Before we reach the plaza, Victor brings our spider to a stop.

"Em, do you want to visit the memorial? I'll take Bawden to Doctor Smith."

The memorial. The twisted metal X where we buried the remains of those who died in the Observatory fire. Victor is asking if I want to visit O'Malley's grave. It's been too long since I've been there, but there's much to do. The dead can wait a little longer.

"No, thank you. Take us in."

Victor parks the spider by the Observatory's main entrance. This entrance was once sealed up tight and obscured by thick vines.

As big as the ziggurat is, we've found only two other ways in. When we shut all three doors, the place is impregnable. We've laid in large supplies of food and water. That's why I make everyone live either inside the Observatory or close to it—if the Springers were to break through Uchmal's gates, all of my people can shelter inside for months, if not years. Borjigin installed Springer war horns across the city, a system he calls the "emergency warning system." If that goes off, everyone is trained to run for the Observatory.

My people are walking in and out of the building. They look like tiny insects scurrying around a huge hive.

Opkick walks toward us, messageboard in her hand. She's followed by Kenzie Smith, our circle-cross doctor. Okereke and Kishor Jepson, both circles, follow along carrying a metal stretcher. Opkick is pregnant. Her swollen belly strains her white shirt. I've only been gone ten days, but she looks much bigger than the last time I saw her.

"Hail, Em," she says. "The boys will get Bawden down after Doctor Smith takes a look at her."

I wearily descend the ladder. Smith reaches for the first rung to start up, looks at me, then grabs my jaw. She doesn't do it hard, but her grip is firm—this is Smith's way, to move a body however she likes, to see what she wants to see, never asking for permission.

"This cut is bad," she says. "Go to the hospital, tell Francine to fix you up."

"I will. Just take care of Bawden first."

Smith gives my shoulder a quick squeeze, then scrambles up

the rungs. That's the closest she'll ever come to showing me real emotion, I suppose, so I'll take it.

Opkick, on the other hand, has no problem expressing herself. She hugs me tight. I hug back, careful of her belly.

"The baby isn't going to break, Em."

I laugh, embarrassed. "I know, but you're so much bigger!"

She smiles wide, rubs her free hand across her stomach.

"Smith says it will be any day now. We're so excited."

Okereke is grinning, and with good reason—he's the father. He's short, but thick with muscle. He has the darkest skin of any of our people.

Smith climbs down from the spider, rubbing a hand through her brown hair.

"It's safe to move Bawden," she says. "Put her on the stretcher, but do it gently."

Okereke and Jepson scramble up. Victor helps them gently lower Bawden, who is still asleep. They put her on the stretcher and carry her into the Observatory.

"It was close," Smith says to me. "If that puncture wound in her shoulder had gone a bit lower, it would have pierced her lung. She wouldn't have made it back alive. Why did you get so close to the enemy? Is something wrong with all those guns you adore so much?"

I'm exhausted. I'm not about to explain my strategy or what went wrong.

"Just take care of the wounded, all right?"

Smith stares for a moment, not hiding her contempt. She thinks proper leadership would mean we don't fight at all. When we do, for whatever reason, she always thinks the fault is mine.

"Get your face looked at," she says. "Don't wait or it could get infected."

She walks into the Observatory.

Victor drops down, laughing lightly.

"Not exactly a hero's welcome, Em."

I shrug. It never is.

"Forget her," he says. "We *won*. Everyone worked well together. No one died. I'm lucky to serve under you."

He puts his right hand on my left shoulder, the circle-star's gesture of respect. I do the same to him, and look up at his dirty face.

"You did well," I say. "If not for you, Bawden would be dead. I might be, too. I'll tell Bishop personally."

At the mention of Bishop's name, Victor's smile fades.

"You're going to see him right away, aren't you."

A statement, not a question.

"I am. Aren't you going to see Zubiri?"

Victor shrugs. "Sooner or later. Don't forget that Borjigin told us to go to the Grand Hall. I'll see you there."

With that, he jogs into the Observatory, spear in hand, slung rifle jostling on his back.

A few months ago, it was all I could do to keep him from running off to see Zubiri every chance he got. I wonder if something happened between them.

Love. It's a mystery to me.

I start to think of Bishop, but it's O'Malley's face that comes to mind. I must visit his grave soon, tell him all about the battle.

But first, I need to have someone fix up my cut.

FOUR

The hospital is busy. It's in the Observatory's second layer. Everything here is white: the pedestals, the cabinets, the walls, the floor and the coffins—sixty-six of them, to be exact, laid out side by side in two rows of thirty-three each.

Smith, Lucky Pokano and Francine Yilmaz—our three circle-crosses—are hard at work fixing the cuts and scrapes suffered during the battle. Ten circle-stars are being treated. So are seven Springers; our docs have gotten good at fixing them up as well.

Smith stands at a pedestal next to a closed coffin that holds Bawden. Lucky is working on Farrar, who had a long cut on his arm. Farrar hid the wound from everyone, like he always seems to do.

Francine leans in close to my face, dabbing at my cut with something that stings.

"Three hours in a med-chamber will fix you right up," she says. "No scar at all."

The circle-crosses call them med-chambers. The rest of us still

call them *coffins*. Finding new words for things doesn't change
what they actually are.

"Just stitch it up," I say. "I've got work to do."

Francine sighs. She's tiny. She's barely grown at all since we
landed. She's filled out some, though, and has a woman's curves.
She has the cutest little nose. Long black lashes frame her big,
dark eyes. The Grownups dressed us like dolls—Francine actually looks like one.

"Em, all your scars . . . we can get rid of those. You'd be so
much prettier without them."

I smile at her. She means well, but she doesn't understand me.
My scars are *mine*. Each one makes me look a little bit different
from Matilda's ideal vision. In the faraway crawl spaces of my
thoughts, I hope that if Matilda ever does overwrite me, she will
hate her own face because of all the damage I have done to it.

"Thank you," I say. "I appreciate your concern. Now stitch
me up."

Francine does as she's told. Fourteen quick, efficient stitches
on my cheek and she's finished.

I thank her again, then walk over to Smith. Icons and lines
float above the pedestal in front of her, information I now know
represents heart rate, blood pressure, temperature, oxygen satu-
ration and a few other things.

"How is Bawden?" I ask.

"She needs two days in there," Smith says. "Three, tops, and
she'll be as good as new. Then you can take her out into the
jungle again and see if you can get her properly killed instead of
just horribly wounded."

Smith annoys me, but I understand her. Her job is to repair
people, to save lives. My job is to protect people, but sometimes
the only way to do that is to kill those that would harm us.
When evil comes, you can't always talk to it—sometimes it must

be destroyed. That's why there are people like Bawden, Victor, Bishop, me, D'souza . . . when real danger comes, people like Smith stay behind us.

"I wish we didn't have to fight," I say, trying to reason with Smith for the hundredth time. "I wish no one attacked us, I wish the jungle was nicer, I wish air tasted like candy and we all got to sleep on a bed of pretty flowers."

I try to reason with her, sure, but I don't try *hard*.

Smith snorts. "One of these days you're going to bring me someone I can't fix. Then we'll see how funny it is."

"You think I *like* this? I hate fighting."

She glances at me. Her mouth twists into a rueful grin.

"No, you don't *like* it—you *revel* in it." She points to my cheek. "You revere it so much you want to show it off. I was made to heal. You? You were made to kill. You are death."

The voice of the boy I love comes from behind me.

"Someone has to be death," Bishop says. "That's how civilization works. What you can't defend will eventually be taken away from you."

Smith rolls her eyes. "If the two of you don't mind, I've got lives to save."

She turns her attention back to her pedestal display. Maybe I'm the leader of my people, but I've just been dismissed.

I leave the hospital. I hear Bishop walking behind me, but I don't turn to look at him. I walk down the stone hall and descend a flight of stairs before I stop.

We're alone.

Now I turn. I haven't seen his face in ten days. That tightly curled blond hair. Those dark-yellow eyes, lovely but bleary from lack of sleep. As tired as he looks, his smile still steals the air from my lungs.

"I missed you, Bishop."

His hands slide around my waist. He lifts me as if I weigh nothing at all. I throw my arms around his thick neck. His lips on mine: warm, eager, wanting. Maybe the kiss lasts for a second, maybe it lasts for an hour.

He sets me down.

"And I missed you."

His hand on my face, his thumb gently tracing my latest badge of bravery. His eyes swim with a mixture of worry and pride.

"Looks like I almost lost you."

I touch the hand that is touching my face. "Never. You'll never lose me."

Not like I lost O'Malley . . .

"I still think it's bad strategy for you to go out and fight," he says. "You're our leader. If the blade that made that cut had struck true, you'd be dead."

He's proud of me, yes, but this particular argument he will never let go.

"I can't ask others to do what I won't do myself. And it went well. If it wasn't for Bawden rushing into the fight, no one in my platoon would have been hurt at all."

Bishop's face wrinkles with surprise.

"Bawden? But she's so reliable."

I shake my head. "She lost it. She jumped out of the spider, screaming that she wanted to kill. She ran into a burning corn-field without any support. Victor and I had to go in after her."

Bishop rubs his chin. I hear his callused hands scraping against his blond stubble.

"That's happening more and more," he says. "Our discipline seems to be fading. I'm worried about it."

I nod. I am, too.

"Still, she can't act like that," Bishop says. "It's unacceptable. I'll speak with her."

I wouldn't want to be in her shoes when that happens. Among the circle-stars, disobeying orders is a heavy sin.

"And what about *Victor*? How did he do?"

The way Bishop said Victor's name . . . with a touch of anger? There seems to be a growing rivalry between the pair. Bishop prides himself on being our best fighter, so I guess it's no surprise, considering how skilled Victor is becoming at all things involving war.

"He was amazing," I say. "He saved Bawden's life. Probably mine as well. He captured two Belligerents, killed another."

Bishop's jaw muscles twitch. He nods.

"Where are the prisoners now?"

I describe what I saw in the Springer city, how Barkah acted. Bishop's face clouds over with anger.

"It's dishonorable to kill captives," he says.

"I know. I tried to bring the prisoners with us, but Barkah wouldn't listen. The way he's been acting lately . . . I couldn't risk a confrontation when we were so heavily outnumbered."

Bishop nods slowly. "The Springers are acting more violent, *we're* acting more violent, the Belligerents gather out of nowhere to attack us . . . I don't understand what's going on."

I take his hand. "We'll figure it out. You look exhausted—anything big happen while I was gone?"

Just as it was important for people to see me lead the attack on the Belligerents, it was important for people to know Bishop can run things if anything happens to me. That's why I left him in charge.

"Only the biggest thing there is," he says. "Spingate said the first alien ship is approaching orbit, or something like that."

We have no idea where it came from. We have no idea what's inside of it.

"I'll go see her right now," I say. "Anything else?"

He looks away.

"Bello tried suicide again. She somehow managed to chip off a piece of her cell wall, used it to cut her wrists."

That damn woman. Why does she have to be so much trouble?

The Springers kill their prisoners—our prisoner tries to kill herself.

"I'll go talk to her," I say.

Bishop gives me that look, the one that says *I told you this would happen.*

"If she succeeds on the next try, any information she has dies with her."

I feel my anger flare. "For the last time, we are *not* going to torture her."

His eyes narrow. "She's the only one who knows why those ships are coming. Now the first one is here. This is *necessary.*"

I rub at my temples. This is giving me a headache.

"No torture, Bishop."

"You always listen to Spingate," he says. "She agrees with me that it's the right thing to do."

"*No!* All right? No torture, and that's final. Don't ask again."

He grunts, then nods.

It isn't just Spingate and Bishop—many people think we should get the information out of Bello by . . . wait, what's the phrase people use to justify this disgusting concept? Oh, yes: *by any means necessary.*

While I'm in charge, that will never happen.

"I'll talk to Bello first, then Spin," I say. "Then I need some sleep. Will I see you at our house later tonight?"

Our house. His and mine. The thought of a night in our place, where I don't have to think about any of this, where I can just be with him . . . it lifts my mood.

Bishop smiles, shakes his head.

"You can't go home yet. Borjigin called that meeting."

"Borjigin said *you* called the meeting."

He blinks a few times.

"Oh, that's right. I called it."

"What's it about? I just got back from a battle. I'm exhausted—I don't want to sit in some damn meeting right now."

"You're going," Bishop says. "You'll understand when you get there. Go to the Grand Hall after you see Spingate. Just do it, Em, it's important."

He kisses me again. When he finally walks away, I feel like part of me goes with him.

Tonight I will allow myself time to relax. Now, though, there is much work still to do.

Spingate's lab is below me. Our prison cells are above.

I head up the steps.

FIVE

stand with a metal tray in my hands. Warmth billows out from between the iron bars of Korrynn Bello's cell.

She's naked, lying on a straw mat on the floor. Two months ago, she tried to hang herself with her blankets, tying them together and looping them over the thick wooden support beam that runs across the ceiling. One month ago, she tried to strangle herself with her coveralls. We don't have enough people to watch her all the time, so we had to take away anything she could use to hurt herself. That includes clothes, which is why we keep it so warm in her cell.

She knows I'm here. She won't look up at me. Her frizzy blond hair hides her face. Her skin is so pale.

"Bishop told me what you did," I say.

My tone is harsh. As my people struggle and sacrifice, fight to build a new culture, to *survive,* this selfish woman tries to take her own life instead of helping us. I do have some sympathy for her—just not very much.

"Kill me," she says. Her voice is a low moan, a whisper of the pain that crawls up from deep in her soul. "That's what you're good at, isn't it, Em? Killing?"

She's trying to make me angry. I won't let her.

"I brought you tea."

"Stop calling it that. Sholtag isn't *tea*. Real tea is amazing. You'll never know what it tastes like."

Of all the things she complains about—and there are too many things to count—she mentions a lack of tea more than any other.

"It's better than nothing," I say.

Finally, she looks up at me. This thousand-year-old thing wears the face and body of my dead friend. Her nose is slightly crooked. Her left eyelid droops, always a little lower than her right. The imperfections of her face are mementos of my rage, when I flew out of control on the shuttle and beat her nearly to death.

Just looking at her is an endless reminder of why I work so hard to stay calm. I can hurt people. I am capable of evil.

She glances at the tray. "*Two* cups? You must want to talk."

I nod.

Korrynn sighs. She stands and walks to the bars. She reaches through and takes one of the paper cups.

She stares at it. "I don't deserve at least a ceramic mug?"

"We both know what you'd use that for."

"But it gets cold so fast."

"Then drink quickly."

I take the other cup and set the metal tray on the stone floor, making sure it's well out of her reach.

We found the paper cups in one of the Observatory's countless storerooms. I take a sip of sholtag. It tastes like wood. Not in a bad way, though. Wood and mint. The Springers drink this all the time. At first I hated it, but I've come to like it.

"Disgusting," she says after taking a sip. She shrugs. "At least it's warm. Thank you." She glances at the palm-plate just outside her cell, on my side of the bars. "Now that we've had a nice drink, how about you let me go for a walk?"

All I have to do is press my hand to the plate. Spingate programmed the prison cell doors to open only for me, Bishop or Borjigin. But now is not the time for a casual stroll.

"The first alien ship is almost here," I say. "Stop playing games, Korrynn. Tell me why the *Xolotl* came to Omeyocan."

I used to call her Bello, which I hated, because that was the name of my friend. At some point, she asked me to call her by her first name. I should be careful what I wish for—calling her Korrynn makes this monster seem like a real person.

She's not. She is one of *them*.

"You know my demands," she says. "Until I get what I want, I won't tell you anything. I'm sure you fixed the antenna. I'm *sure* of it."

Other than carefully supervised walks—where her hands remained shackled for fear she might try to grab a guard's knife or gun—Korrynn has spent every moment of the last year in this cell. In all that time, she has refused to give us the information we need so badly.

"I've always told you the truth about the antenna," I say. "We're trying to fix it, trying very hard. But that doesn't matter anymore. Didn't you hear me? The alien ship is here. Tell me what I need to know, so I can protect us."

She shrugs. "Then find another way to reach the *Xolotl*. Until I can speak with my friends, I won't tell you a godsdamned thing."

Korrynn Bello lifts one hand, palm out toward me so I can see the long, angry cuts on her wrist.

"You're running out of time," she says. "Sooner or later, I'll find a way to kill myself. Or maybe before I can, the aliens will attack and do it for me. If you want what I know, find a way."

I tried to not let her make me mad, but like every time before this one, I failed.

Korrynn Bello knows why the *Xolotl* came to this spot. Whatever that reason is, I assume it's the same thing that drew the Springers, the alien ship almost in orbit, and the two alien ships still on the way.

There are more mysteries she could solve for us. What happened on the *Xolotl* that left so many people dead? Was Matilda really responsible for all those dismembered bodies? Who erased *Ximbal*'s memory, and the memory of Ometeotl, the Control Room's powerful computer?

But Korrynn refuses to talk until she can speak with her friends.

Until she can speak with Matilda.

"I promise you, I'm doing everything I can to fix that antenna," I say. "Please . . . tell me why the *Xolotl* came here. What is it about this place that makes people want to kill and destroy?"

She takes a long sip of sholtag.

"Until I get what I want, you'll never know," she says. "Gods, I am so alone."

And there it is, the phrase she always repeats, the one that sends me into a fury.

"You don't have to be lonely! I've told you that you can be one of us. All you have to do is tell me what you know!"

"You don't understand," she says. "You can't. You are all

children. *Babies*. I need my people. It was never supposed to be this way."

Gods, she makes me so *angry*.

"Some of the others want to torture you to get the information."

Those words slip out before I realize I'm saying them. I yelled at Bishop for bringing it up, yet here I am, letting my anger take over, using torture as a threat.

She glances at my legs, at the knife strapped to my right thigh. Damn—I meant to come here unarmed, but the knife is always on me and I forgot about it.

But Korrynn isn't threatened, by my words or by the knife. She laughs.

"You think you can beat it out of me? Little girl, you don't even know what *real* pain is. Being transformed is worse than anything. Worse than the rod. Worse than when you assaulted me in the shuttle. Worse than when Spingate elbowed me after you stabbed Yong. Worse than when I cut myself, when I tried to hang myself. You want to torture me? Go ahead—I'm tougher than *all* of you."

My skin prickles with goosebumps. My anger disappears.

"What did you just say?"

She casually takes another sip.

"I said I'm tougher than all of you."

"No," I say, shaking my head. "Before that. About when Yong got stabbed."

Korrynn nods. "Yes, when I grabbed Spingate to try and get her off Yong, and she threw her arm back and elbowed me in the face. I don't think she meant . . . meant to . . ."

The naked girl/woman blinks.

She touches her mouth, so lightly, in the spot where Spingate's elbow connected. It connected with that mouth—but not that *person*.

"You weren't there," I say. "That was *our* Bello."

Our Bello, who was overwritten shortly after that. The creature that took over her mind shouldn't have any recollection of that moment.

This Bello, this overwritten thing, she's suddenly confused. She shakes her head lightly.

"No, I . . . well, I don't know what I was saying. I must be thinking of when you beat me on the shuttle. Yes, that's it."

When O'Malley was overwritten, his brain, his soul, everything that made him *him* was supposed to be gone forever. But when I stabbed him, when he was dying in my arms, he smiled at me. He thanked me. In that brief instant, my O'Malley was still in there.

And if Korrynn remembers the moment of Yong's death, maybe my Bello isn't completely gone.

Brewer said the longer we were awake, making our own memories, the less chance the overwrite would work. I've been awake far longer than Bello or O'Malley was—if Matilda ever catches me, tries to overwrite me, what would happen?

Korrynn sets her cup on the floor. She lies on the mattress, turns her back to me.

"I'm tired," she says. "Go away."

I can't stand to look at her anymore. Such a selfish, hateful little creature.

"If this is what a thousand years of life would get me, I hope I die at a hundred."

She rolls over onto one elbow, and smiles at me. When she does, I see the dark space of two missing teeth—another memento of when I attacked her. She refuses to have them fixed.

"The aliens are finally here," she says. "Which means you'll die *far* sooner than that."

Her words send a chill up my spine, crank my anger to new heights.

I walk away, wondering how the person I keep naked and alone in a prison cell continues to have the upper hand.

SIX

The Observatory is the heart of Uchmal.

The Control Room is the heart of the Observatory.

Ometeotl, the living computer, is the heart of the Control Room.

"Welcome back, Empress Savage."

I have barely set one foot in this room and I am already annoyed.

"I've told you to use *my* name, not hers," I say, louder than I normally would, because I'm speaking to the *room,* not a person, and for some reason it always feels like I need to shout to be heard.

"As you wish," Ometeotl answers. *"Welcome back, Em. You have been missed."*

Maybe the computer hidden within these stone walls thinks so, but apparently no one else here does. The people in this room barely notice my arrival.

This is the place where O'Malley was overwritten. The place where I killed him. The place I killed Old Bishop. Other people died here, too: several brave Springers, Old Dr. Smith, the over-written Coyotl and a few Grownups whose names we will never know. This was a place of flame and smoke, bullets and blood, hatchets and hate. But as with so many other things on Omeyo-can, we have changed its form.

The room once held golden coffins designed to wipe out our minds and replace them with the minds of the Grownups. We removed those coffins. In the space where those little death fac-tories stood, we erected a dozen pedestals that are used for edu-cation. We cleaned the walls and ceiling, scrubbed away the char and soot. We painted everything bright white, painted over the mural showing human sacrifice. We removed the twisted metal X where the overwriting process happened.

We turned a temple of evil into a classroom where humans and Springers alike learn how to make a better world.

In a way, we overwrote this room. Take *that,* Matilda.

Every one of those dozen pedestals is in use, yet the students barely give me a glance. They seem . . . upset. Maybe Spingate's lessons are more demanding than usual.

In the center of the room sits the Well, a waist-high red metal wall that encircles the dirt shaft leading down to a power cell. Etched on that wall, the carbon symbol: an outer ring with four dots, an inner ring with two dots, and a solid circle at the center.

That same symbol is at the very top of the Observatory. It was also atop the ruined church where Spingate and I first talked to Barkah. In the past year, we've learned it's the symbol of a for-gotten Springer religion. We don't know what the symbol meant to Matilda and the builders of Uchmal, or why the race she tried to exterminate would have already been using it before the *Xo-lotl* arrived.

Symbols. So important to the Grownups that they embedded

them on our foreheads: the double-ring, SPIRIT, representing religion; the gear, MIND, our scientists; the half-circle, STRUCTURE, the engineers who build machines and make this city run; the circle-crosses of HEALTH, our doctors and teachers; our soldiers, our circle-stars, aptly named MIGHT.

And, of course, the empty circles. SERVICE. Slaves.

But what does the carbon symbol mean to the church?

At the back of the room is a wide, waist-high platform with six more pedestals. On the platform stand Theresa Spingate and Xander Gaston—my two closest friends—and Halim Horn, Spingate's top assistant.

Halim is unique among us: a circle-star that doesn't like to fight. The other circle-stars look down on him for that. Even Bishop. Bishop sees no problem with other symbols wanting to fight *alongside* the circle-stars, but one of his own wanting to be anything *other* than a warrior? To him, that is a betrayal of their birthright.

But it doesn't matter what Bishop thinks about it. Out of our 275 people, we have only *seven* gears. That's seven scientists to handle almost all of our needs. Halim's desire and ability to help Spingate frees her from some things she'd consider to be drudge work.

Halim hides his circle-star symbol behind a white strip of cloth he's tied around his head. On that headband, he's stitched a new symbol: an empty circle, like mine, but with a diagonal slash through it, the ends of the line protruding just past the circle's outer edge. He says the symbol is called an "empty set." It represents his lack of belief in our symbols. I don't think he should be ashamed of who he is, or trade one symbol for another, but that is how he identifies and I have no issue with it.

Spingate and Gaston look exhausted. They *always* do. They

work long, hard hours. They're the only ones who make *me* feel lazy. And having a baby, I gather, doesn't exactly help them get more sleep.

Gaston scratches absently at his thick black beard. He won't admit it, but I'm convinced he grew it to annoy Bishop. Bishop's best effort to grow a beard resulted in a thin scrabble that looks like he glued sparse bits of hurukan fur to his cheeks. He's annoyed someone so much smaller than he can do something he can't.

As if Ramses Bishop needs facial hair to show how "manly" he is.

Gaston's hands work glowing images floating above a pedestal. A cloth sling runs from his left shoulder down to his right hip. Nestled inside the cloth is a lump of noisy (and often smelly) delight known as Kevin Spingate-Gaston.

They named their baby after my O'Malley.

Theresa is also lugging about a baby, but this one is still inside her. She's six months pregnant with their second child. Yet here she is, working away.

"Hello, Spin."

She looks up from her pedestal, seems confused by my face for a moment.

"Oh. Hello, Em. You're back."

Is she glaring at me?

"Spin, are you okay?"

She blinks rapidly, then gives her head a little shake. The confusion seems to clear.

"I'm fine. Come up and join us, please."

I step up onto the platform. I walk to Gaston first.

"Hey," he says. His hands and eyes remain fixed on the pedestal display, but he turns his body so I can get at the baby.

"Wow, Xander, I didn't know you missed me so much."

He grunts once. I pull little Kevin free of the sling and Gaston returns his full attention to his work.

Kevin is so *clean*. So soft. I love the way he smells—except when his diaper needs to be changed, of course. He has Spingate's eyes, Gaston's nose and chin. Without a doubt, though, the thing I love the most about this child's face is his little forehead.

Because Kevin has no symbol.

He is the first human on Omeyocan without one. He has no legacy of slavery or dominance, of being a have or a have-not. He has no memories of what he's *supposed* to be, of a life that others have planned for him. When he grows up, Kevin Spingate-Gaston can choose whatever path he likes.

That makes him a symbol unto himself: a symbol of what this planet can be, what our people can be.

I turn slightly, for some reason showing the baby to Spingate as if she's never seen the boy before.

"He's so wonderful," I say. "He's perfect."

Finally, she smiles. There is the beauty that is my best friend.

"Thank you," she says. "He's growing so quickly."

He is at that. I've only been gone ten days but it feels like the baby has doubled in weight. I bounce him up and down a little. His mouth opens in a toothless grin that is the spitting image of his mother's. She gently pets his head, brushing aside his thin red hair.

"Spin, you and Xander seem a little angry," I say. "Is everything all right?"

"You mean besides the fact that we have three alien ships above us, Zubiri can't get the optical telescope to work correctly, and we have an antenna that won't let us communicate with the *Xolotl,* which we need to do if Bello is going to tell us anything about why all these ships—including ours—came to Omeyocan?"

Her words mirror my own frustration.

"Yes. Besides that."

Her nose crinkles as she thinks.

"I don't know." She speaks quietly, so that only I can hear. "I just feel more . . . *aggressive* lately. I've yelled at Xander for no reason a couple of times. He was a good sport about it at first. He tried to be patient with me, but a couple of days ago he started yelling back. We're getting mad at each other and we don't know why." She nods toward the students down on the floor, working away on their lessons. "Them, too. They're so grumpy. We've all been working so hard. I guess the pressure of the approaching ships is getting to us."

It's that, and more. Much more. The way Bawden acted. The Belligerents gathering to attack us. The way Barkah has changed. I am gifted at solving puzzles no one else can figure out, but for this, I'm at a loss. I push those thoughts away to the back of my mind. Most often, that's where the pieces come together, when I'm not really thinking about them.

"There's something else," Spingate says, her voice a tight whisper. "I've been having nightmares."

"What about?"

She starts to speak, then stops. She looks at little Kevin for a moment, then shakes her head.

"Never mind," she says. "It's nothing. I'm just not sleeping well is all."

Whatever the dreams were, they disturbed her. I know this girl almost as well as I know myself; when she's ready to talk to me, she will. Until then, getting any information out of Theresa Spingate is like trying to get blood from a stone.

But *do* I know her? She's changed. The Spingate I thought I knew would have *never* thought torture was acceptable.

"Well, I hope everyone feels better soon," I say. Then, loud enough for everyone to hear: "What's going on with the alien ship?"

Spingate looks at Halim. "Put it on the main display."

He nods, works the glowing controls floating above his pedestal. The air above the red well flares to life. Spingate and I stand together, waiting. Gaston joins us. Without a word, he gently takes Kevin from my arms and nestles the baby back into the sling.

The image forms. I've seen it so many times in the last six months. A small sphere of blue and yellow and brown represents Omeyocan, our planet. Hovering above it is a red dot labeled *Xolotl*—our ship of nightmares that traveled over a thousand years to get here.

Then there are the three unknowns. A blue dot represents the first alien ship. When we discovered it, Ometeotl labeled it *Beta-One*. Gaston didn't like that generic name, said he wanted his enemies to have a "face," whatever that means. He renamed it *Basilisk*. Farther out, a yellow dot—*Gamma-One*, renamed *Goblin*. And beyond that, a green dot that represents *Delta-One*, renamed *Dragon*.

"The *Basilisk* is thousands of miles from the *Xolotl*, but both ships have a line of sight on Uchmal," Spingate says. "I think the *Basilisk* will settle into final orbit in the next two days. It probably can't safely launch shuttles until then."

Two days. We might be at war in just two days.

"Do we have any way of communicating with it?"

Gaston shakes his head. "Not unless the antenna magically fixes itself. Even if it was repaired, I'm not sure if it would work. Since you left to fight the Belligerents, the electronic interference that's screwed up our communications systems has gotten worse."

I think of the jewels and Borjigin's messageboard problem.

"Could the *Basilisk* be doing that?" I ask. "Or one of the other ships?"

"I don't think so," Gaston says. "Whatever the problem is, it seems to be originating from Omeyocan, not from space."

More bad news. I need the antenna to work so Bello can talk to Matilda. And if war does come, we may need to communicate with the *Xolotl* anyway.

"So even if we fix the antenna," I say, "it won't work because of this interference?"

Spingate shrugs. "Hard to know. The antenna is directly connected to the power plant down in the Well, so a working signal would be exponentially stronger than anything the jewels or the messageboards produce. It might overpower this interference. I've still got Nevins, Peura and Harman working full-time on fixing it. Opkick has been helping them search storage rooms for parts, but so far they haven't been able to repair the damage."

When we first climbed the Observatory's three thousand steps and reached the top layer, we saw a tall stone pillar decorated with our symbols. At that time, we didn't know the pillar housed an antenna meant to let the Observatory communicate with the *Xolotl*. At some point in the two centuries after Uchmal was built, a power surge of some kind damaged the antenna, cutting Matilda off from the spiders and from the construction robots that built this great city.

I stare at the simple blue dot representing the *Basilisk*. The blankness of it tears at me. Because of the radio telescopes spread out across the city and in the jungle I know *where* the alien ships are, but for now we have no idea what they look like.

"How about the repairs to the Goffspear telescope?" I ask. "When will those be complete? I need to see this ship."

"Soon," Gaston says. "Zubiri thinks she's getting closer."

I try to control my anger.

"You've been telling me *soon* for over a year," I say. "Maybe that word means something different to you than it does to me."

His face twists into a snarl. "Then *fix it yourself*. If you know so much, *you* do the godsdamned work!"

I take a step back, shocked at his response.

"*Gaston,*" Spingate snaps, "don't take your frustration out on Em!"

"Oh, it's all right for *you* to be a bastard to *me,* but I can't be one to Em? Sure, *that's* fair."

She points a finger at him. "You shut your stupid mouth. Your attitude makes me *sick.*"

I'm dumbfounded. Since we landed on this planet, these two have been inseparable, their love perfect, patient and kind. Yet here they are screaming at each other.

Gaston takes a step toward her, but before he says anything else little Kevin starts to cry.

The sound shocks Gaston and Spingate out of their sudden burst of anger. Their faces turn red. Spingate steps to Gaston, puts her arms around him. He hugs her back, the baby between them. Comforted in this sudden embrace, Kevin stops crying.

"Maybe you two need a break from work," I say quietly.

Halim comes closer, flashing a disarming grin, hands up as if to say *don't take it out on me* even though he could probably beat all three of us up at the same time.

"Actually, it's time for that meeting in the Grand Hall," he says. "Borjigin said to make sure we weren't late."

Again with the damn meeting?

Spingate runs a hand through her thick red hair. She sighs heavily, as if trying to clear the stress from her body.

"Yes, the meeting," she says. "We should all go now, together."

I point to the blue dot. "This is more important."

"We have at least a day," Gaston says. "If we don't do this meeting now, we might not get to do it at all. I'm told it's very important."

Spingate claps her hands. The students all look up at her.

"Everyone, to the Grand Hall," she says. "Right now."

The students exchange excited looks as they rush out of the room. Does everyone know what this is about except me?

Halim puts his arm around my shoulders.

"Help me out, Em. If you're not on time, Borjigin said he would come down here and yell at me. I'm a delicate soul. I might wither and die."

I can feel the strength in his muscular arm. He is a circle-star, after all.

"You might wither and die," I say. "I find that hard to believe."

"Did I mention how delicate I am? What if I say *pretty please?*"

He smiles wide.

Halim rarely asks for anything. I look at Spingate and Gaston. They're also smiling. Whatever this is, everyone is in on it.

I sigh, and I give in.

"Fine. Let's go."

SEVEN

The four of us walk toward the Grand Hall. It is the largest room in the Observatory. At least the largest one we've found so far—this place is full of hidden doors and hallways. We're still discovering new areas almost every week.

We've had several all-hands meetings in the Grand Hall. It's quite beautiful. Large marble columns support an arched stone ceiling. There were carvings of torture and human sacrifice, but we covered those with large tapestries made by the Springers.

I like the Hall, but one part of it really bothers me—a raised dais with an obnoxious golden throne. I'm sure that's where Matilda thought she would rule. The left side of the throne has a bracket that holds a ceremonial golden knife, its pommel decorated with a double-ring symbol done in rubies. The right side holds a thin red cane—a working "rod," the torture device used to punish people, especially children. Matilda used an identical rod on me when I was her captive. The *pain*. I shiver involuntarily every time I see the thing, which is why the entire throne is covered in a blanket made of hurukan fur. Out of sight, yes, but not out of mind—we all know the throne is there, a constant reminder of the evil that built this city.

None of us have sat in that throne. None of us ever will.

Spin, Gaston, Halim and I walk down the stone corridor. I hear noise coming from the Grand Hall. Loud conversation. Laughter. And . . . is that *music*?

We reach the entryway. One step inside, and I stop cold.

This huge room is full of people and Springers. So many of us, here, maybe *all* of us.

I think everyone has bathed, even those who fought with me against the Belligerents. Bodies washed, hair combed. Most of my people wear Springer-made clothes instead of the familiar black coveralls.

And our Springers . . . hundreds of them, all dressed up. Long robes of fine cloth, in so many wonderful colors. Hems and collars trimmed in bits of gleaming glass. Buttons of polished metal etched with intricate patterns.

Everyone looks so *nice*.

The music stops.

All heads turn to stare at me.

Gaston starts to clap. Spingate joins him, then Halim . . . then *everyone*.

They are applauding. Applauding *me*.

My face feels hot.

"What's going on?"

Borjigin slides out of the crowd. He wears a new blue outfit, beams with pride and joy. He takes my hand and leads me into the Hall.

"People, let's hear it for our leader! Let's hear it for *Em*!"

They clap harder. They hoot and holler. I see smiles from Bishop, Opkick, the shuttle kids, Victor . . . I must be the only person who wasn't in the know.

"Borjigin," I say, "what is this?"

He pulls me in for a hug. "It's a celebration of your triumph in battle. A way for those of us who did not fight to thank those that did. I had it planned all along as a ceremony, but when you told me we didn't lose *anyone,* I turned it into a party!"

He leads me around the room. There are tables full of food: meats and cheeses, pastries, a whole roasted Omeyocan piggy sitting on a huge silver tray. Candies and treats. Platters full of unwrapped grain bars from our food warehouse. The Springers consider those a delicacy. I see another table topped with a pile of small black circular cookies, also from the storehouse, and standing next to that table, of course, is Farrar. He smiles at me, chewed-up cookies caked on his teeth. He always did have a sweet tooth.

There are exhibits, too. Kalle is behind a pedestal, its glowing display showing some kind of wiggling worm thing. I see three shuttle kids with instruments: one with a harp of some kind, one with a brass trumpet, one with several small drums set up around her. Two displays of paintings—not Springer paintings, I'm shocked to see, but *human* ones. A table where black-haired little Bernice Walezak is talking to a dozen people. She wears white robes, smiles like an angel.

Borjigin sweeps his arms wide, a gesture that includes the band, the people, the food, the exhibits . . . everything.

"Important things happened while you were gone," he says. "And there were some things happening while you were here, but you were too busy to notice. I wanted to take a moment and bring all of these things together, so you could see that you're fighting for far more than just survival. Art, science . . . this is the culture we're all building together. Building because of *you,* Em. Because of your leadership."

All this attention, all focused on me. I'm grateful, but I hate it.

Borjigin finally seems to notice how uncomfortable I am. He looks at the people gathered around.

"We have about an hour," he calls out. "Then most of us need to get back to work. Eat, drink, learn and enjoy!"

The crowd applauds again, maybe this time more for him than for me, then they return to what they were doing. The music starts up. The room fills with the sounds of conversation.

I'm used to being the center of attention, but not like this. I'm embarrassed. I'm also very touched.

"Borjigin, you shouldn't have done this."

He laughs. "You never ask for anything for yourself, so I took it upon myself to show you how much we appreciate what you do. This celebration isn't just for you, of course—take a look at your soldiers."

Victor is tearing into a plate overstuffed with steaming piggy meat. A bandage covers the burn wound on his head. He's eating and laughing, talking to Louise Bariso, one of our halves. Bawden is in a wheelchair. The plate on her lap holds a small roasted animal. I recognize it—the same animal Visca found right before he was killed. How I miss him. Maria and Lahfah are laughing and dancing together in front of the little band, along with a young circle-star girl named Ines Darzi. They've all traded in their dirty jungle rags for long scarves of all colors that flow in time with their movements.

The people who fought with me, human and Springer alike . . . just a few hours ago they were putting their lives on the line. Now they are playing, laughing, enjoying this moment like there is no tomorrow. With the *Basilisk* coming in, maybe there *isn't* a tomorrow. They should have fun while they can.

We all should.

Borjigin is clapping in time with the band.

"They're wonderful," I say.

"The Springers made the harp," Borjigin says. "We found the trumpet and the drums in a storage room. Tama, Robert and Karen have been practicing their instruments for weeks."

Tama Church, Robert Williams and Karen Benson are all circles. I had no idea our people could be musicians.

I point to the paintings.

"And those?"

"Axel uses paint provided by the Springers," Borjigin says. "Crystal uses charcoal. They were both hiding their art away, like they thought it would get them into trouble or something."

I shake my head. Axel Shepherd and Crystal Gilbert—both shuttle kids. And, both circles.

"You said there were important discoveries?"

Borjigin takes my hand and leads me to Kalle's pedestal. She waves everyone away so she can focus solely on me. She has such a sweet smile. Unfortunately, what usually comes out of her mouth is anything but sweet.

"Sorry those godsdamned jungle rats burned our crops," she says.

I can't even guess how many hours she invested in developing that cornfield. I don't blame her for being angry, but at the same time I don't need her racism.

"Kalle, we have *guests*," I say. "Can you mind your language, please?"

She huffs, then glances at Lahfah and a few other Springers.

"It's just a word, Em," she says, but not as loud. "Words can't hurt you."

"They can't? Tell that to those who died in Aramovsky's war. Besides, the Springers aren't *rats*."

"Close enough for my taste."

"You've never even seen a rat."

She laughs. "But I remember what they look like. Don't you?"

I do. I didn't at first, but when some people started calling the Springers *jungle rats*, I looked it up on one of the Observatory's pedestals. Once I saw it, I "remembered" it, meaning that Matilda knew about rats when she was a little girl. The only memories that are truly *mine* are the ones that came after I woke up in my coffin, in the dark, screaming and fighting for my life.

"I'm glad you beat them," Kalle says. Her tone is slightly more respectful. "Did you kill them all?"

"No, not all."

"Too bad."

I don't bother telling her that those who survived will probably all die at the hands of Barkah.

She waves her hands above the pedestal. An image sparkles to life—it's the purple vine root. We use its juice to neutralize the toxic mold that makes all food on this planet poisonous.

"I finally had a breakthrough with this thing," she says. "Magnify."

The image zooms in on one spot of the root as if we are plunging into it at high speed. What looked like smooth skin is actually marked with tight wrinkles. We dive further, *through* those wrinkles, into the flesh itself. Tiny dots appear, which grow into irregular cubes packed in together.

"Those cubes are plant cells," Kalle says. "Increase magnification."

The cubes seem to expand. I see that there are dots in the middle of each one, something at the center of the cell. Then I see movement—something long and thin, sliding *between* the cubes.

I point at it. "What is that?"

"It's a microorganism. I first saw them months ago, but assumed they were just a pest of some kind. My recent experiments, however, show that the worms secrete a manganese compound that kills the mold and neutralizes the mold's toxin."

Borjigin nudges me.

"Told you things happened while you were gone," he says.

I stare at the image while my brain catches up with what Kalle just said. I don't understand all her words, but I think I get her meaning.

"So it's not root-juice that makes our food safe to eat," I say, "it's *worm* juice?"

Kalle nods. "A disgusting yet accurate way to describe it, sure."

"Does this worm thing eat the root?"

"No," she says. "I believe the worms eat waste from the plant cells. Without the worms, in fact, I think the roots would die, killing the vines. Do you know what the word *symbiotic* means?"

I shake my head.

"It means that two or more organisms are interdependent. Sometimes it means two species live in close association that may be—but is not necessarily—beneficial to each other. What we have with the roots and the worms is called *obligate symbiosis*. Do you know what that means?"

She's really starting to annoy me.

"Obviously I don't."

She shrugs. "Who can tell with you? You're always so full of surprises. *Obligate symbiosis* means the two species can't survive without each other. Without the worms, the vines die. Without the vines, the worms die."

Borjigin is excited, and getting impatient.

"Tell her the best part," he says.

Kalle points at the image. Her fingertip touches the worm, sending up a little cloud of multicolored sparkles.

"I think I can modify the worms so they become symbiotic with our corn," she says. "And our turnips, and all of our crops. The mold isn't just toxic to us, it's toxic to the plants the Grownups sent down here. That's why everything we grow looks so sickly. If I can get the worms to live symbiotically with our crops, we'll be able to grow our own food."

Despite the unknown threat orbiting us high above, despite the dangers lurking in the jungle, for the first time we have real hope at *permanent* survival on Omeyocan.

"How long will it take to make it work?"

Kalle shrugs. "I couldn't say. Years, maybe. From what I've learned so far, I'm sure I can do it, but it's going to take a shucking long-ass time."

Borjigin frowns at her.

"Kalle, language. You know Em doesn't like that."

She grins at him. "They're just words."

Maybe they are, but I've had enough. I can only take Kalle in small bits.

I walk to the paintings, admire the work. It's really quite impressive. My people can make *art*. I wouldn't have known if I hadn't seen it with my own eyes.

Walezak is leading a few people in prayer. I'm not crazy about religion, but I do notice her robes are white—not red, like Aramovsky wore. Her message sounds peaceful and positive.

I glance at Borjigin.

"You left Aramovsky in his cell, right? And Bello?"

He nods. "I wouldn't remove either of them without your permission. You know that." He looks around the room. "Aside from them, the only ones missing are Zubiri and Okereke. No one could find them. They knew about the party. Zubiri was looking for parts for the Goffspear—maybe she found another hidden room."

I'm glad at least someone is still working.

"Make sure Aramovsky and Bello get some of this food," I say. "But no—"

"No plate or utensils for Bello, I know," Borjigin says. "I'll see to it."

I get a plate. The piggy is delicious. Farrar gives me some cookies for desert. He is all smiles and laughter. Everyone is having so much fun. Yes, the alien ship is close. In a couple of days, we could all be at war. That's what makes this happy moment even more precious.

This is what we are fighting for.

Someone pushes through the people on my right. It's Zubiri.

"I found something," she says.

The brilliant gear has grown. She's almost as tall as I am. Zubiri is still young, but her beauty already rivals that of Spingate. Dark-brown skin, darker eyes. Her black hair is a soft, curly cloud. She is one of the few who prefer the same outfit we were born in: white button-down shirt and a plaid skirt. We found thousands of those outfits in Observatory storerooms, in all sizes—her clothes fit perfectly.

For all her beauty, though, there is no hiding the damage this world has done to her. Her left sleeve is rolled up and pinned closed just above her elbow. She lost the arm in Aramovsky's war. Smith has done wonders repairing Zubiri's ruined face and broken teeth, but the girl will never get her arm back.

"Hi, Zubiri," I say. I tilt my head toward Victor. "Are you and your boyfriend going to dance?"

She starts to shake her head, stops when she glances at Victor. He doesn't seem to notice she's there. Her eyes cloud over for a moment, shimmer with wetness, then Zubiri finishes that paused shake of the head.

"No time for that," she says. "I've found something very important. I need you, Spingate and Gaston to come with me. Right now."

Zubiri is worried. And maybe more than a little afraid.

I glance at Borjigin, not wanting to spoil his party.

He sighs. "Well, I got you to enjoy thirty minutes of fun, which is better than nothing. Go, I'll get everyone back to work in a little bit."

I stand on tiptoe and kiss his cheek.

"Thank you," I say. "I really mean it."

And with that, I gather up Spingate and Gaston.

We follow Zubiri out of the Grand Hall.

EIGHT

From the outside, the size of the Observatory boggles the imagination. It's a thirty-layer ziggurat. Each layer has a hundred steps. Each step is as high as my knee. Standing next to this building, we feel like gnats. Standing atop it, it feels like you can see the entire world.

From the inside, the Observatory seems somehow even bigger. The hallways twist and turn, sometimes in random directions. We've had people get lost not just for a few minutes or a few hours, but for *days*. Ometeotl is able to provide some maps, but—like so many other things the computer should know—much of its memory about the Observatory has been erased. Opkick set up strict rules about who can go where, when, and with whom, just to make sure someone doesn't vanish for good. She's been trying to estimate how many hallways there are, how far they go, and she's still not sure. Many rooms await behind hidden doors—there is much here we have yet to discover.

So it doesn't surprise me that Spingate and I have followed Zubiri for thirty minutes through the stone hallways, and we still haven't reached her new discovery. Gaston went back to the Control Room, worried that if he's not paying constant attention to the alien ship it might somehow do something we're not ready for.

Zubiri won't talk to me as we walk. I've asked four times what's this about; every time she opens her mouth to speak, she seems to choke on the word. She's not crying, but it's easy to see she's biting back heartbreak—heartbreak she thinks *I* caused.

What did Victor say to her?

So I follow her. I'm exhausted and I still haven't changed out of the clothes I wore for ten days in the jungle. I *smell*. I want to go home. But Zubiri has long since earned our respect. If she needs me to see this now, then I see it now.

We're on the tenth layer. We turn a corner and I see Okereke standing halfway down the hall. He's been waiting here this whole time? No, not waiting—*guarding*.

Zubiri walks up to him, stops.

"Open it," she says.

Okereke nods. He presses a small discoloration in the stone wall. Something clicks. A horizontal chunk of stone pops open. In the space behind it, a row of black symbols on a white background: circle, circle-star, double-ring, circle-cross, half-circle and gear. Okereke taps these in a pattern, so fast I can't follow it.

A wide, hidden stone door swings open without a sound. I wonder how many hundreds of times people have walked right past it, not realizing it was there.

Zubiri enters the room. Spingate and I follow her. Okereke remains outside.

On the far side of the small room is a green metal rack. On that rack, at waist height, are five wide spaces. The first space on my left is empty. The next four are filled with gleaming, golden, six-sided objects. Matilda's memories flashfire the shape—like a *pencil*, but flat on both ends. They are big enough for me to fit inside if I tucked up tight. The rack was clearly designed specifically to hold these objects.

There is no dust on the golden surfaces. No dust in this room, either. The door must have stayed sealed shut for centuries until Zubiri figured out how to open it a few hours ago.

Spingate seems to recognize these things. Whatever they are, they frighten her. She stares at the golden objects as if she knows what they are, but speaking their name out loud would somehow bring a nightmare to life

The two smartest people I know are quaking in their boots.

"Enough of this," I say. "What are these things?"

Being in the presence of these objects seems to chase away Zubiri's heartbreak. Most of it, anyway. Whatever Victor said to hurt her, it pales in comparison to this new reality.

"I've been working on the telescope nonstop," Zubiri says. "Crawling around inside of it, trying to figure out why we can't see out of it. The computer memory was wiped, that's why we don't understand how it works, why we have to figure it out for ourselves."

She's anxious, upset, apologizing for something that I already know, something that isn't her fault.

"No one is mad at you," I say softly. "Just tell me what these are."

She takes a deep breath, continues.

"There is a hatch at the base of the telescope. We've been trying for months to get it open, but the access panel is complicated. The telescope is a delicate instrument—you can't just bang on it with hammers, you know."

My patience is running out. "We know. Go on."

Zubiri takes a deep breath, then continues. "Today, Okereke

finally got that hatch open. He did it by entering a pattern sequence he's been working on. He's good with patterns, better than you'd expect from a circle."

Spingate doesn't seem to notice Zubiri's inadvertent insult. I notice it, of course, but for once I don't care—I want to know what this is all about.

"I crawled inside the hatch," Zubiri says. "I thought I would be looking up at a lens of some kind, because I knew I was in the biggest, longest part of the telescope. But there isn't a lens. The end of the telescope . . . it's open. Like the barrel of a gun. And the interior of the barrel isn't round, it's six-sided. Hexagonal. A barrel just a little bit wider"—she nods toward the golden objects—"than one of those."

I can't believe what I'm hearing.

"Zubiri, are you telling me these pencil-shaped things are some kind of giant *bullets*?"

She nods. She's shivering. She's that scared.

"Inside the hatch door, I saw some numbers. I found Opkick. She's been trying to understand the Grownups' cataloging system, why they number doors the way they do, why some rooms are hidden, that kind of thing. She told me the numbers from inside the hatch probably coordinated with the tenth layer, northwest corner. Okereke and I were very excited, so we started searching. That's why we missed your party—I'm sorry about that."

"It's fine," I say. Like I give a damn about the party right now.

"Okereke and I searched the halls," she says. "We found that hidden panel. He entered the same sequence there that he used to get the hatch open, and here we are."

Objects that might be bullets . . . bullets bigger than my whole body.

I step closer to the rack, stand in front of the giant pencil piece that fills the second space from the left. I notice something below the object, on the rack itself. A small plate with engraved letters. It reminds me of the plaque that decorated the foot of my birth-coffin, the one that told me my name. But this small plaque doesn't show a single letter, a period, then a name—it shows a name, then a number.

"*Goff,*" I say, letting my fingertip trace the hard edges of the engraved letters. "And the number 2."

I look at the plaque under the first space, the empty one. It reads *Goff 1.*

The three to my right read *Goff 3, Goff 4* and *Goff 5.*

And then it hits me. I think of the weapon I carry with me almost everywhere, our symbol of power and leadership.

It hits Spingate, too.

"*Goffspear,*" she says. "It's not one word. It's two. *Goff . . .* and *spear.*"

Zubiri nods.

"The telescope isn't just for seeing," she says. "It's for *target-ing.* I think the telescope is a weapons system designed to fire these hexagonal objects. I think we've been wrong about the Observatory all along. It's not some cultural center or temple—I think this place was built to destroy spaceships."

NINE

My house. My favorite place.

Uchmal is large enough to house three million people. Considering that there are only 275 of us, plus around 200 Springers, there isn't much competition when it comes to picking out a home.

Bishop wanted to live in the Observatory. It's "safe," he likes to say. Maybe so, but that place has no windows—I've spent enough of my life locked up in confined places. And I *need* to be away from the Observatory, at least some of the time. I accept my role as leader, but that doesn't mean the constant demands don't wear me down.

I chose the top floor of a small, four-layer ziggurat. It faces the wide road of Yong Boulevard. We're close enough to the Observatory that I can run there in minutes, or be there in seconds if I'm on spiderback.

My house's outside walls are stone panels that swing out easily on hidden hinges. I leave all four sides open most of the time, even when it's cold. I hate feeling enclosed. I want to see, I need to *breathe*.

I've filled the place with handmade Springer furniture, carvings, rugs, tapestries and brightly colored paintings. I got all of it in exchange for a backpack full of grain bars. Springers can't seem to get enough of those tasty treats. I think of the party—I'll have to get some paintings from Crystal and Axel in here next.

My house is just tall enough that I can see past Uchmal's circular walls. Far to the west, the endless jungle ruins of Omeyocan are a constant reminder of both the destruction my progenitors caused and this planet's untamed beauty. To the north and south, the long expanse of buildings and ziggurats. To the east is the Observatory, massive and ever present. Halfway between it and us is Visca's Spire, a tall black obelisk that stretches toward the sky. We named it after the first casualty in our conflict with the Springers. The Spire has elevators, but they don't work. Sometimes people will take the twenty flights of stairs to the top just for the view.

My favorite couch faces to the west. During the rare times Bishop and I are both home, we often sit there, together. Even if it's raining out, we can cuddle up, stay dry, and just stare out at the glory of Omeyocan.

Which is what we are doing right now. His arm is around me. My head is on his chest. We watch the red sun setting over the yellow jungle. We haven't been alone together in ten days. The last of my strength went into—finally—taking a hot shower. We both want something more than a cuddle, but neither of us has the energy to do anything about it.

So the couch it is. And honestly? I couldn't be happier. Clean hair, clean skin, clean coveralls, and I feel like a different person.

Right now I'm not "the leader." I'm not *"Yalani."* I'm just a girl listening to a boy's beating heart.

"I missed you," Bishop says. "And I'm so pooped."

"Me too. To both."

Far off in the jungle, animals chirp and hoot and howl. At this distance, the sounds merge into a soft song. If I wasn't soaking up every last second with Bishop, filing it away in case this violent place takes him away from me, I would have nodded off long ago.

He turns his head, kisses my hair.

"That's amazing news about the Goff Spear," he says. "Does Zubiri think she can get it to work?"

"She says she needs a few days. She's afraid to try, though. The Goff Spear rounds are nuclear weapons. If something goes wrong, she's worried they might destroy the Observatory."

We stare up at the stars. Gaston says one of the twinkling lights out there is the *Basilisk,* but I don't know which one.

Even though my body is finally relaxing, I can't make my mind do the same. It is full of swirling puzzle pieces: the way people are getting mad at each other, the Belligerent attacks, Barkah's change in behavior, aliens in orbit, spaceship-killing bullets . . . somehow these things connect. I hope I figure out how everything fits together before it's too late.

"Em, what do you want?"

The question strikes me as odd.

"Right now, just this," I say. "Just to be with you."

"That's not what I mean. All the work we're doing. I know it will go on for our lifetimes, but you work harder than anyone else. Do you always want to be the leader?"

"No," I say, instantly. "I do it because it has to be done. I want to build up a stable society, then I want to let someone else take over. I just want to be a normal person."

Bishop laughs. "I don't think you're capable of that."

"Jerk."

He laughs again, pets my hair.

"You're so . . . *driven*," he says. "When you stop being leader, all that energy has to go somewhere. What do you want to do then?"

I realize I've never really thought about that. And yet, seeing those circles at the party, making *art*, creating things that would have never existed without their specific mind, their specific vision . . .

Something pops into my head.

"I think I want to be a writer."

"You mean make up stories?"

I close my eyes, sink a little deeper into him.

"Maybe. Or maybe I'll write about real things. Like the history of our people. It's so hard on us, not knowing our past. If I write, maybe Kevin and other children can know what we went through."

He pauses for a moment. I feel him nod.

"That's beautiful," he says. "I hope you can do that."

I love the sound of his voice. There's a burr in it, a huskiness that is just *male*. Usually gender doesn't matter to me. I could give a damn what kind of parts you have, as long as you can do your job. But that's when I am working. In the precious few minutes when I am not, I love that Bishop is everything a man should be.

He clears his throat in the way he does when he's trying to find the right words. My heart sinks—I know what he's going to say before he says it, and it's not something I want to talk about, not tonight.

"You defeated the Belligerents," he says. "You promised me that once they were beaten, we could talk about starting a family."

I'm already so tired, and he somehow finds a way to make me more so.

"We don't know if they're gone for good."

"You're stalling again," he says. "If you don't want a family with me, Em, why don't you just say so."

Because I'm afraid that if I say that, you won't want to be with me anymore.

"Please, Bishop—there's an alien ship coming. Can we talk about this some other time?"

He backs off. He always does. He wants children. I think it's too early for that. And, to be honest, I'm not even sure I *want* children. At all.

"You haven't told me much about the battle," he says, changing the subject. "Do you want to talk about it?"

I think of the Springer being torn apart by my bracelet beam.

"It was hard being out there for so long," I say. "I was always so wet. And *cold*."

I feel him stir.

"Did Victor try and keep you warm?"

Again, that name said with a hint of anger, a touch of disgust.

"What do you mean *did he try to keep me warm*? We all froze our asses off out there. Why would he . . ."

I suddenly feel so stupid. I sit up.

"You think there's something going on between Victor and me?"

Bishop doesn't answer. I can feel the tension in his body.

"There's not," I say. "Victor is a good soldier. He's reliable. But he's just a boy—you're my man."

That seems to relax him somewhat.

"Well, it might be good to tell Victor the same thing."

"What are you talking about? I said I don't like him that way."

"No, but *he* likes *you* that way."

"That's ridiculous."

"He has a crush on you, Em. Everyone sees it but you."

I think about the things Victor said to me. And how he doesn't seem interested in Zubiri anymore. Could Bishop be right? The very thought embarrasses me.

"Well, I'm not interested in him."

"Even though you said he was *amazing*?"

"He fought well, all right? Stop reading into it."

Maybe this is residue from his budding rivalry with the boy. Or . . . maybe the "rivalry" isn't about who is a better warrior— maybe it's about *me*.

I put my head back on Bishop's chest.

"I don't want to talk about it anymore," I say.

I feel him nod.

"Fair enough," he says. "Something else I want to discuss, anyway. For the next battle, you need to let me fight. I was made for war, Em. You're made for greater things."

I don't mention what I was actually "made" for. I'm a circle. I was made to be a slave.

Bishop is just poking me now, bringing up things we've already talked about. Many times. Why can't he just relax with me?

"I needed you here so everyone could see you, watch you manage things while I'm gone," I say. "We have to think about our long-term survival as a people. If anything happens to me, you—"

"Nothing is going to happen to you."

I hear his heartbeat quicken. In combat, he stays remarkably calm and efficient. Alone with me, though, is the only time he lets his guard down, lets his emotions show.

"I know you feel that way," I say. "But Omeyocan is a place of death. Since we landed, we've lost twenty-one people."

I let that number sink in. It's a reminder to him that death could take any of us, at any time.

And probably will.

"If I die, you have to lead," I say. "Or if you don't want to lead, help the person that does. This isn't about me or you—it's about our people. Barkah needs to see me out there, in the battles, taking risks. He has to know I'm not like his father, that I won't sit back and let others fight for me."

Maybe that's the real reason behind my decision to lead our troops into battle. Barkah has thousands of subjects. Regardless of our weapons and technology, I know full well that if he thinks we're weak, he might be able to wipe us out with numbers alone.

Bishop hates that he can't fight. *Hates* it. But like all of us, he does what must be done.

We stare out into the jungle for a long while before he speaks again.

"I have to tell you something. When you were gone, I had trouble sleeping."

"Awwww, you missed me that much?"

"More than you could ever know, but it wasn't that. I . . . if I tell you this, will you promise not to tell anyone else?"

That gets my attention. If there's one thing that defines Ramses Bishop, it's that he doesn't care what anyone thinks.

"Of course," I say. "Anything you tell me in confidence stays with me, forever."

He hesitates. I wait. When it comes to actions, Bishop moves without hesitation, with speed that is simply shocking. When it comes to strategy—or to emotions—it takes him a little longer to know his mind.

"The first few nights you were gone, I slept fine," he says. "But then something changed. I started having nightmares."

We're not together every night, but when we are, he sleeps like the dead. I've never known him to have a nightmare.

Spingate never had them, either.

His voice is a thin whisper. "I was scared, but not because of something else. I was scared of *me,* because I hurt someone."

A shiver ripples across my skin. Just like the shiver I felt when I saw Spingate and Gaston yelling at each other. I know Bishop better than I know myself. I love him, and he is good to me, but I can never, *ever* forget how dangerous he can be.

I sit up again, stare at him. "Who did you hurt?"

He looks down. He won't meet my eyes.

"Victor," he says. "I . . . I killed him."

"What, like an accident? Or a training duel?"

Bishop makes us do combat training every day. We often use real weapons. Sometimes, people get hurt, but experiencing danger is a necessary part of being able to fight efficiently when your life is on the line. Duels are a huge part of that training— one-on-one battles with blunted spears or other weapons.

He still won't look at me.

"Not a duel," he says. "I came up from behind him. I stalked him. I murdered him."

For the briefest moment, I feel an overpowering urge to stand and run. Aside from the snake-wolves, Bishop is the deadliest creature on this planet. Then the urge passes, and I feel ridiculous for being afraid of him.

"It was just a dream," I say.

He nods.

"But it felt so real. I woke up in the middle of it, right after I ran him through. I was screaming. Not from fear, Em . . . I was screaming with joy."

My people are getting more violent. My people are having

nightmares. A sense of dread takes root in my chest. It lies there, twitching, wiggling.

I reach out, caress his cheek.

"It was just a dream," I say again.

But was it?

I nuzzle into him. I feel his hand on my head, stroking my long black hair. I lose myself in that sensation. As big and powerful as Bishop is, this dealer of death has a touch so tender it makes me melt.

I swear, it makes me want to purr.

Like O'Malley's kitten.

The kitten he had to strangle.

My special, perfect moment evaporates.

They made O'Malley's progenitor kill his own kitten, just to prove something that didn't need to be proved. Down here we all work so closely together toward our common goal that sometimes I forget just how awful our species can be.

Bishop's regular breathing tells me he's fallen asleep. Lying on the couch, in the steady hum of my planet, I'm able to let go of disturbing thoughts. I breathe in deeply through my nose. I smell Bishop. I smell the jungle.

My fear slips away, and sleep takes me.

TEN

Rain hammers so hard the jungle leaves moan in pain.

Omeyocan's twin moons glare down.

The rain transforms the yellow jungle to red. It's not water that pours from the sky—it's *blood*.

"Look what you've done, Em."

That voice.

J. Yong.

He's curled up in a ball on the floor of a *Xolotl* hallway, his blood mixing with the endless gray dust to make crimson slush. Red stains his white shirt where I stabbed him in the belly. He rolls from side to side, but his eyes never leave mine.

"Look what you've done," he says.

"I'm sorry! I didn't mean it!"

I know that's a lie.

Yong cries out. His cry becomes a squeal, because he's not Yong, he's a pig—the pig I killed in the Garden.

"Look what you've done, Em," the pig says.

Blood sprays from its slashed throat, a crimson gusher that coats the green grass.

"But I had to," I say. "You were in pain."

The pig's head tilts back, the cut I made widening until the head comes off and tumbles across a nighttime jungle floor. It rolls to a stop—now it's a Grownup's coal-black head wearing the metal and glass mask they use to breathe Omeyocan's air.

"Look what you've done," Old Visca says.

I want to turn away. I can't.

"You were going to shoot my friend," I say. "You were going to murder Barkah. I had to kill you, I had no choice!"

The head is a head one second, a huge Grownup the next. Coal-black skin is cratered, cracked and smoking, because this thing was ripped to shreds and now has been put back together.

"There is always a choice," Old Bishop says. *"Look what you've done!"*

His words are thunder, a concussion that echoes through the city, bounces off ancient stone walls.

The fissures in his body flare with white fire, and once again he is torn to pieces, but each piece moves as if it is a living animal, grows arms and legs and vibrating blurd wings, crawls and scurries and flies back together in a self-assembling puzzle of gore that becomes a Springer . . .

"You murdered me," it says. "Look what you've done."

It's the one I shot in the battle with the Belligerents. When I killed it, I didn't think I saw details, but I was wrong—I would recognize this being anywhere.

"Look what you've done," it says again.

"I had to!" I'm crying. I never cry. My voice is the voice of a weakling, someone who begs. "I'm so sorry, I *had to.*"

The Springer's two-fingered hands slide to its belly, grab the spear sticking out of it. Blue blood sprays out, mixing with the ankle-deep red dust-slush at its feet.

"Look what you've done to me, Em."

Now it is Ponalla, the Springer I killed in the jungle.

"The *first* Springer you killed," Ponalla says. "There were more. Look what you've done to *us*."

Ponalla stands in a field of carnage. Blood rain pours down. All around me are the twisted, ravaged bodies of Springers and humans, shattered remains of ruined spiders. Smoke and fire and flesh and bone.

"Your fault," Ponalla says. "You could have stopped all of it, if you were stronger."

"Aramovsky did this, not me!"

My words come out as cracked little things, as worthless and ineffective as my leadership.

Leadership. The spear in Ponalla's belly . . . it's *mine*. I need it to stop this nightmare.

I grab the spear shaft, but it's not a spear anymore. It's the handle of a knife, thick with jewels and slick with blood.

Red blood.

A knife buried in yet another belly, the belly of a boy wearing black coveralls.

No.

No, I can't take this, I will go insane and I will never wake up *I will never wake up I don't want to see this I don't want to remember!*

"Look what you've done," Kevin O'Malley says.

The stone walls shake around us, the stone floor trembles beneath. His head is in my lap. He smiles up at me with pure love, which makes it even worse. I killed him, but he was *still in there*.

"Look what you've done to me, Em."

I want to tell him I love him, that I will *always* love him and that I'm so sorry, that I didn't know he was still in there, but I suddenly can't even hear my own words. Everything is a roar. The world shudders around us.

His hands reach up, grip my shoulders.

"Wake up, Em," O'Malley says. "Wake up."

His fingers curl in, squeeze hard enough to hurt. He doesn't know his own strength.

Just like Bishop.

"Wake up."

O'Malley shakes me. The world roars louder, and then he vanishes into the darkness of a fading dream.

ELEVEN

"Em, *wake up!*"

My eyes snap open. Bishop, hovering over me, shaking me, fingertips digging into my soft flesh like iron claws. He lets go but the shaking doesn't stop.

A long, low, droning howl, rising and falling, echoing off every building. Borjigin's emergency warning siren.

Another sound, an explosion, its roar so loud I wince, so loud it *hurts,* makes my inner ear flutter like something is kicking it.

"We're under attack," Bishop says, his voice level and spooky-calm. "Move."

I've fallen off the couch. The floor trembles beneath me. Earthquake? But he said we're under attack. . . .

The tremble subsides. I stand. My house is falling apart. The ceiling leaks streams of dust. Deep cracks line my once-smooth walls, like lightning frozen in stone.

Bishop runs to the stairs, but I don't follow him. I have to see what's happening. I sprint to our east balcony and look out.

Uchmal is ablaze.

A dozen fires burn high, illuminating clouds of billowing smoke and dust. Fire makes shadows dance, as if the surrounding buildings are lit up from a dozen tiny suns that have settled on our streets. A ten-layer ziggurat a few blocks down has crumbled like it was stomped on by a giant boot, the peak smashed in, one tiered edge standing thin and tall like a broken brown tooth. The vines that covered the ziggurat are ablaze, leaves burning bright, heat making the long stems twist as if the fresh ruin is carpeted in a blanket of writhing fire-snakes.

We're under attack? The Springers don't have weapons that can do this . . . do they?

Up above, blazing lights . . . long-tailed comets scorch the night sky, plummeting down to strike my city.

I don't know what I'm seeing, exactly, but the source of this destruction becomes suddenly obvious—the alien ship is bombarding us.

One of those comets streaks directly toward me, louder than all the others, a thunder-scream that freezes me where I stand. The fireball smashes into a ziggurat across the street, erupts in an explosion that shuts my eyes, that throws my arm in front of my face before the boiling breath of an angry giant blows me backward. I slam into a table, knocking it over as I spill across the stone floor.

Searing pain on my left shoulder. I slap at it with my right hand even as I lurch to my feet, off-balance. Flames flare: the table is ablaze. Bits of the ceiling break free and drop down. My paintings and tapestries wriggle with fire. The floor trembles so fiercely I can barely stay on my feet.

I dash to my bedroom, jam my feet into boots.

Bishop rushes in, hunched over against the crumbling stone ceiling, arm near his face to protect against the heat and flame.

"Em, come on!"

I follow him through our burning house. Down stone stairs: one flight, then another, then another.

We are out on the street. My city burns. Flames reach up from craters and the husks of smashed buildings. I hear screams, both human and Springer, echoing through the night. The warning siren wails. Above us, tongues of fire streak down to hammer the ground.

Bishop points eastward.

"The Observatory, it's not being attacked."

I see that he's right. The mammoth structure rises up, blocking out the stars, yet it is free of flame. Surely that won't last. Our attackers are raining fire down all around us—they can't possibly miss the biggest building on this planet.

"We need to run for the jungle," I say. "The city's being destroyed!"

"Stick to your emergency plan." Bishop's voice is calm and resonant. "The Observatory is big enough that it can probably survive the impacts."

My plan was to protect us against a Springer attack, not a barrage from space. Most of my people live in the Observatory, so they'll already be there. Those that don't are trained to head for it at the first sound of the siren.

But with comets blazing down, with buildings collapsing, I think of the Observatory crumbling, of being buried beneath a mountain of stone. My breath seizes up. I will not die in the dark, *I will not*. The jungle, the open spaces, that's where we need to be.

I see two people lurch out of a crumbling building. Young circle-stars. Kai Brown, that's his name, and the girl is Ines Darzi. Brown wears black coveralls, while Darzi—one of

D'souza's Demons—is still decked out in the fancy scarves she wore at the party. They stop, kneel by an unconscious girl sprawled out on the rubble.

The girl is hurt. There will be more wounded. In the Observatory's hospital, Kenzie can help them. And if we run to the jungle, we have no central rallying point. My people will be spread out, disorganized . . . defenseless.

We will stick to the plan.

I point to the kids. "Let's help them."

Bishop is much faster than I am. He reaches the wounded girl before I'm even halfway there, scoops her up and throws her over his shoulder.

Darzi's face is badly burned, but her eyes are clear and she is not afraid. A silver bracelet is on her right arm, long point aimed at the ground. The bracelet's crystal glows white, ready to unleash its deadly energy. Brown hovers near, a Springer-made hatchet in his hand.

"Stay with me," I tell them, and we run down the wide Yong Boulevard toward the towering Observatory.

Others join us in our mad rush, stumbling out of buildings or crawling from the rubble. One moment there are the five of us, the next seven, the next ten. Still the comets streak down like swords of flame, punishing our city.

A roar far louder than the others, that thunder-scream telling me a comet is plummeting toward us.

"*Down,*" Bishop screams, and we throw ourselves to the flat stones as a fireball punches into the street not a hundred strides ahead of us. Wind-driven flame washes over our backs. Something smashes into my chin. Rubble showers down around me, hammers into me.

The world goes silent.

For a moment, I can't hear anything. Then, a high-pitched

ringing. Sounds fade back in: the heaving roar of tall flames, the crack and crumble of collapsing stone, the coughing and cries of my people.

We are close to the Observatory, but not close enough.

A pillar of fire rises high into the night sky. Visca Spire is ablaze. A comet took a chunk out of it on the way down. The tower shudders, then something breaks in the middle—the top half tilts sideways, trailing a long arc of orange and red flame. It smashes across the width of Yong Boulevard in a cloud of smoke and ash and hot stone, completely blocking our path.

"Everyone, *up*," Bishop screams. "Grab the wounded, we'll go around!"

It should be me shouting to my people, leading them on, but I have no air in my lungs. Bishop will get us to safety.

I see a girl to my right, struggling to rise. Fancy rags smolder, dance with bits of fire. It's Darzi. I throw myself on her, smothering the flames, then I grab her and pull her up.

"On your feet!"

She wobbles once, but I catch her, steady her, then she's standing on her own power. Blood pours down her face. Her left arm hangs limply. She coughs, then moves to help someone else up.

I see a boy lying facedown across a pile of broken brick. I rush to him, boots slipping on the loose rubble. I fall twice before I reach him. At the back of his head is a knot of white, a tied headband—it's Halim Horn.

I kneel and grab him, turn him over to scream at him to *get up,* to *run* . . .

. . . but he will never do either of those things, not ever again.

Halim's lower jaw is gone, the place where it once was now a void of ragged red flesh and broken bone. His throat, too, is missing—I can see the bones of his neck. His head . . . it's barely attached to his body.

Dead eyes stare out.

Eyes that look exactly like they did in the Observatory: brown, wide, still wet, but now lifeless, hollow, empty.

A glob of red spreads across his white headband.

A hand, pulling at my coveralls. Darzi, screaming at me to move, screaming at me just the way I screamed at her a few moments ago.

I distantly hear another crushing impact, feel the faint caress of billowing heat.

Halim is gone. The boy who didn't want to fight, who wanted to be a scientist, now he is nothing but meat. His dreams will forever go unfulfilled.

I will find who did this . . . I will find them and I will slaughter them.

I stand. Fire all around us. Our world is ablaze. Flame rises up from ziggurats, dances in the streets, whips and whirs with the blowing wind. We have to move, but to where?

Bishop runs to my side. He still has the girl over his right shoulder, and now a boy over his left. The two limp bodies look like toys.

"Em, help me find a safe way through the fire."

Again that dauntless calm. Bishop is iron, cold and hard. His steadiness soothes my fear and rage.

The fires are closing in. Heat bakes us, grows hotter by the second. I don't see a way clear. Smoke sears my lungs, stings my eyes. We'll be cooked alive.

A new noise, coming from the far side of the crumbled, burning spire that blocks the street. Through the shimmering heat, I see something approaching.

Something *big*.

I recognize the new noise: an engine.

The remnants of Visca Spire billow outward, broken bricks

tumbling and flame-kissed stones spinning as the fire is pierced by a moving wall of metal.

Trailing flames from its strange front end, Big Pig thunders across the rubble. It slows suddenly—huge black tires squealing and sliding on broken stone—then shudders to a halt.

The driver's door opens.

"Everyone, *come on*," Victor screams at us. "Go go go!"

People rush for the truck. I push Darzi toward it, then grab at Brown, who is slow to rise. His leg is broken. I throw him over my own shoulders in a fireman's carry, the way Bawden taught me to do.

Bishop is next to me, urging me on, his steps strong and sure despite his double-shouldered burden.

The heat hammers at us, tries to drain the life from our very bodies.

Then Victor is there, pulling Brown from my shoulders. Coughing madly, I stagger toward the back of the truck, no longer sure of what's happening around me. Someone lifts me. Hands pull me up. I wipe tears from my stinging eyes. I'm in the truck's big bed, which is full of dirt and people. Darzi, Brown, Bishop, people from my neighborhood, others Victor must have rescued along the way.

Zubiri is here, her white shirt filthy from the dirt and the smoke. She has a thick leather bag over her shoulder, and from it she pulls out clean white bandages. She ties off wounds, not with Smith's delicate touch, but rather with an urgency born of desperation. She's coughing hard, not even bothering to cover her mouth as she moves from wounded person to wounded person.

The truck lurches. We grab for the sides, for each other, for anything that will let us hold on as Victor turns it sharply.

I grip the top of the truck bed's wall, pull myself up to look over. Fires all around. They aren't spreading, though, and some are already dying out. The vines are damp from the rains. If they had been dry, Uchmal would be a sea of flame.

The truck hits something in the road, bounces over it roughly enough to make me lose my grip. I fall back to the dirt. All around me, the lurching ride makes people struggle to maintain their balance.

Zubiri crawls across the dirt toward me.

"Em, you're cut," she says. She pulls a white bandage from her bag and presses it to my jaw. "Hold this tight, keep the pressure on it."

In a daze, I reach up to do what she says, then realize I'm already holding something in that hand. Something soft. In a distant, dreamy state, I look to see what it is.

A strip of bloodstained white cloth.

Halim's headband, embroidered with the null-set symbol.

I feel the truck slow sharply, again hear the screeching of tires. We stop. The heat is gone. Cool night air caresses me, soothes my scorched skin. The Observatory—it looms over us. If we can get inside, maybe we'll survive to see the sun rise again.

People call to me. Hands gently pull me to my feet, then lower me to the ground. Someone slides under my arm, helps me walk.

There is no fire here.

The Observatory's vines dance with shadows cast by the flames we've left behind.

TWELVE

The circle-crosses patch up our wounds until the attack stops. We don't know if it will start up again, so those of us who can walk rush from the Observatory and into the nighttime streets.

Usually, I lead. Sometimes in violent situations, Bishop takes over. Now, it is neither of us—Borjigin tells everyone what to do.

He is on spiderback, messageboard in hand. While Kenzie tended the wounded, Borjigin was making a list of who is missing and where they live. He assigns people to dig, to carry water to workers, to call out for the missing by name, to use spiders and trucks to move rubble.

Most of the fires have already burned out. The city is made of stone and brick. What wood and cloth there is—furniture, doorframes, things like that—is already consumed.

Everywhere, the smell of smoke. Of scorched stone. And another scent I know all too well, one that I had hoped I would never know again: the smell of burned flesh.

A few of the Springers who live in Uchmal are here with us.

The rest are digging madly in a nearby area, as that's where most of them lived. As bad as my neighborhood looks, I'm told theirs is even worse.

I don't see Maria anywhere. If she's dead . . .

Borjigin assigns me to a crew with Farrar and a young gear named Milton Cathcart. Farrar swings a pickaxe to break up the stones of a collapsed entrance. Milton and I shovel away the broken chunks as fast as Farrar makes them. Milton works hard, but babbles the entire time, saying that the comet-missiles were probably big rocks "superheated" from punching through the atmosphere. He uses words like "potential energy" and "giga-jewels." I don't know what those things mean. I keep shoveling.

I hear a murmur of alarm, people shouting that we're under attack again. A Springer war horn echoes through the city—and this one isn't from our emergency system.

Bishop shouts commands, telling us to form lines and set up firing positions. People scramble to take cover. I hear the rattle of rifles being cocked, barrels bracing on heavy stone, mutters of "Springer backstabbers" and "godsdamned jungle rats."

Are the Belligerents attacking? We're at our weakest, this would be the ideal time for them to strike, but how could they have gotten through the gates?

Far down the wide, straight swath that is Yong Boulevard, toward the Observatory, I see movement through the swirling smoke. Springers, *hundreds* of them, marching in a tight formation. Flat carts rolling on wooden wheels. Some of the carts have wooden frameworks on top. At first I think they are the trebuchets the Springers used in the Battle of the Crescent-Shaped Clearing to hurl boulders at our spiders, but these frameworks don't look the same.

Something big quickly moves from the back of the column to

the front . . . *two* somethings. I can't make them out . . . hurukans? Yes, hurukans, with riders. One rider carries a flag that
waves slightly in the wind.

But the Belligerents don't have hurukans, at least not that
we've seen.

All around me, my people settle in for this unexpected fight.
Those who have bracelets and rifles take aim. Those who don't
hunker down and clutch tight to axes, knives, hatchets, spears
and other weapons, ready to rush forward on command.

Spears . . . I don't have my spear. It was in my house. I am
without our symbol of leadership.

A short gust of wind clears the smoke for an instant, and in
that instant I see the hurukans and their riders—it's Maria, atop
Fenrir, and Lahfah atop her mount. Riding behind Lahfah, carrying the flag . . . it's Barkah.

I drop my shovel. I step out into the street, feet crunching on
rocks and cinders.

Bishop screams at me to take cover. I raise my hand toward
him, palm out, silently telling him to leave me be.

Maria must have opened the gates, let the Malbinti soldiers in.

Barkah has one arm around Lahfah's waist. He's wearing a
long blue coat with silver trim, finery that seems out of place
amid this wreckage.

His flag . . . it's white.

Just like the one I carried the first time I met him.

"Bishop," I say, "tell everyone to hold their fire."

Bishop barks orders. My people slowly rise from cover, their
weapons pointed at the ground.

Barkah slides off Lahfah's hurukan. He hops toward me,
stops just a few steps away. At least two hundred Springer soldiers stretch down the street behind him. He sets the flagpole
butt on the broken stone street. The white fabric flutters slightly.

He coughs from the smoke. I know his moods, his expressions. He's holding back rage, but there is also anguish and sympathy swirling within him.

"Hem . . . we help?"

I nod. Perhaps I will never fully understand this alien, but right now he is exactly what we need. I put my right hand on his thin left shoulder.

"Thank you," I say. Then, I look for Borjigin, see him on his spider, and shout up to him.

"Barkah and his people are here to help us—tell them what to do."

THIRTEEN

We don't bury our dead.

We burn them.

After the fight in the Observatory where O'Malley, Coyotl and others died, and the fire that reduced them all to ashes, we've chosen funeral pyres as the way we say goodbye.

We gather around a bomb crater not that far from where my home stood. Okereke covered the bottom of the crater in a neat layer of logs and kindling. Our nine fallen friends lie on top, side by side, shoulder to shoulder.

I wish I had my spear.

Humans and Springers alike line the crater's edge. Barkah is here, dressed in fine regalia. Lahfah is next to him—she's *filthy*, covered in soot and ash.

The Springers who died in the attack have been taken out of the city, to be buried in the jungle. Barkah's people have their traditions, we have ours.

Walezak is giving a nice little speech. Something about the glory of dying in the service of your fellow citizens. I have a feeling similar speeches have been given for thousands of years, maybe as far back as humanity goes. The living can make it all sound heroic and magical, because the dead can't argue. Anyway, I'm not really listening. I have one line to deliver, so I pay just enough attention that I don't miss my cue.

Walezak is so small, yet she delivers her speech with volume, conviction. She stands there in white robes, a lit torch in one hand held up high.

"So we bid you farewell," she says. "And we say *thank you* for being part of our lives."

All heads turn to me. My cue, I almost missed it.

"May the gods welcome them home."

My people echo my words: *"May the gods welcome them home."*

Walezak tosses the torch into the crater.

Borjigin has been experimenting with what he calls *accelerants,* a too-fancy word for "things that burn really fast." When the torch hits, flames *whoosh* up instantly, making all of us take a step back.

"Sorry," Borjigin calls out.

I look around, but the burst of flame didn't hurt anyone.

In the pit, Birthday Children bodies burn. When they are reduced to ash, circles will fill in this hole. We'll put up some kind of memorial, as we did with the melted X that marks the resting place of O'Malley's ashes and the ashes of those who died with him.

I'm done here.

Some people ride spiders or other vehicles back to the Observatory.

I think I'll walk.

I'd rather be alone for a little while.

FOURTEEN

Our world has descended into chaos. I can't shake the feeling that I'm missing something, something that makes these puzzle pieces fit. No one I talk to has answers.

But there is one person I haven't spoken to yet. I haven't spoken to him in a long time.

There are twelve cells in our jail, set in two facing rows of six each. Stone walls, iron bars. No windows. We use these cells as punishment for various crimes. Most people serve only a few days here, sometimes a few weeks. All except for our two permanent guests—Korrynn, and her former partner in deceit, Aramovsky.

I have to walk past her cell to get to his. She's asleep, or at least pretending to be. I'm not here to talk to her anyway. Aramovsky's cell is on the same side of the hall as hers. They can't see each other, but they're close enough to talk if she ever chooses to do so. She rarely does.

I stop at his cell.

"Hello, Aramovsky."

He's lying on his bed, arm over his eyes. At the sound of my voice, he sits up instantly.

"Em. Walezak told me about the attack. Did we lose anyone?"

Walezak is the only person who visits him for anything other than delivering food. One double-ring providing emotional comfort to another.

Aramovsky has changed so much since we put him in here. The hatemonger who started a war claims to have seen the error of his ways. He says he wants to make amends for what he's done. He seems sincere about that, but I will never trust this man.

Because of Aramovsky, O'Malley is dead.

Yes, I am the one who drove a knife into Kevin's belly, but that never would have happened if Aramovsky hadn't betrayed us. Aramovsky made a deal with Matilda; in exchange for power, he sold us out.

"Nine," I say.

Nine people, gone. We're down to 266 survivors. The deaths crush me. I am the leader; this loss of life is my fault.

"Nine *humans*, that is," I say. "Because I'm sure you won't be the least bit upset by the fifteen Springers who also died in the attack."

He winces, as if those words sting. He's always been a great actor.

"I take no joy in their deaths," he says. "The Springers are our friends."

I don't bother telling him that Barkah's efforts saved human lives. His soldiers attacked the rubble, clearing it away far faster than we could have done on our own. The carts were cranes, which Borjigin used to stabilize damaged walls long enough to rescue two of our people who were buried in the wreckage. On our own, we wouldn't have reached them in time. And then there's the obvious fact that we were devastated by the attack—Barkah could have easily wiped us out for good. Instead, he helped us in our time of need.

Aramovsky stands and walks toward me. He grips the vertical bars of his cell, leans his face closer. He's not wearing a shirt. He's as tall as he was when we first woke—maybe even a little taller—but his skinny days are long gone. There isn't much to do in his cell, so he exercises constantly: push-ups, sit-ups, stretching, things like that. Muscles ripple beneath his dark skin.

"Em, I know you told me not to ask you anymore, but I have to. When can I get out of here?"

He's in this cell for two reasons. The first is for the things he did. The second is because if his Springer "friends" get their hands on him, they will chop him into tiny pieces.

"Not now," I say. "It's not safe."

He sags a little. How is it possible I feel bad for Aramovsky? It's his fault O'Malley is dead. And Coyotl. And Beckett. And the fourteen kids who died in the Battle of the Crescent-Shaped Clearing. And the hundreds of Springers who died there as well. So much blood on Aramovsky's hands, yes, but to be stuck in this stone cell for over a year? If it was me in there, I wonder if I would be positive and optimistic, like him, or if I'd try to kill myself, like Bello.

"I want your thoughts on our situation," I say.

"Of course," he says instantly. "Anything to help."

I tell him about the bombardment, about the other two ships that will be here soon. I tell him about the Belligerents and Barkah's inconsistent behavior. I tell him about how Spingate and Gaston act toward each other, about her nightmare, and Bishop's—and mine.

Before I know it, I am telling Aramovsky *everything*. The

words pour out of me. He might already know much of this from Walezak's visits, but I don't care—saying it all out loud is a relief. Hearing my own words helps me mentally catalog the vast problems we face.

He listens attentively, nodding occasionally, asking small clarifying questions. He's always been a good listener. It's part of what helped him come to power.

When I finish, his eyes crinkle in thought.

"I know you don't want to hear it," he says, "but this is the influence of the God of Blood."

I want to kick myself. Why did I think this superstitious fool might have real answers?

"The same God of Blood that stood by when we put you in this cell for a year? Doesn't sound like he has all that much power."

Aramovsky shakes his head. "It doesn't care about me. It doesn't want to protect anyone. It creates chaos, Em. It wants hate. It wants its namesake—it wants blood."

Chaos. The same word I was thinking when I came here.

"So the God of Blood *told* you to start a war?"

I say it snarkily, trying to anger him, but he doesn't take the bait. He stares at me, solemn and grim.

"It doesn't work like that. The God of Blood is a trickster. It doesn't *speak* to you, it shapes your emotions. Only after you defeated me did I see what I had done, did I see how my envy of you grew to become bitter jealousy. Only after I was in this cell did I see how hate slowly took me over, guided everything I did. Now I am constantly on guard against its deceptions, its influence. I've learned how to fight it when it tries to manipulate me. You say our people are acting more violent? Then be careful, Em. I know you don't think the God of Blood is real, but I assure you, it is. I succumbed to it. Others will, too."

I don't believe in gods, yet Aramovsky's words stir fear deep inside me. He believes what he's saying, every last word.

I think of how the Belligerents suddenly gathered together, individuals from several tribes joining to try and drive us out of Uchmal. Their species against ours.

Is that so different from Aramovsky's war?

"You hated the Springers," I say. "Why? Why did you want to kill them?"

He shrugs. "Because they were different from us."

There is no shame in those words. I can see he no longer feels that way about the Springers, yet he shares his reason for starting a war as if it were no more important than talking about the weather—he's simply stating a fact.

"Thank you for the talk," I say.

"Did it help?"

"No."

But maybe it did, a little. I don't know why.

"Em, if the aliens attack again, I volunteer to help fight. I don't want to die in here knowing that I didn't make up for the awful things I did."

"You *can't* make up for them."

Those words hit him hard.

"At least let me try," he says. "Please. Every war needs cannon fodder, right? Better that I die than someone who doesn't deserve it."

The pain in his eyes. He hates himself. He wants to be better.

No. I trusted him once. He betrayed me. I will never trust him again.

Aramovsky is in prison, and there he will stay.

FIFTEEN

My wounds are bandaged. So are Bishop's. He hurt his leg in one of the explosions. He didn't show pain or let it slow him down, which is no surprise.

I've gathered my council. These are the people that I most rely upon. Bishop, of course, because we are at war and he speaks for the circle-stars. Spingate and Gaston, because they are the only ones who can tell us what happened. Zubiri, because she is smarter than everyone else. Borjigin, because he runs our city, and during last night's attack he proved himself as a leader beyond any doubt. Barkah, because he represents his tribe of Springers. He and Lahfah are going to stay in Uchmal for a few days, be part of our strategy sessions. His tribe is allied with ours, after all, and we have been attacked.

We're gathered in the Observatory's Control Room. We stand around the Well's waist-high red wall. A glowing hologram of Omeyocan floats above it, complete with the colored dots that represent the *Xolotl* and the alien ships.

"*Goblin* and *Dragon* have sped up," Gaston says. "They accelerated significantly after the *Basilisk*'s attack. *Goblin* will probably be here in a day, the *Dragon* maybe the day after that."

Not the news anyone wanted to hear. We thought we had months before we'd have to worry about those ships.

Gaston clears his throat, stands straight and rigid. He stares at a space somewhere above my head.

"The bombing is my fault," he says. "The *Basilisk* wasn't close enough to safely launch shuttles, still isn't, but I didn't account for kinetic bombardment. It's a lot easier to launch rocks than it is to launch personnel. I should have prepared us for that. I did not. I failed."

His head is back and his chest is out, not in pride, but in acceptance. He's trying to take the blame. His stance is the stance of a man who refuses to make excuses.

As if he could be to blame—I'm the leader, not him. The *failure* is all mine.

"You're not the only one who should have thought of it," I say. "If I had asked you if it was possible the ship might bomb us, would you have accounted for it then?"

He seems suddenly unsure. He was ready to bear all the responsibility, not pass it off on someone else. Xander Gaston is a good person.

"Answer me," I say.

He nods. "I might have, yes."

"You *would* have," Bishop says. "Yes, you should have thought they would bomb us. Em should have thought of it, too, and I *definitely* should have thought of it. I didn't. There's nothing we can do about that now. Assigning blame doesn't bring back the dead."

Spingate reaches out and takes Gaston's hand.

"That battle is over," she says. "Time to get ready for the next one."

Gaston's rigid posture breaks. He slumps, so much so he nearly collapses. He was ready to be chastised, to be punished—not forgiven.

Spingate is correct—time to move on and prepare for whatever comes next.

"Borjigin," I say, "update us on the wounded."

He consults his messageboard.

"Eleven people left in the hospital," he says. "All will be out by tomorrow, except for Delilah Szwarc, who will be in there for a few days. Smith had to amputate her leg."

I can't help but glance at Zubiri's missing arm. Some wounds are beyond even the medical miracles left to us by the Grownups.

"We're still gathering information on damage to the city," Borjigin says. "Looks like sixty-six impacts, total. Most were in the residential area. The Spider Nest took a hit, but the maintenance and repair machinery inside is still functioning. We got lucky there. One of the meteors struck our main food warehouse. It was destroyed. Food supply isn't a major concern, though, as we'd already set up secondary warehouses as a contingency against war or natural disasters. We've still got at least a year's worth of rations, which I'll further subdivide and store in many places across the city."

The puzzle pieces spin in my head. The aliens hit the Spider Nest and the food warehouse. Important buildings.

"Gaston," I say, "is there any way they could know what we had in the Spider Nest and the food warehouse?"

He purses his lips, thinking.

"Depends on their technology," he says. "We know the Spider Nest can't fly, but they might not know that. It's easily identifiable as an orbital-capable ship. Could be the reason they targeted it, to take out a potential spacecraft we could use to attack them."

"But they didn't target *Ximbal*," Bishop says. "No craters anywhere near our shuttle."

Gaston nods. "Right. And the food warehouse is a stone building, like thousands of others in Uchmal. I don't think they could have known what was in there. The food warehouse is big, sure, but larger buildings went unscathed."

The puzzle pieces spin faster.

"Could the aliens see *us*?" I ask. "Where people go?"

"Probably," Gaston says. "Even with really good optics, though, we'd be very tiny, with no detail. Kind of like if you stood on a tall ladder and looked down at an ant hive."

Ants. We've never seen those ourselves, but we know them from our progenitors' memories. It's hard to see individual ants . . . they kind of blend together. But a bunch of them, moving in the same direction, that makes ant *trails* far easier to see than the individual ants themselves.

"People use the Spider Nest and the food warehouse all the time," I say. "And there were people walking to and from the residential areas. Maybe the *Basilisk* chose its targets based on foot traffic, assuming the busiest places were the most important?"

"Except they didn't hit the Observatory," Spingate says. "It has more traffic than any other building."

She's right.

"So much for my theory," I say.

"*Hypothesis*," Spingate says.

I glare at her, annoyed. "What?"

"A *hypothesis* is an attempt to explain something. A *theory* is what happens when you test the hypothesis and confirm it is accurate."

Gaston rubs hard at his face. "Theresa, must you be such an annoying know-it-all?"

She snarls, is about to yell at him, but I cut her off.

"There was *no* damage to the Observatory?"

Borjigin shakes his head. "Not a scratch."

The puzzle pieces refuse to fit. My frustration builds. What am I missing?

"There's only one reason to not target the Observatory," Bishop says. "They don't want to destroy it—they want to capture it. To do that, they need to land troops. We'll have to fight them in the streets."

"Or shoot them down," Gaston says. He looks at Borjigin. "How many tower cannons are operational?"

"Four," Borjigin says. "But we were working on two more that might be salvaged."

Gaston shrinks down the map, showing us the whole city. "We can mount them equidistant around the wall. That gives us the best chance at hitting incoming landing craft, no matter which direction they come from."

Bishop rubs his hands together. "Gaston's right, Em. We need those last two cannons online."

"Make it happen, Borjigin," I say. "Take whoever and whatever you need."

He nods. "I'll get it done."

"There's something else strange about the bombs," Spingate says. "I sent Cathcart out to collect data on crater depths as well as the distance impact debris was thrown. The biggest crater was just over three meters deep. I won't go into the math right now, but based on the explosive power we observed, that indicates the impact of an object about twenty-five centimeters in diameter, assuming it was something about the density of iron. Ometeotl, show the animation I made."

A flash from the blue dot representing the *Basilisk;* a pale blue line streaks away from it.

"We think the alien projectiles were rocks or metal of varying density layers," Spingate says. "When these balls hit the atmosphere, they started to burn up." The streaking blue object turns white. Tiny flames flare up, leave a growing tail behind it. "The atmosphere slowed them some. Most meteors break up while still descending. These did not."

As the white streak descends, the display of Uchmal zooms in closer. In seconds, we're looking at a wide area around Visca Spire. The streak hits nearby, causing a billowing explosion of fire. A shock wave races out, rippling the street stones and hammering nearby buildings. A smoldering crater marks the impact site.

Spingate arches her back, making her belly stretch out a bit farther. She sighs with fatigue. She's still got three months to go, but I get the impression carrying a whole extra person inside of you can wear a girl out.

"Here's what I don't get," she says. "If the aliens had used bigger projectiles, they would have done exponentially more damage. I mean, a projectile just *twice* the size would have destroyed dozens of city blocks and made craters over six meters deep. Why didn't they use bigger projectiles? Why did they go easy on us?"

"*Easy?*" Bishop can't believe what she just said. "Twenty-four of us died."

His count includes both the human and Springer deaths. That bit of respect isn't lost on Barkah.

"*Easy* was the wrong word," Spingate says. "What I mean is, why didn't we have far more casualties? If the aliens really wanted to wipe out Uchmal and everyone in it, all they had to do was throw bigger rocks."

I feel a familiar buzz at the back of my head. The size of the rocks . . . it's one of the missing pieces I need. I know I don't have enough information to see the big picture, not yet, but four things stand out: *the shuttle, the Observatory, shallow craters, they only attacked parts of the city where we go the most.*

I look to Barkah.

"Did any meteors hit Schechak?"

"No hits," he says. *"No in city, no in jungle."*

The aliens weren't attacking the *planet* . . . they were specifically attacking *Uchmal.* But why do that and not hit the Observatory? Why wouldn't they attack Uchmal's largest building, where most of our people live and work?

I stare at the map. What am I missing? I need to get up high, as high as I can, and see if my eyes can show me something this map can't.

"Everyone, get back to your jobs," I say. "I'm going to the peak."

SIXTEEN

climb the circular metal steps that take me to the Observatory's top layer. The walls glow soft white around me. Just above, I see a bit of the sky, mostly hidden by a large stone slab supported by four golden poles.

When we first climbed the Observatory's three thousand steps, that slab was flush with the Observatory's top layer. The slab supported a tall pillar decorated with Bishop-sized symbols of the Grownups: circle at top, then circle-star, double-ring, circle-cross, half-circle and gear. Aramovsky pressed his hand to a palm print inside that gear: the platform rose up on those poles, revealing this staircase that led down into the gargantuan building.

I feel the morning heat even before I finish the climb. Maybe two hours until the reddish sun is directly overhead, and already the day is the hottest we've had in weeks. I step between the golden poles and onto the top plateau. The first thing I notice is the large carbon symbol engraved across the stone beneath my feet. I always notice it, because O'Malley was the first of us to see it. Even though we still don't know its full significance, it always makes me think of him.

This spot truly is the top of our world. I can see forever. The sweltering sun bakes mist from the yellow jungle ruins. The tallest trees look like grass. Uchmal's city walls and buildings are like a child's toys.

Snow-capped mountains rise up to the west. To the north, the lake that feeds the river flowing into our city. To the northeast, the crescent-shaped clearing where Aramovsky fought the Springer king, where I defeated the Belligerents. The clearing has a black smudge in the center—the remnants of Kalle's cornfield.

All of it, from north to west to south to east and back again . . . this is my home.

The lake . . .

Sometimes when I see that blue surface, I have the tiniest bit of Matilda memory. A red canoe. My grampa, smiling, laughing. It should be a happy memory, but it isn't. It bothers me.

I push the splinter of memory away and walk to the plateau's edge. Far below, I see the plaza, a thumbnail-sized tan square. On it, *Ximbal* is a tiny gleam of silver. No damage to the shuttle or the plaza. If I believed in the gods, I'd thank them for that miracle. Although, if gods *were* real, then I'd have to ask them why they let the attack happen in the first place. The best "miracle" would be no attack at all, wouldn't it?

The area all around the Observatory is untouched. Beyond that, though, I see the attack's carnage.

Beautiful Uchmal, the stone city built for the Birthday Children, is pockmarked and ravaged. The residential area is ripped apart like fresh-turned farmland. Bits of buildings stick up like cracked brown bones. Rings of black surround each crater, where flames were hot enough to dry out the wet vines and set them ablaze. The slightest breeze stirs blackened ash into tiny, spinning whirlwinds.

Down there, nine of us died.

Down there, a flying stone ripped away Halim's throat.

Down there, somewhere, is my spear.

I want it.

Maybe the wood shaft burned up. Maybe the blade melted. I don't care. I will find it. Even if it is a melted lump of metal, I will have Borjigin hammer it into a new weapon—a weapon I swear I will use on the aliens who did this to us.

Matilda destroyed the Springer city. She killed thousands. Maybe millions. I know that if there really are gods, if there is justice, her descendants might have to pay for her crimes. I know this, yet I don't care; the Birthday Children did *nothing* to deserve such punishment. We are not responsible for the actions of those who came before us. If we must suffer for our own sins, so be it, but we will not give up our blood for crimes committed by others.

Something about the bomb craters bothers me.

Why didn't they attack the Observatory?

If the aliens destroyed the places where we walked the most, congregated the most, why wouldn't they hit the place where most of us live? It makes no sense.

I look up at the stone slab. A rope ladder dangles from it. I climb. When I reach the top, I see three boys lying on their backs, eyes closed. Nevins and Peura are gears, scientists like Spingate and Zubiri. Harman is a circle. Like me. I've spent a little time with him. For lack of a better way to say it, he just isn't very smart. He's here to help the other two, to be their assistant.

Nevins couldn't be more skinny, while Peura has steadily gained weight since he awoke. Both boys have straight black hair and chocolate-brown skin. If it wasn't for the difference in their bodies, they could be mistaken for brothers. Harman is already taller than I am, thick with muscle. When he's full grown, he'll be a red-haired giant, bigger than Farrar, maybe even bigger than Bishop. The poor boy burns so easily, though— he's going to be feeling the effects of this little nap all over his small nose and freckled face.

The thick pillar lies on its side. When I first saw it, I thought it was stone. I was wrong. It's some man-made material—tough and strong, but hollow.

The contents of the pillar are spread about the slab: bits and pieces of disassembled machinery. Those bits once made an antenna capable of communicating with the stars. Some of the parts are shiny, almost new, but many are melted blobs. Tangles of colored wires are spread out like spilled wax. This collection of pieces is a puzzle, yes, but not the kind of puzzle I could ever solve.

"Having a good nap, boys?"

They lurch to their feet so fast I'm surprised they don't pee themselves. They look terrified, as if I am a hurukan and not a girl that is barely taller than any of them.

"Em," Harman says. "I . . . we . . . there was thinking and we . . . and you . . ."

He's stammering nonsense. Not the smartest of the three, but at least he had the courage to actually speak.

"I need this antenna fixed," I say. "*Now*, not later, not after you've had a nice rest."

They look at each other, frightened anew.

"But Grandmaster Spingate told you," Nevins said. "She said she did. We can't fix it. We *can't*."

I point to the spot where they were just lying.

"So you think you can just go to sleep instead? People are dying, you lazy fools!"

They shrivel in place, shoulders hunched, eyes cast down. Maybe they'd *rather* have a hurukan sneak up on them than face me when I'm angry.

"We were trying to think," Peura says. He has a communication jewel in his left ear. His voice is thin and light, little different from the wind that usually whips across this tiny plateau. "Zubiri told us to do that from time to time. To stop and just *think*. We've done everything we know how to do, Em. Some of the parts are broken for good. It's just . . . well . . . some things can't be fixed."

I think of Halim. He was broken, too. His parts could not be fixed.

Yelling at these boys isn't going to magically make them smarter.

"So you were thinking," I say, lowering my voice, making it softer. "Did you think of anything?"

The three of them shake their heads as if they are one body.

"We need help," Peura says. "Can Zubiri help us for a while?"

If the telescope really is a weapon, I can't spare Zubiri from that project, not even for an instant.

"I guess you better lie back down for a while and think some more," I say. "I don't care what Spingate told you. Zubiri is busy. *You three* need to fix this antenna. Everyone's lives depend on it."

I don't know if that last part is true or not. Reaching the *Xolotl* and letting Bello talk to her friends might make a difference; it might not. If it could possibly help our survival, though, these boys must find a way.

There is always a solution. *Always.*

"Get back to work," I say.

I turn toward the rope ladder, then pause. The cityscape seems to shift. The buildings are already tiny bumps to my eyes, yet they change, they blend together into a shapeless brown mass.

The craters . . .

How could I have not seen it right away?

The shape isn't perfect, but now that I've seen it I can't *un*see it: a wide circle with the plaza at dead center.

The meteor attack didn't avoid a specific building . . . it avoided an *area.*

Peura rushes to me, tugs on my sleeve. He's holding his left pointer finger against his communication jewel in his ear, as if he has to focus hard to understand what he's hearing.

"Spingate wants you in the Control Room," he says. "Zubiri fixed the telescope!"

SEVENTEEN

The elevator stops. I step out into a Control Room alive with activity. A glowing image of the Observatory hovers above the Well. It's an image I've seen a hundred times, but there is something new: halfway up each side, on the ninety-degree corners, are glowing orange dots.

Spingate, Zubiri and Gaston are standing on the platform. Spin adjusts her sling; little Kevin is fussing, crying softly. Spin whispers something comforting, but the baby doesn't stop.

I quickly walk past the students at their pedestals. No lessons today—each display shows some part of the Observatory. I catch glimpses of a weapon I have not seen before, boxy and tan with a long black barrel sticking out of it. No, *six* barrels, all bunched together.

I step onto the platform. Spingate looks up from her work. She's afraid; something has disturbed her right down to her core.

"Zubiri did it," she says. "Or Ometeotl did, because of the attack—Zubiri isn't sure yet. The telescope is working—we have visuals on the alien ships. *All* of them."

Her words hang in the air. I glance at Zubiri. She nods slightly. I've waited months for this—we all have.

I point to the floating Observatory.

"Then why are you showing that instead of our enemies?"

"The attack activated systems we didn't know existed," Gaston says. "Those orange dots are antimissile batteries. Opkick and the halves are examining them now, seeing if any of them still work. If the aliens bombard us again, we might be able to hit their meteors before they impact, break them up so they don't cause as much damage."

I feel a rush of mixed emotions—hope and excitement that we might be able to defend ourselves against the next strike, anger that these systems sat idle while nine of my people died.

"Why didn't they activate during the attack?"

"*I did not know they existed, Empress.*" Ometeotl's voice echoes through the room. "*The orbital bombardment overrode some of the programming blocks that were put into my system long ago.*"

I'd give anything to find out who screwed up the computer's memory. I don't believe in torture, but for that person? I might make an exception.

"All right," I say. "Show me our enemy."

"You need to see the *Xolotl* first," Gaston says to me. "Theresa, put it up on the main display."

He isn't asking Spingate, he's *commanding* her. In *Ximbal's* cockpit, where his authority is unquestioned, this is what he sounds like. I've never heard him use that tone with her anywhere else. She obeys instantly.

"On main display," she says.

The air above the Well sparkles to life. Multicolored flecks gather and glow, swell to blobs, then shrink, rush together and take shape.

A cylinder.

Copper in color, pitted, scratched and gouged all along its length.

I think of the drawing Spingate made in the dust, so long ago, when she said we had walked in a circle.

The part of the cylinder facing Omeyocan ends in a flat, squashed cartoon face surrounded by a ring of small images I can't quite make out. It reminds me of the Mictlan symbol stitched into our black coveralls and our red ties. Just past the cartoon face, a tiny tube sticks out of the cylinder, ending in a small sphere. The sphere is barely a speck compared to the *Xolotl*'s massive size, yet I know what it must be: the Crystal Ball, the place where we first learned we were on a spaceship and not in an endless dungeon.

At the cylinder's far end, a slightly smaller cylinder juts out, points away from the planet. This section is a mishmash of pipes and machinery, gray and silver and teal tapering to a narrow black cone.

Gaston steps off the platform and walks to the Well. He hops onto the red wall, walks around its flat, narrow top with the grace of a circle-star.

"This is where we were when we woke up," he says, pointing to a section of the *Xolotl* near the Crystal Ball. The area he indicates is small, barely more than the tip of the huge ship. He then points to the middle of the copper-colored tube.

"We have no idea what's in here," he says. "That's the part the Grownups sealed off. The part past the end of the Garden, perhaps."

He reaches out, grabbing the image of the *Xolotl,* rotating it. He spreads his hands, making a section bigger. I see a long, deepening groove that ends in a flat gray door that would open like a set of huge jaws.

"Landing bay," he says. "Inside that door is where our shuttle was. And this"—he runs his fingers across the gray, silver and teal section, lets them linger on the tapering black cone—"is the *Xolotl*'s main engine. This is what brought us here."

His voice is full of awe. Aramovsky has his gods, Gaston has this.

"They trained me to command that ship," he says. "Now that I've actually seen it, Em, so much of my training is flooding back. Just like with *Ximbal*. I had to show you that to show you this—put the *Basilisk* on the display."

The *Xolotl* blinks out.

The air above the Well sparkles. An image coalesces . . . it's the same image I was just looking at.

"You put the *Xolotl* up again," I say.

Gaston shakes his head. "Look at the colors."

What is he talking about? It's the *Xolotl*. The long, copper-colored cylinder, the section with machinery and pipes, the tapering engine cone, the . . .

The section with the machinery, the pipes . . . the colors are different. Gleaming, dark reds. Cobalt blues. And the front of the ship, the flat, circular end that points toward Omeyocan, it doesn't have the squashed cartoon face . . . the front of this ship is gray. On that gray disc, in thick, black lines, are the two rings and seven dots of the carbon symbol.

I glance at the Well wall, knowing a matching symbol is etched into it—black on red instead of black on gray.

"The two ships are almost the same," I say.

Zubiri steps off the platform, slowly walks to the Well. She stares up at the image, her wide-eyed face bathed in reflected light.

"Our ship and the *Basilisk* came from completely different

areas of space," she says. "Millions of light-years apart, yet they look like almost identical designs. How can that be?"

Spingate and Gaston say nothing. They don't know, either.

"Maybe it's a coincidence," I say.

Zubiri shakes her head. "Impossible. Theresa, please show her."

"Putting *Gamma-One* on the display," Spingate says.

Gamma-One. The *Goblin*.

The *Basilisk* fuzzes out.

This image that replaces it is smaller, perhaps because the *Goblin* is farther away from us. It is not quite as detailed as the first two, but there is no mistaking what I see: a thick, copper-colored cylinder, a smaller section sticking out the back, tapering to a black engine cone. The *Goblin*'s circular front is deep green, semi-translucent like glass. Etched on it in yellow lines is a curling symbol with thornlike points. I don't know what that symbol is.

"Now show me the *Dragon*," Gaston says. Standing atop the red wall, fists on his hips, silhouetted in the display's light, he looks so commanding. He reminds me of Bishop. He reminds me of *me*.

The image blurs, fuzzes, crystallizes, becomes clear. The smallest of the four ships I've seen so far is the least detailed, yet there is zero doubt—the *Dragon* looks like the *Goblin*, which looks like the *Basilisk*, which looks like our *Xolotl*.

The *Dragon*'s flat circular front is pure white. No symbol. The part tapering away from the copper-colored cylinder's far end is also white. The black engine cone looks identical.

"They're *all* the same," I mutter. "Different colors, but basically the same ship."

"*Grandmaster Spingate,*" the room says. "*New contact detected. Labeling it Epsilon-One.*"

My heart sinks, weighed down by a sense of defeat, a feeling that no matter what we do we will eventually lose.

Zubiri turns her back to the red wall. She sags slowly, sits on her heels. She starts to cry.

"It will never end," she says. "Never."

"Silence on the bridge," Gaston snaps.

The sharpness of his voice startles me. Zubiri as well—she stops crying, looks up at him in confused surprise.

I don't know what a "bridge" is, but Gaston seems to think he's in one.

"Show me the new contact," he says. "Global model, and in scale."

"Processing, Captain Xander."

The image of white-fronted *Dragon* dissipates in an angry shower of sparkles. Those sparkles rush together to form the familiar blue, green and brown orb that is Omeyocan. Big at first, wider than the width of the Well, but the planet shrinks as if we're flying away from it. I see the *Xolotl,* now highlighted in glowing red, then the *Basilisk,* highlighted in glowing blue. As the planet shrinks, those ships quickly become nothing more than colored dots.

Omeyocan reduces to the size of Gaston's chest. The two moons blur into view, then shrink in time with the planet.

A green dot appears: the *Goblin.* When our planet is the size of Gaston's head, I see a white dot—the *Dragon.*

When Omeyocan is as tiny as Gaston's eyeball, I see a fifth colored light. This one is purple.

"The purple dot represents Epsilon-One, Captain," the room says.

Gaston stares. "We'll call it the *Eel.* Show me the *Eel's* projected time to arrival in orbit."

A long, curved purple line appears, connecting the new dot to Omeyocan.

"At current rate of speed and factoring in deceleration, the Eel *will reach orbit in fifteen months, ten days, Captain Xander."*

Gaston's shoulders sag. His veneer of leadership fades away.

One of Matilda's school lessons flares to life in my thoughts. They taught her about *solar systems.* Planets and their moons, all orbiting around a central star. That's what this display reminds me of, except the "star" is Omeyocan, and the "planets" are alien ships.

Alien ships coming to destroy us.

Zubiri's cheeks gleam with tears, reflect the colored lights of this horrible reality.

"We're in hell," she says. "Ship after ship after ship . . . they will keep coming. We'll never beat them all."

A high-pitched wail comes from the walls and ceiling.

"Alert, Captain Xander—incoming projectile fire from the Basilisk.*"*

Gaston hops off the Well and runs to join Spingate on the platform.

"Show me," he says as he slides to a stop at the pedestal next to hers. Spingate's hands are already moving, grabbing floating images of light, moving them, twisting them.

"Attack-level magnification," Ometeotl says.

The glowing display of Omeyocan swells like we are plummeting toward the planet. We don't see the entire orb anymore, just a curve of it. At the center, so small I barely recognize the huge city wall, I make out Uchmal and the surrounding jungle. High up above, the tiny blue dot of the *Basilisk.* Thread-thin blue lines reach out from it, streaking down toward our city.

"How many projectiles in the first salvo?" Gaston asks, his hands moving just as furiously as Spingate's.

"*Seventeen,*" Ometeotl answers. "*Time to first impact, thirteen minutes and seven seconds.*"

"Are the missile-defense batteries active?"

"*Chancellor Borjigin confirms three of the four batteries are functioning, Captain. I have full control of physical systems. Targeting and tracking system active.*"

"Fire at will," Gaston says. "Shoot the godsdamned things down."

"*As you command, Captain. I will initiate automated defense fire as soon as the projectiles enter the stratosphere.*"

Spingate's hands are a blur of light and color. I have no idea what she's doing. I feel stupid and useless.

"Batteries one, two and four active," she says. "A total of thirty-one combined antimissile bursts available. That's not enough . . . should we only target the projectiles aimed at the Observatory?"

Gaston snarls, thinks for a moment. I can almost see the anger simmering inside of him.

"If we only protect the Observatory, they might figure out we're low on ammo," he says, talking out loud as he works through the problem.

There are no easy answers here—for once, I'm glad the decision is not mine to make.

"The *Basilisk* is close enough to safely launch landing craft," Gaston says. "But it hasn't yet. We have to assume that's coming, make sure we can shoot down at least some of those ships. Ometeotl, target the first twenty projectiles, regardless of where they are aimed. Save the last eleven antimissile bursts for incoming aircraft only. If the Observatory or *Ximbal* are directly targeted, use those reserve rounds."

"Affirmative, Captain."

He's making an impossible choice, protecting our people and our only working spaceship, possibly at the expense of being able to shoot down the alien ground troops. I could jump in, I could tell him what to do, but in all honesty, he knows more about air combat than I ever will. I trust him.

Gaston glances at Spingate. "Battery three, the one that doesn't work, are there any rounds in there?"

Spingate moves icons. "Another twelve rounds."

"That gives us a little more breathing room," Gaston says. "Ometeotl, tell Borjigin to have people evenly distribute the ammunition from battery three to the other batteries."

Zubiri starts crying again. Maybe she's a genius scientist, but right now she looks like a terrified little thirteen-year-old girl.

Twelve minutes until the streaks of fire split our sky and shatter our city.

Twelve minutes . . .

"Zubiri," I say, "the telescope is working—does that mean the Goff Spear works? Can we shoot it?"

She looks up at me, eyes wet and wide.

"I haven't verified that yet. The Goff rounds are nuclear weapons—without testing, we can't take a chance that they might malfunction and detonate inside the Observatory."

"A second enemy salvo has launched," Ometeotl calls out. *"Seventeen additional projectiles, time of impact estimated at twenty-one minutes, fourteen seconds. Total incoming projectiles—thirty-four."*

Gaston points at Zubiri. While she looks like a little girl, he suddenly looks like a grown man.

"Load the Goff Spear," he growls. *"Immediately."*

She shakes her head, screams back at him in a broken voice.

"I just told you, I haven't had time to test it! For all I know, it could blow up instead of launching. It could kill us all!"

Gaston looks at me, nods once, returns to his mad work above the pedestal. I'm the leader of our people, but with that brief glance I realize that in here, *he* is in charge, and he has just given me orders.

I walk to Zubiri and haul her to her feet.

"Let's go," I say. "We're loading that weapon."

EIGHTEEN

’m breathing so hard from sprinting here. I feel the Observatory shudder. Our antimissile batteries, shooting at yet another incoming meteor. I marvel at weapons so powerful that just firing them can shake this man-made mountain of stone.

Zubiri isn't breathing as hard as I am—for a scientist, she's in better shape than I would have thought.

"Lock it down," she says to Okereke. "Johnson, use those clamps on top, make sure they're secure."

We're in the room with the Goff Spear rounds. The golden hexagonal chunk known as Goff 2 lies in the strange cart. It fits perfectly, like an egg in an egg carton. Okereke and Johnson fasten a hinged bracket down on top. They close clamps, tighten screws. The cart's solidity, the padding, the tight fit, the springs that support the wheels—the Grownups didn't want the hexagonal object jostled in any way.

I think of what Zubiri said ten minutes ago in the Control Room: *For all I know, it could blow up instead of launching. It could kill us all.*

We can cower in our stone mountain and hope we aren't hit, just like the Springers hid in their underground cities. Or we can take our chances and fight.

Attack, attack, when in doubt, always attack.

Sometimes the voice of my father is wrong. This is not one of those times.

"Move faster," I say. "*Move!*"

Okereke, Johnson, Ingolfsson and a younger circle boy named Daniel Roth roll the cart down the hallway. Okereke is singing a song; the circles' steps land in time to the beat.

The cart has a long handle with four handholds. There is no motor on it, nothing like the engines that drive the spiders or the trucks. I wonder if the Grownups wanted to make sure people had to really *think* about using this weapon. Is that why the rounds are so far from the telescope? Is this weapon so horrible that they wanted to make sure people had more time to consider if it should be used at all?

Up ahead, Opkick is standing in front of an open elevator I haven't seen before. This one is wider than the one that leads down to the Control Room—just wide enough for the cart that carries the Goff round.

"That elevator leads to the loading chamber," Zubiri says. "Only a few minutes now."

She's jogging behind the cart, next to me.

The floor beneath us shudders again—another round fired in our defense, or an enemy meteor punching home?

Opkick waves madly for us to hurry. She has her message-board pinned under her armpit, and a hand cupped under her pregnant belly.

"Come on," she calls out. "You're slowing down!"

Her words give the circles new energy. Okereke increases the song's rhythm. The circles increase their pace to match.

We're almost to the elevator when the building shakes again, but far harder this time. Dust trails down from the ceiling. I see a tiny bit of the wall's surface chip free and fall to the floor. The cart's wheels run over it, crushing it to powder.

The elevator opens to a place I haven't seen before.

For some reason, I expected a big, sprawling room, like the landing bay up on the *Xolotl*. This room is cramped. No wasted space. Just wide enough to roll the cart in.

Heavy, curved, gleaming metal brackets—not gold, but a similar color, perhaps it's brass—support the bottom of a large cylinder made of the same material. The cylinder angles up steeply, through a channel cut into the Observatory's stone. It really does look like the barrel of a massive rifle.

The floor here is steel. The walls, too, at least where we can see them; equipment I don't recognize covers everything. Flashing lights, knobs and switches, levers as long as my arm. Two pedestals are active, images already swirling above them.

Zubiri pushes past me.

"Stay out of the way," she says. "Okereke, open it. The rest of you, unfasten the brackets and get ready to load the round, but don't do *anything else* until I tell you to."

Okereke steps to a round hatch mounted on the side of the massive gun barrel. At the center of the hatch, a panel with our familiar symbols. He taps out a pattern; I hear the loud clank of bolts sliding free. He grabs a handle and leans back hard. It takes all his strength to pull the hatch open. Most doors in this

building open effortlessly. Some even open on their own. Okereke's struggle is yet another reminder from the Grownups: *Are
you sure you want to fire this weapon?*

Zubiri climbs through the open hatch. She moves well despite
her missing arm, but her motions are still awkward. She looks
around, craning her head this way and that. Unseen lights play
off her dark-brown skin. She flips white switches, turns black
dials.

"It's ready," she says. She crawls out, steps to me and takes
my hand. Her fingers are warm. They squeeze in time with her
words.

"Em, *please*. We shouldn't do this. My progenitor wasn't
trained to operate this weapon. If I get something wrong, the
bomb could blow up right here or it could jam in the barrel. It's
been at least *two centuries* since this equipment was checked.
The aliens haven't attacked the Observatory—we're safe here
for now."

Zubiri isn't a warrior. I am. I don't know why the *Basilisk*
hasn't hit the Observatory yet, but when it does we will be done
for. I don't care if using this weapon is risky—we need to stop
these attackers while we still can, before they launch shuttles of
their own and invade.

"Load it," I say. "Right now."

She doesn't want to. She does anyway, telling Okereke and
the others exactly what to do.

I leave the cramped space and sprint for the Control Room.

By the time I rejoin Spingate and Gaston, I'm exhausted, soaked
in sweat.

I rush to join Spingate on the platform. "What's our status?"

"Five defensive rounds left," she says. "Not counting the eleven Gaston is keeping in reserve."

For once, she isn't wearing her sling. Joandra Rigby wears it instead. She's a circle who sometimes works as Kevin's babysitter, when both Spingate and Gaston really need to focus on their work. Joandra is down on the floor, holding little Kevin in her arms. His crying screech is impossible to ignore.

Gaston stands by the Well's red wall. His outstretched arms are bathed in light, dozens of glowing symbols floating on or near his hands. He's looking up at a mix of images: a top-down map of Uchmal with flashing red circles; live scenes of broken and burning ziggurats; meteors streaking down followed by their long orange tails of fire; the *Basilisk,* tinged in blue, and far away from it, the *Xolotl,* tinged in red.

He looks down at me. "What's the status on the Goff Spear?"

"They were loading it when I left," I say. "It should be ready by now."

"We're in bad shape," he says. "We've stopped a lot of incoming rounds, but several got through. Impacts all over the city."

"Grandmaster Zubiri reports that the Goff cannon is ready to fire." Ometeotl's words give me hope. *"The* Xolotl *and the* Basilisk *are both in range."*

On the display of Omeyocan, the blue and red dots flash rapidly.

"Target the *Basilisk,"* Gaston says.

His voice reminds me of Bishop's when we're in combat. The two boys are so different, yet when lives are on the line both of them are calm and reliable.

On the hovering display, the *Basilisk*'s blue light pulses faster.

"Target solution confirmed, Captain."

"Then hit that bastard," Gaston says. "Fire!"

Nothing happens. I feel the room vibrate.

"Four defensive rounds left," Spingate calls out. "After that we'll need to use our eleven-round reserve."

"Ometeotl, I said *fire*," Gaston says. He's not so calm anymore. "Shoot the damn weapon!"

"Of the people present in this room, only Empress Savage may authorize firing of the Goff Spear."

Gaston stares down at me, his eyes wide with rage and his upper lip curled into a wicked snarl. He looks like a madman.

"Tell it to shoot, Em! *Kill them!*"

I start to do just that, an automatic reaction to the chaos unfolding around us, but I pause. Yet again, Zubiri's words rip through my thoughts. If the Goff Spear malfunctions, will I cause all of our deaths?

The room shudders. Cracks appear in the walls. Trails of dust puff down from the ceiling.

"That was close," Spingate says, looking at her pedestal display. "Only a few blocks from the Observatory."

We didn't attack the *Basilisk*. It attacked us. The aliens inside that ship started this fight.

If it's war they want, they messed with the wrong girl.

I have a spear, and I will use it.

"Ometeotl," I say, "fire the weapon."

"By your command, Empress Savage."

The floor, walls and ceiling thrum. They pulse like the heart of a planet-sized stone giant. A buzzing sound drowns out everything except for baby Kevin's piercing wail. My hair stands on end. I feel the vibration in my bones, in my teeth.

There is a whooshing sensation, as if the room's air is sucked out for a split second, then rushes back in. My eardrums flutter in complaint.

The thrumming stops.

The display above the shaft changes. Gaston's multiple scenes vanish, replaced by the lone image of the *Basilisk*.

From Uchmal, a long red streak flashes toward it. At the head of that streak, a metal ball that sizzles and bubbles and shimmers with godlike energy.

It seems to take forever for the red streak to close the distance.

The *Basilisk* fires weapons at the ball, to no apparent effect. The massive ship starts to move, but it is far too slow, far too late.

The red streak punches into the *Basilisk*'s copper hull.

I have a moment to think *That didn't work,* then the enemy ship's hull starts to swell. Another childhood memory of Matilda's: pork sausages on my father's grill, heating and swelling until the skin splits and bubbling meat pushes through. The *Basilisk*'s copper hull *tears*—flashing red energy pulses out, somehow solid and gas and liquid all at once, curling like the dissolving tentacles of some demon monster.

The copper hull snaps in the middle: the ship breaks in two. The halves slowly spin for a moment, then they, too, break up, shattering into a hundred pieces.

Only moments ago, there was a ship with who knows how many living souls aboard. Now, there is a cloud of wreckage.

"Gods," Spingate says. Her voice is a whisper, but I hear it clearly.

Kevin stops crying.

"Ometeotl," Gaston says, "status report."

The room's dispassionate voice confirms my fears.

"The Basilisk *is destroyed. No escape ships detected. Entire crew presumed to be dead. Enemy salvos one and two have either impacted or were destroyed in flight. No incoming projectiles remain."*

Gaston shakes a fist at the shattered ship.

"I hope it *hurt*." His voice is hoarse with bloodlust. "I hope your last moments were full of panic and terror, you gods-damned bastards!"

I think of the room that holds the Goff Spear rounds. One was missing. I wonder if what we saw just now happened be-fore, in the two centuries before we arrived, to some other alien ship that we will never know about.

I stare at the display, at the spreading wreckage. How many intelligent beings just died at my command? Yes, they bombed us, but how many of them had no choice in that matter? How many of them had nothing to do with this war, nothing to do with the decision to attack?

How many civilians did I just kill?

An arm around my shoulder. It's Spingate.

"You had to," she says. "We didn't have any choice."

She always seems to know what I'm thinking. I resist for a moment, then let her pull me in.

As she hugs me, rubs at my back, I see Joandra holding little Kevin, jostling him lightly to comfort him.

Babies.

When the *Basilisk* blew up, were there families?

Were there babies?

If there were, now they are dead.

I have killed them all.

I am the wind . . . I am death.

NINETEEN

There is one final meteor shower. Everyone comes out to watch.

We find ourselves in a world of flame: Uchmal burns around us, while high above the wreckage of the *Basilisk* rains down, a thousand streams of blazing light that scar the nighttime sky.

Humans and Springers ascend the Observatory steps. Hundreds of us, climbing together, as if taking step after step is some kind of quiet ritual celebrating our mutual survival.

Some stop after only a few layers. Some make it only halfway. Some of us, like me, march steadily upward. I have never felt this tired. My soul feels dead.

Ten layers climbed.

Then twenty.

At twenty-five, the vines are stunted things. Past twenty-six, we're too high for the vines to grow at all. I don't stop until I've climbed all thirty layers—*three thousand* steps—watching my city burn as I go.

The day's high heat was the worst thing that could have happened to us. Steady sunlight dried out the vines that have clung to Uchmal's buildings for centuries. The results are tragic. All around and below us, the black night is turned to day by spreading flame. Fire follows the vines that cover almost everything, jumping from yellow leaf to yellow leaf, from blue stem to blue stem, from tree to tree, sheathing every ziggurat and building in a shimmering cascade of blazing orange.

The Observatory is isolated from the fire, it seems, thanks to the project that cleared plants and dead leaves from the plaza and the surrounding streets. I think of how I argued with Borjigin, told him that was a waste of energy. I'm grateful he kept bothering me until I gave in.

Those who made the climb with me stand at the pinnacle of a mountain island rising high from a sea of fire. It's not just Uchmal—beyond our circular walls, parts of the jungle burn as well. Not as intensely, though. Perhaps the ground there holds water longer than our stone streets, slowing the blaze. I hope the Springers out in the jungle are safe. We have no word from Schechak. Barkah and Lahfah were with us in Uchmal when this attack began. They have no idea what's happening in their city, and they won't know until the fires burn out. Right now, the Observatory is the only safe place.

High above, the *Basilisk's* remains continue to rain down. The flaming pieces break apart as they fall, creating showers of smaller glowing trails. Spingate told me most pieces will burn up completely before hitting the ground. I watch them with an insane mixture of emotions: primitive satisfaction that I have killed those who tried to kill us; anguish that I have taken lives, maybe *thousands* of them; fear that the fires below will not stop, that they will spread across the planet, turning everything to ash; a haunting sense of failure I couldn't find a way to end this without violence.

There are about thirty people and maybe ten Springers on the Observatory's top layer. Bishop is up here, as are Borjigin and Bawden, Lahfah and Barkah.

I was wary of Barkah's ambition, but not any more. He had the perfect opportunity to destroy us—he chose to help us instead. My tribe and his are bound together now, temporarily united by the presence of a third that wants all of us dead. For now, at least, the fates of our two peoples seem intertwined.

The Springer king hops closer to me.

"Hem, tragedy," he says. *"Why?"*

Why. The question I need answered more than any other. Why did the *Basilisk* come here? Why did the other ships? Why did the Springers?

Why did the Grownups?

"I don't know. I wish I did."

I look into his two good eyes. Those green orbs are filled with rage and sorrow. He's silhouetted by the burning horizon.

"Underdirt," he says. *"If we go underdirt, you with us."*

The words are slightly off, but my heart breaks with their meaning. If he and his people have to return to their subterranean villages and towns, Barkah is inviting us to go with them. He's offering my people shelter.

"Thank you," I say. I point at the long flames streaking the sky. "The attackers are dead. *Nahnaw.* We destroyed that ship."

He points straight up, to the stars.

"Two more come," he says. *"Tomorrow, will prepare underdirt."*

Three more, actually, although *Epsilon-One*—the *Eel*—is more than a year away. *Goblin* and *Dragon* will be here in days. Every ship that has come to Omeyocan has brought a cargo of war. There is no reason to think the next two will do anything different.

I see a boy on the far side of the top layer, facing north. Huan Chowdhury. He made the climb.

Why? Barkah asked. Why have so many races come to this planet? That is the most important question right now. That is the missing piece of the puzzle.

Huan has spent a year digging, studying. He might be the only person who can venture a guess.

I sit down next to him. Our legs dangle over the edge, heels bouncing against the top layer's stone sides. The fire has spread to the northern part of Uchmal. Buildings seem to shiver beneath a living sheen of flame.

"It's horrible," I say.

Huan jumps a little. He didn't notice me sit down.

"It is," he says. "Just horrible."

Huan and I are both Birthday Children, which means we're basically the same age even though I'm physically six or seven years older than he is. He always seems to be smiling, but he's not smiling now—fear makes him look like a different person.

"There are three more ships coming," I say. I'm sure he already knows. News spreads fast here. "Plus us, and the Springers."

"And the Vellen," he says.

Vellen is the Springer name for the race that came before them. Strange, one-eyed creatures with backward-folded legs, a middle set of arms and a second set of smaller arms that grew from the sides of their heads.

"And the Vellen," I agree. "That's seven races. I need to know why you think they came to Omeyocan."

He shakes his head. "I don't know, Em. I'm just a circle."

I nod. "So am I."

He glances at me, checking to see if I'm having fun at his expense. I'm not.

"But you're our leader," he says.

I point to my forehead symbol. He knows it's there, looks anyway. Maybe he forgets that I'm an *empty*, just like him. Sometimes I do, too.

He starts to talk, stops. I see in him what I see in so many circles: self-doubt.

"Go ahead, Huan. A bad guess is better than no guess at all."

He gazes out at the sea of fire.

"I don't think the races came here on their own," he says. "I think they were drawn here. Maybe . . . *lured* here. There's something about this place that calls to the races. I feel it. Do you?"

I do. I felt it when I was in the Crystal Ball and saw Omeyocan for the first time.

"This feeling, or call or whatever it is," Huan says, "I think it creates a desire to not only possess Omeyocan, but also make sure no other race can have it. That's why the Springers wiped out the Vellen. That's why the Grownups tried to wipe out the Springers."

He points up, to the rain of fire slashing our skies.

"That's why the *Basilisk* attacked us. That's why the *Goblin* will attack us next."

Huan's words don't solve the puzzle, but they rearrange some of the pieces. That buzz in the back of my brain again. I feel like I almost have it. *Almost.*

"The Grownups traveled for over a thousand years to get here," I say. "Who knows how long the other races traveled. If everyone came because they were called . . . who did the calling?"

Huan shrugs. "Nothing I've found tells me why the Vellen came. Or the Springers." He shivers, rubs at his shoulders the way Bello used to do when she was afraid. "I don't know why I came up here. This building feels spooky."

Spooky. He said the same thing about the Well shaft in the Control Room, where he started his archaeological project.

So many races coming to this place . . .

Races that slaughter each other . . .

The *Basilisk* bombed us, but it didn't target the Observatory . . .

The puzzle pieces stop spinning. They click home. They *fit*.

At least seven races aiming for the same place, but that *place* isn't actually Omeyocan. It isn't Uchmal. It isn't the Observatory.

It's the very ground the Observatory is built upon.

"Go back to the Well shaft in the Control Room," I say. "Start digging there again, immediately."

His head snaps toward me.

"No," he says. "That place scares me."

I gesture to the burning city. "Scares you worse than this?" I gesture to the stars. "Worse than the other ships coming to destroy us?"

He starts to nod, then half shakes his head. He doesn't know how to react.

"It's not a request," I say. "It's an order."

I see the terror in his eyes.

"*Please,* Em. I don't want to. There's something wrong down there."

"So find out what that *wrong* is. Our lives might depend on it."

He holds my stare for a few moments, then gives up and looks away. He'll do what he's told. I won't give him any other choice.

"Huan, go be someplace else," says a voice behind us.

It's Spingate. She's standing over us. Huan takes advantage of the chance to escape, scurries away.

"You start at dawn," I call after him. "Be there or I'll come find you."

Spingate sits in Huan's place. She does so carefully, cradling her swollen belly with one hand.

"We need answers," she says.

I nod. As if I needed a gear to tell me that.

Spingate seems distant, cold. There's no hint of the warmth that was once as much a part of her as her red hair.

"We know who has those answers," she says. "Bello is one of *them*. She knows why the *Xolotl* came here."

I can't stop my annoyed sigh. "I've asked her so many times I'm sick of it."

"Then stop asking. *Make* her tell you."

Her eyes bore into me, insistent, almost commanding. I feel my heart tearing into a thousand pieces. It's bad enough when Bishop asks for this. Not Spin, too . . . *not her*.

"You think we should torture Bello," I say quietly.

She shrugs. "If that's how you want to phrase it."

My temper flares, but I control it.

"I *phrase* it like that because that's what it's *called*. We won't stoop to torture, Spin. We're better than that. We're civilized."

Expressionless, she turns her attention to the burning city.

"You don't understand," she says. "I'm a mother. You're not. We were lucky tonight. The *Goblin* will arrive soon, and when it does, that luck might run out. They could hit us harder than the *Basilisk* did. My son could die. My unborn child could die. *Everyone* could die. Why? Because of your precious honor?"

I rarely cry, but the way her words carve at my soul I'm surprised I don't cry now.

"Honor has nothing to do with it. Torturing people is *wrong*."

She slowly shakes her head.

"I hope your version of right and wrong doesn't wind up killing my family."

She stands, heads to the plateau's edge. She starts down the wide stone stairs, opting for the three-thousand-step descent instead of taking the elevator.

A flashfire of memory. A flash, and a fizzle. Matilda knew Spingate. Brewer told me that before, but this is different. I *feel* it this time. I can't place the memory . . . an image of Theresa Spingate being . . . *cruel.*

Something about that intangible memory makes me wonder— if Bello was a gear, not a circle, would Theresa still be willing to torture her? Or is it only because Bello is an *empty*?

I stand, brush off my legs and butt. The wind has increased. A swirling gray snowstorm of ash filters up from the sprawling fire.

The ash looks just like the *Xolotl*'s endless dust.

PART II

SIGNALS AND SILENCE

TWENTY

I circle left, Bawden circles right.

Our boots press into the fine white sand of our training circle. We point wooden practice spears at each other.

"This isn't dance class," Bishop calls out.

He wants us to attack. I've sparred with Bawden enough to know she's blindingly fast with a block and counterattack. I'm trying to figure out her footwork, wait for the right moment to strike.

All around us I hear the *clack-clack* of spears and farm tools bouncing off each other or thudding into bodies.

After we destroyed the *Basilisk,* the *Goblin* slowed its approach, stopped, then moved a little farther *away* from Omeyocan. We've shown what we can do, and the ship reacted accordingly.

Still, we've prepared hard. Our weapons are cleaned, loaded or charged. We've set up primary plans for responding to any landing craft. Barkah and Lahfah have returned to Schechak.

In short, we are as ready as we can be. If we're attacked, we don't know when we might be outside again. Bishop insisted on one last training session here on the plaza, so we might enjoy the sunshine while we still can.

I agreed, but not for his reasons. I've been so busy running here and there, answering endless questions, pushing Huan to keep exploring the shaft, and seeing to a thousand other things that can't happen at all without *my* input . . . I'm frustrated. I want the release that hard training brings; I want to forget, just for a few moments, the endless pressure we're all under.

In other words, I want to *hit* something.

Bawden finally thrusts. I parry, blocking her attack. She grins.

"Come at me, little empty," she says. "Prove you're a real warrior."

"Taunts won't work, sweetheart," I answer as I circle. "Your mouth says such mean things, but your eyes tell me how much you love me."

Bawden laughs—when she does I snap out a knee strike. She barely blocks it.

Hardness settles into her eyes.

Farrar, our other trainer for the day, shouts at us. "Didn't Bishop tell you you're not dancing? Finish your foe, *now*."

I think I have her timing. I thrust at her face. She ducks and spins. I've fought her before, know she'll sweep my legs as she completes that spin, so I jump before she does—her spear's wooden blade whizzes harmlessly beneath my feet. I land and lunge in the same motion before she can bring her spear up to defend, put my blade behind her feet and throw my shoulder into her chest.

Bawden falls hard on her back, air whuffing out of her lungs.

My wooden spear tip is at her throat. She freezes.

"Point, Savage," Farrar says. "Way to be predictable, Bawden."

She glares up at him. "I won two out of three!"

"Which will look nice on your gravestone."

Bawden slaps the sand in frustration. I guess it's not as fun when she loses. I offer my hand. She takes it and I pull her to her feet.

"Rotate partners," Bishop calls out.

There are six sand-filled circles at the plaza's edge. This is where we train. We practice with spears, blunt knives, rifles with dull bayonets, and whatever random things Farrar brings—sticks, broken bits of masonry . . . even rocks. Once he made us fight with belts. Belts *hurt*.

The main thing we do, though, is spar. One-on-one, two-on-one, on our feet, from our backs, one arm tied down as if we were wounded, you name it. These are the skills that will keep us alive in combat.

"Lucky," Bawden says. "I'll kick your ass next time, Savage."

"Looking forward to it."

With that, we both move to the circles on our respective rights.

I find myself facing Victor Muller.

Inside, I cringe. I've *never* beaten him.

He's shaved his head. The medical coffins healed his scalp burns, but he was left with a big missing patch of hair so he cut it all off. His locks were beautiful, yet somehow he looks even *better* with nothing but stubble.

Victor smiles at me, wide and genuine and a little awkward, and I'm suddenly reminded that Bishop thinks this boy has a crush on me.

"Bow and begin," Bishop calls to everyone.

Victor and I bow. I grip my spear, hunting for a weakness in the boy's stance. There isn't one.

He lunges and thrusts. I parry. His spear whirls so fast I don't even see his second strike—the wooden blade presses into the side of my neck.

"Point," he says. "Your hair looks nice today, Em."

My hair's in a tightly braided ponytail, just like always.

"You tell Zubiri her hair looks nice?"

He shrugs. "Haven't seen her. She's very busy."

We return to our starting spots. Victor is so *fast*. Beating him seems impossible. But there has to be a way. There is always a way.

We bow. This time I don't wait—I lunge, feinting at Victor's head before sweeping at his thighs.

He doesn't buy the feint at all, doesn't even move. He blocks my clumsy strike. I start to back away, but he thrusts at my eyes. I blink before I realize I'm doing it, feel his foot behind my heel. I'm falling, but his move tells me where his leg is. I surprise myself with my speed, jam the butt of my spear into his kneecap.

I feel the *thonk* of impact, hear him yelp in pain.

I hit the ground and roll to my feet.

As soon as I'm up, his spear shaft smacks into my chest, drives me backward. I stumble, then his fist drives into my stomach so hard it lifts me off my feet. I drop my spear, land awkwardly on my hands and knees.

Victor's wooden blade touches the side of my neck.

"Point," he says. He smiles wide, extends his hand. "Nice shot to my knee! You're getting so much better, you—"

Bishop levels him with a flying tackle.

The two boys spill into the next circle over, knocking those combatants aside.

Bishop lands on top. He drives an elbow into Victor's mouth—a tooth arcs away.

"You don't TOUCH her," Bishop screams, the roar of a mindless animal.

He rears back for another strike. Before it lands, Bawden rushes in, drives the butt of her spear into Bishop's forehead. The *thonk* echoes across the plaza.

Inside of me, rage explodes.

I stand, step and throw in a perfect motion—my spear closes the short distance in an instant. The wooden point bounces hard off Bawden's sternum. She cries out, crumples to the ground.

Victor staggers to his feet, blood pouring from his snarling mouth. Just as Bishop rises, Victor tackles him, driving them both to the sand again.

In an instant, our disciplined training session erupts into a melee. Kids grab each other, cursing, punching and kicking. Blood and spit flies.

Farrar wades into the carnage, tossing people aside like so much trash. It takes him only seconds to break up the fights.

All but one.

Bishop is straddling Victor, hands locked around the smaller boy's throat. Farrar grabs Bishop, throws him face-first onto the sand before locking a thick arm around Bishop's neck.

"Stop fighting," Farrar growls.

My brain doesn't seem to work. What just happened to me? To *all* of us?

Despite the weight of Farrar on his back, Ramses Bishop struggles to rise.

"I'll *kill* that little bastard!"

I rush to them, grab a handful of Bishop's blond hair and force him to look at me.

"Bishop, *stop*! Victor and I had a fair fight!"

He seems confused for a moment. He stops struggling. I see realization wash over his face.

Farrar looks at me, questioning, as if this might be a trick.

"Let him up," I say.

Farrar does.

Bishop stands, wipes sand from his face.

None of us know what to do.

Victor is on his hands and knees, coughing, spitting blood. Bawden rolls from side to side, hands still covering her chest.

I threw a practice spear, but I didn't think about that. If I'd held the real thing, I'd have done exactly the same—the blade would have punched through her sternum and pierced her heart.

Bawden attacked my man: I instantly wanted her dead.

I see someone hurrying toward us from the Observatory. It's Joandra Rigby, little Kevin clutched in her arms. Even from a distance, I see she's nearly in a panic.

"Everyone," I say, "get back to the Observatory, now. Get Bawden and Victor to Doctor Smith."

Joandra reaches us, chest heaving.

"Em, Gaston wants you, right now! He said the *Dragon* is attacking the *Goblin*!"

TWENTY-ONE

Bishop and I rush into the Control Room. We ran here as fast as we could, neither of us discussing what just happened. He had no right to attack Victor like that. I was hit, yes, but getting hit is part of training. The way Bishop reacted, the way *I* reacted when Bawden tried to stop him . . . I'm disturbed to my core.

The Control Room is abuzz. Gaston is up on the main platform. The smaller pedestals are all filled—he's put people to work analyzing the information we're getting from the telescope. Bariso and Schuster are there, as is Henry Bemba, three halves delegating tasks to the collection of circles and even a few Springers.

Schuster is wearing black coveralls, like the rest of us. No dress. We're well past the time for wearing anything but clothes suitable for war.

Above the Well, I see two *Xolotl*-shaped ships. One is the yellow-tinged *Goblin,* with its yellow curved-thorn symbol on the circular front. The other is the green-tinged *Dragon.* Tiny green dots are heading away from the *Dragon* and moving toward the *Goblin*.

Bishop and I join Gaston on the platform.

He glances at us, then back at the display above his pedestal.

"Damn, Bishop," he says. "What happened to your head?"

The spot where Bawden hit him is already swelling, a big red bump with a circle in the middle the exact diameter of a spear shaft.

"Never mind that," I say. "What's going on? Where's Spin?"

"She's sick," Gaston says. "She could barely stand. Must be from the baby. She can't do anything about what's happening between these ships, so I told her to go lie down."

Spingate is *always* in the Control Room. It feels odd here without her. But considering the way she talked to me on top of the Observatory, maybe it's for the best that I don't see her now.

"The *Goblin* was moving away from Omeyocan," Gaston says. "It wasn't leaving, just making sure it was out of Goff Spear range. That brought it closer to the *Dragon*. *Dragon* recently changed course and headed straight for the *Goblin*—now the *Dragon* appears to be attacking it with smaller ships."

The swarm of green dots reminds me of blurds buzzing over the river's surface.

I pull my braid around over my right shoulder, stroke it nervously.

"I don't see the *Xolotl*," I say. "Where is it?"

"Matilda apparently doesn't want any part of this," Gaston says. "The *Xolotl* is beyond the horizon; we can't even see it right now."

Joandra Rigby enters the Control Room. She's not as fast as Bishop and I, especially when lugging around a baby. She sits on the platform's edge, tries to regain her breath.

On the display, I see something moving on the *Goblin*. It's the landing bay doors—which must be huge but look tiny in relation to the massive ship—opening like the jaws of a monster.

"Defensive action," Gaston says. "*Goblin* launching fighters of her own."

A swarm of yellow dots slides out of the landing bay and heads to meet the oncoming green cloud. The yellow dots seem slower than the wave they fly out to meet. Slower, and fewer.

Midway between the two great starships, the green and yellow swarms collide. Two half-solid masses become a single yellow-green cloud that sparks and flashes and flickers. It takes me a moment to realize the combined cloud is thinning—lights of both colors are blinking out.

A strand of green, maybe five dots in all, rips from the roiling cloud and heads straight at the yellow-tinged *Goblin*.

"*Dragon*'s fighters already control the combat zone," Gaston says. "They're sending a few units to strafe the *Goblin*."

I glance at Bishop. He notices my look, meets my eyes, shrugs, goes back to watching the display. He knows war, yes, but not this kind—space is Gaston's domain.

The five green dots spread out and attack the *Goblin* from five different angles, a predator's claw clutching down on its prey. Lights flicker across the *Goblin*'s surface.

"That's counterfire," Gaston says. "*Goblin* gunners trying to shoot down the incoming *Dragon* fighters."

One of the *Dragon*'s green specks disappears. Then another. Flashes of orange blossom on the *Goblin,* and this time it's not from counterfire—the *Dragon*'s fighters are landing big, explosive hits. Another green dot vanishes. I think that the *Goblin* might survive this assault, then I glance back to the roiling cloud—it is now almost completely green.

"*Dragon*'s fighters are clearly better than the *Goblin*'s," Gaston says. He sounds worried.

In seconds, the last few yellow dots blink out, leaving only green. The remaining *Dragon* fighters close on the yellow-tinged *Goblin*. Counterfire isn't even half of what it was to begin with—the *Dragon*'s fighters are taking out the *Goblin*'s guns.

"*Numerous breaches on the* Goblin*'s hull,*" Ometeotl calls out. "*The* Dragon *is launching a second wave.*"

Six new green dots leave the *Dragon* and head straight for the *Goblin*. These new dots are fatter, thicker.

"I think those are boarding craft," Gaston says. "The *Dragon*'s crew doesn't want to destroy the *Goblin,* they want to capture it. Ometeotl, give me more detail."

"*Detail is at maximum, Captain Xander.*"

He mumbles something under his breath, a curse word that would have gotten him severely beaten when we were in school.

The fat dots reach the *Goblin,* land on the long, tapering part that sticks out the back.

"The boarders will try to breach that hull," Gaston says. "If they do, it will be hand-to-hand fighting against the *Goblin*'s crew."

We watch for a long time. The *Goblin*'s counterfire flickers diminish further, then cease completely.

I imagine a desperate battle of knives and guns and energy blasts, a battle fought between two unknown species.

More killing—and we still don't know the reason for it.

"*The* Goblin *is changing course,*" Ometeotl calls out.

The besieged ship starts moving toward the *Dragon.* I don't know why I pick sides, but I hope the *Goblin* attacks. Maybe both ships will be destroyed.

When it gets closer to the *Dragon,* the *Goblin* slows, then stops.

It doesn't attack.

The two mother ships sit side by side, round front ends facing toward my planet.

"Captured," Bishop says.

Gaston nods. "Looks that way."

Was the *Goblin* going to attack us, like the *Basilisk* did? If so, is it possible that the *Dragon* took out that threat as a gesture of good faith, because those aliens want to be our allies?

I wish that were true, but it seems unlikely. We don't know what this brief battle means for us. I have a feeling we won't have to wait long to find out.

Little Kevin wakes up, lets out a happy squeal. The sound is like a trigger that releases our pent-up stress. Not all of it, but enough that I relax a little. If a baby can . . .

Wait . . . something is wrong.

Kevin. When Spingate isn't working, Kevin is *always* with her.

Spingate isn't here.

But I am. She would have known I'd be here for this.

Bello . . .

Without another word, I sprint for the elevator.

TWENTY-TWO

The moment I step through the door into the cell block, I hear Aramovsky shouting for help.

I see him at the end of the hall, his face pressed between the bars, one arm waving madly.

"Em, *stop Spingate!* The God of Blood has her!"

I slide to a halt in front of Bello's cell, the soles of my boots skidding across the stone floor.

A naked Korrynn Bello hangs from the ceiling support beam by a rope tied tight around her wrists. Her toes dangle just above the stone floor.

Theresa Spingate stands in front of her. Flecks of blood dot Spingate's face. In her hand is a thin cane—the rod from the Grand Hall throne. It's smeared with thick blood, a red identical to that of the cane itself.

Bello's head hangs down, thin blond hair half-hiding a left eye that is already swollen shut. She spins slightly from left to right, the rope creaking in time. Her lower lip is split and ragged. Blood trails from the lip, from a gash on her forehead, from her horribly broken nose, down her cheeks, under her chin and down her too-white body, a path of crimson that drips from her toes into a puddle on the stone floor.

. . . plop . . . plop . . . plop . . .

I press my hand to the palm-plate—the cell door won't open. Spingate reprogrammed it.

"Theresa, open this door!"

She looks at me, but I'm not sure it's me that she sees. Her eyes are wide, her teeth are bared. Her hand is a white-knuckled talon gripping the red rod. I remember Matilda using that device on me, the searing agony it caused every time she touched it to my body.

Spingate is my best friend, the person I know better than anyone—with her face twisted up like that, she is almost unrecognizable.

The God of Blood has her. . . .

"Bello must talk," she says. "She hasn't yet, but she will."

There's cold-blooded anger in Spingate's words, but also a trembling of doubt. Maybe she thought torture would be easy.

"Spin, open this godsdamned cell, *right now!*"

Her voice holds doubt; mine does not. My words are roaring muskets firing at close range.

She glances at Bello.

"Bello will break. She'll tell us what she knows. She *has* to. Why don't you understand?"

My best friend is talking, but it's not really *her*. Theresa is a puppet, controlled by an invisible entity, by pure evil.

"Something is affecting us all," I say. "Something is *changing* us. Listen to me—we don't torture people. We're not like the Grownups!"

Spingate didn't just use the rod to shock, she *beat* Bello with it. Severely. And still Bello wouldn't talk. How can a woman who is so weak she cries from loneliness resist this kind of physical punishment?

I realize Bello isn't spinning anymore.

She isn't moving at all.

The drip-drip of blood falling from her toes is slowing.

. . . *plop* . . .

. . . *plop* . . .

I have to get in there.

"Spin, if she hasn't talked yet, she's not going to. Her will is too strong. Please open the door. *Please!*"

Spingate's face furrows in confusion.

"My children, Em." Her voice is thin, distant. "I need to protect them. Bello knows why the aliens are here. While she stays silent, our people die. Don't you see? My son could be next."

I point to Bello. "Spin, *look* at her."

Spingate does.

"You're doing this for your children," I say. "What if it works? What if torture becomes accepted in our culture, part of who we are. Imagine our world ten years from now—then imagine that it's *Kevin* hanging by his wrists, that someone is hitting him with the rod, over and over and over again."

Spingate stares. She blinks. That blankness washes over her, the same one I saw on Bishop's face after he attacked Victor.

"Imagine it's your son," I say. "Bleeding. *Screaming.*"

Spingate looks at the red rod in her hand like she doesn't know how it got there. A drop of blood falls from the end, splats against the cell floor.

She looks at me. Horror twists her face—horror brought on by realization.

"Em . . . what did I just do?"

She drops the rod. It clatters against the stone. She shuffles to the cell bars, reaches through and presses her hand to the palm-plate. When she takes her hand away, it leaves smeared finger-prints of blood.

The door lock clicks.

I yank it open and rush inside. I draw my knife from the sheath on my thigh and slash the rope. Bello drops like a bag of meat, like she has no bones.

She hits the floor. She doesn't move.

I rush to her. I slice the ropes from her wrists, then sheathe my knife. I feel her face: it's cool to the touch.

I press my ear to her chest: no heartbeat.

I lay her flat on her back, put my hands on her sternum and drive them down, once, twice, three times, just like Smith showed us to do. I press my mouth to Bello's and breathe out hard.

She doesn't respond.

I do chest compressions again, again push air into her lungs.

She doesn't respond.

Over and over I do this, feeling the rage building inside me, sensing my soul eroding, flaking away—how could my best friend *beat a woman to death*?

Hands on my shoulders. A man's hands.

"Let me try," Aramovsky says.

Spingate let him out.

I fall to my butt, get out of his way.

Aramovsky's chest compressions are stronger, his larger lungs force in more air than mine ever could. He is methodical, pumping away, desperate to save Bello.

Still she doesn't respond.

A sheen of sweat breaks out on Aramovsky's dark skin. Of course it does—it's hot in this cell, and he's working so hard.

She's not moving.

I start to crawl backward, wanting to get away from the body. . . .

My hand comes down on something round—the rod.

"Come on," Aramovsky hisses as he keeps pumping. "Come on, Bello, *fight*!"

I hear crying, and for a moment my heart surges with hope, because that's what Bello does, *cry,* until I realize it's not her—it's Spingate.

She's standing in the open cell doorway. Tears streak her blood-flecked face. Her lower lip quivers.

Really? *Now* she feels bad?

I pick up the rod.

Aramovsky sits back, wipes sweat from his forehead with the back of his hand.

"It's no use," he says. "Bello is dead."

I feel myself nodding as I stand.

"Of course she is," I say. "Because this goddamned *gear* killed her."

I step toward Spingate. She stares at me, shakes her head.

"Em, I . . . I didn't mean . . ."

"Yes, you did, you bitch," I say, then I jam the rod tip into her neck.

Spingate's body convulses. She makes a strange gurgling sound.

"Yes, you did," I say, and I pull the rod away.

She collapses backward into the space between the rows of cells, her arms wrapped protectively around her round belly.

"Yes, you *did*." I step out of the cell, touch the rod to her cheek. She convulses anew, that strange sound coming from deep in her throat. Her face wrinkles tight in agony. Her splayed fingers stretch out, half-curled, grabbing at nothing.

I'm going to kill this bitch. Her and her unborn baby, which will probably turn out just as evil as she is. Spingate tortures circles? She *murders* my kind? I'll show her. I press the rod harder against her face, use it to pin her head against the stone floor.

A blur of motion: the rod is ripped from my grasp.

I turn to face Aramovsky. Sheened in sweat, he holds the rod in his right hand.

"The God of Blood has you," he says. "Fight it."

I draw my knife. The images on the Observatory walls, of double-rings torturing people, burning them, *skinning* them. Aramovsky, who started a war, who sent me out to die. He should have killed me when he had the chance.

"*Fight it,* Em," he says, snarling out the words. "You are the strongest of us, don't let it control you."

I drop into a fighting stance, looking for a way past the rod he holds.

Aramovsky tosses the rod into the cell.

He puts his hands to his sides. He closes his eyes.

"Kill me if you must," he says. "But if you do, the God of Blood will own you forever."

I see the veins in his neck pulsing beneath his skin.

One slash of my blade will open up those veins. Aramovsky's blood will spray everywhere.

Just like the pig's did.

It will flow and puddle.

Just like Yong's did.

The God of Blood has you. . . .

I blink. I hear nothing. All I see is a defenseless man standing before me.

My knife clatters against the stone floor.

I glance at Spingate. She's curled up on the floor, shaking, drooling blood.

I glance at Bello. Naked. Lifeless. *Dead*.

Aramovsky opens his eyes.

"Now you know, Em" he says. "Now you know what it's like."

TWENTY-THREE

Bishop and I can do nothing but stand and watch. One of us usually leads, but right now the fate of our people relies on Giles Borjigin.

We're atop a wall tower. A thick stone battlement runs along the outside edge of the circular floor. The battlement is taller than I am, but there are notches cut into it so people can look out. To the north, I see the river snaking off through the jungle ruins, slicing between the canyon of trees rising up on either side. To the south, I can see all of Uchmal—blackened, burned, coated in ash.

Opkick is up here, with us, as are five filthy circles awaiting their next task. Two of the circles, Elisa Hinog and Kurt Armbruster, have been trained to fire the cannon and will make sure it's working properly.

We can't spare circle-stars to crew the wall cannons, as we need them in the city streets, battling with rifle and spear and spider. Halves, gears and circle-crosses have important jobs to do when the fighting begins; we can't spare them, either.

What we *can* spare—as always—are circles.

The circles up here are filthy because they've spent all morning raising a five-meter-high dirt ramp against the city side of the tower.

Up that ramp walks a metal giant.

Borjigin is inside, piloting the massive, two-legged, fifteen-meter-tall construction machine that we found in the Spider Nest, the same giant that he turned into a war machine at Aramovsky's command. In that battle, I ordered Spingate to fire shuttle missiles at the giant, which caused the death of the four people inside.

I remember their names: Abrantes, Cadotte, Aeschelman, Cody.

They burned alive. Because of me.

I feel Bishop's hand on my shoulder, squeezing, reassuring.

"Are you thinking about when we stopped Aramovsky?"

I nod.

"You did what you had to do," he says quietly. "It was war."

Using the word *war* frames my decisions, but it doesn't justify them.

We watch the giant machine continue up the ramp.

"I don't think that's an excuse," I say. "Spingate did what she thought she had to do—she's a murderer because of it, not a hero."

Bishop shakes his head. "Whatever Spingate is, her mind is too valuable to waste away in prison. You need to let her out and put her back to work."

"She tortured a human being to death," I say. "She'll stay where I put her."

Which is in a cell, right next to Aramovsky's.

Aramovsky claims something took Theresa over, fanned the

flames of her deepest fears, somehow *forced* one of the smartest people I know to listen to her most primitive, hateful instincts.

She killed Bello. Spingate will be punished—she is responsible for her actions.

But you felt it, didn't you? You felt the God of Blood. You could have killed Spingate just as easily as Spingate killed Bello, killed Spingate and her unborn baby . . .

No, there's a difference. I *didn't* kill. But is that only because Aramovsky was there to interfere?

I glance at Bishop. He went into a rage and almost killed Victor. If Victor had died, would I have put Bishop in a cell?

If I'd been holding a real spear instead of a practice one, Bawden would be dead—would I have put *myself* in jail? Would I have let someone else put me in there?

"You're being stupid," Bishop says. "This isn't the time for your morals if those morals get in the way of our survival. Spingate is special. Her mind is irreplaceable. What's more important—the accidental death of an enemy, or the deaths of our people that might occur because she's locked up instead of being in the Control Room where she belongs?"

I don't know the right answer to his question.

Spingate has always been among the most reliable of the Birthday Children. Smart, self-sacrificing, dedicated. Honorable. The fact that she, of all people, did what she did? It intensifies the sense of anger and dismay spreading through our people.

Spingate. Bishop. *Me.* The fight on the training ground. The Belligerents. Barkah and his prisoner.

Is something really making us all do evil things?

Or are we all just evil to begin with?

"Here we go," Bishop says, nodding toward the giant. "We better get clear."

We press our backs against the curved battlement wall, making space for Opkick and the circles to work.

Borjigin spent months rebuilding his giant, using tubes, wires and other parts I don't understand from the hundreds of dead machines rusting away in the Spider Nest. He even painted over the giant's scorched metal frame, turning it from fire-smudge black to a light blue dotted with bright bits of steel. Cables and cords of green and black snake through the framework. The left arm ends in a bright blue, three-fingered pincer. The right ends in a scoop shovel big enough for five people to stand in comfortably. Right now, though, it holds today's prize—a long wall cannon, silvery metal blazing reddish in the afternoon sun.

Opkick shouts instructions to Borjigin. The scoop rises above the battlements. The three-fingered pincer gently lifts the cannon from the scoop and sets it down in the center of the tower. Opkick barks commands to the circles, who scramble to fasten the cannon to bolts mounted in the stone.

"That's the last one," Bishop says. "I hope they're enough."

The wall surrounding Uchmal has sixty-four towers. Once upon a time, Borjigin tells me, every tower had a cannon. Out of all of those, he and the other halves were able to cobble together enough parts to make six working weapons. He's spaced these evenly around the wall. If the city was a clock face and due north was twelve o'clock, we have cannons at 1, 3, 5, 7, 9 and 11. We're standing in the one o'clock tower. The three o'clock tower is the one above the East Gate, and so on.

"Use the signal flags," I say. "Tell the Observatory the cannon is in place."

Bishop pulls an orange handheld flag from inside his coveralls: he steps to the tower's south edge and moves the flags in a simple pattern.

Twenty blocks away, someone atop a four-story ziggurat

waves a much larger orange flag, mimicking Bishop's pattern. Moments later, I can just make out a third orange flag, another twenty blocks closer to the city center.

"It works," Bishop says. "Good. Between the flags and the horns, we'll be fine."

We've given up on the communication jewels. They don't work at all now, not even close to the Observatory. Borjigin still doesn't know what's causing the interference, and he doesn't have time to figure it out.

If the aliens land and we have a ground war, our combat units need to communicate with each other. Bawden came up with the idea of using signal flags to relay messages through the city. Lah-fah brought us more war horns—we'll also use those to coordinate troop movements, just like the Springers do in the jungle.

Centuries ago, this city had a huge arsenal with which to defend itself, but time is the great destroyer. Machines and weapons went untended. Rust ate metal. Delicate parts corroded. Synthetic materials broke down.

Other than bracelets, rifles, spears, knives and farm tools, we don't have much: the Observatory's automated defense, six tower cannons, seven spiders, four heavy trucks converted from hauling dirt to hauling infantry, the Big Pig and some small un-armored vehicles.

And, of course, the Goff Spear and its three remaining rounds.

We have four platoons of human soldiers. I lead one platoon. Bishop, Farrar and young Darzi lead the others. A platoon consists of three spiders—each with a crew of three—and twelve infantry.

Infantry. That's a funny word. It's supposed to mean trained soldiers. We have circle-stars, yes, who have programmed memories and fighting skills, but most of them are physically only thirteen years old. They are children with guns. And we don't even have enough of them, so each platoon is rounded out with a handful of circles. Shuttle kids, mostly, also physically thirteen years old, but any combat training they've received has come in the last six months.

We have help from Barkah. Four companies of his Malbinti warriors are hidden throughout the city. Two hundred soldiers in each company, armed with rifles and muskets. Inside our own walls, armed Springers now outnumber us over three to one. A risk, yes, but if Bishop is right and the aliens land ground troops, it's a risk worth taking.

There are more of Barkah's forces out in the jungle ruins, ready to defend Schechak. Eight companies organized into two battalions, sixteen hundred warriors ready to fight whatever comes their way. Assisting them are the hurukan squads: D'souza's Demons and Lahfah's Creepers. The snake-wolves are best suited for jungle warfare, so that's where they are stationed unless things really get out of hand here in Uchmal.

If our new enemy lands among the trees, they are in for a serious fight.

A long wail, rising and falling, reaches across the city—the emergency warning siren.

Did the people in the Control Room detect incoming ships?

Everyone atop the tower looks to the sky, searching this way and that. My heart races. We've prepared as best we can, but we're not ready.

I hear it before I see it; the distant roar of a rocket echoing across the jungle canopy. Something about that sound is oddly familiar. Is it one of those "fighters" from the *Dragon*? Or, worse, a swarm of them?

Bishop points north. "There!"

Far out at the horizon, I see a black dot.

Bishop shouts at the circles installing the silver cannon.

"Get that weapon online! Right now!"

Other wall cannons might have an angle, but it's flying straight at us—our tower will have the best shot.

It comes in low, skimming the yellow treetops. The noisy ship trails a thick, roiling cloud of black.

Wait, the sound of that rocket . . . how do I know that sound?

"Cannon is online," Opkick shouts.

Bishop points at Elisa and Kurt.

"Man your weapon!"

They're shuttle kids. Barely thirteen years old. They looked shocked. They have trained and trained, but this isn't a drill. This is real.

Elisa sits in a metal chair mounted on the cannon's right side. She pulls a targeting rig close to her face, starts working the controls. Kurt steps to the weapon's left side, where he'll monitor a dozen different settings.

The enemy ship is coming in low, fast and loud.

The white crystal atop the silver cannon begins to glow.

A blazing white beam fires from our left, coming from the eleven o'clock tower. It misses the incoming ship, leaves a shimmering reverse-image streamer dancing across my vision. I see a small fireball rise up from the jungle, where the beam touched down.

Now I realize why the ship is flying at tree level—it's below the top of the city wall, meaning most of our cannons can't get a line of sight on it.

Just one ship . . . why just *one*?

"Weapon charged," Kurt shouts. His voice breaks on *charged*. He's so young he's still in puberty. He sounds as scared as he looks.

"Targeting," Elisa says. She's shaking.

Icons flash on her display: an image of the ship, a crosshairs lined up on it. That ship . . . it's larger in the targeting display, I can make out details I can't with my naked eye.

It's not sleek, as I expected . . . it's black, and it's . . .

. . . it's *lumpy*.

It's the same ship that brought Bello down a year ago, that took Matilda and Old Gaston back up to the *Xolotl*.

"*Stop,*" I scream as I rush at Elisa, yank her hands away from the controls. I turn to Bishop. "That ship is *ours*! Signal all batteries to cease fire!"

He doesn't second-guess me, even for an instant. He faces south, starts making sharp signals with his flag.

A beam of light lashes out from the southeast, from the three o'clock tower. This beam grazes the lumpy ship's back, lashing up a splattering wave of molten metal. The ship starts to tremble. It dips down into the trees, vanishes for a second, then arcs back up above the canopy in an eruption of leaves and vines.

The shuddering ship struggles to rise—it's not going to make it over the vine-covered wall.

I grip the slot in the battlements, pouring my will into that ship.

Climb. Climb, dammit!

It's going to smash into the wall just to our right. It climbs. I wince as it reaches the wall—the ship's belly grinds against the stone edge and bounces over, trailing a cloud of pulverized stone, spinning vine leaves and billowing smoke.

The lumpy ship tilts hard right and drops toward the wide, north/south street that is Latu Way. It whizzes by blackened stone buildings on either side. Cones of fire shoot out from all over the lumpy ship, fluttering and flickering in an effort to keep it level. It slows dramatically as the already-ruined undercarriage slams into the street with an ear-splitting spray of sparks. Metal grinds against stone.

The ship slides to a stop some twenty-five blocks south of our position.

A massive shadow above my head makes me duck. The huge scoop-shovel of Borjigin's giant touches down on the battlement's floor with barely a clank. In the giant's "head," through light blue bars and a slot cut into metal plating, I see Borjigin's face.

"Em, *get in*," he shouts. "Let's go!"

Bishop and I scramble into the scoop. Borjigin lifts it clear. The giant machine turns. Long strides take it down the earthen ramp and onto Latu Way. Each thundering step makes the big machine tremble, rattling us in the scoop. Bishop and I hold on tight as big legs chew up the distance.

I flick my wrist left and then right. Bishop does the same. Our bracelets glow with the promise of death.

We reach the ship in minutes. It's twisted and broken. It will clearly never fly again, but it's mostly in one piece. Thin smoke curls up from a dozen tiny tears and cracks. The nose cone is badly dented.

Bishop waves at Borjigin to get his attention, then points to the ground. A hatch opens on the back of the giant's head. There is a long ladder running down the giant's spine, but Borjigin ignores it—with agility I would have never expected from him, he balance-walks along the giant's shoulder and down its arm toward us. He jumps into the scoop, then waves at someone still inside the chest.

"Put us down!"

A whir of machinery, the hiss of hydraulics.

The scoop hits the ground. We scramble out onto the street.

The lumpy black ship seems much bigger up close. Eight to ten people would fit inside it comfortably.

Bishop runs to the nose cone, looks through a crack.

"I think there's someone moving in there!"

Borjigin sprints to the side of the ship, finds a door just behind the cockpit. The door is badly bent and refuses to open enough for him to enter. Bishop and I join in—the three of us yank and yank until the door pops opens with a shriek of complaining metal.

I scramble into the ship's shadows, Bishop at my heels. Sunlight filters through cracks in the hull, lighting up beams of swirling smoke.

A black form falls out of the pilot's seat.

It's a Grownup, gnarled and thin, wearing the metal frame and clear mask that lets its kind breathe on Omeyocan. I can't make out the face through all this smoke.

I aim my bracelet. Bishop does the same.

The Grownup is trembling, coughing so hard its thin body shudders. Its skinny legs are twisted, misshapen and limp.

It lifts its head.

A sunbeam finds its way through the cracked hull to light up the Grownup's visor and the face behind it. Two bulbous red eyes look at me, eyes that whirl with a soft, red glow.

"Little Savage," it says between violent coughs. "Do be a . . . be a sweetie, and . . . don't kill me a second time."

It's Brewer. I can't believe it.

I lower my arm. "What are you doing here?"

He raises a trembling coal-black arm, points a bone-thin finger behind Bishop and me.

"Beware the Cherished who bears gifts," he says. "Or who gifts bears with chairs that itch."

Bishop and I both turn and look deeper into the ruined lumpy ship. Through the swirling sunbeam smoke, I see a long shape, thick straps holding it tight against gray foam padding.

I recognize the shape.

"You've got to be kidding me," I say.

Bishop looks from the shape to me, then back to the shape again.

"What is it?"

I saw something like it up on top of the Observatory, only that one was broken up into a hundred pieces. This one? This one is new. This one is *whole*.

"It's an antenna," I say. "Brewer brought us an antenna."

TWENTY-FOUR

'm in the hospital. Kenzie Smith and I stand next to a closed white coffin. Inside it, Brewer.

"He's in bad shape," Kenzie says. "His left side took the brunt of it—broken tibia, fibula broken in *three* places, fractured femur, broken hip bone. A couple of cracked ribs for good measure, although I've never seen ribs like his before. Whatever they did to make Grownups live for so long changed their bodies immensely."

Brewer passed out as soon as we tried to move him. I'll never forget his scream of pain. Bishop used his signal flags to call for vehicles and medical help.

Nevins, Peura and Harman rushed to the crash site almost as fast as Kenzie did. Once Brewer was safely away, they crawled into the lumpy ship, excited beyond any level of self-control. They *oohed* and *aahed* over the antenna, squealed with delight at finally understanding where a few of their mystery parts were supposed to go. Some bits broke in the crash, but the boys are confident that between the new and the old they now have enough working pieces to make a functioning antenna.

"How long until he's out of there?" I ask Kenzie.

"Depends on if you want him on his feet or in a wheelchair. That hip will take weeks in the med-chamber, if I can heal him at all. His bones are so brittle."

"I don't care if he can walk, as long as he can talk."

He risked his life to deliver the antenna. Why? Can he tell us why the *Xolotl* came to Omeyocan? Can he tell us why the alien ships are here?

"There's something else," Kenzie says. "He's dying."

"Of course he's dying, he's a thousand godsdamned years old."

She shakes her head. "He's got small-cell carcinoma. It's metastasized."

Kenzie stares at me for a moment, all solemn, waiting for a response.

I shrug. "I don't know what that means."

She waves her hand over the top of the white pedestal next to the coffin. An image sparkles to life: the outline of a thin man, legs together, hands at his sides. The image is white. His chest is dotted with spots of deep green. There are spots of green all over him, including his head.

"He has lung cancer," she says. "And it has spread to his lymph nodes, his liver, his bones . . . his brain. He must be in excruciating pain."

I look at the white coffin, as if I can suddenly see through it to the gnarled, ancient man inside. I think back to when I first spoke to him, up on the *Xolotl*.

"Lung cancer," I say. "Would that make you cough?"

"At his stage, yes. A lot."

"So cure him. The coffins can fix that, right?"

Kenzie shakes her head. "Med-chambers can do a lot, but many conditions are beyond the technology."

Zubiri's arm. Delilah's leg. Some things can't be healed.

"How long until he dies?"

Kenzie thinks this over for a moment, runs a hand through her hair.

"Based on what I know, what I see, he should have been dead a year ago. I honestly don't know how he's still alive. He can't have more than a few weeks left. A few days, probably."

If he dies before he can tell us why he came . . .

"Fix what you can as fast as you can," I say. "Then wake him up."

I turn to leave.

"Wait," Kenzie says. "I need to talk to you about Spingate. She's extremely upset."

My jaw tightens. "She's a murderer. Her feelings are not important to me right now."

"You won't let her see her own child. It's killing her."

"Which means the baby is safe," I say.

Kenzie rubs her eyes. "Theresa wouldn't hurt little Kevin."

"And I wouldn't have thought she could hurt Bello, either."

This is taking a toll on Kenzie, draining her. She looks at me with an expression I've become all too familiar with—she wants this to make sense. She wants answers.

Answers that I don't have.

"Theresa is the sweetest person I know," Kenzie said. "How could she have done that to Bello?"

"I don't know," I say.

Kenzie glances at the lines of coffins. She shivers.

"What's happening to us, Em? When is this going to stop?"

I've never seen her this distraught.

"I have no idea," I say. "I'm doing the best I can."

She forces a smile. "I know. But please, reconsider not letting Spin see her baby. All right?"

I think of Bello, hanging by her wrists, and Spingate, holding the bloody rod. Was that really a one-time thing, or could it happen again?

"I'll think about it," I say.

Kenzie looks off, nods, then goes back to work on the pedestal display next to Brewer's coffin.

TWENTY-FIVE

We're atop the Observatory.

Dawn sets the sky aglow.

Brewer sits in a wheelchair, blanket over his legs, staring out at Omeyocan's endless expanse. A strong breeze sweeps clouds of vine ash across the city, makes Gaston's black locks flutter, pulls a few tickling strands of hair free from my braid.

Gaston, Bishop, Aramovsky, Kenzie Smith and I are here with Brewer. Kenzie insisted on coming so she could keep an eye on her patient. I brought Aramovsky because he knows religion, which I suspect is at the root of everything we face. And because I think he may have stopped me from killing Spingate. I was that lost in my rage. I'm not about to set him free, but I think he's earned some time out of his cell.

Gaston won't look anyone in the eye. He's deeply ashamed of Spingate's hateful act. I think he feels responsible, somehow, as if it's his fault he let her out of his sight.

I stare at Brewer, try to sort through my feelings. He's horrifying to behold; gnarled, wrinkled and spindly, the embodiment of the evil that's been done to us. But he is also the person who protected us, spent centuries keeping us from being erased. Without him, we might never have awoken at all, let alone escaped the *Xolotl*.

Looking at him now, though, in person, not over some pedestal connection, I finally see the *real* B. Brewer—an ancient, broken man staring out at the lost dream of his life.

Bishop carried the wheelchair up the spiral staircase with Brewer still in it. Bishop moved as gently as he could, but with each step Brewer let out a little whimper. A broken hip must be an awful thing. We asked Brewer several times if he wanted to stop. He didn't.

Because more than anything else, he wanted to see the planet that had been promised to him so long ago.

His eyes are bigger than ours, rounder. They stick out slightly from his head, almost touching the clear mask that covers his face. Combined with the fleshy folds that hang where his nose and mouth should be, the Grownups look hideous.

"I waited twelve centuries for this view," he says. "Give or take a century."

His voice is soft, muffled by the mask. The mask filters out the poisons from Omeyocan's air. Poisons for *him*. We're different—we were created to live here.

"Or take," he says. "Take a flake and cake a rake."

I glance at Bishop. He's pulling slightly at his lower lip, staring at Brewer, a worried look on his face. I understand how he feels. Up on the *Xolotl*, I wondered if Brewer was crazy. Now I'm sure of it. Since Kenzie let Brewer out of the hospital coffin, the man has been babbling, repeating words, making nonsensical rhymes.

On the slab above and behind us, we hear Nevins, Peura and Harman installing the new antenna. The irony digs at me—we tried desperately to fix the antenna so Bello could talk to the *Xolotl,* and now that she's dead the *Xolotl* has sent us an antenna.

If Spingate had waited just one more day, Bello would still be alive.

Soon, Peura tells me, we'll be able to talk to the *Xolotl.* I'm hoping for that, yes, but for much more—if we can reach the *Goblin* or the *Dragon,* maybe we can communicate with those aliens before it is too late.

Maybe I can make peace instead of war.

Until the boys get the antenna working, though, this crazy, ancient man is our only connection to the bigger picture.

"So *dirty,*" Brewer says. "Dirty dirty gurty city."

Was Uchmal supposed to be his paradise? He endured centuries of pain to reach this place.

"It's not as bad as it looks," I say. "Most of the buildings are fine. Only the vines burned."

Huge craters dotting the city contradict my words.

"Grungy mungy," Brewer says.

I glance to the sky. It's an involuntary tic now—whenever I'm outside I look up, wondering when the next attack will come.

Before we brought Brewer up here, Gaston told me both the *Goblin* and the *Dragon* had passed below the horizon, out of sight of our radio telescope. We don't know where those ships are. They might be landing troops on the far side of the planet for all we know. But if they do that, those troops will have to march or fly thousands of miles to reach us. Bishop says that's not strategically sound. He thinks they'll land closer, if not in the city itself—which means we'll soon see those ships again.

"Brewer," I say, "you asked us to bring you up here. Now we need you to focus and answer some questions. Can you do that?"

"Do not speak to me as if I am the child, girl. Respect your elders who are also the same age as you but not really. Ask and ye shall receive bereave conceive."

I take a breath, steady myself. So many questions. That we might finally get answers nearly overwhelms me. I'll focus on the most important questions first.

"Why did you bring the antenna?"

"Because you asked me to."

I glance at Kenzie.

"You mean *Matilda* asked you to," she says softly to Brewer. "Yes?"

Brewer coughs. "Potato, tomahto, vibrato."

He's working *with* Matilda now? The ship she used to escape Omeyocan is the same one he came down in, so that much adds up.

I step to the right side of Brewer's wheelchair, squat down on my heels.

"You kept Matilda and the others from overwriting us. You were her enemy. Why are you working with her now?"

He looks down at me. His red eyes seem strange . . . kind of unfocused, clouded.

"I know why *you* want that girl, Matilda, but we could be the last humans in existence," he says. "We *must* keep the children alive. We must help them against the aliens. I remember how to fly—I'll take the spare antenna down to them."

He's looking right at me, but he thinks I'm *her*. Does he not know where he is?

The last humans in existence. Just mad babbling? He's crazy, but the way he said it doesn't *feel* like mad babbling. In all this time, I've never really thought about where other people might be—it's just been *us*.

We can't be the only ones. Can we?

"Brewer, you already flew down to Omeyocan," I say. I gesture to the horizon. "Just look."

He stares at me for a few seconds, then gazes out over the jungle.

"Beautiful," he says. "Did you know I waited twelve centuries for this view?"

I stand, huddle with Kenzie, Bishop, Gaston and Aramovsky.

"Damn, Smith," Gaston says. "Could you have drugged this loser up any more?"

"Be quiet," Kenzie snaps. The wind whips at her brown hair. "You don't know a damn thing about medicine, Gaston. I don't think this behavior is from the painkillers. Not all of it, anyway. I think Brewer is senile."

Senile. I know that can happen to old people, and Brewer is over a *thousand* years old. Whatever was done to make him live this long, his body and his brain are finally wearing out.

I again squat by his side. I don't want to touch him, but I take his hand anyway. My skin crawls, as if I'm picking up a fist-sized centipede. His grip is weak. His gnarled skin is cold.

He squeezes my hand, gives it a little reassuring shake.

"It's all right, Matilda, I'll go," he says. "With what happened last time, they'll kill you as soon as they see you. They'll kill any Cherished on sight. Except me, maybe. I'm the only one Little Savage might spare."

Brewer thinks he's talking to Matilda, but he's right—I do want to kill her. If I'd done that when I first had the chance, O'Malley would still be alive.

Frustration bubbles up within me. This isn't *fair*, godsdammit. Bello wouldn't talk and now she's dead. Brewer came down and now he's senile?

Aramovsky leans close to me, whispers.

"If he thinks you're Matilda, pretend to be Matilda. Get as much information as you can."

Aramovsky's voice: so calm, so steady. It's actually kind of soothing.

Pretend to be Matilda. I'll give it a try.

"Brewer, tell me what the antenna will do for them again?"

"The children are under siege," he says. "If we can reach them, we can help the whelps with orbital observation."

He waves his free hand like he's dismissing some annoying comment.

"Yes-yes-yes in a dress, I know I destroyed the antenna in the first place, but you had that coming. Now isn't the time for quibbles *or* nibbles. If humanity is to survive, this must be done."

He sabotaged the original antenna? Why? Another mystery to solve, but one for later.

"Eyes in the sky," Bishop says, excited by this concept. "If we face ground troops, knowing where they are is critical."

This time it's Gaston who whispers to me.

"Find out why the *Xolotl* won't fight. If Matilda wants to keep you alive, the best way is to destroy those trying to kill you. Why doesn't she engage?"

This would be so much easier if Brewer knew where he was, perhaps *when* he was. I think of a way to phrase the question.

"We should just destroy those other ships," I say. "Don't you agree?"

The ancient creature laughs—a harsh, wet cough cuts the laugh short. Bits of gray paste splatter against the inside of his visor.

Brewer's head lolls back. His eyes scrunch tight. Painkillers or not, he's clearly fighting against horrific agony.

He takes a moment to gather himself, then answers.

"Destroy them with what? The six decrepit Macanas Vick that Tick Tick wastes his time with?"

Macanas . . . Vick Tick Tick . . . he's talking nonsense.

"Macanas," Aramovsky says, almost shouting the word. He's wide-eyed, immersed in a flashfire moment. "Those are . . . I know those. They're fighter craft, interceptors, made for space combat."

The name means nothing to me, but Brewer nods.

"I monitored the fighter battle between those two mother ships," he says. "Our Macanas are completely outclassed, if they work at all. *Destroy those other ships,* you say. Somehow, Matilda, you still don't appreciate what that last battle did to the *Xolotl.* I mean, it only happened *two centuries* ago, so maybe you haven't had time to process it."

I again glance to the sky, feel that imaginary clock ticking down. Something drew those ships here. That same something must have drawn *us.*

I ask the most important question there is

"Why did we come to Omeyocan?"

He slowly turns his head to look at me.

"The prophecy," he says. "The Founder said the scourge is coming. We're going where Tlaloc wants us to be. I'm not like you, Matilda—I was *born* into the church. When the ship leaves, my father says I have to be on it. I don't have a choice."

Now he thinks the *Xolotl* hasn't even started its original journey? Maybe looking at my face, the young face of Matilda Savage, is confusing him further.

And . . . he said he didn't have a choice? I'd assumed the Grownups were the cause of everything, that it was their decision to make this journey. Could it be they had no more control over their destiny than we did?

Aramovsky steps to the wheelchair, squats down on the side opposite me. He stares at Brewer like Brewer is the only thing that exists.

"You said you were born into the church. What church?"

Aramovsky doesn't sound calm anymore. He's agitated, as if he's on the verge of remembering something very important.

Brewer looks at Aramovsky. The bulbous red eyes narrow.

"You're playing with me, Boris."

B. Aramovsky . . . the *B* is for *Boris*.

Aramovsky grips the chair's wheel, squeezes hard.

"Tell me, Brewer. Right now. *What church?*"

"*The* church, of course," Brewer says. "The Church of Mictlan."

The moment those words leave his mouth, my memories flashfire, make connections that have been right in front of me all along. *The Church of Mictlan*. The symbol on our red ties, stitched into our black coveralls. The squashed-face symbol on the *Xolotl*'s round, flat front.

"Our clothes were school uniforms," I say. "Our classes, our training . . . *all* of us were in the Church of Mictlan."

I've mocked Aramovsky for his religion, called him a fool, but it turns out religion is what brought us here in the first place. Is he the fool, or am I?

"How many people were in the church?" Aramovsky asks, both eager and astonished.

Brewer squints one red eye, thinking.

"The Founder claims a million at the cotillion in dresses of vermilion," he says. "But there's a reason the ship will only take forty thousand, because that's all there is. Don't argue with me, Boris—you take the religious history courses far too seriously. Sometimes you don't use your own brain."

Forty thousand? The Birthday Children are not even three hundred strong—forty thousand on the *Xolotl* seems like an unimaginable amount.

"You mentioned *the scourge*," Bishop says. "I can . . . I can almost remember that. What is it?"

"The Abernessia," Brewer says. "They are coming. The Founder told us so. They bring hellfire and damnation, a pestilence to punish humanity. But when they reach Solomon, we'll be long gone."

Solomon . . .

Another flashfire rips through me, through all of us.

We were little kids, eight years old, taking a shuttle from a planet—from Solomon, our *home*—up to the *Xolotl*. Solomon, burning behind us, alien warships raining fire down upon it. Cities wiped out. Millions of people dying.

And I . . . I was crying. *Screaming.* I look at Gaston. He was there with me. So was Aramovsky. And Spingate and O'Malley . . . Okadigbo and Yong and . . . and *Brewer.*

B. Brewer's coffin. The emaciated little boy inside, skin dried taut to the skull. Repressed memories flesh out that face, bring hair back to life, reincarnate a mischievous smile, an infectious laugh. I look at the wrinkled, ancient thing sitting in the wheelchair.

"We were *friends,*" I say, breathless. "We all took classes together. We played together."

Brewer nods, and when he does I see the Grownup and the child in the same body.

"We are a *lacha,*" he says. "Twelve that will have immortality together, as the Founder foretells, as Tlaloc promises. I am sorry, Matilda—to be Okadigbo's attendant forever and ever? How horrible. Bello has it rough with Theresa, but you have to admit nobody is as awful as Okadigbo."

He laughs. He coughs. He settles into his chair.

The wind sends yellow waves across the jungle canopy.

What is *Tlaloc*? I still don't know, but one word Brewer said resonates—*lacha*. It means "twelve." Twelve coffins in our room. Twelve people who were together since childhood.

It never occurred to me there was a specific reason we woke up in the same room. I don't remember the details, but my progenitor's connection to Brewer is far deeper than I knew.

Brewer pats my hand.

"But honestly, Matilda, you need to stop making goo-goo eyes at Kevey-Wehvey. It's silly for you to think you can be with him."

Kevey-Wehvey . . . *Kevin.*

O'Malley was in our *lacha.* Could I have been in love with Kevin O'Malley since I was just a little girl?

"Why is it silly?" I ask.

Bishop puts his hand on my shoulder. "Em, we need to focus on the important things right now."

I slap his hand away, glare up at him. "Stay *out* of this, Bishop."

I shouldn't care about some schoolgirl crush a thousand years gone, but I can't help it. I do everything for everyone else, all the time. This is for *me*. I'm a woman without a past—I want my history back.

I squeeze Brewer's hand. "Why is it silly? Tell me."

He sighs. "Silly nilly billy willy. Kevin is above your station! Are you looking for yet another reason for Okadigbo to be mean to you? You're my best friend in all the ship, Matilda, but your father and I agree on this."

His words wash over me like a wave of ice-cold water, shatter me, break free new flashfires in an assault of emotions; when I first woke up in my coffin, when I thought it was my twelfth birthday, I was afraid I'd be late for school, that my mother would punish me for that.

Because when I was twelve, I lived with her.

But our ship fled Solomon when I was *eight*.

"My parents . . . they were on the *Xolotl*?"

Brewer nods.

My breath catches. The universe condenses to a single point the size and shape of Brewer's ancient face.

"Are my parents still alive?"

He blinks, confused.

"Of course not," he says. "Don't be stupid, Matilda."

I move to the front of his chair, lean in close, my hands gripping the handrails.

"Brewer, listen to me. I am not Matilda. I'm *Em*. I need you in the here and now. You flew a ship from the *Xolotl* down to Omeyocan. Don't you remember? *Please*."

Out of the corner of my eye, I see Kenzie shaking her head.

"You can't just will him out of it," she says. "That's not how senility works."

But this time, it *does* work. Brewer blinks. His eyes focus on me.

"Oh dear," he says. "It happened again."

The disgusting folds of flesh where his mouth should be . . . they're trembling. He's upset. He's *scared*.

"My intellect is all I have left," he says. "And it's fading. Slipping away, just like my life did. Do you know what that's like?"

Does he want sympathy from me? From *me*, who never had a life at all, let alone one that could slip away?

I feel sorry for him. I hate him. I want to help him. I want to kill him.

Brewer tries to lean away from me, but he can't; he's trapped in this chair. I hover over him, a cat poised above a helpless mouse.

I grip his left forearm. Harder than I intend, I think, because he flinches.

"*You* lived this long," I say, my words simmering with anger. "As did Matilda. So why couldn't my parents?"

Brewer relaxes slightly. "Ah, I see said the blind man. Little Savage, your mother and father were *vassals*. Only the Cherished were chosen for rebirth."

Deep down, I knew my parents were gone, and yet I can't stop sadness from crushing me. I should have been smarter— I shouldn't have *hoped*. They've been dead for a millennium and more. The only way I will ever know them is through Matilda's memories.

And I have so few of those.

"You said you and my father agreed about Kevin. You talked to my dad?"

"Of course," Brewer says. "After we departed, he took you, me and Bello to services in the Flatland every Sunday."

My life already seemed so cruel. Now I learn that this madman knew my father, yet I never will.

"I remember sitting on my father's lap," I say. "He didn't have a circle on his head." Another bit of that memory flutters to the surface. "Come to think of it, I didn't have one, either."

Brewer raises a trembling hand to wipe his wet mouth-folds, but his visor blocks it.

"That recollection must be from when you were very young," he says. "The church assigns our stations on our sixth birthday."

Aramovsky's fingertips drift to his forehead, trace the symbol there. Gaston and Bishop do the same with theirs, an automatic reaction.

I was assigned my "station"—my circle, my *empty*—at the age of *six*? I was marked as a slave before I had any understanding of how life works.

"So my father wasn't in the church, then?"

"He was," Brewer says. "Vassals are the lowest level. They don't get stations. I suppose we might think of them as *regular people.*"

Aramovsky drops to his butt. He's staring off, shaking his head. It's all too much for him. I understand, because it's all too much for me.

"The vassals were slaves," he says. "Like the circles?"

Brewer tries to wipe his mouth again, hits his visor again.

"So long ago," he says. "Hard to remember. Empties were slaves, yes, but far above vassals. Empties are the Cherished just as much as I am."

He raises his arm, looks at it.

"We Cherished did *this* to ourselves. We cheated death, kept it at bay so we could survive the journey and be rewarded in paradise with our new bodies."

The centuries have not been kind to the Cherished, Brewer once said. He was talking about his withered body. The Cherished created us—their *receptacles*—to house their consciousnesses so they could be young again.

Gaston has been quiet so long I forgot he was here. Finally, he speaks.

"The trip from Solomon to Omeyocan took centuries, as you're so damn fond of repeating. If the Grownups were modified to survive the trip, how did the vassals survive?"

Brewer laughs, and this time, at least, he avoids that awful cough.

"Xander-dander, smart in the air and dumb on the ground, as always. The vassals didn't survive. They grew old. They died."

The horrifying images of the *Xolotl* flash through my thoughts. Severed arms, piles of skulls, stacks of bodies, and . . . babies.

Babies.

"Families," I say. "The vassals had families?"

Brewer nods. "The birds and the bees if you please. Many people had children. Even some of the Cherished did. Don't you remember your own daughter?"

I take a step back, shake my head. He thinks I'm Matilda again. And Matilda had a child? *I* had a child?

I feel Bishop's stare. He's *smiling*. A warm smile, one of love— one of hope.

"Children," Brewer says. "That's why most vassals joined the church, really. On Solomon, those people had no future. Their children would have lived short, brutish lives, just like they did. The Founder promised safety, education—hope for a better to- morrow. And when her prediction about the scourge started to come true, believers flooded in. People came from all over human space. New Rodina, Capizzi Seven, Tower, Madhava, the Quyth Orbital Stations . . . even Earth. So many cultures came to join."

Aramovsky lies flat on his back. He stares straight up at the sky.

"But the trip here took centuries," he says. "The vassals had to know their children wouldn't even *see* Omeyocan. Neither would their grandchildren, and so on."

"Hundreds of thousands of people were born and died on that ship without knowing anything *but* the ship," Brewer says. "Over thirty generations that saw neither Solomon nor Omeyo- can."

My life is far from perfect, but I have to wonder if I have it better than those people did. What would it be like to be born on a ship, to grow up and one day realize that you would live your whole life within its hull? To know that by the time the *Xolotl* reached Omeyocan, you would be five, six, ten, *twenty* generations back, completely forgotten.

It would fill me with rage.

Puzzle pieces click together.

"They rebelled," I say. "The vassals wanted receptacles. They wanted the same transformation the Grownups had, so they could live to see Omeyocan."

Brewer folds his spindly fingers together.

"Some of them, yes. They mutinied because they didn't know their place in life. They wanted the same privileges as we Cherished. But you knew that, Matilda. You fed on that selfish desire, used it to become the rebellion's leader. To this day, I still don't know if you actually thought they were in the right, or you just wanted to seize power. And your *blasphemy* when you won, making new Cherished and promising them they would live side by side with us on Omeyocan. Disgusting."

Gaston glances at me. "That must be why some of us woke up with bigger bodies. The new batch, the ones who woke up with twelve-year-old bodies and not just twelve-year-old minds, their growth began after the rebellion, when the *Xolotl* had already been traveling for centuries."

"Correct," Brewer says. "The original *lachas* incubated for far too long, but the rebels' timing was just about right."

I realize I'm caught up in the moment. I want to hear everything, but I've let myself be distracted away from the information we desperately need.

"All the ships that came here look the same," I say. "How did the Church of Mictlan get the *Xolotl*?"

Brewer looks at me—I see his eyes cloud over.

"Ships? What other ships?"

No, I will not let him slip away.

I reach to grab his arm again, but before I can, Kenzie grabs mine.

"Em, *stop it*," she says. "He needs rest."

Rest? Is she insane? I'll—

From the pillar platform come the excited shouts of three teenage boys.

Peura leans out over the edge, looks down at us. His chubby face is electric.

"It's working! I sent a test ping, just two short bursts of static followed by two long bursts. We got the same message back. Em, the *Xolotl* can hear us!"

And then, the city moans—the emergency siren.

No, not now, NOT NOW!

Gaston grabs my arm.

"Let Theresa out of her cell, *now*. I need her in the Control Room with me."

He sprints for the spiral staircase that leads to the elevator.

Nevins, Harman and Peura scramble down the rope ladder. They must have hit a switch, because the slab is already slowly lowering on its gold pillars.

Bishop scoops up Brewer's chair. Aramovsky and Kenzie walk with him, hands out, hovering to catch Brewer if Bishop stumbles, but Bishop does not.

I'm the last one down. As I descend the metal stairs, the slab closes above me, sealing out both the morning's light and most of the emergency siren's haunting drone.

That sound means only one thing: one of the alien ships is closing to attack range.

TWENTY-SIX

took Aramovsky back to his cell. He argued, said he wanted to go out and fight with everyone else, but I reminded him we would be fighting side by side with the Springers, and that they would probably kill him on sight.

When I put him in, I let Spingate out. She'd heard the alert horns, knew why I was there. We didn't say a word to each other.

Bishop is in the streets, getting our units into position. If the aliens land troops, we need to be ready.

Harman and Nevins stayed in the spiral stairwell below the antenna pillar. If the aliens attack the pillar, they are willing to rush out and make repairs.

Gaston is once again in his favorite spot, standing atop the Well wall.

Above the Well, the glowing display of Omeyocan, slowly spinning. A yellow dot comes slowly closer—the *Goblin*.

"No sign of the *Dragon*," Spingate calls out. "Or the *Xolotl*."

Gaston huffs. "Big surprise. As usual, when a fight comes, our progenitors are nowhere to be found."

Spingate is on the platform. Her belly, swollen. *I would have killed her and the baby both.* Milton Cathcart is with her, his eyes fixed on the icons floating above his pedestal. He's assumed Halim's duties, I suppose. Spingate has little Kevin in her sling. In a back corner of the room, Joandra Rigby leans against the wall, arms crossed. She's glaring at Spingate, glaring with pure venom.

Joandra, too? Is there anyone not turning into a horrible person?

I'm down on the floor, standing with Peura at a student pedestal. He's trying to reach the *Xolotl.*

"Ometeotl," Gaston calls out, "do we have a targeting solution?"

"Not yet, Captain Xander. The Goblin *is not yet in range. ETA to firing solution, forty-two seconds. Grandmaster Zubiri reports that the Goff Spear is loaded and ready to fire."*

A red ring appears on the display, the image of Omeyocan at its center.

"That red line is the Goff Spear's outer range. Once the *Goblin* crosses it, we can destroy it."

The yellow dot is coming closer. It looks like we have a few minutes before it reaches the red line. I don't want this battle to end the same way as the last. I'm hoping the *Xolotl* can help us somehow.

Peura's hands are covered in light. He's moving glowing icons, working the controls. I wish I knew what he was doing so I could assist—I feel so helpless.

He shakes his head. "The *Xolotl* isn't responding to pings, or anything else. I think it's beyond the horizon."

"Because it's *gone*," Gaston calls out. "Didn't you hear me? Those cowardly bastards ran away as soon as the *Goblin* started approaching. Matilda wants nothing to do with a space battle."

Matilda wants me to live, but not so badly that she's willing to fight those that attack us. Why am I not surprised?

We're on our own.

We've *always* been on our own.

Movement by Gaston's feet draws my attention—a black rope, looped over the Well's edge. I hadn't noticed it before. From inside the Well comes Huan Chowdhury's voice.

"Gaston, get out of the way!"

Gaston looks down into the shaft.

"You okay, Huan?"

"Get out of the damned way or I swear I will stab you in the balls!"

"I'll take that as a *no*," Gaston says, then walks a few steps along the circular top, his attention again returning to the display above him.

I squeeze Peura's shoulder. "Keep trying," I say, and walk to the Well.

Huan Chowdhury climbs up the rope, climbs up *fast*. He falls more than swings over, lands hard on the floor. I take a knee next to him.

"You're trembling," I say. "Did you see something down there?"

He's in a fetal position, shaking hands close to his chin. He wears a canvas climbing harness over his black coveralls. Every inch of him is covered in dirt and mud. His big teeth chatter. Not from the temperature, from fear.

"Huan!" I give his shoulders a shake. "I don't have time for this! What did you see?"

"Didn't . . . didn't see anything. Just felt something, down there with me."

He's acting like this because he got spooked?

I grab his harness, use it to sit him up. I thump his back against the Well wall, maybe a little too hard. People like me face down guns and hatchets, fight the *real* enemy, while people like Huan cower at shadows? Whatever he has to tell me, it better be good.

"You didn't see anything," I say. "Tell me what you *felt,* then."

"Been going through the tunnels." He's talking slowly, forcing his words through quivering lips. "End of the tunnel . . . wasn't hard dirt . . . I was able to push through it into another tunnel complex, one I hadn't seen before. It's *wet.* Wet and warm"—his eyes lock onto mine—"it felt like *breath.*"

My bottled-up anger swells, it pushes, looking for a way out.

"And that's it? You felt a warm draft and you panicked?"

He shakes his head hard. "No, it was more than that, I . . . I heard a voice. It was my mother. She said *Don't be afraid.*"

His mother? She's probably been dead as long as my mother has. Could he have heard Springers? They were in the Observatory long before we were. Maybe there's another way into those tunnels. But no, if it was Springers, there's no way Huan could mistake them for his own mother. He must have imagined it.

"Forget the voice," I say. "Did you actually *see* anything?"

He shakes his head again. "No. I was too scared, I ran."

He missed his godsdamned mommy. I needed this idiot boy to find information critical to our survival, and all he can do is piss his pants because he's afraid of shadows? What would he do if he ever faced *real* danger?

I yank Huan to his feet, shove him toward the door.

"Get out of my sight, you coward."

Still trembling from the fear of what he saw down there—and, perhaps, his fear of *me*—Huan sprints out of the Control Room.

"*Goblin* approaching firing range," Gaston says. "Em, if you're done intimidating little kids, think maybe we can focus on the alien race that's trying to kill us?"

The yellow dot of the *Goblin* creeps closer to the red line. When it gets there, I will give the order to fire—thousands of intelligent beings will die. It is an order I do not want to give.

There has to be another way.

I run back to Peura. The boy is still trying. He's on the verge of hyperventilating.

"You can't reach what isn't there," I say. "Instead, can you use the antenna to talk to the alien ship?"

"I . . . I don't know. I'll try."

"Don't bother," Gaston says. "We'll blow that ship out of the sky before they can launch an attack. Besides, they're aliens—even if we can reach their ship we can't communicate with them."

Gaston doesn't even want to try to stop this battle from happening? That's not like him. Or rather, that's not like the Gaston I used to know. Is this really how he wants to be, or is this unknown anger affecting him like it affected Bishop and Spingate?

Like it affected *me*.

I lean in close to Peura. "Don't worry about Gaston. Just try, all right?"

He nods, and once again his hands are a glowing blur.

On the big display above the Well, the *Goblin* has almost reached the red line.

"Ometeotl," Gaston says, "show me the *Goblin*'s probable maximum firing distance, and also maximum probable distance from which it can launch atmospheric-capable craft."

Two more lines appear. A purple one—marked MISSILE ZONE—appears a bit inside the red one that signifies Goff Spear's outer range. A blue line—marked LAUNCH DISTANCE—is farther inside the purple.

Gaston reaches out and touches the purple line, his fingers kicking up multicolored sparkles. He turns to look down at me.

"If the *Goblin* gets here, they can start firing. We don't know if they'll ignore the Observatory like the *Basilisk* did."

"Peura, *hurry,*" I say quietly. "We have to talk to them now!"

He looks at me, wide-eyed, shaking his head. Stupid Em—this kid's nerves are shot, pressuring him isn't going to help.

"Take a breath and keep trying," I say, forcing myself to sound calm. "Just do your best."

Peura nods and gets back to work. I see sweat beading on his forehead, wetting his black hair.

"The Goblin *is entering Goff Spear range,"* the room calls out.

On the display, the glowing yellow dot touches the red line.

"Em, we're ready," Gaston says. "Give the command to fire."

I close my eyes. I don't believe in gods—I don't even believe the God of Blood is real and I *felt* it compel me to do violence—but for the first time I pray, pray to a god I know nothing about.

Tlaloc, please, help us—please don't make me murder thousands, make them talk to us.

There is no answer.

"Em, stop screwing around," Gaston says. "The *Goblin* is almost in missile-launch range."

I open my eyes. Sure enough, the yellow dot is past the red line and approaching the purple one.

"I'm sure I reached them," Peura says. "I'm sure of it. No response." He looks at me, shaking his head. "Em, I *know* they received our signal. If they wanted to reach us, they could."

Gaston glares down at me. "Em, *give the godsdamned order to fire!*"

The *Goblin* is almost to the purple line.

Every race that's come here has come to kill. The race populating the *Dragon* seems to control the *Goblin,* and even if they didn't, why would either race be any different from the Vellen, Springers and humans? These aliens are coming because of the same signal that brought us.

I tried to communicate. They didn't respond.

If I wait, my people die.

Kill your enemies and you are forever free. . . .

"Ometeotl," I say, "fire the Goff Spear."

The room thrums, pulses. I hear that buzzing sound, drowning out all other noise. Like before, my hair stands on end, my teeth and bones vibrate.

The room's air is sucked out and rushes back in.

The noise ceases, as does the thrumming vibration.

A red streak flashes out from Uchmal toward the *Goblin.*

"Increase magnification on target ship," Gaston says.

The display above him changes. We see the *Goblin*'s green front, the yellow symbol etched there. I realize that I will never get a chance to know what that symbol means.

The wait is agonizing. The red streak draws closer. It seems an eternity before our weapon connects. The *Goblin* swells, swells, swells . . . then rips apart.

"Target destroyed," the room says.

Cathcart and Peura whoop with joy. Gaston shakes his fist at the image of the ship breaking into a hundred pieces.

But something is wrong. . . .

"Possible contact," Ometeotl says. *"Significant interference from the detonation. There may be a solid mass beyond it."*

"Oh no," Gaston says. "Ometeotl, tell Zubiri to reload the

Goff Spear, right now! And ask her how long until we can fire again!"

Spingate takes a reactive step back from her pedestal. Her arms wrap protectively around little Kevin.

"What's happening?" I ask.

No one answers.

I walk to the Well wall and look up at Gaston.

"Gaston, what is it?"

He points to the wreckage of the *Goblin*.

"The *Dragon*," he says. "We couldn't see it because it was in the blind spot behind the *Goblin*."

Through the cloud of wreckage, I see the *Dragon*'s plain white flat front coming closer.

Our radio telescope's waves radiate out in an ever-expanding sphere—when that sphere hit the *Goblin*, anything behind the ship was invisible to us.

The evil of what I just witnessed . . .

"They used the *Goblin* as a screen," I say. "They knew full well we would destroy it. They sacrificed thousands of lives to get closer to us."

"Zoom out," Gaston says.

The image above him changes: Omeyocan, the blue LAUNCH DISTANCE line, beyond that the purple MISSILE ZONE line, the red line of the Goff Spear's outer range.

The *Dragon*'s green dot passes through the red line.

"*Grandmaster Zubiri is reloading,*" Ometeotl says. "*Eight minutes, twelve seconds before the Goff Spear can fire again.*"

"Gods," Spingate says. "That's not enough time."

We watched, transfixed, as the green dot passes through the purple MISSILE ZONE line.

And keeps going, without firing any weapons.

I understand their strategy—the *Dragon* is going to launch

landing craft, then retreat out of our range before we can destroy it. They will try, anyway—they don't know how long it will take us to reload. Whatever race is on that ship, it's a race that is willing to gamble.

The *Dragon* closes in on the purple line.

"Ometeotl," I say, "do you acknowledge my absolute authority?"

"Yes, Empress Savage."

"Then I transfer authorization to fire the Goff Spear to Captain Xander Gaston."

"Order understood and implemented, Empress Savage."

The green dot reaches the purple line.

As soon as it does, dozens of tiny green dots fly away from it.

"Ships launched," Ometeotl says. *"Twenty-one small fighter craft and six larger craft—most likely transports. Approximately seventeen minutes until they reach Uchmal."*

I can do no more here.

"Gaston, don't activate the antimissile batteries until you get my signal, understand?"

He nods without looking at me. "I know the plan, Em. And if I get a shot at *Dragon*, I'll kill it. Now get out there and kick some ass."

Is this the last time I will see him? The last time I will see Theresa?

I look to the platform. Theresa's eyes meet mine.

"I believe in you," she says. "Please come back to us."

I hope I do.

Without another word, I leave to join my troops.

TWENTY-SEVEN

I rush from the Observatory into the morning light. Beneath the *Ximbal*'s wings, Bishop waits with two dozen members of our army. Humans and Springers both. These are the squad leaders who will soon rush to their units and give the final commands.

Uchmal is about to become a battleground.

High above, Omeyocan's atmosphere eats up the *Goblin*'s pieces. That ship traveled an unknown, impossible distance to bring its people here. Now it is nothing but streaks of burning metal.

I've wiped out another race.

Em Savage: bringer of extinction.

Our emergency siren fills the air, but already another sound is fighting it for dominance—the echoing roar of approaching aircraft.

Far off to the west, high in the sky, I see a cluster of tiny black dots.

We don't have long.

I sprint across the plaza to our shuttle. The squad leaders part, close in behind me as I stand next to Bishop.

I face my fellow soldiers. Sunlight glints off muskets and rifles, bayonets and knives, hatchets and long-pointed bracelets, farm tools and spears. Farrar is stone-faced. The younger circle-stars look excited but worried. They might soon be fighting for their lives. I wish Maria was here, but her unit is out in the jungle.

Oddly, I feel no doubts about the coming battle. We will not back down. We will not run and hide.

I was born a circle. A slave. Now I am a leader. A warrior. A general.

I am a killer, and it is time to kill.

"We didn't ask for this fight," I say to my soldiers. "The antenna is working. We tried to contact the *Goblin,* talk to whoever or *what*ever is on that ship—we were ignored."

My soldiers exchange glances. They're scared, of course, but now they think this fight might have been avoided if only the enemy had spoken with me. That makes my soldiers *mad.*

Good. Anger is better than fear.

I pound my fist against my chest, three times, punctuating my words.

"Let . . . them . . . *come*! We are ready. We, who have sweated here, bled here, *died* here. We who have been here for centuries, and we who were *created* for this planet."

The Springers who understand my words translate for those who do not. Heads nod. Faces tighten with commitment, with the hard knowledge that war has come to our doorstep.

"Remember our strategy," I say. "We know this city, they do not. Use upper floors to your advantage. Enter a building, identify your exits, then find windows and fire down upon your enemy. When they come up to get you, melt away and do it again. *Remember the signals*—horns and flags both. Once the fighting starts, things will break down. You'll have to think for yourselves. You—"

"*Hem!*"

The single, hoarse syllable cuts me off.

I turn. Lahfah is mounted on her galloping hurukan, a handful of Springers hopping along behind. All of them are filthy, their jungle rags so covered in ash that wisps of the stuff trail along behind them.

She's supposed to be out in the jungle. I start to get angry, wonder what she's doing here, then she raises her hand high—she's holding a spear.

My spear.

Lahfah brings the hurukan to a halt a few steps away. She dismounts, offers me the spear. The shaft is lightly charred in a few places, but still looks solid. And the blade . . . it's undamaged. The edge catches a glint of red sun, and I know that Lahfah just sharpened it.

I take the weapon. Char instantly blackens my fingers and palms, but I don't care—I have my spear.

How long has she been searching the ruins for this?

She knows what the spear means to me, to all of us. With it comes belief—I was ready to fight, now I'm ready to *win*.

"Thank you," I say.

"War," she answers. From the mouths of Springers or humans, it seems, that word sounds identical.

From a pocket of my coveralls, I pull out a strip of white cloth streaked with dried blood. I tie it around my head. My soldiers stare at it, take in Halim Horn's null-set symbol.

"Today, we are not Springers," I say. "We are not humans. We are not circles, circle-stars or anything else. We, *all of us*, we are the people of Omeyocan."

I raise the spear. This piece of wood and metal that has come to symbolize so much to both races. Every eye stares up at it, draws strength from it.

"Today, we will fight for what is *ours*," I say. "Why will we win? Because *we live here!* To your positions!"

For a moment, the combined battle cry of two peoples drowns out the incoming rockets' roar, then my soldiers rush to their assigned places.

Victor and I crouch on a fifth-floor balcony in the southwest quadrant. We're high enough up that I can see over the walls. I watch the incoming ships streaking in from the west above the jungle canopy—twenty-one thin fighters that are all sharp angles and points, and six fat troopships packed with enemy soldiers.

The ships are almost in range of our tower cannons.

Bawden is on the ground floor with our spider, hidden from view.

In buildings to the north and southeast of me, lookouts in balconies stay low, watching my every move. They're waiting to relay my signals.

The roar of the incoming ships is so loud there is almost no point in talking—I'd have to scream in Victor's ear to be heard at all.

Our towers open fire.

Bright white cannon beams lace the sky. One of the smaller enemy ships explodes in a cloud of reddish-orange flame. The wrecked vessel tumbles down and disappears into the yellow jungle.

Unlike Brewer's lumpy ship, the fighters shoot back. They pulse with amber flashes, give birth to tiny missiles trailing long cones of gray smoke.

Those missiles close the distance in seconds. Two of them smack into the five o'clock tower, *boom, boom.* The top of the tower vanishes in a billowing fireball, thick chunks of stone spin away in all directions.

I know who was manning that gun: Isaac Hachilinski and Cassie Nauer. Two shuttle kids. Two circles. They lived barely a year, and now they are gone.

The wave of attacking ships passes over the wall. Another fighter explodes. A tower beam lances through one of the fat troopships—trailing flame, it plummets into a ten-layered ziggurat.

Missiles snake into the seven o'clock tower. The fireball sends stone flying, launches the silvery cannon—now twisted and warped—whirling end over end into the city, where it crashes into a soot-caked building.

Joannes Tosetti and Liselot Wieck. Dead.

We've already lost two towers. The fighters roar above me, a swarm of death heading for the center of the city. I can wait no more.

I lean toward Victor, hold up one finger.

He stands and waves his orange flag: down-left-down-up-left. The north lookout sees this. She stands, faces the Observatory, then uses her own flag to mimic Victor's sequence.

As enemy fighters bank and swerve above Uchmal, flag waver after flag waver quickly relays the simple message back to Gaston and Spingate, safe in the Control Room's depths.

Halfway up the Observatory, long black antimissile barrels slide out of hidden slots.

Our mountain of stone becomes a giant monster swatting at the gnats buzzing through the sky. The air fills with crisscrossing streaks of missile smoke, white tower cannon beams and the ragged red flashes of the antimissile batteries.

Fighters explode, one after another.

South of my building, a fat troopship angles toward a wide street. One second it is flying smoothly, descending to unload whatever it carries, the next a stream of red fire reaches out from the Observatory's southwest corner. The troopship erupts into a thousand flaming pieces, a deadly hail of bouncing metal that scatters in all directions.

When this battle began, only fifteen of the Observatory's antimissile rounds remained. I knew waiting to use those might cost us tower cannons, but we had to make sure the enemy ships were so close they couldn't be missed, we had to make every antimissile round count. That strategy resulted in the deaths of at least four of my people—in a way, I sacrificed them to lure the enemy in.

I am a killer. That is who I am.

That choice may haunt my dreams later, but for now it seems to have worked. The surviving fighters point their noses straight up and accelerate on columns of flame; they must be heading back to the *Dragon*. I count only ten of them—we destroyed the rest.

Victor thumps me on the back. "Em, it worked! The skies are clear!"

Springer horns sound from the southeast. Three long notes, then two short, then two long—the alert signal for ground fighting.

At least one troopship landed.

We've knocked their ships out of the sky, but the battle isn't over.

Now the fight moves to the streets.

TWENTY-EIGHT

awden guides our spider through the streets. Victor grips the cannon controls. My bracelet hums with the promise of death.

This won't be like the battle with the Belligerents. They were dangerous enough with their muskets and bayonets, but this time our enemy came from the stars.

What weapons will we face?

My squad's other two spiders crawl along behind us, our circle-star infantry behind them.

Up ahead, rifle and musket fire echoes through the streets, off tall stone buildings darkened by fire and dusted with ash. I hear the crackling sizzle of bracelet beams, the *whuff* of spider cannons, shouts of rage . . . and screams.

Screams of wounded humans and Springers. A third kind as well. This kind chitters. It clicks. It hums.

The screams of our enemy.

And, above it all, far off in the distance, the low rumbling of rockets. I look up, search, but the skies above Uchmal remain clear.

The sound of battle grows louder. We're closing in. I can *smell* it, too, the stench of gunpowder and burning machines.

Bawden turns a corner.

The street is partially blocked by the wreck of a sleek fighter craft. Thick black smoke billows from its shattered shell. Part of the fighter remains stuck in a building three stories up, smoldering with unseen fire.

Next to the wreck lie two dead bodies—one human, one Springer, both with horrific, gaping wounds of mangled flesh and splintered bone. They died so recently that their blood still spreads, red swirling with blue, both mixing with the street's ash, dirt and gravel. I don't recognize the Springer. The human is facedown, thankfully—one less name I have to know right now.

Bawden drives past the wreck and the bodies, stops the spider at the next intersection, just close enough for me to look around the corner.

Two blocks down the street, a troopship. Where our shuttle is streamlined, silver and sleek, the alien ship is thick, segmented and spiny. Its dark gray color eats up the morning sun. Unknown symbols on its hull gleam in rich shades of violet.

Like maggots spilling forth from a rotten fruit, enemy soldiers scurry around the troopship, looking for cover against blistering rifle, musket and bracelet fire that pours down from buildings on either side of the street. The enemy soldiers move fast. I can't quite make out what they look like, because their colors shift and swirl, matching those of the street or building or ship or wreckage around them.

The aliens return fire. Their bulky black rifles stutter with orange muzzle flashes, bullets ripping fist-sized chunks from the stone walls around the windows.

I see something moving on top of the troopship—an armored turret with a stubby barrel. It reminds me of our tower cannons. The barrel lets loose a gout of flame and a deafening boom; down the street, a third-floor balcony erupts in a blossom of fire and stone, and I know that more of my people are dead.

The enemy ship . . . it looks undamaged. If it landed, can it take off again? Can it fly?

I grab Victor.

"When we charge, *don't hit the ship*. We're going to capture it. See if you can take out its cannon up on top."

I lean out over the armored ridge and shout back to the rest of our squad. The other two spiders are close behind, the circle-stars crouched around their legs.

"We're going in! Spiders, protect our flanks, and *do not* target the enemy landing craft. Circle-stars, follow us in. The enemy has camouflage armor that lets them hide easily. That will make them hard to find if they escape, so make sure none of them do!"

I slide back into the spider's protected cockpit, knowing that some of my circle-stars are going to die today.

Attack, attack, when in doubt, always attack.

I draw a deep breath, feel my lungs expand. I take a fraction of a second to center myself. These could be my last moments of life. If I die, I want to die a good death.

It's time.

My held breath erupts as a roaring battle cry.

"Bawden, *chaaaaaaarge*!"

I duck low and hold on tight as our war machine turns the corner and hurtles toward the enemy. Bullets hammer against the metal spider, *ping-ping-ping*, so many hitting so fast it sounds like a musical instrument. Behind us, my circle-stars fire rifles and bracelets between our spiders' legs.

My heart kicks so hard each beat makes my vision twitch. My mouth tastes like sand. It will only take seconds to reach the enemy, yet each instant drags out for eternity.

I don't want to get shot, I don't want to die. . . .

Victor fires the cannon—the troopship's turret explodes in a thousand pieces.

A roaring boom: our spider tilts hard left. I slam into Bawden, but hang on. The spider levels out, each step a lurch that tosses me forward, then back, but we keep advancing.

I rise up just enough to aim my bracelet.

A frozen moment, a blur of images. An alien close ahead, armor shifting from tan to black to brown to ash-gray, the colors of the city. Limbs that are too long, joints too small. A dancer's graceful fluidity. Spikes and curving protrusions—part of the armor, or part of the creature beneath? Black rifle firing, muzzle flashes lighting up the alien like an orange strobe light.

I flick my fingers forward.

My bracelet's beam blinds me for an instant. By the time I can see again, the alien is no more. I've reduced that elegant creature to splatters of flesh, spinning bits of armor and a fading mist of yellow blood.

The sounds of war and death: relentless, unforgiving. Rifles, muskets, bracelets, beam cannons, the *rat-tat-tat-tat* of alien weapons, explosions, roaring fire, screams of agony. I'm terrified beyond measure, waiting for a bit of metal to punch through me and end my short life.

Victor fires the spider cannon again. The beam slices into the street, turning paving rocks into a blurring cloud of stone shrapnel, sending a pair of aliens spinning through the air.

The armored aliens rush forward to meet our charge. They

should be retreating into the buildings, finding places to hide and fight from cover. They have better weapons, yes, but we outnumber them and hold higher ground—their behavior makes no sense.

Bullets ricochet off the spider's armor.

I fire again, killing another enemy soldier just as their charge meets ours.

Our spider's front leg slashes down, long metal claw impaling an alien, punching through color-shifting armor as if it were paper. The alien's click-hum-chitter scream of death is awful, a sound I know will never fully leave my ears.

We're through their charge and closing in on the troopship. Behind me I hear the battle cry of my young circle-stars as they meet the line of armored aliens. Rifles fire, knives slash, spears thrust. People die. The air splits with a numbing howl of war so horrific the God of Blood must be dancing to its tune.

The landing craft's rear end is open, a monster's maw with a wide ramp serving as the tongue. At the top of the ramp, two aliens fire away at us.

"Bawden, drive us inside!"

The lurching spider pivots as she obeys.

Victor unslings his rifle. He crouches low, his body mostly protected by the spider's ridge. His legs bend with each lurching movement, keeping his head and chest impossibly level. He fires the rifle, flicks the black loop lever beneath it forward with a *clack* that reloads the weapon, fires again, his movements fast and sure.

One of the aliens falls from the ramp.

I mimic Victor's stance. I hold my spear tight in my left hand, raise my right arm, aim at the alien and fire. My shot goes wide, hits somewhere inside the landing craft.

Bawden's lips curl back into a primitive snarl—our spider

scurries up the ramp and into the fat bug-ship. Open sky gives way to gray ceiling.

The last alien leaps into the cockpit, smashing into all of us and knocking me hard against the armored ridge. Victor grapples with it, the alien's armor a swirling pattern of cockpit, black coveralls and Victor's face.

Bawden is between me and the alien. She draws her knife and thrusts—the blade skids off color-shifting armor. I drop my spear and lunge over her, grab the alien's arm. It twists, trying to throw me off. Victor snatches his rifle up from the spider's metal deck, jams the barrel under the creature's chin—*bang*clack*bang*clack*bang*, three bullets rip through the helmet.

The dead alien falls into Bawden, who stumbles into me and knocks me backward. I tumble over the spider's armored ridge.

The back of my head slams against metal.

Everything swirls around me . . . I try to rise . . . I can't . . . blackness drags me under.

TWENTY-NINE

Odors engulf me: antiseptic, wet charcoal, scorched stone, blood, smoke, grease . . . burning flesh. This is what pain smells like, what *death* smells like.

And *damn,* does my head hurt.

I'm still in the landing craft, sitting on a crate of some kind. Kenzie Smith is stitching a gash on the back of my head.

I was out for a while, apparently. By the time she woke me up, the battle was over.

Bishop could be alive, dead, injured . . . I haven't heard from his unit.

The inside of this alien ship looks strange, but the design is obvious in concept: it was built to carry hundreds of tightly packed troops from one place to another, with little thought given to comfort. Everything is the same flat, dark gray as the outside.

The spider is still in here. Seeing it crammed into this tight space, I'm even more impressed with Bawden's driving skills. I wonder if the dead alien remains in the cockpit where Victor killed it.

The spider hull bears hundreds of new dents, yellow and brown paint dotted with gleaming spots where bullets hit home. The leg closest to me is badly bent, metal torn apart on its top segment. I hope Borjigin can fix the damage quickly and get 05 back into service.

"Finished," Kenzie says. I feel a sting as she wipes at the newly stitched cut. She walks around in front of me. Her fingertips gently turn my head this way and that. Every motion feels like a sledgehammer thudding into my brain.

"Your skull is thick," she says. "Usually, that's the cause of many problems, but in this case it helps."

She's making a joke. That means I'm all right.

Something flies over the spider's armored ridge and clanks against the metal floor. The something rolls once, stops when it hits my foot. It's the alien's helmet, with three gore-smeared bullet holes in the top. No swirling colors now, it's just a dull shade of gray.

Kalle's head peeks over the spider's ridge.

"Em, come up and see this!"

I start to rise. Kenzie puts a hand on my shoulder.

"You can go when I'm *finished*," she says.

I knock her hand away and stand. The sudden movement makes my throbbing head flush with new pain.

"I'm good for now," I say. "I'll see you in the Observatory later."

Kenzie huffs.

"You never listen to the people you *need* to listen to," she says. "Thick skull indeed. I should have tended to the seriously wounded first, but here I thought I should take care of our *leader* before anyone else. Silly me."

With that, she picks up a big bag of medical supplies and trudges down the ramp, out of the ship.

I watch her go with a sense of longing—I should have asked for a painkiller. My head hurts so bad I can barely think.

"Em!" Kalle's shout echoes off the troopship's walls, makes me wince. "I said get up here!"

I press my fingertips to my temples. I look up at the tiny tooth-girl. She smiles and vanishes behind the ridge.

The fact that she's here at all tells me we control the city. That's good, but there's still much to do. I need a casualty report. What's our ammunition situation? Did we take any prisoners?

I need to get out there and see what's going on. But when I do, I'll learn how many of my people died. I just can't handle that yet. Seeing what Kalle has to show me will delay that news for a few moments.

Slowly, I climb the spider's rungs and slide over the ridge into the cockpit. The dead alien lies in a fingertip-thick pool of thick yellow fluid. Kalle is kneeling in the stuff; it's all over her black coveralls, her hands, even her face.

She grins up at me.

"Isn't this amazing?"

The alien's armor lies scattered about. Kalle removed all of it. The once-graceful creature is now nothing but a pile of dead flesh.

Its skin looks stiff. Maybe *shell* is a better term than *skin*. I've never seen a color like this. Some of the jungle's brighter flowers might come close to it. Matilda's memories call up a name: *fuchsia*. The color is so bright and beautiful—it seems out of place on an unmoving corpse.

Two arms, two legs and a head, but any similarity to humans ends there. The legs and arms have three sections, not two, and they're *thin;* my arms are to this creature's what Bishop's are to mine. The alien's joints seem so small they might break at the slightest movement.

Narrow chest, a waist so tiny I could wrap my hands around it with forefingers and thumbs touching. Standing up, this creature must be a whole head taller than me, but I would outweigh it by quite a bit.

The spikes I saw weren't a part of the armor, they came *through* it. The spikes are long and delicate, like curved rose thorns that jut out of the alien's arms and shoulders.

Matilda's memories fire. The narrow joints, the shiny shell, the long curves. There's only one thing in her past that even remotely resembles this creature. That insect, stinging her— stinging *me*—when she was only four years old. The burning sensation . . . the fear.

"It kind of looks like a Solomon wasp," I say.

Kalle stops her work, looks the corpse up and down.

"A little bit," she says. "Better nickname than *jungle rat,* I'll give you that."

I don't have the energy to yell at her.

Compared to this willowy form, our human bodies are thick and brutish. Victor's bullets mangled the top of the alien's head, but I can still make out a face. At least I *think* it's a face. Long and thin. A slate-blue ridge runs down the middle.

I point down at two thick bumps halfway up the face, one on either side of the ridge.

"Are those eyes?"

Kalle nods. She uses her finger and thumb to pry one open. Beneath the lids is a corn-silk-yellow eye. Other than the color, the eye looks so much like a human's that I lean away in an unconscious reaction of horror and surprise.

I expect the eye to move, to focus, to see me.

It won't, of course—not unless these things can live with the tops of their heads blown apart.

Kalle lets go. The lids slowly close.

First the Springers, now this. Life—*intelligent* life—must come in many, many forms. What did the aliens on the *Basilisk* look like? We will never know.

I leave Kalle to her gruesome work. I'm shaken to my core. That creature . . . so *beautiful,* yet it came here to kill us.

I walk down the ramp. The stench of war hits me anew. Long curls of smoke drift in from some unseen fire. Dead wasp-aliens litter the ground. There are Springer bodies, too. And, of course, the fallen of my own people. A circle's face stares out blankly. I recognize him—*I. Tosto.* Strange first name, what was it? Oh yes: *Iseult.*

Iseult has a hole in his chest the size of my fist.

My platoon's other two spiders are heavily dented, but it looks like they didn't take any serious damage.

Our wounded—human and Springer both—are laid out all over the place. Kenzie and Pokano bark out orders to tend to this cut, that broken arm. Victor, Bawden and the other circle-stars jump to obey, to help their fellow soldiers.

Tina Schuster scurries from person to person—dead and alive alike. She's doing a head count. Soon she'll give me that casualty report. Maybe my brain will stop throbbing by the time she does. I hope so, because when I see that report, my heart will hurt far more than my head ever could.

Behind me, I hear the metal feet of a spider coming down the street. My three are accounted for, which means this one is from another platoon. I start to turn, but I freeze.

The spider has to be from Bishop's unit.

What if he's not in it?

What if it's someone come to tell me he's gone?

I've lost O'Malley . . . I can't lose Bishop, too.

The spider stops behind me.

I force myself to look.

Bishop stands alone in the cockpit, smiling at me.

Relief hits me so hard it buckles my knees. It's all I can do to keep from collapsing.

He swings a leg over the ridge and drops down. My sense of command and responsibility vanish as I run to him, throw my arms around his neck. He squeezes me tight, so tight I can't breathe, but I don't *want* to breathe, I want him to hold me like this forever so I know he's real and he's *alive* and he's *mine*.

Bishop steps back. He places his right arm on my shoulder. I place mine on his.

"Hail, Em."

"Hail, Bishop."

He's as happy to see me alive as I am to see him, but there is work to be done.

"Three troopships landed inside the city walls," he says. "One was heavily damaged. Barkah's Springers got to that one first. They took no prisoners. My unit found the other troopship. We had them surrounded, but they kept fighting. It's almost like the aliens didn't want to live at all, like they came here to die."

Just like the ones I fought. There is something to that, something I need to figure out quickly.

"Was the landing ship damaged in the fight?"

He shakes his head. "Not much. I figured if it landed, it could fly, so I charged it on foot, killed the two aliens inside and captured it." He pats my shoulder, gives me an admiring grin. "I sure wish *I'd* been smart enough to drive a spider inside of it."

I see the pride on his face. It makes me feel good.

We didn't plan to capture any ships, but under fire he and I had the same instinct. Now we have two troopships. Can we learn to fly them? Or do they have fuel that would work with *Ximbal*'s engines? If either answer is yes, our new enemy has made a critical mistake.

"What about the *Dragon*?" I ask.

"Gaston sent a runner with news. It was out of range by the time the Goff Spear was ready to fire again. We can't hit it, but at least we won the day. We're victorious."

I glance around, take in our casualties.

This is victory?

"There's something else," Bishop says. "Gaston's runner also had a message from the hospital—it's Brewer. His end is near, and he wants to see you."

THIRTY

The hospital has never been this full.

Most of the white coffins are closed, wounded circles, circle-stars and Springers inside. I still don't have casualty numbers, but the battle cost us dearly.

Smith, Yilmaz and Pokano try to be everywhere at once, constantly checking dozens of wounded. The three of them must be exhausted, but they fight on, show no signs of slowing.

I sit in a chair next to an open coffin at the room's far end, away from the bustle. Inside the coffin: Brewer. The pedestal display beeps in time with the slow beat of his heart.

The time for questions has passed. This is about him now.

"Of all the people I'd want by my side when I die," he says, "you're last on the list."

Kenzie told me there's nothing left that can be done.

B. Brewer is in his last moments. Yilmaz gave him drugs to take away most of his pain. Considering he's spent an eternity in agony, that's a blessing.

His mask is gone. A thin, clear tube runs into the fleshy folds where his mouth should be.

"If you'd like someone else, I'll get them for you," I say. "Suit yourself."

His wrinkled body jiggles with laughter, the bone-scraping-bone sound I remember all too well, but there is something new in it. This is *real* laughter, the kind made from joy—not from sarcasm.

"Oh, my-my-my," he says. "Did you hear that, Mattie? An actual laugh. And it didn't even hurt."

His voice is soft, weak. He knows he is dying, yet he seems to enjoy these final moments. To suffer for so long, then to be free of pain . . . that must be like heaven itself.

He called me *Mattie*. A small part of me remembers that name—that's what he called Matilda when they were little. When they were childhood friends.

He again thinks I'm her. If that's who he wants at his side, I'll play along as best I can.

"I'm sorry for everything," I say. "I know that doesn't help, but I am."

He stares at me for a moment. His big red eyes are fading to pink.

"Do you know why you're the last person on that list, Mattie? Because everyone else on that list has been dead for a long, long time."

He raises one thin, gnarled hand toward me. I take it, hold it gently, afraid I might break him. His skin feels paper-thin. Only a trace of warmth remains.

"Where did we go wrong?" he asks. "We did what we were told. We obeyed. We served. Why didn't we get the reward that was promised to us?"

His words dig at my soul. He never had a choice. And because he stood up to Matilda—for reasons I still don't understand—he lost his chance to be reborn.

"Because people lie," I say. "They tell us what we'd like to hear so they can get what they want."

His other hand rises up, pats my knuckles.

"At least I got to see Omeyocan," he says. "So many did not."

I hear his heartbeat slowing.

"I wish there was something I could do," I say.

He gently pulls his hand away.

"There is . . . one thing," he says. His voice is so soft now I have to lean close to hear him.

"Anything, Brewer. Anything at all."

Color briefly flares back into his eyes. "Tell me it was worth it. Tell me all the pain, the sacrifice . . . thc *loneliness* . . . tell me it was worth it. Tell me my life *mattered*."

People lie, yes, but this time, at least, I can tell the honest truth.

"You saved us," I say. "Yes, your life matters, because you used it to give life to others. The Birthday Children will never forget what you've done. They will never forget *you*."

For an instant, the red eyes sharpen. They see me, recognize me.

He doesn't have a mouth, but I think he's smiling.

The eyes fade from red to pink.

The heartbeat changes from a slow beep to a flat, unwavering tone.

Brewer's eyes turn white.

He is gone.

THIRTY-ONE

We gather around a crater to say goodbye once again.

It's a bigger crater than last time, because we have more bodies.

Three rows of them this time.

In all, we have seventy-two dead: Brewer, eight young circle-stars, nine circles, fifty-four Springers, lined up shoulder to shoulder in no particular order. Brewer lies at the center of the middle row. Coal-black, withered and gnarled, he's flanked on one side by a circle-star boy of thirteen, and on the other by a Springer missing part of her head.

The Malbinti usually bury their dead, but not this time. Barkah insisted that his soldiers fell fighting for Uchmal, so they should be memorialized as people from Uchmal are. They fought together, they died together, they will burn together.

It's a touching sentiment, further cementing the bonds between his people and mine.

Humans and Springers line the crater's edge. Barkah already

gave his speech. Now Walezak is giving hers, the ceremonial funeral torch held high.

I wonder how many more of these mass burials we'll have.

Considering there are only 249 Birthday Children left, there won't be that many before we're all gone.

"So we say goodbye," Walezak says. "And we say *thank you* for being part of our lives."

This time I don't miss my cue, but I no longer give a damn about words that came from some meaningless religion. With everyone watching, I walk to Walezak and take the torch from her hand.

"You will not be forgotten," I say. "Those responsible for your deaths will pay. I swear it."

I toss the torch into the crater.

Flames catch instantly, a *whoof* that engulfs the corpses as one. Borjigin seems to have his accelerants under control. That's good, at least—we need every weapon we can get.

THIRTY-TWO

The *Dragon* has again vanished beyond the horizon.

Bishop is in charge of redistributing our troops, filling in gaps left by casualties. Borjigin is repairing our spiders, Opkick is distributing ammunition, and so on. It's a team effort, really.

Except that right now, the effort doesn't involve me.

I sit in my room in the Observatory, sharpening my spear. I'm waiting for Peura to come get me. The *Xolotl* is in range again. He assured me that it won't be long until he makes contact.

Right now, I want to be alone. I need a few minutes to think about our situation.

My personal things were destroyed when my home collapsed. This room contains a straw mattress made by the Springers, one extra pair of boots, two extra black coveralls, and my weapons.

We are at war—what other possessions do I need?

Just one: the white pedestal that stands in the corner, waiting to be activated.

I run the sharpening stone along the blade, as Coyotl once

showed me. The sound of stone on metal is comforting. This is something I can control.

I miss Coyotl. I miss so many people.

The Wasps launched six landing craft. Each one held 666 enemy soldiers—an invading army of almost four thousand. Half of them died when their ships were shot down by tower cannons or the Observatory's antimissile defenses.

Two craft landed successfully. One crash-landed. Schuster counted a total of 1,612 alien troops that made it out of those ships.

We killed them all.

Bishop and Farrar are raving that we "only" lost seventy-one soldiers, are elated about a "kill ratio" of almost twenty-three to one. They're sad for our losses, of course, but at their core they're built for war; they accept that every battle brings casualties.

Which is part of why I want to be alone. The fact that Bishop is *excited* about our "major victory," as he calls it, disgusts me. The battle had an effect I didn't see coming: my people seem much calmer. The tension and the increased need for violence have eased away. That in itself disturbs me, as if our desire for blood is quenched.

For now, anyway. I have a feeling that desire will build up again, and soon.

I need answers. Brewer is gone—I must get those answers from someone else.

From someone I never wanted to speak to again.

A knock on my door.

"Come in."

The door opens. Peura enters. His lips are horribly chapped. He's been chewing on them, a nervous tic. Poor kid is a wreck.

"The *Xolotl* is in range," he says.

I stand. I think of putting the spear in a corner, but change my mind—for this conversation, I'd rather hold it.

"Connect me," I say.

We step to the pedestal. He waves his hands over the flat top. Glowing symbols appear. He moves them, turns them, then steps back. His hands grip each other, squeeze so hard the fingers look bleach-white.

"It's ready," he says. "Just tap the pedestal, and it will call the *Xolotl*. I don't know who will answer, or if anyone will answer at all. Do you want me to stay and make sure it works?"

"No. Stand in the hallway, please. Close enough I can call you if I need you."

He leaves, closes the door behind himself.

I tap the pedestal. Sparkles of color flare to life, a glimmering, shining cloud that appears out of nowhere. The sparkles immediately coalesce into a gray shape that darkens, then turns black.

It is the head and shoulders of a Grownup.

A Grownup with one eye.

Matilda.

"Thank the gods," she says. "You're still intact."

Genuine relief in her voice, but those words—not *you're alive,* but rather, *you're intact.* To her I am not a person, I am an object. A vessel to be filled.

Her good eye whirls with intensity, with blatant hunger for my mind, my body, my life. The other eye is covered by a hard, shiny piece of white plastic. That's the eye I ruined when we fought.

The very sight of her makes my skin crawl.

"Yes, I'm *intact,* no thanks to you. You fled when the *Goblin* came close. You're the same coward you have always been."

"Oh, *please,*" Matilda says. "Our ship has already been through one battle, darling-dear, which was one too many. Or did you think the vessel that brought those hopping vermin simply dropped them off and then flew away?"

That explains why we've never seen any sign of a Springer mother ship. The Grownups must have destroyed it about the same time they bombed the Springer city.

"So you can't help us," I say. "You can't help defend this planet you've spent your too-long life pursuing?"

"We're trying to build a tanker ship. If we can deliver fuel to the shuttle, you can come up here, out of danger."

The laugh that escapes me sounds like that of an insane woman.

"*Out of danger?* How in hell's name do you think me walking into the viper's nest, coming *to you,* puts me out of danger? You, who sent a senile old man to do your dirty work, want me to come up there and, what . . . *trust* you?"

She waves a hand, dismissing my words.

"Brewer doesn't have a receptacle. His brain is rotting away. He's useless."

"And now he's gone."

She pauses.

"Brewer is dead?"

"He is," I say. "Natural causes."

She sent him here, knowing his days were numbered, but his passing seems to catch her unawares, as if reality suddenly doesn't match how she thought she'd feel.

"It's irrelevant," Matilda says. "He's lucky that I gave him a final way to serve and didn't have someone slice his throat."

I feel a mad grin spread across my face.

"You would have someone else do it, because you've never done your own dirty work, right? You don't know what it's like to put that knife in, to twist it, to watch someone die at your hand."

Her spindly fingers curl into a shaking fist.

"*Who do you think you are?* I *made* you! You are *nothing*. You don't *exist*! Did you take *my body* out to fight the invaders?"

I lean close to her image, so close that if we were actually face-to-face the spit of my scream would splatter against her good eye and plastic patch both.

"You're godsdamned right I did! I led my people. I'm willing to die for them, if need be—unlike *you,* you sniveling coward!"

Her twisted knot of a fist becomes a frail finger aimed at my face, jabs out and hits my forehead in splashes of multicolored sparkles.

"You put my perfect body at risk defeating that little token force! I've waited *twelve centuries* for that body, you horrible little worthless *bitch*!"

Matilda vibrates like a leaf in a tree. Spit hangs from her mouth-folds. Her one red eye blazes so bright it lights up the gnarled black skin around it.

I was just as furious as she was, but my fury was blasted clean away by two words.

"*Token force?* What does that mean?"

She leans back. She wipes the wetness from her mouth-folds. The glow of her eye returns to normal.

"It means the ships that landed in Uchmal were a diversion, you stupid infant. They screened your radio telescopes from seeing the *real* force, which they landed a few hundred kilometers to the northeast, well beyond the ruins of the vermin city."

She's lying. She has to be. We *won*. But . . . during the battle . . .

"The other rockets I heard. I thought those were an echo."

"They were not," Matilda says. "There's some kind of interference coming from Omeyocan that is screwing with our sensors, so we don't have exact numbers, but Gaston thinks at least twenty troop transports landed."

Gaston. *Her* Gaston, the one she fled the planet with.

Wait . . . *twenty?* No, it would be twenty-*one*, another gods-damned multiple of three, I know it, and if those troopships are the same size as the ones that landed in our streets, that would be a force of . . .

"Fourteen thousand." The words leak out of me, little more than a whine of escaping air. "They landed *fourteen thousand* troops?"

"So it appears," Matilda says.

"Why didn't they just land with the others? Those numbers would have overwhelmed us."

"Because they didn't know what your defenses were," Matilda says. "Basic strategy, darling-dear—send a probing force to find out what your enemy has and how they will react."

I think of the Wasps we fought in the streets of Uchmal. Even when outnumbered and outgunned, they didn't run for cover. They fought hard, yes, but they fought like they knew they were going to die. Their behavior now makes sense—they were on a suicide mission. They were a sacrifice to hold our attention, to tie us up and keep us from seeing the real threat.

Now that threat is safely on Omeyocan. Even with Barkah's army, we're outnumbered five to one. The Wasps have better weapons, better armor . . . how can we possibly defeat them?

"Tell me where they are," I say.

"Why, so you can go get my body destroyed? I don't think so. And I couldn't tell you if I wanted to. We detected their launch and were able to roughly extrapolate their landing area, but that is all. Thanks to that interference, we can't see anything on the planet. We don't know where the bastards are."

We need to find the Wasps and find them *now*. We have to

gather information on our enemy. I can send Maria. No, I'll go with her. I have to see for myself what we face.

I will do that, but I don't know when I might talk to Matilda again. There are things I *must* know.

"Tell me why you came here," I say. "The church, all of you. Dad, Mom . . . why did people come here?"

"Didn't you ask Brewer?"

"I'm asking *you*. Just tell me. Give me this one thing."

She stares at me. A gnarled hand reaches up, lifts the hard eye patch and tosses it away. She's going to tell me, but the price is looking at what I've done to her, at the ragged hole where her eye used to be.

"We came because of the Founder's prophecy," she says. "I met her once. Do you remember that?"

I shake my head.

"The first time I entered the Mictlan compound. I didn't speak to her, I only saw her. As ancient as she was, she was just mesmerizing. So much *power*. The Founder heard the call from Tlaloc, then built the church up from nothing."

That name again: *Tlaloc*. Is it a real thing?

"The call for what?" I ask. "To come to Omeyocan?"

"That and so much more. The call foretold the Abernessia invasion, gave us the location of Omeyocan and the schematics for the ark that would take us there."

Wait . . . she said "schematics." . . . that word means plans, blueprints. . . .

"The *Xolotl* . . . the church didn't design it?"

"The ship jumped between *galaxies,* darling-dear. Beyond any technology known to man. Only the word of the gods could bring such a miracle."

I thought gods were made up, but something sent a call across the universe, a call that drew my people here. Did that call radi-

ate out from Omeyocan like the signals from our radio telescope? If so, that signal spread equally in all directions . . . it
must have hit other races.

The call contained *schematics* . . .

Which is why all the ships look the same.

My tongue feels swollen. My stomach roils. Humans were
called here; so were the other races—called here by *something
on this planet.*

"The alien ships look exactly like the *Xolotl*," I say. "Is that
what the Springer ship looked like?"

Matilda nods.

Religion brought us here. Did religion bring the other races as
well? Do the ships orbiting our planet have their own "found-
ers" who sent thousands of their kind here to fight and die?

"That *call* your church is based upon, the call wasn't just for
humans," I say. "The other races heard it, too. That's why all the
ships look the same."

Matilda laughs. "Did you figure that out yourself, darling-
dear? As the Founder foretold, paradise is promised, but never
given. Paradise must be earned with blood and sacrifice."

She knew this was a planet of endless war. When did she learn
this—before the *Xolotl* departed, or at some point during the
journey? Did Brewer know? Did *all* the Grownups?

There is so much more to learn, but I'm wasting time. Somewhere in the jungle, our enemy gathers.

"I have to leave," I say. "I'm giving orders that none of my
people are to talk to you or anyone on the *Xolotl*. I don't trust
you, Matilda."

"Don't go into the jungle," she says. "Please, Em, don't go
out there."

Now she uses my name?

"I have to go. That's what a leader does."

Matilda shakes her head.

"We might be able to send fuel down to you in six days. Just don't . . . you can't . . . all . . ."

Her image is fuzzing out in bursts of colored static.

". . . they're trying—" she says, then her image puffs away.

Did something go wrong with the broadcast?

The air above the pedestal again flares to life.

But it's not Matilda.

It's a man.

Not a blackened, gnarled Grownup—an *adult* man. Older than me, yes, but the way we're supposed to get old.

His image crystallizes. His smile is one of pure joy, total amazement.

"I can't believe it," he says. "It's you."

His long black hair is tied up in a topknot. I see a few strands of gray in there. Small wrinkles line his eyes. Something comforting about looking at his face.

He wears a blue robe tied over one shoulder, simple but clean, with folds that seem very precise. The word *toga* pops into my head. Around his neck hangs a thin steel necklace dotted with bits of colored glass.

"It's *you*," he says again, laughing.

"You know me?"

"Well, I know *of* you. Victor was right. I can't believe it! You're Matilda Savage."

He says her name with reverence. I am not her and I will never be her, but I can explain that later. If there *is* a later.

"And who are you?"

"My name is Marcus."

He pauses, looks down. I see his hands—he's counting on his fingertips. I hear him mumbling something over and over.

Eight, eight, eight, eight . . .

No, he's not saying *eight* . . . he's saying *great*.

"I think I need maybe thirty-five *great*s." he says. "Hard to say for sure."

He smiles, warm and wide.

"I'm Marcus Savage, your great-great-great—and then some—grandson."

THIRTY-THREE

Brewer told us the *Xolotl* was built to house thousands of people.

Babies . . .

Generation after generation after generation.

"You're a vassal," I say.

Still smiling, Marcus shakes his head.

"Our ancestors were, yes, but that word doesn't apply anymore. The New People are free people."

Vassals had children. So did some of the Cherished.

Matilda's daughter that Brewer spoke of . . . could she have had kids of her own? Could Marcus Savage be my actual flesh and blood?

Do I have family after all?

"I'm not Matilda. I'm *Em*."

"Well, of course," Marcus says. "Victor told me."

That name stops me cold. I feel like I'm being pummeled senseless with words and concepts, a flurry of strikes coming so fast I can't parry or duck.

"Victor . . . *Muller*?"

Marcus nods. "Would you like to talk to him?"

I stare blankly. I don't know how to react, I don't know what to think.

Marcus takes a step to his left.

A Grownup steps into view.

"Hello, Em. That is the name you prefer, is it not?"

"Sure. That's fine."

The gnarled creature shakes its head slowly.

"So *young*." His voice is raspy, like that of all the Grownups, but there is a strange tone to it. . . . he sounds . . . *happy*?

I'm looking at the ancient version of the boy in my spider crew. This Grownup, "Old Victor," he has the same gnarled skin of Matilda and Brewer, but it's lined with dozens of gray streaks—scars. They crisscross his arms and shoulders, mark his face. Some of the scars are ragged, like bolts of lightning forever frozen in time, but others are intricate patterns—carefully planned designs, not the remnants of random wounds.

On his wrinkled black forehead, the ragged gray lines form a circle-star.

"I haven't seen you like this in centuries," he says. "You are so beautiful. And your hair . . . has it really been a *thousand years* since I touched it?"

A shudder washes through me. That this *thing* would ever touch me fills me with disgust.

This is all too much.

"I don't understand what's happening," I say.

"We knew Brewer took an antenna down to you," Old Victor says. "We've been waiting for you to use it. When you did, we cut into the broadcast signal."

"So you're not working with Matilda?"

Marcus laughs. "Hardly."

"I was on her side once," Old Victor says. He holds up a hand, turns it, showing me the gnarled skin. "I won the right to do *this* to my body. So did many who fought for her. But I saw the error of my ways and have fought against her ever since."

I adjust my grip on my spear. I suddenly feel like an idiot, standing here holding it, posturing with it. I want to be in the jungle, with Maria. I want to *fight*. Fighting is simple. This? I don't even know what "this" is.

"The *New People*," I say. "How many of you are there?"

"Five thousand, three hundred and sixty-four," Marcus says without a moment's hesitation. "Including the child that was born yesterday."

Over *five thousand* people are still living on the ship?

"Not possible," I say. "We didn't see any adults like you when we were on the *Xolotl*."

Marcus holds his hands shoulder-width apart, like someone showing the size of a fish he caught. "Say the *Xolotl* is this big." He shortens the space between his hands until they are almost together. "You saw only *this* much of it."

"Brewer controlled the abandoned section in the prow," Old Victor says. "That's where you were. Matilda controls the middle section, which includes the bridge. We control everything beyond that. Until you took the shuttle, we didn't even know there were any receptacles left onboard."

I open my mouth to ask him about his own receptacle, then stop. If he's telling the truth, there's a possibility he doesn't know about our Victor. Maybe that's safer.

I suddenly want Spingate here with me, to explain this. The size of the *Xolotl* is already beyond my ability to imagine.

"But five thousand people . . . how can you feed that many?"

Marcus laughs. It's a delightful sound. I think he laughs often.

"The *Xolotl* originally supported eight times that many," he says. "Feeding five thousand isn't hard. Many fields and orchards have died out, but more than enough remain. And we get meat from cattle, chickens and pigs."

Pigs. The same kind that killed Latu, no doubt. One pig was enough to feed twenty of my people. And Brewer showed us images: hundreds of cows in pastures, *thousands* of chickens in cages.

The Wasp troopships we captured. Gaston is trying to learn their controls. Zubiri is studying the fuel they carry, seeing if she can convert it for *Ximbal*'s use. If either of them succeed, could we fly back to the *Xolotl* and bring some of those animals down here? Could we raise herds of our own?

I'm getting ahead of myself again. If we can't defeat the Wasp army, what's the point of bringing down livestock?

Five thousand people . . .

"We're at war," I say. "We need help. This city is big enough for all of you, for a *hundred times* your number. Help us fight and we can—"

Marcus holds up a hand, stopping me in mid-sentence.

"Em, the New People can't survive on Omeyocan. You're modified to breathe the air—we're not."

Marcus and his kind weren't "created," like I was. They are susceptible to the same poisons that can kill the Grownups.

But still, so many people . . .

"The Grownups—I mean *the Cherished*—they can survive down here for a time with masks. Could you use masks and help us fight? What weapons do you have? We need spiders, bracelets, cannons . . . anything you've got."

Old Victor shakes his head. "There are few weapons aboard. And no ships left with which to deliver them."

"But Brewer said there were fighter craft."

"There are," the Grownup says. "But they are interceptors, made for space only. They can't fly in atmosphere. I'm sorry—we can't help you."

I had a momentary flicker of hope: more soldiers, more weapons. Old Victor's words extinguish that flame, leave me even more dejected than before.

"Then we have nothing to discuss. I have a war to win."

"You *can't* win," Old Victor says. "We know about the second wave of troopships. You need to find a way to come back up here and leave Omeyocan behind."

Marcus smiles. "We will welcome you with open arms."

Leave Omeyocan?

Wait a second . . . that's what Matilda wants, too.

I finally contact her, refuse her demands, and these two just so happen to "cut in" to her signal?

My anger flares, instant and overwhelming.

"You're working with Matilda."

Marcus shakes his head. "No, of course we aren't! We just don't want to see you get killed!"

"Omeyocan is my *home*." My voice rings with hate, drips with violence. "We've bled for it, *died* for it. How dare you suggest we abandon our birthright!"

"Yes, you have bled." Old Victor's tone is that of a soldier who has seen much. "Yes, you have died—if you stay, you will continue to do so. Even if you beat this ground army, another alien ship is coming. More may come after that. I believe this war is not meant to be won, it is meant to be continuous."

His words echo my own fears. We can win the next battle and still lose the war. And if we win *this* war, will there just be another? We're running out of equipment. There aren't even 250 of us left—we're running out of *people*.

"Tell me why the ships come here," I say. "Why all this war, this killing?"

Old Victor's shriveled shoulders shrug.

"The scriptures ordained that the promised land would not be given—it had to be earned with blood and sacrifice. That was the message that the Founder received from Tlaloc. The alien races obviously received the same message."

Tlaloc, the mysterious "god" that called the races here.

Blood and sacrifice . . .

. . . god . . .

. . . blood . . .

The God of Blood. If this Tlaloc is real, could it be the God of Blood that manipulated Aramovsky, that enraged Bishop, that caused Spingate to murder Bello, that almost made me kill Spingate? I *felt* it, guiding me, pushing me. How long can I deny it is a real thing?

"The killing won't stop," Old Victor says. "Find a way to escape while you still can."

No. This is a trick, and I will not fall for it.

"You want me to leave the place I was *made for,* and come up there so you can hand me over to someone whose sole purpose in life is to wipe me from existence? No thanks. You bastards created us specifically to live on Omeyocan. This planet breathes in our very bones. We'll beat the Wasps. We will survive."

Old Victor's red eyes seem to dull a little. He sags in place. He's getting tired.

"Omeyocan is a place of forever war. I beg you, Em, believe me."

"If this planet is so awful, then why don't you take the *Xolotl* and run away?"

"Matilda's power is weakened, but she still controls the bridge," Old Victor says. "That means she controls where the

Xolotl goes. She doesn't just want you, Em, she wants Omeyo-can. She wants what was promised to her. Bring your people up here, together we can overthrow her and we can finally leave."

Ah . . . could that be the *real* reason they want us to come up? They want us to fight their battles for them.

I wish Brewer were still here. Maybe he could tell me if Victor is genuine. But without Brewer, there's no way to know.

"You're either a liar working for Matilda, or a coward who fears her," I say. "Either way, we're not going anywhere."

I'm suddenly grateful I hold the spear after all. I thump the butt against the floor.

"We will defend our home."

I don't wait for them to spew more lies. I go into the hall and tell Peura to break the connection, to make sure no one but me contacts that ship.

I tell him what will happen to him if he disobeys me.

From the terrified look on his face, I know he will not.

I leave him to his work and set out to find Maria.

THIRTY-FOUR

D'Souza's Demons and Lahfah's Creepers gather on the plaza. Six snake-wolves—three from each platoon—stand idly by, pincers picking up unwrapped grain bars from a pile and popping them into their wide mouths. They love that food even more than the Springers do, it seems. It keeps the mounts calm as their riders talk to me and Barkah.

We stand over a beautiful, hand-drawn leather map spread out on the plaza tiles. The map has Uchmal at its center. It's not as detailed as the electronic maps, of course, but we can carry this one with us into the jungle. Barkah drew it. He has so many talents.

Maria makes a sweeping gesture that takes in the areas to the south and the west.

"The Khochin and Podakra tribes live here, so we won't run into them," she says. She taps a spot just north of Uchmal. "This is Schechak. We're going around that." Finally, she taps a spot far to the northeast, beyond the area drawn on the map. "This is all Galanak territory. We're looking for the Wasps, but we have to be careful—the Galanak hate the Malbinti."

Lahfah, Barkah and the two other Springers present all spit on the ground. The Malbinti is Barkah's tribe—they hate the Galanak right back.

"So we stay *quiet*," Maria says. "Stick to your grid pattern. There is no excuse for you to miss our scheduled rendezvous. If you don't show up, the rest of us will assume you're dead and look in your assigned grid for the enemy. We have an *enormous* area to cover. Everyone understand?"

Human heads nod, Springer tails slap against the plaza tiles.

"And *do not* engage," I say. "If you're attacked, *run*. Our mission is to find out what the Wasps have, not to kill them one or two at a time, understand?"

Nods and slaps.

"I'll ride with Maria," I say. "I'm in command, but if she gives an order, you all follow it without question. Let's go."

The riders walk to their mounts for a final check of harnesses and gear.

Barkah hops to Lahfah. He doesn't want her to leave, to put herself at risk, but he understands what's at stake. Besides, if he tells her not to go, she'll go anyway, and that will make him look bad.

Barkah is exceptional at not looking bad.

He's wearing a violet coat decorated with blue glass beads. He's taken to painting his tail in streaks of orange and blue, which somehow makes him seem even more regal.

Lahfah, on the other hand, wears jungle rags, with knives and hatchets stuffed into her belt. Barkah looks like a king. His queen looks like a killer.

The two of them nuzzle close. They intertwine their tails.

They press closed eyes together. That's the Springer version of kissing.

I wish I had someone to kiss *me* goodbye, but Bishop doesn't want to talk to me. He's furious I'm joining the scouting mission. He says my leadership is too valuable to risk, that I should stay behind Uchmal's walls.

He's right. I know he is, but I have to get out of here. I need the open spaces.

I tried to leave Bishop in charge—he declined. He has too much to do prepping for the city defenses.

So, while I'm gone, Borjigin is our leader.

I walk to Maria and Fenrir. She's stroking his tawny flank, cooing to him like he's a housecat and not a 640-kilo apex predator with pincers that could snap her head clean off.

"Come pet him," Maria says.

"I'd really rather not."

"You're going to be on his back for days," she says. "Maybe weeks. I hope you understand just how *much* jungle is out there."

"Of course I understand."

I don't, really. I just visit the jungle—Maria *lives* out there.

She takes my right hand and presses it against Fenrir. The beast stirs slightly—I try to pull away, but Maria is stronger than I am and she keeps my hand on the beast's fur.

Fenrir is . . . *warm*. He's dirty—and oh my *gods* does he stink—but his fur is soft.

"Don't flinch," Maria says.

I start to ask *why*, then see movement on my left—razor-sharp barbed pincers hover inches from my face.

I stay very, very still.

Between the pincers are Fenrir's little pink nostrils. They open and close, open and close—then they bump against my fore-head.

"He likes you," Maria says.

When the thick snake trunk moves the pincers away, I sneak a hand down to my privates to make sure I didn't pee myself.

"Eyes up," Maria says. "The murderer is coming."

Sure enough, Spingate is walking our way.

I stride toward her. I miss her desperately, and at the same time don't want to see her at all. She knows how angry I am; she wouldn't have come if she didn't have critical information to share.

When we're a meter apart, we both stop.

"Make it quick," I say.

She's scant steps away, yet we seem as distant as Omeyocan is from the *Xolotl*. Theresa Spingate was my closest friend. Now she is a stranger to me.

"Gaston has figured out most of the troopship controls," she says. "He thinks he'll do a test-flight tomorrow morning. And good news from Zubiri as well. She and Henry Bemba are build-ing a processor that will convert troopship fuel into a form that works with *Ximbal*'s engines."

"How long will that take?"

"Zubiri estimates a day or two, she's not sure."

Could that work be completed before the Wasp army gets here? The shuttle has weaponry—when the Wasps attack, we'll need that firepower.

Or, we could fly *Ximbal* up to the *Xolotl*, evacuate the city . . .

I shake my head, hard. We are *not* leaving our home.

Spingate glances over my shoulder at Maria and Fenrir.

"Bishop told me you were going," she says. "I didn't believe him. He loves you, you know. You two should have children."

"I don't need relationship advice from you. Or advice of any kind."

She looks down. My tone is a rebuke. I know her well enough to understand that she didn't come here just to tell me about the troopships and Zubiri's experiment.

Her hand absently rubs at her belly.

"Em, you have to understand . . . I didn't want to hurt Bello."

Her voice wavers. She's still trying to come to grips with what she's done.

"You didn't just *hurt* her," I say. "You *murdered* her."

Spin lets out a breath as if I just kicked her in the stomach.

This is gutting her, and I'm glad. She tortured a woman to death—I *want* my words to hurt.

"I couldn't have known Brewer would bring an antenna down the next day," she says. "Lives were at stake, Em. I had to—"

"How much fuel will we have when Zubiri is finished?"

My words are sharp, biting. I don't care about her excuses. I only care about facts.

She looks off, wipes at her eyes.

"Some will be lost in the conversion process, but there should be enough to fill the *Ximbal*'s main tank. We're taking it from the crashed troopship, so that won't affect the fuel supply of the two working craft."

If Gaston can fly the ships we captured, that would give us three working aircraft. I could quickly move our people to multiple areas. I could move Barkah's troops, too. The ruins, the deep jungle . . . if we can find our enemy, we might be able to flank them, or even hit them from behind.

Spingate is staring at me. I feel a stab of guilt for being so cruel to her—she's *haunted* by what she did in that jail cell. If I was really her friend, wouldn't I be there for her instead of making it worse?

She misses what the two of us have lost.

So do I. So much.

No . . . *no!* I will not feel this way. It's not like she broke up with Gaston and needs comfort—Spingate tortured Bello to death.

And you would have done the same to Spin if Aramovsky hadn't stopped you . . . you would have done WORSE. . . .

Maybe I'm wrong for acting this way, but that doesn't matter right now—I need to find our enemy.

"You told me what you came to tell me," I say. "Anything else?"

Her eyes glisten with tears that don't quite fall.

"No. Nothing else."

I turn away, but her voice stops me.

"You don't understand," she says, her tone biting and aggressive. "You *can't.* Not until you have children of your own."

She storms off toward the Observatory.

Whatever signal left this place, whatever "the call" really was, I wish I could go back in time and stop it from happening. Omeyocan is a place of hatred, of death, and . . .

. . . the signal . . .

. . . *the call* . . .

Puzzle pieces spin, circle, rotate, flip, all trying to fit together. . . .

The Church of Mictlan, founded to build the *Xolotl,* to bring people to this planet. The other races receiving the same signal, using the same schematics to build ships that look almost exactly like ours . . .

The way the Wasps fought . . . they didn't care about taking cover, they came right at us. They should have run. They should have surrendered. Instead, they fought like their own lives weren't important, like they were sacrificing themselves for something greater . . .

Aramovsky used religion to start a war, to make people *want* to kill.

I look at the Observatory.

So much damage to Uchmal . . . but no damage to that massive building.

Or to the area around it . . .

The signal . . . the call . . .

The pieces finally click together.

Two attacks from two different races, yet no damage in this particular spot?

The aliens didn't attack the Observatory because the call, the signal, it came from the Observatory itself.

Or, rather, from whatever lies *beneath* it.

THIRTY-FIVE

A pair of flashlights illuminate the narrow tunnel.

There are no ceiling supports of wood or stone. These tunnels weren't engineered, they weren't made by flowing water.

This is the kind of tunnel an animal would make.

Something *dug* this.

I sent D'Souza's Demons and Lahfah's Creepers on the scouting mission—but told Lahfah herself to wait for me. Once I'm done with Huan, she will take me north. We know the rendezvous points for the check-ins, so as sprawling and vast as the jungle is, we should be able to connect with Maria.

Unless the Wasps get her first.

"Huan, I don't give a damn if you're afraid—keep moving."

If only I was as brave as I sound. There's something about this tunnel . . . something *wrong*.

Huan Chowdhury glares back at me. My climbing harness matches his. The rigs' metal loops secure us to ropes when the inclines are too steep to walk, or when they drop straight down. I'm filthy, he's filthy.

"You better watch your ass, Em. You get lost down here"—he smiles, rests his hand on the handle of the knife in his belt— "and they might never find you ever again."

The growl in his voice . . . is he threatening me? I didn't bring my spear—it's too cramped down here for it—but I have a knife, too, and I know how to use it.

Test me, little boy, and I'll add one more kill to my list. . . .

I stop walking. What kind of a thought was that? You don't *kill* someone for words. And Huan's thinly veiled threat . . . that's not like him at all.

Whatever release we gained with the fight against the Wasps, it's gone.

Because the God of Blood is in us.

"Huan, we both need to relax," I say. "The violent urges are coming back. Do you feel them?"

He glares at me, suspecting I am trying to trick him. Then he rubs his eyes. His face scrunches up.

"Yeah," he says. He grabs his chest, fingertips digging into straps and black canvas. "In here . . . I'm so angry and I don't know why."

I've felt this thirst for violence before. Strong in the jungle. Stronger in the city. Stronger still in the Observatory, and strongest in the Control Room.

But in these tunnels, it's even worse.

There is something evil down here. The source of all the hate and anger . . . we're closing in on it.

Whatever it is, could it also be the thing that called so many races across the stars?

And it's not just anger this time . . . there is also *fear*. My body screams at me to *get out* of this place, to just *run*.

I will not run. I will not give in.

"You were right," I say to Huan. "It is spooky down here. *Damn* spooky."

He looks at me doubtfully. "Are you mocking me again?"

I shake my head. "No, and I'm sorry I did before. It's terrifying down here. I should have believed you. We all should have."

I see the anger melt from his face. In that moment, Huan isn't a little boy anymore—he's a man finally getting the respect he deserves.

"Thank you," he says.

Something unspoken passes between us. Whatever must be done down here, Huan and I will do it together.

We continue on. At the tunnel's end, there is a Huan-sized dark shadow in the muddy wall.

"That was the spot I told you about," he says. "I was able to push through into a new tunnel. A few meters farther in, there's a bend to the right. That's where I heard the voice."

He doesn't want to continue. Neither do I.

But we have to.

I slip through the muddy opening into a larger tunnel. Huan hesitates, then follows.

It's hotter in here. Hotter and more humid, just like Huan said.

And then I feel it, just barely—a push/pull of air, soft, repetitive, insistent.

As if something was breathing.

I'm so afraid it's hard to think. It's like an entity is in my heart and head, *making* me afraid the same way I would make a puppet dance.

"Huan, I'm really sorry I called you a coward."

He nods, a simple movement that tells me I'm forgiven. I believe him now, that's all that matters to him.

We continue on. The soles of our boots squish in mud. Our flashlight beams play off of water slowly dripping from the ceiling and thin rivulets running down the walls.

Up ahead of Huan, I see the tunnel bend sharply to the right. Huan points with a shaking hand.

"That's where I heard her," he whispers. "That's where I heard my mom."

We have to go on, but I can't bring myself to take another step forward.

Then I hear it—a soft human voice echoing off the wet dirt walls.

"Don't be afraid. . . ."

Not a woman's voice . . . a man's.

My body trembles. I want to run away, but my feet have frozen solid to the tunnel floor.

"Don't be afraid," the voice says again, closer now. "I'm right around the corner. I'll approach slowly."

The voice of an older man. It sounds a little like Marcus.

I grab Huan's arm.

"You said it sounded like your mom!"

He's shaking his head, nonstop.

"It *did*! I swear it did!"

"Don't be afraid," the man says a third time. "I'll step around the corner now."

He does.

It's a man. Old*er* but not *old*. Jeans and a blue button-down shirt.

Black hair.

Black mustache.

Matilda's memories are sparse, scattered and mostly fuzzy. Very few of them burn so clear they are real to me, like I experienced that moment myself.

One of those memories has come to life.

A memory of being a little girl, crying, sitting on a man's lap.

I stare at that man now.

A single word escapes my tight throat.

"Daddy?"

THIRTY-SIX

He can't be real. He *can't*.

My father smiles.

"Hello, peanut."

His words crush me, steal the strength from my limbs. I lean against the tunnel wall to stop myself from falling.

Peanut.

That's what he used to call me. Call Matilda. Call *us*.

I know he's not *my* dad. Matilda was born—I *hatched*. In the deep fiber of my being, though, she and I are the same person. Which means no matter what this thing is, I feel a connection to him so powerful and so real it doesn't matter who came from where.

This is my father.

Am I imagining this?

"Huan," I say, "what do you see?"

"A man." Huan sounds almost as shocked as I am. "A black-haired man with a mustache."

"You've done well, peanut," my father says. "We know that

many of you died on the journey here. That is to be expected. Only the strong survive, and only the strongest merge."

This is madness.

"You're dead," I say, my voice cracking on the words. "You've been dead for a thousand years."

That smile . . . so warm, so loving.

"Think of me as an echo. An echo of a concerned parent, if you will, perhaps no different than the memory in your thoughts that lets me take this form."

This is a memory? I don't understand.

"Can you read my mind?"

"Not in the way you mean," he says. "I drew from your experiences to find a form that is important to you."

He can't read my mind, but he can read my memories? I don't know how those things are different.

He is anguish and heartbreak dragged from my past and sculpted into reality. My *father*. So many times I've wished I could meet him. Now here he is, but he's not real. Whatever this thing is, it is cruel.

A tiny part of me is glad I'm not looking at an "echo" of O'Malley. I don't know if I could take that.

Maybe this thing would have chosen my mother, but I don't remember what she looks like. I don't know her face.

Am I going insane? This whirlwind of emotions

    —love and hate and terror and killing rage—

      whips at me, makes it hard to see, impossible to think.

"Em," Huan whispers. "Em, *say something.*"

My fingers flex on the handle of my knife.

Have to focus . . . I'm here for answers.

"My people received a signal," I say. "Very long ago."

My father shrugs. "*Long* is a relative term, peanut."

"Don't call me that!" I draw my knife, shake it at him even

though I'm not sure if there's anything really there that I can cut. "Did you send that signal, or not?"

"I did. But not for myself. As I told you, I'm an echo. I'm not real. You know one like me. . . . his name is . . . ah, now I have it—his name is Ometeotl."

The Observatory computer.

"You're a *machine*," Huan says. "A godsdamned robot?"

My father glances to the tunnel ceiling, a painfully natural, *human* expression—he's thinking over Huan's words.

"No, not a machine, but perhaps *robot* is close. I am a small piece of a sentient, biological organism."

He smooths his mustache. He does this because I remember my father doing the same thing.

But . . . why *my* father?

"You take a form only I know," I say. "Were you Huan's mother before?"

My father nods. "I was. Now you are both here, and of the two of you, peanut, I sense you're the natural leader—you are the stronger one."

He isn't talking about physical strength. He can look into our thoughts. Or, perhaps, into whatever passes for our *souls*. I don't know what lies in Huan's heart, but I know the blackness that buzzes within mine.

"Stronger," I say. "To you, that means *more violent,* doesn't it?"

My father's smile widens.

"Violence and strength are the same thing. In all the history of all the worlds before this one, and in all the history of all the worlds yet to come, the violent *always* win. Those who are capable of committing violence, or getting others to commit violence for them, or who build systems that create mass violence, more *efficient* violence—those beings eliminate the opposition and, therefore, create the future."

He's spouting some kind of philosophy. I don't care about that.

"The signal wasn't for you," I say. "So who was it for?"

He beckons us to follow him.

"Come. I will show you."

He wants to take us deeper into this place of hate and fear.

I want to run away. I want to be with my friends, touch their faces, hear their voices, celebrate all that is *real* and *solid* and *true*.

But if I don't get answers, those friends could die.

And I realize something ironic, something twisted and dark— I never met my real father, but I often feel his spirit within me.

He would expect me to be brave, to follow through.

If you run, your enemies will hunt you.

I will not run.

I sheathe my knife. "Lead on. Show me who did this to us."

Huan glances at me, that guarded look again in his eyes. He hears the barely controlled rage in my voice. I've been hurt before, badly, but this is different—something has *invaded* me, forced its way into the most private place anyone can have.

And that something is going to pay.

My false father leads us into the tunnel on the right. A few meters farther is a narrow opening on our left.

"Do not be afraid of what you see next," he says. "This could be the destiny of your people."

He walks through the opening.

Huan and I follow, into a small cavern. Two flashlights aren't nearly enough to light up the whole space.

Our beams play against something large, something with the satiny gleam of dull metal.

Metal . . . that *moves*.

THIRTY-SEVEN

"Tlaloc," Huan whispers. "What is this?"

Something unrecognizable fills this cavern, presses against the ceiling and walls. It's *bigger* than the cavern, with much of its bulk hidden by darkness, dirt and mud. I can't see all of this thing, but it has to be massive, maybe as large as five shuttles laid end to end.

Matilda's memories flashfire, try to match words to what my eyes take in.

Some of those words are for real animals: *whale . . . eel . . . hanash . . . lamprey . . . centipede . . . Rewall . . . Lisa's cardon . . .*

Other names represent creatures of legend, things that never existed at all: *Jörmungandrm . . . Quetzalcoatl . . . death worm . . . Bakunawa . . .*

Then her memories lock onto something repulsive and disgusting, something that's so close to what I see I can't possibly call it by any other name.

Grub.

A gleaming copper color instead of translucent white. If there is a head, I can't see it. All I see is the long body wedged into the mud slimed across it. The Grub is as much a *part* of this cavern as it is inside of it. The thing twitches, wriggles, sending undulations down its length in trembling waves of fat. I see things fluttering beneath the copper skin, see the coursing pulse of barely visible liquid that can only be its blood.

My father steps toward this . . . this *leviathan* . . . and I realize that his boots leave no footprints in the mud. He's not real. He's just an image, projected onto the ground before us, or directly into our minds, I don't know.

"This is the reason you're here," he says. "This is the next generation of my kind. One species, and *only* one, will merge with it, complete the cycle. I sent a call across the universe, inviting any who heard it to come and compete for this ultimate blessing."

"You're wrong," Huan says. "I remember sermons from school, from church . . . we were destined to find the promised land. But that thing isn't *land*. And the other ships that came here, the other races—how could they respond to the same call that brought us when we all speak different languages?"

My false father nods as if to say *That's an excellent question.*

"Our race first rose to the stars five hundred million years ago," he says. "Our ability to communicate with any intelligent species is too complex for you to understand, but I will try to explain. There are commonalities in the mental processes of sentient creatures. Certain energies generated from conscious, intelligent thought have similar patterns." He gestures to himself. "I'm using those patterns now to create this image. I have also used such patterns to appear in different forms."

One moment he is my father, the next he is a Vellen, like the statues I saw in the Springer church. My height, the one big eye, the backward-folded legs, the larger middle set of arms just above the hips, the thin arms coming out the sides of the head, ending in delicate hands.

The strange creature speaks with my father's voice: "*This* race landed and built a city above this spot, but they could not defend themselves."

The form shifts again, becomes a green-eyed Springer wearing beautiful clothes of purple trimmed with silver lace and dotted with real jewels—not bits of melted glass. No Springer has clothing this fine, not even Barkah.

"This race destroyed the first, even stood where you stand right now."

The Springer shifts back to the form of my father.

"Sadly for them, they were not strong enough to survive *your* race's arrival. The closer my child comes to rising, the more powerful the urge to compete for his love."

When we first lived here, we had problems with the Springers, yes, but nothing Barkah and I couldn't handle. About six months ago, things got worse. Then the Belligerents came. Were they somehow drawn toward Uchmal by this *urge to compete?* And in the past few days, incidents of violence amongst my people— the fight on the training ground, Spingate torturing Bello, me almost killing Spingate . . .

I don't understand how this can be, but the facts seem obvious; the Grub is doing something to our heads. It is the cause of the hate and violence that's tearing us apart.

"Now a new race has landed," False Father says. "You will destroy them or they will destroy you. Or perhaps the Springers that you stupidly allow to live will be the ones who wipe you out. When my child rises, we shall see who is there to merge with him."

Huan's hand moves to his belt, rests on the handle of his knife.

"Huan, *don't*," I say.

"He's making us fight each other," Huan says. "Like animals."

False Father nods. "Trials determine the strong. For a species as primitive as yours, to merge with us is the ultimate gift. Your kind rules planets—our kind rules space itself."

"*Merge*," I say. "What does that mean?"

"When my child rises, he will be weak. Defenseless. The strongest species will protect him until he can protect himself, then be a part of him when he leaves this planet."

Huan's nose wrinkles in confusion. "Leave? You mean on a ship?"

False Father shakes his head.

"Our kind do not need ships. We move through space as easily as you walk on land. But the nature of our biology requires that smaller, intelligent organisms merge with us, tend to us from the inside. Together, my child and the winning species will explore the stars, see the wonders of the universe. And someday, the descendants of that species will be there when my child breeds. On some distant planet in some other galaxy, my child will lay its three eggs, just as I did."

My dad died over a thousand years ago. The thing that looks exactly like him turns slightly, gazes lovingly at the giant, coppery Grub.

"An echo of my child will send out a call of its own. That call will reach intelligent races, who will build new ships. They will travel to that planet. They will compete against each other. The strongest will survive, and will join with my grandchild."

Huan's grip tightens on the knife handle.

"So your squirming, jiggling baby doesn't need a ship, it *is* a ship," he says. "We'd be, what . . . its crew?"

False Father thinks on this for a moment.

"Merging is far more than that," he says. "Once my child travels to the stars, he will not be able to live without you. And you will change, too, to where you cannot live without him. He will protect you from the vastness of space. In return, you tend to his needs."

Two species that can't survive without each other.

Just like the tiny organisms that live in the vine roots.

That's what we would be to this massive thing: *worms*. We would be a part of it. It would be a part of us.

Symbiotes.

Huan adjusts his stance. His boots make sucking sounds in the mud.

"So you want us to be *babysitters*?" he says. "You're so powerful you can draw all these races and make them fight, but you can't protect your babies?"

"As it is with any intelligent race," False Father says. "Can the newborn human babies protect themselves?"

I think of little Kevin, soft, helpless. If left on his own, he would quickly die.

"Our parents protect us," I say. "Most of our parents do, anyway. But not you—you abandon your children?"

"Our ancestors reached the stars and stayed, but at a price. When our kind leaves a planet, our bodies change permanently. We retain the ability to survive planetside only long enough to deposit our three eggs and"—he gestures to himself—"leave an echo which can send a call and communicate with those that answer it. After we lay eggs, we undergo a final change and we become too delicate to survive in heavy gravity. We end our lives as creatures of the cosmos, seeing all the beauty we can before we pass on."

"You're like insects," Huan says. He points to the Grub.

"That's some kind of larva, right? It will change, like a maggot turning into a fly. Your species is nothing but damned *bugs*."

False Father spreads his hands.

"Our kind has survived half a billion years. We have watched hundreds of races like yours evolve, flourish, reach the stars, then fade and die out. After humanity has vanished from history, my kind will still be spreading across the universe, finding new worlds and merging with new races."

Wait . . . what he said . . .

"You said *three* eggs." I point to the wriggling monstrosity. "There's two more of those?"

"They hatch one at a time," False Father says. "The next two are buried deeper. When this child leaves the planet, the next child will hatch, develop and eventually rise."

"Multiples of three," Huan says, his voice dreamy, distant. "Everything is multiples of three . . ."

Three eggs. My *lacha*—my *twelve*. The coffins on *Ximbal*, 168 of them. The Church of Mictlan references multiples of three over and over again. And it's not just us: six Wasp troop-ships, 666 soldiers in each one, twenty-one troopships landing somewhere in the jungle.

I wonder if the cultures aboard the *Basilisk* and the *Goblin* celebrated the same number.

"The signal," I say. "The call you sent out. Did it contain this information? Did our Founder really understand what was waiting for us here?"

"Impossible to know," False Father answers. "An infinite number of races has interpreted an infinite number of calls an infinite number of ways. I can communicate directly with you because you're here, because you are close enough that I can sense and interpret your thought patterns. Exoplanets are far too distant for that. We can only send, we can't receive, we can't communicate. The signal we broadcast has two parts. My part is mathematical—ship designs, galactic location and more. The second part of the signal comes from my child, a nonlinguistic impulse our kind has sent out for over half a billion years— a primitive, basic urge to *come,* to *fight,* to *join,* to *love.* To *serve.*"

Maybe the Founder knew what awaited us here, maybe not. She clearly understood, though, that other races would come to this location, that there would be a brutal war. She prepared for it—when we were just children, Okadigbo was trained to use the Goff Spear.

"Why humanity?" I ask. "Why the Springers? The Vellen and the other races?"

"My kind evolved on a planet similar to this one. So did the first race that joined with our kind. As adults we travel the stars, but our"—he smiles at Huan—"our *larvae* and *pupae,* they need oxygen, they need gravity. The call included this planet's atmospheric composition—the races that could survive here came. Finding new races to merge with us is part of why we have spread so far and survived for so long, but those races must be able to survive inside our skin as did the first race. That is why those that join with us must be a carbon-based, oxygen-breathing species."

Carbon. The symbol on the Well wall. On the Springer church. On the *Basilisk's* flat prow. The symbol was part of the signal that went out across the stars. Some races, including my own, made that image part of a new religion, a religion dedicated to obeying the call of a powerful being.

Of . . . of a *god.*

Tlaloc. The God of Blood. It's real. And it's right in front of me.

I look at the Grub. This glistening nightmare is what makes us want to fight, want to kill. This is what is making us *hate*. Maybe it only magnifies the natural urges we have inside of us, but if this thing wasn't here would Spingate have killed Bello? Would the Belligerents have come at all?

It's been down here the whole time.

That's why the other races didn't bomb the Observatory—because they knew, or maybe *sensed* is a better word, that their god lived down here. That must be part of the signal the Grub sends out.

"So what happens now?" I ask. "Do you expect us to just . . . what . . . come down here and climb in? What if we choose not to do that?"

False Father smiles at me.

"My child has been growing stronger. You've felt it. Soon, it will rise, and when it does, every sentient being around will be *compelled* to protect it."

I want to believe that isn't possible, but look what has already happened. Six races have reached Omeyocan. A seventh is on the way. Who knows how many more are coming? There is a power here beyond comprehension. Maybe it's advanced technology, maybe it's something else, but if this species has existed for half a billion years it is because their strategy *works*.

I thought gods didn't exist.

I was wrong.

"What if more than one race is *worthy*?" I ask. "We're working closely with the Springers. Your *child* tried to make us kill each other—it failed."

"Your two races have already fought," my false father says. "Multiple times. Do you think that was a coincidence? You've overcome the urge for now, which is a testament to your strength. When my child rises, however, those urges will become irresistible. The races will fight. One race will win, the others will be eliminated."

His words chill me. If he's right, not even Barkah and I will be able to keep our people apart. And if we fight each other, there is no way we can defeat the Wasps.

We're doomed.

I thought the Grownups were evil, but they're pawns. Just like we are. The Cherished, the Springers, the Wasps . . . we've all been manipulated and drawn in by a lie so massive it spans *galaxies,* maybe even the universe itself.

We were brought here to fight to the death, for the privilege of being *worms.*

The hiss of a knife sliding out of a sheath.

Huan rushes at the Grub. Screaming, spitting, Huan raises his blade and drives it down.

A *crack* of energy louder than any gunshot makes my body vibrate.

Huan is flung backward. He splashes into the thick mud next to me, slides to a stop.

I kneel beside him. His body is trembling so hard his teeth rattle. Smoke rises up from his face and hands, which smolder with fresh burns.

"Huan! Are you all right?"

A stupid thing to say. He's hurt bad.

I look up at my father. If he was real, I would gut him.

"My child protected himself," he says. "Your friend is lucky to be alive—that was a fraction of my child's power. The next attacker will not be as fortunate."

"You said it couldn't defend itself!"

He smooths his mustache. "Not against all attacks, no."

Fury fills me, *encases* me. I want to *hurt* . . . I want to *murder.*

I drag Huan to his feet. He's shaking so bad he can barely stand.

"Can you walk if I help you?"

Grimacing, he nods.

Supporting his weight, I turn my back on the Grub and the Echo.

"Good luck," False Father calls after me. "My child will soon rise. If you are strong, if you are *smart,* you will kill the Springers before that happens, because when it does, they will come to kill you."

I stop and turn, careful not to drop Huan. I look at the image of the man that raised my progenitor.

"Don't worry, *Father*—I promise you I'll strike first."

And I will. But not against the Springers.

Whatever it takes, I'll find a way to destroy the thing responsible for all of this.

I will kill the God of Blood.

THIRTY-EIGHT

I stand next to the throne in the Grand Hall. Huan is with me. We look down at the faces of my people.

So much to tell them. So little time.

Huan leans against the throne because he can't stand on his own. Physically weak but mentally strong, he refuses to go to the hospital until this is done. He grits his teeth against the pain.

I tell everyone about my talk with Matilda. I tell them of Old Victor, somehow manage to not look at our Victor when I do so. I tell them about Marcus and the five thousand vassal descendants. I leave off the strange fact that he's *my* descendant, because that's not important right now. I tell them there are no weapons on the *Xolotl* for us, how we can't count on any help from our mother ship.

I talk about the tunnels. The Echo. The signal.

Then, I tell them about the Grub. The size of it, how it's making us violent . . . how we're supposed to fight to the death so one race can *merge* with it. How it might soon rise.

Faces stare back. Incredulous. Afraid. Disbelieving. And more than a few, *angry*. At me, for telling the truth?

Maria and her squad are scouting, and a few cannon crews are in the towers serving as lookouts, but the rest of my people are here. Bishop, Kalle, Bawden, Farrar, Borjigin, Kenzie, Schuster . . . everyone. I even had Aramovsky brought down from his cell, although I hope that doesn't turn out to be a mistake.

The Springer residents of Uchmal are here, too, although I notice they aren't mixed in with us like they were before. They're clustered closer to Barkah and Lahfah. The distrust between our peoples is growing once again.

"That's it," I say, finishing my tale. "That's what we saw."

For almost a minute, there is only silence.

Walezak is the first to speak.

She steps forward from the crowd. "You're a *liar*."

Huan points to the burns on his face. "Look what it did to me. Em speaks the truth."

Walezak's lip curls into a hateful sneer.

"You did that to yourself! Or you had Em do it to you! The gods called us here. *The gods,* not some imaginary monster that supposedly has to be born on a planet and then lives *in space*. That's ridiculous!"

Kalle steps forward, calm as can be.

"There are some parallels to the amphibian life cycle," she says. "Like toads, for example—eggs and tadpoles can only live in water, while adults of most species spend their lives on land. If the organism Em found does begin life on a planet, then lives out in the void, I suppose we'd classify it as an *astro*phibian."

Walezak stares at Kalle like Kalle is speaking a different language.

"Granted, it would have to be an extremely complex life

cycle," Kalle says. "But that kind of drastic physical change isn't that dissimilar from what insects or blurds go through. Like a caterpillar becoming a moth. If what this *Echo* told Em and Huan is true, the creature begins as an egg. When it hatches, it becomes a larva—the form it is now. Sometime after it rises, it must metamorphize into a form that can leave the planet. Let's call that form a *nymph*. Maybe it has a couple of nymph stages, actually—a *protonymph* that leaves the planet, then a *deutero-nymph* that lays eggs. After that it changes again, into the final, nonbreeding adult form."

Spingate steps out of the crowd. Her breathing is ragged.

"Em said it's *making* us do things," she says to Kalle. "Is that even possible?"

Kalle nods. "Definitely. Some parasites can change the behavior of their hosts, force them to do things that seem crazy. Maybe this Grub's larval phase is parasitic, making the races fight to determine a dominant species, and then, when it's a nymph, it becomes symbiotic."

Tears trickle down Spingate's face, but she stands tall and stiff. Watching how this news strikes her, it rips my heart into pieces. She's been hammered down by the guilt of killing Bello; it must be wrenching to hear that maybe, just *maybe,* it wasn't entirely her fault.

"But *how*?" she says. "How could that thing control us?"

"Maybe some kind of alteration to our neurochemistry," Kalle answers. "For all we know, it could be releasing spores that infect us, change the way we think and act. Or more likely, it's some mechanism far beyond our understanding. Em said the Echo claims its species is five hundred million years old. That's *two thousand* times longer than humans have even existed. I mean, the Grub's species could have evolved some form of control we don't know about, or they could have engineered this

ability into their own offspring—like how the Grownups engineered us to survive on Omeyocan when they can't survive here
themselves."

Kalle is just guessing. That's clear to me, clear to everyone.
But the matter-of-fact way she describes the possibilities—
combined with what Huan and I saw—erodes disbelief.

And if anyone should believe in intelligent life being modified,
if not created from scratch, it is the Birthday Children.

Someone begins to cry. I can't see who.

"But the church," Borjigin says. "I don't remember much of
it, but . . . how could the church be steered wrong like that?"

Still leaning against the throne for support, Huan shakes his
fist.

"Because it was a *trick*!" His words bounce off the room's
stone walls. "Our religion is a *fake*. Don't you get it? The thing
below our feet sent a signal, and when the Founder got that signal she founded the church. She made a religion so she could
control people!"

Everyone starts yelling at Huan, or at each other. The Grand
Hall is awash in fury and confusion.

Bishop steps out from the crowd. The crowd immediately
quiets down.

"Whatever this *Grub* is, we have to kill it," he says. "If it's
making us do bad things, we must destroy it."

Farrar shakes his head. "We don't dare. Just because we've
seen it doesn't mean it's not really a god. Look what it did to
Huan. If that was just a warning, what happens if we make an
organized attack against it? I don't like the idea of making a god
mad."

He has a point. If I send people down there, they might die,
and right now we can't afford to lose anyone. I'm caught between two threats: the Grub rising and the Wasp army. Because

of the Grub, I should get my people out of Uchmal, but we can't abandon the Goff Spear, not with the *Dragon* still up there. And the city has walls, cannons on those walls—this is the best place to defend against the Wasps.

Now Aramovsky shuffles forward, hunched over as if the weight of his past actions is too much to bear.

"We have to face facts," he says. "It's not a real god. And Huan is right. Our church . . . it's all make-believe."

No one speaks. Not even Walezak. Everyone in this room knows of Aramovsky's devotion to religion. To hear him say such things is almost as jarring as me talking about the creature below the Observatory in the first place.

"We can argue all we like, but look into your hearts," he says. "Look at where we are, what's happened to us. Everything Em describes matches what we've seen with our own eyes. The church . . . the Founder made it up."

Someone else starts to cry. I don't blame them—I almost want to cry myself. Even though I know what's happening, the way Aramovsky talks makes everything seem more real.

The Birthday Children never had a choice.

And those that didn't give us a choice, they themselves were duped.

I've never felt so hopeless.

Bawden steps out of the crowd. She stares at her feet.

"But that means our parents were tricked," she says. "*Everyone* in the church was tricked. How can that be?"

Aramovsky finally stands straight, addresses everyone with just a hint of his former vocal power.

"Because the Founder needed to build a ship," he says. "For that, she needed people. *Lots* of people. And money. I don't pretend to know the details, but I can't deny the truth any longer— the Founder invented a religion so people would follow her blindly, do what she needed them to do. And people fell for it. *Thousands* of them."

A heavy mood settles on the Grand Hall. Heads hang. My people don't know what to make of any of this. Neither do I. We are in the eye of a storm of madness, trying to comprehend a power that is beyond anything we could know.

The Grub is a problem we *must* solve, but as shocking as it seems, right now it is not our biggest problem.

"No one is to enter those tunnels," I say. "We'll deal with the Grub as soon as we can. For now, everyone keep preparing the city defenses. Lahfah, let's go, we have to ride hard to catch up with Maria."

Bishop gawks at me in disbelief.

"You can't leave. We have to deal with this, right now."

"It will wait," I say. "If we don't find out what the Wasps are bringing against us, we might not live long enough to deal with the Grub at all."

And on top of that, I just need to *go*. I need the jungle around me. I need to be free of this place.

I raise my spear and thump it on the stone dais. The reverberating *thunk* draws all eyes to me.

"I'm leaving, immediately. Borjigin, while I'm gone, you're in command. Bishop, Farrar, Bawden, if *anyone* tries to go down into the Well, you are to put them in a jail cell. Do you understand?"

"We understand," Farrar and Bawden say in unison.

Bishop glares at me for a moment. I glare back. I won't give in to what he wants. The church might be fake, but the Wasps are real. We can argue about what the past means after we secure our future, and the only way to do that is to know what's coming.

Finally, Bishop nods.

"I understand," he says. "What about Aramovsky? Put him back in his cell?"

I look at Aramovsky. He's a beaten man. His religion took us to war. His religion caused so many to die. And now he knows, finally and for certain, that his religion was a lie.

"He's spent enough time in jail," I say. "Put him to work."

I descend the dais steps and head for the exit. Lahfah joins me.

I hope we find Maria before we find the Wasps.

PART III

VIOLENCE AND VISIONS

THIRTY-NINE

ahfah and I left near dusk. We rode through the night. The
twin moons lit our way as we passed through seemingly endless, overgrown ruins of hexagonal buildings. The sun was just
beginning to climb when we finally entered untouched jungle.
As big as Uchmal is, it is but a dot in the sprawling expanse of
the former Springer city, which is itself but a speck in the infinite
jungle.

It took all of the next day to reach the rendezvous point,
where we connected with Maria and the other hurukan riders.
They hadn't found the enemy yet, but they'd seen a big column
of smoke on the distant horizon. I gave everyone a quick update
on what Huan and I found. No arguments from the riders, no
debate—they're not ignoring my shattering news, but they know
that if you don't pay full attention to the jungle, the jungle can
kill you.

So can the Galanak.

So can the Wasps.

We'll worry about the fake church when we get back. For now, we focus on the dangerous task at hand.

I ride with Maria on Fenrir. I want Lahfah with me, too, so I changed up the two squads. Demons, Creepers . . . none of that matters right now. Nedelka Holub, a circle-star girl, rounds out our squad. We're riding northeast, toward where Maria saw the smoke. The other three riders head due north, working their grids.

Fenrir streaks through the jungle, powerful and silent. I hold tight around Maria's waist so I don't slide off and crash into the underbrush.

Our way seems perpetually blocked by thick trees, dense bushes and dangling vines, yet the hurukan slides past all of it as if the yellow plants and brown trunks are mist, as insubstantial as the projected image of my father. I've taken hundreds of spiderback rides through the jungle, but there is a huge difference between riding a machine and being on the back of a powerful predator.

Lahfah is off to our left, flashing in and out of the jungle's cover. Nedelka is somewhere on our right. I hope she's keeping up.

The Grub . . . I saw it, yet I can still scarcely believe it. What are we going to do? Huan could have died. We could send people down with guns, but my instincts tell me that will get them killed. My false father said the Grub couldn't defend itself, but it did.

No . . . he said it couldn't defend itself *against all attacks.*
What did that mean?

Fenrir cuts sharply left, banking around a thick stump caked with blue moss, and my butt slides to the right. I start to slip, but Maria reaches behind her and shoves me back into place. She's so *strong.* A year in the jungle, a year taming these beasts . . . it has made her a different person.

She talks to me over her shoulder.

"You loosened your grip. Did your mind wander?"

I'm embarrassed, but I tell the truth. "It did."

"Pay attention. Hold on tighter. You're not going to break me. If you fall off and die, Bishop will have my head."

I do as I'm told. We're just riding, but it feels good to hold Maria tight.

The jungle envelops me. She's right, I need to focus. And unlike an all-powerful alien baby, this is something I can actually control: *war*. Our enemy is out here somewhere.

Maria leans back, pulls on the reins. Fenrir instantly slows—I can't believe something so big can stop so quickly, so smoothly. Up ahead, Lahfah and her mount silently slip through a pair of wide yellow leaves and come toward us. The muscles of Lahfah's mount ripple beneath its tawny fur. The long trunk is raised high. I can see its pink nostrils flaring open and closed.

D'souza sniffs the air.

"We're close," she says.

I inhale deeply. It's faint, but I smell it, too—the unforgettable odor of burned Springer flesh.

Lahfah's lithe mount stops next to ours. Nedelka and her hurukan melt out of the jungle without a sound, join us.

"Smoke smell old," Lahfah says quietly. *"Fire dead?"*

We scan the trees above us, but there is no trace of smoke.

"The fire must have burned out," Maria says. "But if we can still smell it, we can find it. Spread out. Stay in visual distance."

She leans forward, scratches the side of Fenrir's furry head. The snake trunk curls back toward her. Even though Maria said the beast "likes" me, I can't help but flinch away from those lethal pincers.

"Fenrir, my lovely," Maria says. "Do you smell that? Smell?"

The little nostrils on the trunk's end open and close, open and close. The pincers clack together twice—Maria has taught it that *one* means "no," and *two* means "yes." These animals are not only big and lethal, they are *smart*.

"Good boy," she says, then sits up. "Em, you better hold on for real this time."

I wrap my arms tight around her stomach. Not that long ago, Maria D'souza was just a circle—an "empty," like me. She taught herself the Springer language. She tamed these huge animals. She became a strong leader. I love Bishop with all my heart and respect his abilities as our greatest warrior, but Maria D'souza is my hero.

She snaps the reins.

"Fenrir, *seek*!"

And with that, the beast plunges through the jungle.

FORTY

Since I awoke in my coffin, I've seen so many horrors.

But nothing like this.

The four of us stand side by side at the edge of a burned-out Springer village. A small stream runs through the center. Seven or eight bodies are piled up in that stream like a log jam. Water flows up and around the corpses, carrying with it streaks of blue blood and clumps of ash.

Thin wisps of smoke curl from blackened boards and timbers. Even ten strides away, even though the fire has been out for hours, we still feel the heat.

I don't know if the wooden buildings were built after Barkah and I made peace, or if this place is far enough away from Uchmal's spiders that these Springers never had to live below ground. I don't think it matters. The village is *broken:* burned-out huts, smashed pottery, scattered muskets and hatchets.

And bodies. So many bodies . . .

Most of the corpses smolder, blackened and scorched by the same fires that leveled this place. The smell of charred flesh is so strong that I press my mouth against my inner elbow, try to breathe through the thick fabric of my coveralls.

Some of the bodies are whole. Others are in pieces, blown apart by bullets or hacked up by blades. A few are smashed into bloody piles of flesh and clothing—something *big* ran them over. Wide, parallel, ankle-deep trenches run through dirt, mud, burned wood, even the bodies themselves.

"Are those truck tracks?" Maria asks. "Like maybe they have a Big Pig?"

No one answers her.

All the colors of the Springers are represented among the corpses: blue adults, purple teenagers, red children. Some of the corpses are so small I could hold them with one hand.

These were civilians. This wasn't a battle—it was a slaughter.

Lahfah speaks in Springer. Maria and Nedelka listen closely. I'm the only one here not fluent in that language.

"What did she say?" I ask Maria.

"She said this is the work of . . . the best translation is *barbarians*. Lahfah has experienced war. Even before we came, the Springer tribes fought with each other. She's never seen anything like this. She says it's like the stories handed down from her ancestors about the destruction of their big city."

From when Matilda's machines attacked. From when my kind came from the sky and wiped out everything they could find, murdering thousands.

Now the Wasps are doing the same thing.

If they'll do it to the Springers, they'll do it to us.

It's easy to see where the attack came from. The tracks stretch northeast into the jungle. Trees were cut down—long fallen trunks stretch away from either side of the path; squat stumps lie between the parallel tracks.

And it's easy to see where they went: southwest, toward Uchmal.

Nedelka's hurukan stirs, tries to turn back to the jungle. She snaps on the reins, keeps her mount in place.

"We should head back to Uchmal," she says, her voice quavering. "This is horrible."

Maria looks at me, waits for my orders.

"We have to know what we're up against," I say. "Follow them."

FORTY-ONE

We don't know exactly how many troopships landed, but we do know they carried more than just soldiers.

A year ago, I was with O'Malley. Aramovsky had won the election and become leader. He'd taken my spear. He'd sent me out—alone—to talk to the Springers, hoping I would fail, hoping I would die. O'Malley snuck away from the others, risked his life to be by my side.

O'Malley wasn't a fighter. He wasn't good in the jungle. He had nothing to offer other than his love.

I miss him so much.

He was with me when we felt the ground shaking, when I climbed the tallest tree I could find and saw the long lines of the advancing Springer army. That sight made me feel like my people had no hope.

I am again high up in a tree, looking out at an army—but this time, the enemy I see is far more terrifying.

Nedelka is on the other side of this ridge, watching our

mounts. Maria and Lahfah are in the tree with me. The tree is halfway up a steep hill, not at the top, where we'd be more visible against the backdrop of a darkening sky.

Because if we're seen, we're dead.

Utter destruction marches through the valley below us. Six huge armored vehicles roll along in a single-file column, their flat treads leaving the now-familiar parallel tracks. They are terrifying machines, much larger than our spiders. And so *loud;* we heard them long before we got close, which let us move off their trail and through the jungle so we weren't seen by rear scouts. The rolling hulks are painted in irregular stripes of yellow and brown. Each of them has a cannon mounted on an armored turret, long barrel pointing forward like the stinger of a deadly insect.

"I think I know what those are," Maria says. "Tranks. No . . . *tanks.*"

The lead vehicle has a horizontal saw mounted on its front. The column of tanks weaves around the biggest trunks, but most of the trees are simply mown down.

Far to the left and right of the tanks are machines similar to our spiders, also painted in jagged streaks of yellow and brown. These are fatter, though, with eight long legs instead of five.

Maria points to the one closest to us.

"Em, do you remember what a *tick* looks like?"

The word stirs up Matilda's memories. The eight-legged machines do look a bit like those nasty insects.

We count twelve "ticks." Four groups of three: one group far out front, a group on either side, and a group in the rear.

Behind the tanks are six lightly armored trucks, similar to Big Pig. These look like they are made to carry cargo more than fight—food, weapons and ammunition, I assume.

Each truck tows something that disturbs me deeply—the biggest cannons I've ever seen. The black barrels are long and thick. They strike me as oversized rifles or muskets—I'm guessing they fire projectiles instead of energy. *Big* projectiles, by the looks of things.

Tanks, supplies, artillery . . . and infantry. Wasp foot soldiers seem to fill the valley below me, their armor blending with the vines and trees. If they weren't moving, I'm not sure I'd see them at all. They carry deadly rifles like the ones we faced in the city battle. A few of them carry thicker, fatter rifles that are as big as the soldiers themselves.

"So *many*," Maria whispers. "Lahfah, what's your count of their infantry?"

I think Maria forgot to speak in Springer, but Lahfah answers quickly.

"*Thousand eight*," she says. She rubs at her middle eye, then corrects herself: "*Eight thousand. That how said?*"

I nod. "That's how you say it, yes."

When Matilda told me of the Wasp troopships landing in the jungle, I estimated some fourteen thousand enemy soldiers. Obviously the trucks, tanks, ticks and cannons took up much of the available space on those craft, but still . . . *eight thousand* foot soldiers. Even with Barkah's troops, we're outnumbered three to one.

And then there's the fighter craft that flew back up to their mother ship. When the ground troops attack Uchmal, I know those fighters will be there.

"How long will it take us to get back to Uchmal?" I ask.

Maria breathes deep, considering. She says something in Springer to Lahfah, who thinks before replying. Maria nods.

"The snake-wolves are getting some rest now," she says.

"We'll have to take breaks on the way back, but if we push hard we can reach Uchmal by this time tomorrow."

I nod toward the enemy force.

"And them?"

Maria stares down into the valley. The tanks roll along. The troops march through the jungle.

"They have numbers, but that costs them speed," she says. "If they keep moving at the pace we see now, they'll reach Uchmal in two days."

Which means we'll have just one day to prepare.

A *single godsdamned day* to prepare against tanks, troops and cannons, but at least we have that day. That doesn't make strategic sense to me—why didn't they land closer and hit us before we could get ready?

A Springer horn echoes from the north, in the jungle on the far side of the marching army.

From the southwest, in front of the advancing Wasp army, a second war horn answers the first.

My blood runs cold.

"*Galanak,*" Lahfah says. "*Tribe attacking.*"

The Galanak. The largest Springer tribe we know of. That village we saw was probably in their territory.

The Wasps react. They shout at each other in their piercing clicking tongue. Orders of some kind. The tanks stop. The infantry spreads out, making a wide circle around the trucks. The troop movements are uncoordinated, as if many of the soldiers are unsure of how they are supposed to act. Wasps with copper streaks on their shoulder armor scream at the confused ones, push them in the right direction.

"They're new to this," Maria says. "Like our circles were when we first started training them to fight."

The tick groups rush into the jungle, eight legs a blur as they vanish among the dark trees and thick underbrush.

The southwest horn sounds again, closer this time.

The tanks spread out, creating space between them. Turrets pivot to point toward the threats in front of them and on their right flank.

The Wasps obviously have better weapons and equipment, but as a whole they are uncoordinated and slow to respond.

Matilda's words come back to me: *Find out what your enemy has and how they will react.*

I watch. I learn. I *memorize.* Seeing how the Wasps respond to this threat is a huge stroke of luck. If I know their strategies, maybe I can find holes in them.

Both horns bellow again, followed by a sound I know all too well—a guttural war cry from thousands of Springers. Louder than the one I heard in the crescent-shaped clearing a year ago. This Springer army must be far larger than the one we faced.

A massive volley of musket fire; muzzle flashes in the heavy jungle cover reveal a long line of Springers spread through the underbrush. A few Wasp soldiers fall. A few others panic and run away. The copper-striped leaders grab them, hit them, throw them back toward their units—or just shoot them as a warning to the others.

"*Galanak yinilah nahnaw,*" Lahfah says.

I glance at Maria.

"Death-revenge," Maria says. "The Galanak tribe wants payback for the village."

"How many soldiers do the Galanak have?"

Maria translates for Lahfah.

"*Thousand fifteen,*" the Springer queen says, then corrects herself. "*Fifteen thousand soldiers. They all come.*"

I hear another musket volley. More movement, as if the jungle itself has come to life and is slithering toward Wasp soldiers that take cover and form rough lines of their own.

The Galanak outnumber the Wasps. Fifteen thousand Springers are closing in, giving me a surge of hope that the Wasp invasion might be routed right here, right now.

Then the tanks open fire.

Deafening echoes flood the valley. I instinctively move to cover my ears, almost fall, grab at branches to stop myself from tumbling down.

Fireballs erupt in the Springer lines. Trees shatter. Bits of vines soar into the air. In those brief flashes of light, I see Springers torn apart, ravaged bodies spinning away in all directions. Between detonations, I hear the screams of the terrified, the wounded and the dying.

The tanks pour it on, blasting huge, flaming holes in the tortured jungle.

Another war horn sounds: three short blasts, a pause, three short blasts.

The Springers that can still move rise and flee.

Blurs of machinery tear through the darkening jungle, rush past the crackling flames. The ticks are giving chase. Their weapons flash staccato bursts that shred flesh and wood alike.

Then, a different kind of scream—the Wasp foot soldiers rise from cover and shout as one as they move into the jungle after their attackers. When they pass fallen Springers, they shoot them repeatedly or draw long knives and hack at them, over and over again. The wounded Springers cry out. I don't need to understand their language to know they're begging for mercy.

They get none.

The armored aliens slaughter them.

Sounds of battle fade, not so much from distance as from the obvious fact that there's no one left to kill.

Maria, Lahfah and I stay perfectly still in our tree, stunned into silence. The battle lasted only a few minutes, tearing the heart out of the jungle. Fallen trees. Broken stumps. Burning vines. Smoldering craters. And everywhere . . . *bodies.*

"Thousands," I say, ever so softly lest these killers hear us. "There were *thousands* of Springers."

"And they were waiting," Maria says. "Springers chose the ground, had the position they wanted. And they still didn't stand a chance."

Lahfah says nothing. She's making a strange noise—the Springer equivalent of crying.

The Wasp troops are inexperienced. They won with greater firepower, not greater discipline. Now I understand why they landed so far from Uchmal. They needed enough distance to make sure we couldn't hit them as they unloaded, but there was a bigger reason—the Wasp soldiers don't have combat experience. Before this army hits our well-defended walls, before these soldiers face my battle-hardened people, the Wasp commanders want their troops prepared to face enemy fire and to know what it's like to kill.

They *wanted* the Springers to attack.

When we fought the Wasps in Uchmal, we outnumbered them.

When the next battle comes, *we* will be outnumbered.

We will be outgunned.

The *Xolotl* can't help us.

No one can.

I close my eyes, lean my forehead against the tree's rough bark.

Reality is what it is whether we like it or not.

The reality is we can't win this war.

I have always searched for ways to keep my people alive.

Now there is only one way left.

I know what needs to be done, but I can't do it without the help of my partner, my friend, my lover—I must talk to Bishop.

"Let's get back to Uchmal," I say. "As fast as we can."

FORTY-TWO

The sun is setting when we reach Uchmal. This time it's not just Borjigin waiting for us at the city gate—thankfully, Bishop is there as well, standing tall in spider 01.

I slide off Fenrir and run to him, he hops down from the spider and runs to me. He takes me in his arms. For one sweet moment, we're not leaders, we're not soldiers—we are a boy who desperately missed his girl, and a girl who desperately missed her boy. We hold each other in full view of Borjigin, Maria, Nedelka and Lahfah, and we don't care.

I'm filthy and exhausted from the long, hard ride. I smell like Fenrir. But there's no time to clean up, no time to rest.

"The Wasp army is coming," I say to Bishop. "I need to talk to you, in private. Right now. Let's take your spider."

He runs a hand over my dirty hair, pulls me in for another fast, desperate hug.

"As you wish," he says, and walks to the machine.

Maria slides off Fenrir, leans close to me and whispers: "I wish he was taking *me* for a little private time."

Our world is ending, yet I can't help the blood rising to my cheeks.

"It's not like that!"

Maria grins at me. "Too bad. It *should* be like that."

Yes, it should, but there isn't enough time.

"Please take Lahfah and find Barkah for me," I say. "Tell him I need to talk to him in my room, alone, in one hour. It's important."

Her smile fades a bit. She gives me a *what is this about?* look, but she doesn't question me.

"I'll take care of it," she says, then kisses my cheek. "Now go see your boy."

I run to join Bishop.

The waterfall's roar fills my ears. White mist crashes down, lit up by Omeyocan's twin moons. Blurds zip in and out of the spray. I wonder if they are playing.

"*Now* can you tell me what this is about?" Bishop asks. "We don't have time for dramatic nonsense. Why did you ask me to come here?"

We're standing in the spider's cockpit. As we drove from the gate to the waterfall, I told him about the Wasp army, the battle, how outnumbered we are. He's anxious to get back to our people and start planning for Uchmal's defense. But before that, I will say what must be said.

"We're here because this is where we first kissed. Where we first saw a spider. It was here that everything changed for us—and it's here that everything will change again."

Bishop shakes his head in exasperation. I'm clearly trying his patience.

"Em, I love you, but you're playing games. Every second matters. Get on with it."

I take his hands in mine.

"We can't beat their army," I say. "We have to leave."

Bishop thinks for a moment, choosing his words carefully.

"That might be the best strategy. If those cannons you saw have a greater range than ours, they can sit back and hammer the towers. The Observatory's antimissile batteries are almost out of ammo. If we lose the tower cannons, the Wasps can march right in or land troops anywhere they like. Maybe you're right—we take everyone to the ruins, go underground with Barkah. Then we fight a guerrilla campaign. We hit them where we want, when we want."

"Like the Belligerents did? We wiped them out, remember?"

That stops him for a moment.

"We're smarter than they were," he says. "Barkah's people hid from the automated spiders for *centuries*. We can hide from the Wasps the same way."

I shake my head.

"That's not the life I want our people to live. When I said *we need to leave,* I didn't mean leave Uchmal. We need to return to the *Xolotl.*"

His eyes narrow in confusion.

"But you said there's no weapons on that ship. All the *Xolotl* has to offer is a few old fighter craft. What would be the purpose of going up there?"

He is a warrior through and through, bred to defend his people. The thought of running is so contrary to who he is that he can't even process what I'm telling him.

This will be hard for him to hear. Almost as hard as it is for me to say.

"The purpose would be to leave Omeyocan. For good. I'm giving the order to abandon the planet."

Even this simple statement takes him a few moments to comprehend. I watch his face change from loving to guarded.

"But this is our home."

I shake my head. "It never really was. This place is poison."

His eyes narrow with anger.

"This world is *ours*. We've fought for it. We were made for it. We can't leave."

I put my hands on his shoulders.

"We leave or we die, Bishop. You have to see that."

He flinches away as if he suddenly can't stand my touch. That move was a reaction, he didn't think about it at all, yet it makes my heart drop.

"I can't believe you want to give up. You? Em Savage? Miss *if you run your enemies will find you*? You've gotten us through worse! You overcame Aramovsky's lies. You stopped the Springer war. You're the reason we escaped the *Xolotl* in the first place. That place was *hell*, and now you want to take us back?"

His voice is rising. He's never yelled at me before, not even once.

"The Wasps have weapons we can't beat." I keep my voice level. I don't want to aggravate him further. "And there's another alien ship coming, remember? The Wasps won't be the last enemy we face. But that doesn't matter—the Grub is driving people crazy. It's made us hate each other, fight each other. It's made us *kill* each other."

"Spingate was weak," he says.

"When you strangled Victor, was that just weakness?"

"He *hit* you!"

"In a training session," I say. "In a fair fight, the way he's done a hundred times before. You almost killed him! You attacked him from behind, like a coward."

Bishop leans back as if I'd just slapped him.

"I am no coward."

"No, you're not. You're also not a murderer, but on the training ground you almost were. And if I'd had my normal spear close by, Bawden would be dead. That's the Grub's influence. If it can make you and me give in to rage, what do you think it will do to the others when its power grows?"

He crosses his arms.

"Then we kill it now, before it gets stronger."

"We *don't* . . . *have* . . . *time*! The Wasps will be here tomorrow. The Grub could rise at any moment, and when it does, I don't think any of us will be able to resist. I saw it, I *felt* it. When it rises, we won't just be fighting the Wasps, we'll be fighting the Springers, too. And we'll be fighting each other."

"If anyone comes at me, I will *destroy them*!" His face twists into something primitive and hateful. He snarls, slams a fist against the cockpit's back wall. "I've killed before and I will kill again! Do you hear me? And if you try and stop me, Em, I swear to the God of Blood that *I will kill* you!"

His words hang in the air like the waterfall's mist.

I stand very still, say nothing.

Bishop blinks. He's confused. His hateful face grows slack. His cheeks flush bright red.

"Em, I'm . . . I don't know . . . I didn't mean to say that."

I force myself to take his hands again.

"It's all right," I say softly. "That's what the Grub does to us. It makes us hate. Maybe you didn't like Victor to begin with, but you *love* me—you just threatened my life. Now do you understand?"

He looks at the waterfall, refuses to meet my eyes. Maybe the Grub is affecting him, but Ramses Bishop doesn't believe in excuses; he said the words, which means he's at fault for saying them.

"We have a way out," I say. "Did Zubiri tell you how long until our shuttle is fueled?"

Bishop nods. "She thinks tomorrow around midnight."

It's just past sunset now. Maria thinks the Wasps will be here around this time tomorrow—midnight will be too late. I know Zubiri and Gaston are working as fast as they can. We'll have to find a way to slow the Wasps down.

"What about the captured troopships?"

"Sooner than the shuttle," he says. "Nevins is scheduled to do the first test flight tomorrow at noon, Cathcart right after that. Then they have hull integrity checks, or something like that."

He continues to stare at the waterfall.

"Bishop, look at me."

I reach for his face, to cup it, to hold it—with a sharp wave of his arm, he slaps my hands away.

Tears in his eyes. He feels betrayed. The person he loves is asking him to abandon everything he stands for.

"If you want to run, coward, then *run,*" he says. "Take your godsdamned shuttle and leave. I will stay. I will *fight.*"

I knew it would come to this. He won't be the only one that feels this way. Bishop is an icon among us—if he stays, many will follow his lead. As a people, we must not be divided. Despite Bishop's bravery, despite his skill as a warrior, despite his dedication to protecting our home against anyone and everyone, if he stays, he will die.

And so will those who stay because of him.

That I will not allow.

"Bishop . . . do you love me?"

The words crack his anger, but don't destroy it.

"You know I do. Don't dare use that against me."

I already feel like a villain, because I *am* manipulating him, but I need him on my side no matter what it takes.

"Staying is suicide," I say. "For you, for anyone who won't leave. If you love me, Bishop, if you *truly* love me, then trust in me."

Physically, Bishop is the strongest of us. But this isn't a test of physical strength—this is a test of will. When it comes to that, I am more powerful than anyone.

"We're going to take control of the *Xolotl*," I say. "If we have to kill Matilda and her people to do that, then so be it."

He finally looks at me. "What about the descendants of the vassals? Will we have to kill them as well?"

I thought Old Victor and Marcus were in league with Matilda, but now I believe that was the God of Blood warping my thoughts. If we have to fight them, we will, but I hope we don't have to.

"They told me they want us there," I say. "Together, we can make a new culture."

If I want Bishop on my side, I must be merciless. I must use every weapon I have. I hate myself for this, but lives depend on it.

"A new culture," I say. "Not just for you and me . . . for our children as well."

He lets out a half breath. He's stunned. He stares at me with his yellowish eyes . . . those big, soulful eyes.

"Children," he says. "Do you mean it?"

I reach out, slowly, and take his hand, expecting him to slap it away again. He does not. He's the most powerful man I know, yet now his hands are limp, almost lifeless. When I slide my fingers between his, they barely flex at all.

"Do this for me," I say softly. "Our people need to see that you and I are unified."

His fingers curl around mine. His eyes narrow, his jaw clenches. He nods.

"I support you, Em. Now and forever. When you announce your plan, I'll be at your side."

I have him. This is the right thing to do, and yet inside I feel so utterly *wrong*. I don't know if I want children. If we make it out of this alive and I choose against having kids with Bishop, will he ever forgive me?

I don't know.

What I do know is that the dead can't forgive anyone.

I will keep Bishop alive.

Him, and as many of my people as I can.

"We have to go," I say. "As soon as we're back, call a general meeting. I want everyone in the Grand Hall, even the tower crews. Man the cannons with Springers until the meeting is done."

Bishop nods. He guides the spider toward the Observatory.

I look back at the waterfall. I watch our special place fade into the distance, knowing that I will never see it again.

FORTY-THREE

My people are gathering in the Grand Hall. I stand alone in my sparse room, practicing spear forms. Before I tell the Birthday Children what comes next, there is someone I must speak to first.

"Hem?"

Barkah stands in my open door.

"Come in, please."

I realize I don't have any chairs. There is nowhere for us to sit.

Tension between our peoples is growing again, yet he came alone, as I asked. No bodyguards. This is a sign of Barkah's trust in me.

Trust that I am about to betray.

Not that long ago, he and I stopped a war. We saved lives. Now I will ask him to put those lives at risk, and to make an impossible decision—a decision I would not know how to make myself.

He wears new clothes. Long purple robes that fall just short of the floor, trimmed in yellow and green patterns. His copper necklace gleams. There are smears of red and gold above and below his eyes. His eye patch matches that color combination. He and I are both leaders, yes, but we're very different—the worse things get on our planet, the more time he spends on his appearance.

He already knows much. The Grub. The rising that could be just days away. The two additional eggs. The new ship that is a little over a year out. The fact that more ships will probably come after that. Lahfah will have informed him about the marching Wasp army.

Now I add to that list of bad news.

"Barkah, we're leaving the planet. All of my people will fit in our shuttle. We are returning to the ship that brought us here. We have enemies there, enemies that will fight us. And someday we'll need to colonize a new planet. That means we need to take our weapons with us, our bracelets, our rifles, even the spiders. We will leave tomorrow, before the Wasps arrive, so they can't damage our shuttle. Do you understand?"

His two good eyes lock on mine. I'm again surprised at how much they look like ours. Similar shape, yes, but it's not that— there is an intelligence that bubbles within. It isn't like looking into the eyes of an animal. With any Springer, there is a *connection,* an understanding that we are more than our urges and instincts. I think of my false father, what he said about intelligent beings having similar patterns of thought. I think of the Wasp I killed—if I had managed to capture it, would looking into its eyes have given me the same feeling of connection I get from looking into Barkah's?

The Springer king takes a long time to respond. I wait.

When he speaks, I hear anguish in his voice.

"We fight, together," he says. *"We win, together."*

He thought we were unified, our peoples fighting for the same thing. We were. Things change.

"There is no way to win. If we stay, my people will die."

I don't know if he understands all of my words. From the look in his eyes, though, he gets my meaning.

Barkah nods.

That is not something the Springers do. He learned that gesture from us. He does understand, and also accepts his new reality—his strongest ally will not be here to help him anymore.

Telling him that was hard, but it's nothing compared to the news I give him next.

"The ship we're traveling to was made to hold forty thousand of us. There are only five thousand people on it now. We captured two Wasp troopships. Each one carried six hundred and sixty-six armored troops, but if we pack tight, each could carry a thousand Albonden. If you want, we can take two thousand of your people with us. We can take *you* with us."

I don't speak much Springer, but I know what they call themselves: *Albonden.*

Two centuries ago, the Albonden ruled this planet. They lived in a city so large it dwarfed Uchmal. Springers numbered in the millions, at least, perhaps *tens* of millions. Matilda shattered that civilization, slaughtered the Springers, drove the survivors underground to live like insects in the dirt. Perhaps the Springers will go underground again and survive, just as they did with us, but I doubt it.

If the Wasps don't wipe the Springers out for good, the next race to arrive will. Or the race after that. Taking two thousand of his people with me is the least I can do to make good on a debt inflicted by my progenitor, a debt I could never begin to fully repay.

Barkah takes only a few moments to make his decision.

"Will send two thousand with you," he says. *"Lahfah say enemy arrive sundown tomorrow. You leave sooner?"*

Now for the final piece of my request.

"Our shuttle won't be ready in time. We need to delay the enemy advance long enough to prep all three ships and to safely load your people. We'll attack the Wasps at noon, try to slow them down. Will you fight with us?"

This time his decision is instant.

He offers his hand, another behavior he picked up to better communicate with us. Three fingers, not five, but biological differences don't matter—he knows what the gesture means to me.

I take his offered hand, squeeze it tight. He squeezes mine.

"We fight," he says. *"Together. One last time."*

I pull him close, hug him. I know he should stay with his people, lead them, but I don't care—I'm selfish and I want my friend to live.

"Come with us, Barkah. This planet is doomed."

He holds me tight.

"Will think on it," he says. *"Now, we prepare for war."*

With that, he leaves.

I've told him what his people face, and what decision I've made.

Now it is time to tell mine.

FORTY-FOUR

My people have gathered in the Grand Hall.

All 249 of them, all armed and ready for war.

Another forty-seven faces should be here, but their bodies belong to Omeyocan.

Bishop and I pulled Gaston, Smith, Spingate, Borjigin and Maria aside. I told them of my decision. All but Maria instantly agreed. Spingate and Gaston are eager to leave this world behind—they long for somewhere safe to raise their children. I think Kenzie understands Omeyocan is a place of death, and she's tired of watching people die. As for Borjigin? I can't say his reasons—maybe he sees his Coyotl everywhere he looks, like I still see my O'Malley.

Maria didn't agree, but she didn't object, either. She loves it here. She could survive in the jungle indefinitely. She could live on her own, or with the Springers. I think that she wants to stay, but she believes in my leadership so strongly she supports my decisions even if it means doing something she doesn't want to do.

I stand on the dais, next to the throne, flanked by my five closest friends. Our symbols aren't supposed to matter, but that's wishful thinking—symbols *always* matter. The people standing by my side are our most respected gears, circle-star, half and circle-cross.

I have no double-ring up here with me. There are only two of that symbol anyway. Walezak glares at me constantly, blames me for turning people against the gods. Aramovsky is lucky to be out of his cell at all; I'm not about to give him a place of honor.

I face the rest of our people. They are on the floor, gathered in a semicircle. The smaller kids, like Zubiri and Kalle, sit cross-legged; taller kids stand behind them. The tallest of us—Farrar, Bawden, Aramovsky, Victor, Okereke and the other adults— look over their heads.

Everyone waits for me to speak. A year ago, I wondered why they listened to me at all. I don't wonder anymore. I'm the one who leads by example. I'm the one who fights from the front.

I'm the one willing to make the hard choices.

And no choice is harder than this.

"We are in great danger," I say. My words echo off the Grand Hall's stone walls and vaulted ceiling. "Greater than ever before."

Even though I'm sure the gossip has already spread, I quickly cover our tactical situation with the Wasp army. I remind everyone of the Grub and what it's doing to us. I remind them that another ship is coming, and that more may follow.

I speak the hard truth: if we stay, we might never be free of violence.

"That is reality," I say. "I know it's hard to hear, *impossible* to hear, but reality is what it is whether we like it or not."

I see sadness, anguish, fear. More than anything else, I see *anger.* So much of it that I don't want to tell them what comes next.

But I must.

I take a deep breath and deliver the hardest news of all.

"Our dream of paradise is dead. That is why we are leaving. *Ximbal* should be fully fueled by sunset tomorrow. When it is, we're abandoning Omeyocan and returning to the *Xolotl*. We will take control of that ship and leave this world behind."

Stunned silence. Some people still look angry, but most look confused, as if I'd spoken Springer instead of English.

Farrar raises a hand.

"How long do we stay out in space?" he asks. "When do we come back?"

Heads nod. The question was on everyone's mind.

I clear my throat. No backing down now.

"I'm afraid I didn't make myself clear. We're leaving Omeyocan behind *forever.* We will travel the stars in search of a new home."

Confusion fades. On some faces, relief—those people would rather take their chances out among the stars than stay in this terrifying place. On other faces, disbelief . . . even *betrayal.*

Plenty of us, perhaps a third of our number, clearly do not approve of my decision. I don't care. I'm saving their lives.

Victor gently pushes through the kids in front of him, steps over the first row. He thumps his spear butt against the stone floor. Its sharp blade points up to the vaulted ceiling.

"My home is here," he says. "I will not leave."

Kalle stands up next to him.

"I'm not leaving, either. I can't even believe you mean what you're saying, Em. We can beat them."

More than a few murmurs of agreement.

"It's not just the Wasps," I say. "It's not just our difficulties with the Springers. It's not just that more races might come here to fight us." I point down to the ground. "Below us is a creature of pure evil. It's making us want to fight, to kill each other. We're leaving as soon as the *Ximbal* is fueled and Gaston finishes teaching Nevins and Cathcart how to pilot the Wasp troopships."

Kalle tilts her head. "And why would we need the troopships? If we decide to leave, wouldn't all of us fit in *Ximbal*?"

"Because two thousand Springers are coming with us."

Tempers erupt. People are yelling at me, shouting obscenities. Some because they don't want to leave Omeyocan. Of those that do, many can't stand the thought of taking another race with us. I underestimated how quickly my people could forget about Barkah's help after the first meteor attack. It's the Grub, affecting us all, playing on primitive emotions of self-preservation, of hate.

If only the shuttle was ready right now. The longer we wait, the more likely we are to erupt into violence with each other.

I raise my spear and I shout.

"Be . . . quiet!"

The grumbling dies down. This scene has played out several times since we arrived—I will talk and they will listen. I only need to stay in charge a little bit longer. Once everyone is on the *Xolotl*, once we take control, they will see that leaving Omeyocan was the right decision. If they want a new leader after that? So be it. In truth, I'm tired of being in charge—I could use a rest.

"There is more than enough room on the *Xolotl* for all of us," I say. "And there are five thousand people like us up there—little kids, teenagers, adults, old men and old women. They have invited us to join them. We will be part of a much larger community, a community that has already survived on that ship for *twelve hundred* years. That's longer than Uchmal has existed. Longer than the Springer city that came before it. The people we will be joining, they know how to survive."

The vassal descendants were an abstract thought before. Now that we might join them, the idea of stability, of being with more people than we knew existed, it has an undeniable appeal. On some faces, I see anger and frustration shift toward hope.

Bawden steps forward.

"What about Matilda and the Grownups that control the ship? And what if my progenitor is alive?"

"We are *taking* that ship, by force," I say. "I'm not going to lie to you and tell you I have it all figured out, because I don't. But know this—the *Xolotl* will be ours. Anyone who tries to stop us will be dealt with. And I won't allow any of you to live under constant threat, so if your progenitor is still alive, your progenitor will be dealt with."

In my head, *dealt with* means *executed.* We're not the ones who created life so that it could be overwritten, so that the creators could live forever no matter what the cost. Any progenitor that would harm us must be killed.

Including Matilda.

Especially Matilda.

"The Wasps might reach Uchmal before *Ximbal* is ready to leave," I say. "We're going to have to slow the Wasps down. Your individual unit leaders will go over your duties soon. For now, take thirty minutes and pack anything you want to take with you on the shuttle. You're allowed to keep anything that fits in one standard backpack, and that is *all* you can keep."

Victor takes two steps closer to the dais.

"I'm not packing anything," he says. "Because I'm not leaving."

I'd hoped there wouldn't be trouble. That was naïve of me.

"You're going," I say. "Everyone is. That's an order."

He shakes his head. "If you're leaving, then you are not my leader. I refuse your order."

Bishop points a finger at him. "Shut your mouth, Muller. The decision has been made. We don't have time to debate."

"There is no debate," Victor says. He does not sound angry—he sounds resolved.

I have to get through to him.

"I can't let anyone stay behind," I say. "Anyone who stays will die, don't you understand that?"

He adjusts his grip on his spear.

"That's what you think will happen. You are making the decision you think is best, but that decision is not best for me. I will fight for Omeyocan, or I will die here."

Another murmur rolls through the crowd, a murmur of surprise and support.

For a moment, I think Victor chose those words to mock me, to parrot something I said before we first stepped off *Ximbal* onto our new world—*The Birthday Children will survive on Omeyocan, or the Birthday Children will die here.* Then I remember properly; Victor can't be mocking me, because I never actually said those words out loud.

I only *thought* them.

He and I are so very much alike.

"No one stays behind," I say, letting my volume rise. "Everyone is getting on the *Ximbal,* and that is final."

Victor nods, as if he expected me to say that.

"You are making the coward's decision," he says. "I challenge your leadership."

Bishop starts forward. I grab at his arm, expecting him to

stop, but he shakes me off with barely a shrug. He strides down the dais steps, stands nose-to-nose with Victor.

People near them back away, giving the two circle-stars room.

"We don't have time for a vote, you idiot," Bishop says. "The enemy is almost at our gates. Em has made her decision and that decision is *final*."

Victor shakes his head. "She doesn't decide for me. If your girlfriend wants to abandon our home, then she is no leader of mine."

Bishop snarls and reaches for Victor's throat.

Victor moves faster than I've ever seen a human being move. He steps back, and in a fraction of a second the tip of his spear is at Bishop's throat.

Bishop freezes, a shocked look on his face.

"Not this time," Victor says. "This time I don't have my back turned."

He's going to kill my Bishop.

Without thinking, I sharply rotate my hand right, then left, activating my bracelet.

"*Don't,*" Victor snaps, his voice still calm but now much louder. "Raise that arm, Em, and I'll slice his throat before you can fire."

The Grand Hall is still. No one moves. All Victor needs to do is give his spear one slight push.

The anger that vanished from Bishop's face seeps back in.

"Put it down," he says. "Put it down and let's settle this, one-on-one."

Victor slowly shakes his head. "Instead of me putting mine down, how about you pick up yours? No practice spears this time—we use the real thing. If you win, I do what Em says. If I win, I decide what's best for me, and you let everyone else decide what's best for them."

A *duel*? Is that what he's suggesting?

"Stop this," I say. "Put the godsdamned spear *down,* right now. We don't settle our differences by killing each other over them."

Victor's eyes don't leave Bishop. Neither does his spearpoint.

I've had enough of this. I step toward them.

"Victor, I'm warning you for the last time, you—"

Bishop raises a hand, not toward Victor, but toward me.

"Stay out of this, Em," Bishop says, his words a low growl. "This little pup wants to meet me in the circle? I accept his challenge."

Victor takes a step back. Bishop smiles at him.

All around, heads nod. Murmurs of approval, a tone of excitement, eager expressions.

My people *want* this fight. Do they hope one of the boys will die?

"This is madness," I say. "Don't you all see? The Grub is messing with our heads. We don't solve problems by fighting. This isn't *us!*"

Bishop heads for the exit. He's on his way to the plaza, to the sand-filled training circles.

Victor gives me a sidelong glance.

"People do solve problems by fighting," he says. "It's called *war*. This isn't any different."

With that, he follows Bishop, and everyone follows him, hungry to see blood spilled. Even Maria and Borjigin rush out.

I said *no* and it didn't make a difference. My words are suddenly meaningless.

In seconds, I am left standing with only Gaston and Spingate.

What do I do now?

The feeling of hopelessness drives through me. Everything is falling apart at the last moment.

"We have to stop this fight," Spingate says.

I shake my head. "We can't."

But maybe I can stop them from killing each other.

We head for the training ground.

FORTY-FIVE

An army of bloodthirsty alien warriors is bearing down on us, and my people watch two of our own fight. If I give orders for everyone to return to their posts, those orders will be ignored—my leadership will be even further compromised.

I can do nothing but watch, just like everyone else.

The night is clear. No clouds. Omeyocan's twin moons blaze down. A few people brought torches. Flickering firelight illuminates the training pit sand, reflects off razor-sharp spearheads. Bishop and Victor circle each other, legs bent, spear tips out in front of them. Bishop is bigger than the younger boy, but the way Victor *moves:* lithe, smooth, no wasted energy.

Victor is a great fighter. I have fought both against him and side by side with him. I know how fast he is. Someday, perhaps in a few years, he could be the best of us, even better than Farrar and Bishop.

Today is not that day.

I just hope Bishop doesn't accidentally kill him.

They warily move around the training circle's edge, booted

feet pressing into the sand. People are packed in around them, only a few steps away from the circle, so close that if either fighter is knocked out of the ring the crowd will be able to push them right back in again.

The faces of my people, twisted by bloodlust. They lean forward, grab at each other, shake fists and shout for the fight to begin. Has the Grub done this to us, made something in our minds that did not exist before? Maybe. Or is this desire to see violence something that has always been there, just below the surface, hiding among our orderly society?

Bishop takes a short step forward and thrusts. Victor parries it with a clack of wood on wood.

The crowd screams in glee.

Bishop's feet are wide, his knees bent. He keeps a low center of gravity, just as he taught me to do. Victor's weight rides on the balls of his feet. His head dips a little with each of Bishop's steps—he's trying to lock in the bigger boy's timing.

Bishop shoots forward, thrusts at Victor's chest. Victor dodges left; the blade hisses by. Bishop instantly adjusts, flicks his blade up at Victor's face—a reaction so fast I barely see it—but the younger warrior is even faster. He leans back, avoiding the slash even as his own spearpoint slices through Bishop's shoulder, trailing blood behind it.

The crowd roars like a wild animal.

Bishop winces as he bounces away, again circles to his left.

Victor presses the attack, lunging forward and thrusting at Bishop's heart. Bishop moves to parry, but the thrust is a feint—in a blur of motion, Victor angles his spear down. The tip slashes through the coveralls of Bishop's right thigh.

The duel has lasted only a few seconds, yet Bishop's blood drips from a pair of wounds, red streaks that stain the white sand.

Victor isn't just *fast,* his speed is *blinding.*

My people scream so loud. They love what they see. They want more.

This can't be happening. Bishop is hurt, bleeding . . . could he really *lose?*

The younger boy dashes in again, forcing Bishop to move right. Bishop puts all his weight on his wounded leg; he winces and stumbles. Victor strikes, squatting low and sweeping the spear along the ground. The shaft cracks into Bishop's ankle—he falls, hands outstretched, his spear skidding away.

Bishop lands on his hands and knees, kicking up a spray of sand. Before that sand arcs back down, Victor has closed the distance.

He thrusts at Bishop's neck.

Everything stops.

I'm paralyzed, waiting for a gush of blood to paint the sand crimson.

But there is no gush, just a tiny bead of red where the point of Victor's blade presses into the side of Bishop's neck.

Bishop doesn't move.

The crowd is silent.

I'm speechless. *Thought*less. Everyone is.

Victor Muller beat the unbeatable.

"Yield," the boy says.

His message is simple and unmistakable. Just as his fighting style radiates efficiency, so too does this final action. There is no doubt what will happen if Bishop tries to rise.

Someone breaks the silence with a guttural shout: *"Kill him!"*

The crowd surges back to life, howling with rage and delight.

Bishop remains still. Only his eyes move, flicking to the spear that lies in the sand just an arm's reach away.

Kill him! the people scream, over and over, *Kill him!* I'm stunned to see those calling for Bishop's death include Farrar, Bawden, Kalle, Borjigin . . . Maria.

The Grub is warping even the strongest of us.

Bishop fought for these people, bled for them, protected them. He has been our pillar, strong and unbreakable, but just like that, they want to see his blood spilled onto the sand.

Victor's hands tighten on his spear shaft.

I step to the edge of the circle.

"Bishop, yield," I say.

When he doesn't respond, I scream it: *"Yield!"*

He looks at me. I can see it in his eyes—he can't believe he lost. The blade did not slice into his belly, but he's gutted just the same.

"I yield," he says.

The crowd screams for his blood anyway.

Victor takes a step back, thumps the butt of his spear into the sand. Emotion finally overwhelms him. His face wrinkles with disgust—not at Bishop, but rather at the crowd.

"All of you, *shut your godsdamned mouths*!"

His words are a slap across hundreds of faces. They stare at him, dumbly. A wave washes over them, reality crashing in. They finally understand what they sounded like, how they howled for the blood of a man who would have given his life for any of them.

My people are ashamed of themselves.

The Grub has power over us, yes, but not *complete* power.

Maybe there is still time.

Farrar and Bawden drag Bishop from the sand. Kenzie kneels by him, goes to work on his wounds.

Victor raises his spear.

"We're at war. The normal rules don't apply. No vote, no debate—I defeated Em's champion, that makes *me* the leader."

I wouldn't have thought I could be shocked to my core again, yet with those simple words, I am.

To my disbelief, heads nod.

This is how we function now? Just like that, the best fighter is our leader?

"The shuttle goes nowhere," Victor says. He speaks to all of us, but stares straight at me. "You will not take that weapon away from us."

This cannot happen. I won't allow it.

"I'm taking *Ximbal*," I say. "And *everyone* is coming with me. I don't care if you defeated Bishop, Victor, you're coming, too. We're all leaving this place together."

"You will not take the troopships, either," Victor says, as if I hadn't spoken at all. "We need everything we've got to beat the Wasps. Don't bother arguing, Em—we don't have time for it. I'm the leader now. You will do what I say."

A word pops into my head, something from Matilda's childhood. Something my father used to say. Something I would have never even thought of saying for fear of the rod.

"Victor, that is pure *bullshit*."

I hear people gasp. They look at each other, wondering if they just heard me right. We've been on our own for over a year with no adults, no Grownups, we have fought and died, remade this city in our image, and yet one bad word can stun people? The beatings they must have given us all when we were little to make us petrified of a few simple words . . .

Victor shakes his head. "Cursing won't make a difference."

"No, it won't," I say. "But violence will." I look around at the crowd. "That's what you all love now, isn't it? Violence? *Blood?*" I tap my temple. "Have you all become so simpleminded that some evil thing beneath our city can change who you are, how you think? We are stronger than this!"

Victor strides toward me. He stops a few steps away, his eyes narrowed more with annoyance than fury.

"This is over," he says. He holds out his hand. "I'm the leader now. Give me your spear."

His works perfectly fine, as we've just witnessed, but mine is different. Charred, chipped and beat up, it remains our symbol of leadership. If Victor takes it, then this is truly over. And if that happens, his actions will condemn my people to death.

I step to the training circle's edge. I spin my spear once, twice, then slam the butt into the sand.

"You want my spear, little boy? Then *take* it from me."

His eyes squint in doubt.

"Em, are you serious? Are you challenging me?"

I turn in place, looking at this crowd of people who are so easily manipulated.

"Would you all like that?" I ask them. "Would you enjoy seeing Victor and me duel, because you're so *entertained* by pain, by death?"

Some of them hold my gaze, but most look down. I'm magnifying their shame. Victor's words cracked the God of Blood's hold on them—my words are shattering it into a million pieces.

"Em, don't be stupid," Victor says. "I just beat Bishop and there isn't a scratch on me."

I hold out my right hand palm-up, curl my fingers in three times.

"You want scratches? Come get some."

A hint of betrayal in his eyes. And then, I remember his crush. Was the fight against Bishop just for leadership . . . or, in Victor's mind, was it also for *me*?

Maybe he thought he would rule, and I would be happily by his side.

He thought wrong.

"Make your choice," I say. "Get in the circle, or shut your mouth and do what you're told."

His expression hardens.

"The enemy is coming," he says. "We don't have time for more duels. If you insist on this challenge, I have no choice but to make an example of you."

I spit into the sand.

"You talk too much, Victor. Let's settle this."

FORTY-SIX

take off my boots. I want to feel the sand between my toes. It is cool and soft.

The shaft of my spear is charred and cracked, but still solid. This weapon has seen me through hard times. I need it to see me through one more.

Spingate pushes through the crowd, steps into the training circle. Dancing torchlight makes her red hair shimmer.

"This is *crazy,*" she says. "Single combat isn't how we pick leaders! We can have another vote."

She doesn't think I can win. No one does.

Victor gives his spear a spin to the right, then to the left.

"Isn't time for a vote," he says. "This last fight, then no more. Anyone who challenges me after this will be put to death."

He's so confident. Barely more than a boy, but the way he fights, the way he *speaks* . . . it's almost as if he's destined to be a leader. Is Old Victor proof of that?

If leadership is Victor's destiny, that destiny will have to wait.

"Spin," I say, "get out of the circle."

She does, shaking her head in both disgust and despair. Gaston takes her hand.

"Em, don't do this," he says. "You're going to get killed. This is ridiculous."

Other people chime in. Some murmur I have no right to challenge Victor at all, that Bishop's loss settled things. I don't care—I'm getting my people off this planet.

If violence rules, then I will rule by violence.

I nod at Victor. "You ready?"

He nods back. "May the best fighter win. I'll try to go easy on you."

Victor is committed to this course of action, but he clearly doesn't want to fight me.

Something I can and will use against him . . .

If we'd dueled a week ago, he would have easily defeated me—he's too fast, too strong. But in that week, I won a battle only to learn I'd lost the war. I learned about *diversions*.

I dart forward, thrust for his heart.

Victor dances right—my blade slices empty air, I'm too top-heavy, off-balance. I stumble, use my weapon to stop myself from falling—the spear tip sinks deep into the sand.

Before I can pull it free, Victor's blade streaks for my throat. I twist left—his thrust misses me by a hair.

He steps back, a small smile lifting the corners of his mouth.

"Nice speed," he says. "You're fast, but not fast enough."

You hurt my man, now I'll hurt you in more ways than one. . . .

"I love you," I say.

The words are so quiet I don't know if he hears them, but he sees them on my lips. From the way his eyes widen, I know he understands what I said. The words are like a slap to his face, stunning him for just an instant.

My spear blade is still buried in the sand. I lift and flick at the same time, launching a streak of tiny white grains straight into Victor's face.

The move is so subtle and quick he doesn't have time to duck or even blink. For an instant, his fighting form is forgotten as he twists his head away, lets go of the spear with one hand to rub at his tightly scrunched eyes. He quickly realizes his mistake, again grips the shaft with both hands and points his spear to the last place he saw me—but I've already moved to my right.

I slash down, slicing across the back of his hand. Blood spills out, streaming red jewels that sparkle in the torchlight before they hit the white sand, bead up in grainy clumps.

You tried to take what is mine, now you will pay with your life. . . .

Squinting and blinking, Victor pivots, swings wildly. I easily block the strike and step in fast, erasing the distance between us. I twist my hips and turn my shoulders, transferring strength and momentum into my weapon—my spear butt comes up in a sharp arc that hits Victor in the balls so hard it lifts him off his feet.

He grunts, stumbles. That shot would have dropped most boys, but, half bent over, he shuffles backward, still trying to defend himself. He's squinting, looking for me, trying to blink the sand out of his eyes.

The lust for brutality courses through me. I don't fight it—it fills me with strength, with pure *power*.

I'll end you, I'll KILL you. . . .

I close in for the finish.

Victor somehow recovers enough to plant his feet and thrust forward, spearpoint driving toward my guts, but the shot to his groin has slowed him. I slip past his blade, slam my right knee into his stomach: he doubles over, air whuffing out of his lungs.

He can't see—now he can't breathe.

I drive my elbow into his nose; I hear and feel it *snap*.

Victor falls to his side. His spear rolls away. His hands flounder in the air, as if they can't decide between rubbing his eyes, clutching his broken nose, holding his balls or stemming the blood gushing from his slashed hand.

Victor Muller is defenseless.

And now he'll pay for what he's done.

"You thought you could take what is mine," I say. "You thought *wrong*."

He raises his bloody, shaking hand toward me. "I yield!"

I laugh. *"I don't care!"*

Will I slash his legs and arms, watch him bleed out, crying, begging for mercy? Or stab him through his throat, so I can see the look in his eyes as he dies the same way he tried to kill Bishop? Or should I make him go slowly, with a deep, *deep* gut wound, so he can try to stuff his own intestines back into his belly?

A blade in the belly . . .

The same way I killed Yong.

That makes me pause, but only for a moment. Yong attacked me. He deserved to die. So does Victor—I *hate* him, I want to hear him *scream*.

I raise my spear.

Spingate calmly steps between us.

"Don't kill a defenseless person," she says. "It will haunt you forever. Trust me, I know."

I should kill her, too, kill them *both*.

"This is what the Grub wants." She taps her temple. "The God of Blood is corrupting you, it's doing to you what it did to me."

The Grub . . .

Yes, it's affecting me. Why shouldn't it? The Grub is *guiding* me, guiding me toward my true self.

Victor lies there, helpless. Just one stab to his belly . . .

Yes, the *belly,* the same way I killed Yong.

The same way I killed O'Malley.

My temper vanishes, leaving a void that is filled by a rush of cold reality.

Victor is in a fetal position, wounded hand still upstretched toward me, blood pattering down to the sand. His nose is broken and bleeding. He can barely see.

He's defenseless.

He *surrendered.*

And I was going to murder him, because of that thing with the wet metallic skin, the disgusting blob wriggling beneath the dirt, the abomination that wants us to *hate.*

I lower the spear.

Spingate's eyes brim with tears.

"You did it," she says. "You did what I couldn't."

She wishes she'd been stronger. I see it in her, see her desperate desire to take it all back.

But she can't.

Spin stepped in front of me knowing exactly what could have happened. I look around, realize that no one else did a damn thing. Even Bishop stayed quiet, didn't yell at me to stop—only Theresa acted.

My best friend risked her life to save my soul.

I drop my spear. I grab Spingate, hug her as tight as I can.

"Thank you," I say. "Thank you."

I let her go, kneel next to Victor.

His eyes still blinking madly and watering from sand, he looks at me with a clear mix of admiration and disbelief.

"You defeated me."

"I had to."

His voice drops to a whisper.

"When you said . . . said that you . . ."

Even as beat up as he is, there is hope in his voice, hope that I meant those three magic words: *I love you.*

"I lied," I say. "I had to get you off guard."

That admission hurts him far worse than the physical damage. He can't hide his need for me, not anymore, but he recovers almost instantly. Victor somehow finds the strength to make his blood-smeared lips smile.

"We're at war," he says. "Winning matters. *How* you win does not. I'm yours, Em. Where you lead, I will follow."

Then Kenzie is there, gently pushing me aside.

Okereke and other circles bring stretchers, take Victor and Bishop away.

I look at my people. I slowly turn in place to take in those who gleefully watched us fight like mad beasts.

It shouldn't have happened like this, but it did. I will not let this moment go to waste.

"Anyone else question my right to lead?"

Hundreds of heads slowly shake from side to side.

"Good. Let's get to work."

FORTY-SEVEN

I hold our strategy meeting in the *Ximbal*'s pilothouse. The walls appear clear, showing us the Observatory and people rushing about the plaza in the reddish glow of the rising sun.

With me are Bishop, Maria, Gaston, Zubiri, Barkah, Lahfah and, yes, Spingate. We've all worked through the night, preparing for the upcoming battle. They look as exhausted as I feel.

Bishop wears only shorts. He's on crutches. Bandages are wrapped around his shoulder and thigh. Kenzie says he needs another hour in the med-chamber. He won't be at a hundred percent, but he'll be ready to fight.

We stand around a waist-high, glowing disc of a map. On it, Uchmal is no bigger than a button, and Schechak, just to the north, is but a pin. Both sit within an area the size of a dinner plate that represents the jungle ruins of the ancient Springer city. Beyond the ruins, a huge area of land that includes the valley where I saw the Wasp army. Small words float above shaded areas marking the Springer tribes: *Malbinti, Khochin, Galanak, Podakra*.

Eleven columns of smoke dot the Galanak territory, making a zigzag line that points roughly toward Uchmal and Schechak. At the end of that line, a red dot flashes—the location of the Wasp army, just confirmed by Malbinti scouts.

Gaston points to one of the smoke columns.

"That's the village D'souza's Demons found. Some of the other fires were reported by the second hurukan unit, and the rest are close enough that we can see them from the top of the Observatory."

The second unit found villages that looked just like the one Lahfah, Maria and I saw.

"Galanak, nahnaw," Barkah says.

The destruction has upset him, shaken him so much he doesn't bother with English. He speaks quickly to Maria. She listens, solemnly nods, then translates.

"Barkah says the Wasps destroyed most of the large Galanak towns. Combined with the routing of the Galanak army, he thinks that tribe is almost completely wiped out. The word he uses for all this best translates to *apocalypse.*"

The Wasps are clearly coming for us, but they're slaughtering any Springers they find along the way. This isn't war—this is extermination.

"How long until the Wasps reach us?" I ask.

Maria studies the map. She chews at her lower lip.

"Looks like they've sped up," she says. "A lot. At their current pace, I'm afraid they'll be here a couple of hours before sunset."

Gaston crosses his arms, shakes his head. "Way too soon. *Ximbal* won't be fully fueled for at least three hours after that."

And here I didn't think things could get any worse. We'll be too late. Unless . . .

"Maybe we don't need a full tank," I say. "How long to load just enough to get us to the *Xolotl*?"

Gaston stares at me like I just said the dumbest thing anyone has ever spoken.

"Um, that's a really, *really* bad idea, all right? That doesn't account for any contingencies, or if we can't actually board the *Xolotl* and have to come back down. We need a full tank."

Maria points to the red dot on the map.

"I hate to ruin the story for you, Gaston, but here's how it ends—the Wasps take over Uchmal. Period. We can't beat them. If we don't evacuate before they get here, you, Spingate, your baby and everyone you know will be chopped up into little pieces. *Coming back* is the least of our worries."

Gaston sneers at her. He looks at the gathered faces, perhaps expecting someone to back him up. No one does. Not even Spingate.

"We're out of options," she says to him. She speaks softly, patiently. "If we produce the minimum fuel needed to reach the *Xolotl*, how long will that take?"

He rubs at his face. I'm sure there are all kinds of worst-case scenarios rolling through his head, but Spin summed it up perfectly—we're out of options.

"Sunset, at the earliest," Gaston says. "And that's not me being difficult, that's physics. We can only convert the fuel at a fixed rate. The process can't be rushed."

I bang my spear butt lightly on the floor, twice, to make sure I have everyone's attention.

"I know that isn't what any of us wanted to hear," I say. "But we spent all night planning a delaying strategy. That strategy *will work*. It has to. We need to make sure the Wasps don't reach Uchmal until after the sun sets. We have to slow them down, *and* leave enough time for us to get back to the shuttle. Got it?"

Everyone nods. Everyone except the Springer king. He stares at the map.

"Barkah," I say, "they're going to do to Schechak what they did to the Galanak villages. You need to evacuate everyone."

Maria starts to translate, Barkah waves her off. He understood what I said.

We stay quiet, give him time to think.

He turns to Lahfah, rattles off a fast, sharp sentence in Springer. I recognize a few words—he's asking his queen if she agrees with Maria and me that the approaching army is truly unbeatable.

Lahfah doesn't hesitate. She speaks softly, quickly. No laughter in her voice now.

Barkah again stares at the map.

Finally, he looks at me.

"*Malbinti march south,*" he says. "*Abandon Schechak, immediately.*"

If all goes well, my people will be gone from this planet in a few hours. We can't help the Malbinti against the Wasps. I wish them well.

Bishop takes over. He maps out our plan to use our spiders as fast attackers, to position our soldiers in small ambush groups to pick away at the incoming troops from multiple directions. Maria's hurukans will serve as fast-moving decoys—if all goes well, the Wasps will think there are two dozen of them, not just the six we have. Borjigin's machines will quickly ferry troops around the jungle to flank the Wasps, something Bishop calls a "force multiplier." Barkah points to the areas on the map where he can bring his larger numbers to bear.

They cover many angles, but the map itself draws my focus away from the conversation.

The valley . . . how the Wasps moved through it . . . how they spread out when the Springers attacked, but before that they were in a more concentrated formation . . .

"The Goff Spear," I say, blurting out the words so loud everyone stares at me. "Zubiri, is there any way to aim the Goff Spear at the Wasp army?"

If she holds any animosity toward me for her troubles with Victor, she doesn't show it.

"The Goff Spear is built to fire at orbital craft," she says. "We can't aim at a ground target. Besides, these are very particular weapons, designed to penetrate the extremely thick armor of the *Basilisk* or the *Xolotl,* but the part that goes *boom* is a nuclear warhead—we definitely don't want them going off down here."

My frustration flares. We have a weapon that can destroy massive spaceships, but we can't use it to win this battle?

"What about the rounds themselves?" Spingate asks. "Can they be rigged to explode on their own?"

Zubiri huffs. "Didn't I just tell you it fires *nukes?*"

"Answer Spingate's question," I say. "Can you rig them?"

The one-armed girl glares at me, but she nods.

"It would take me about eight hours, I think, to modify it. Let me show you why this is a horrible idea. *Ximbal,* show damage radius of a Goff round detonation, centered on the estimated position of where the Wasp army will be in eight hours."

The flashing red dot moves much closer to Uchmal, becomes the center of an orange circle, which itself is surrounded by a larger gray circle.

Schechak is at the edge of the orange circle.

Uchmal is inside the gray.

"The explosion would produce a massive fireball," Zubiri says. "Every living thing inside the orange circle would be burned alive. The gray area represents what's called a *shock wave*. The walls of Uchmal would likely crumble. All but the biggest buildings would collapse. And then there's the fallout, which, depending on wind direction and speed, would poison a thousand-kilometer-long, two-hundred-kilometer-wide swath of jungle for decades to come. Any creature inside that area in the first few hours after detonation would likely die within weeks from radiation."

She crosses her arms, glares at all of us. "Any questions?"

There are none. My friends look at the map, stunned by the destructive power at our hands.

But I'm not stunned; I feel pieces fall into place.

The *Basilisk*'s assault, ignoring the area around the Observatory . . .

My false father, saying the Grub could defend itself but not against *all* attacks . . .

He meant attacks like this.

"A nuke could have wiped the Springer city off the map, but Matilda didn't use nukes," I say. "If the *Basilisk* used nukes, they could have taken us out easily. They didn't. The Echo's signal, it must include some kind of absolute command to not use big bombs that could hurt the Grub."

Has Matilda known about the Grub all along, or did she obey the call's commands the same way the *Basilisk*'s crew did?

I made a promise to myself, that I would kill the God of Blood. The nuke would do that. But it doesn't matter. We clearly can't use a weapon that would kill us, too. Unless . . .

"A *timer*," I say. "The Grub is drawing the Wasps to Uchmal. If we could set some kind of timer, we could have the nuke go off after we leave—we could wipe out the Grub *and* the Wasps at the same time."

Zubiri shakes her head. "With that weird electrical interference going on around here, there is no way I would trust a timer. The thing could go off before we leave, or not at all. Same thing with any kind of remote detonation—we can't risk it."

It feels like an answer is so close. Frustration creeping in, filling me up.

Gaston smacks his fist into his hand, so loud it startles everyone.

"*Impact*," he says. "Our shuttle takes off vertically. What if we make some kind of simple bomb rack, rig the nuke to detonate on impact. We go straight up, *way* up, so when we drop it we have enough time to get clear. Then, bang—dead Wasps, dead Grub." He glances at Zubiri. "Could you engineer it to detonate on impact?"

Everyone stares at the young woman who has already lost an arm to war. She seems to shrink under our combined gaze.

"I could," she says in a voice almost too quiet to hear. "But there's no time to engineer any kind of guidance system. All we could do is drop it, let it fall on its own. For the shuttle to have enough time to get clear, we'd have to drop from a high altitude. Even a slight wind could push the nuke off-target. I'm pretty sure that if the Grub is within the orange zone, we'll kill it, but the shockwave zone? I don't think so, it's too far underground."

Bishop nods with excitement. "But if it does work, we destroy the Wasps and the Grub, then we land somewhere else on the planet. We start over."

"*No*," Spingate says before I can respond. "Without the Goff Spear, we can't stop future races from landing. Even if we kill the Grub, the call has already been sent—at least one additional ship is coming. Maybe more. It's not like those ships will just turn around and go home. For all we know, the next race will scour the planet to wipe out competition, a larger version of what the Wasps are doing now."

She's right. Killing the Grub won't make this planet safe. Our only real chance for survival is to leave Omeyocan behind.

I make my decision.

"Zubiri, get to work on converting the rounds as bombs. Give Gaston the information he needs so he can have the bomb rack built."

"Hem, no." It's Barkah. He's still staring at the map, at the massive zone of destruction if we detonate the nuke. *"My people will die."*

"Then you better tell them to march south as fast as they can go," I say. "The Wasps have already slaughtered thousands of Springers. Once we leave, they're going to keep coming after you. As horrible as this bomb is, it might kill enough of them and their equipment that your survivors have a chance to go on, instead of being hunted down and slaughtered."

He looks from the map to me. I wait for him to answer, although it doesn't really matter what he says. I will do what must be done.

Finally, sadly, he nods. *"Kill them,"* he says. *"Kill them all."*

We are unified. I take a deep breath, hold it, let it out slow.

"We have our mission," I say. "Now let's slow these bastards down."

FORTY-EIGHT

t's late morning. We have only a few hours left. I walk around the plaza, shouting encouragement to my people. They place their backpacks on a scale, one at a time under Tina Schuster's watchful eye, then stack them in neat piles. She's carefully tracking the weight allowance Gaston has given her.

At the *Ximbal*'s rear is a half-rusted tanker truck. A black hose leads from it into an open door in the *Ximbal*'s underside. Louise Bariso and Noam Peura are in charge of loading the fuel.

"How much longer?" I ask them.

Peura checks something on a messageboard.

"Five hours," he says.

Five hours. Can we give him that much time? Maria and her hurukans are scouting the jungle, trying to find the invading army.

Across the plaza are the two captured troopships. Through their cockpit windows, I see Cathcart in one, Nevins in the other, preparing for the flight. Thirteen-year-old boys, each responsible for the lives of a thousand Springers.

Throngs of Springers are gathered around the troopships, panicked crowds jostling for their place, pushing at burly Springer soldiers who are trying, desperately, to keep the boarding process orderly. Scattered piles of belongings litter the ground—things the refugees wanted to bring with them, but there simply isn't room for anything other than the clothes on their backs. Red children, purple teens, blue adults. I notice that none of the refugees have the deep-blue skin of elders. I suppose that makes sense. This could be the future of Barkah's entire race—he won't send those that would live only a few more years. I can't imagine how difficult it was for him to choose the scant few of his kind that will leave Omeyocan behind.

Barkah is among them, shouting in his native tongue, directing traffic. Maybe this is only a fraction of his people, but two thousand panicked Springers makes for a grand swirl of chaos.

I jog to him. He has on yet another new coat, this one emerald green and trimmed with polished bits of steel. It covers him from thick neck down to his big feet.

"Hem. How long?"

How long until the shuttle is ready to depart. "Five hours."

He glances at the troopships, at his panic-stricken people, then back at me.

"That is enough."

"If their fighters don't attack before then, sure. Are your units in position?"

He nods. His battalions are already in the jungle. Those soldiers will not be coming with us—they will fight until we retreat for the evacuation, then head south to join the rest of the refugees fleeing Schechak.

Our forces are ready: twenty-four hundred Malbinti warriors, seven spiders, all twenty-seven remaining circle-stars, a hundred young circles, and one big surprise.

I hear something, to the north . . .

Faint, distant, but undeniable—the far-off, echoing scream of Wasp fighter craft.

"Hem, they come," Barkah says.

I shout to Schuster, tell her it's time to deploy our forces. She barks orders in turn. In seconds, I hear the deep thrum of a truck's engine.

I turn to Barkah. "Are you ready?"

He shouts something I don't understand. Three of his biggest bodyguards hop out of the crowd of Springers, accompanied by a young red female carrying an embroidered pillow. Barkah takes off his necklace, the symbol of his office, and sets it on the pillow.

Barkah slides out of his emerald-green coat. His arms and chest are tied up in the yellow, blue and green rags of Springer jungle camouflage. The female takes his coat, bows and hops away.

One of the bodyguards hands Barkah a leather equipment belt. The Springer king buckles it on, takes a hatchet and a knife from another bodyguard and jams the weapons into the belt. The final bodyguard hands my alien friend one of our long-pointed silver bracelets.

Barkah slides the bracelet onto his forearm. He twitches his hand right, then left. I see the bracelet's white crystal start to glow.

Finally, the Springer king takes off his embroidered, jeweled eye patch and tosses it aside. From a pouch on his belt, he pulls out another and ties it in place. This patch is plain gray. Stitched on it, in heavy black thread, is a null-set symbol.

Gone is the regal king with his fancy clothes. Before me I see the warrior I first met in the jungle, the brave soul that killed a hurukan with spear, musket and hatchet.

He's not sitting back this time: he's here to fight.

"Ready, Hem. You?"

From a pocket, I pull out Halim's bloodstained headband. I tie it around my head, aware as ever that it hides my circle.

Belching smoke, Big Pig rolls to a stop next to us. The heavy vehicle will carry us to our jungle battleground. Dozens of troops—Springer and human both—hang over the thick metal walls, slapping them in a primal rhythm. The Springers wear jungle rags. The humans wear black coveralls, with yellow-leafed blue vines tied around their chests, arms and legs. A thick paste of mud and ash covers the exposed skin of both races.

Two different species, yet every single soldier in that truck wears a headband decorated with the null-set symbol. Some are neatly stitched. Others, crudely done with paint. A few are inked in blood.

I wish there was an afterlife, so Halim could look down and see the impact of his small gesture.

Today, we are all truly one people.

I climb into the truck. Barkah and his bodyguards scramble up behind me.

Big Pig's engine rumbles—we drive off to war.

FORTY-NINE

I am deep in the jungle ruins. Perhaps a hundred people of Omeyocan—Springer and human both—surround me. The jungle canopy arcs above, life-giving vines hanging down. No blurds here, no piggies, no animals of any kind, because wildlife seems to have the good sense to clear the hell out.

If only we could be as smart.

Big Pig dropped me and mine off, then carried Barkah to his own regiment. Far north, we hear Springer war horns, volley fire from rifles and muskets, the deadly bark of Wasp machine guns and the thundering echo of tanks letting off round after round. Barkah has engaged the enemy, but we have no idea how he's doing.

My unit waits for me to speak. Eyes of many colors look at me with fear, excitement and anger. *Always* anger. I am not so foolish to think our newly unified sense of purpose comes only because we now have a common enemy—the God of Blood drives us to fight, and fight we will.

"The Wasps are coming," I say. "Our scouts estimate they'll be at the walls of Uchmal in two hours. Our ships will be ready to leave in four, so we *must* slow them down."

I turn as I talk, looking every single being in the eye, a technique I learned from Aramovsky. These soldiers' thoughts swirl with rage and hatred, both from the Grub's influence and because their home is being invaded. I need to connect with them, make sure they understand I'm *here*, fighting by their side.

I still don't know why I became the leader, but I have learned what a leader must do.

"They have better weapons, but we know the jungle," I say. "We'll use that to our advantage. We get close, hit them hard, then fall back and lure them into our trap. Our goal is to take out as many tanks as we can, understand?"

Heads nod. Springer tails thump against the ground.

Tanks are the enemy's lead element. If we let them roll right in, they'll blow open the city gates and cruise down our streets with infantry close behind. If we attack the tanks, the Wasps will react to defend those tanks. That, we hope, will tie up their ground troops and slow their cannons, keeping them from moving into firing range until our evacuation is complete.

We know they still have the troopships that brought them here. We haven't seen those yet, don't know where they are. All we can do is hope they fear our tower cannons and hold their troopships in reserve.

"Keep fighting until we hear the retreat signal—three long blasts in a row," I say. "When that sounds, all human troops return to the plaza, *fast*. All Springers, leave the battlefield. Head south to join your people. Everyone understand?"

Nods and thumps. Focused eyes. Determined faces.

The Springers here with us will not leave the planet. They

know they are quite possibly fighting for the future of their species. And I know that if we drop the nuke, they probably won't have enough time to make it out of the blast radius. We might only have this one chance to destroy the Wasp army—I will sacrifice thousands of my allies so that millions of them can survive.

If I am very, *very* lucky, these are choices I will have to live with the rest of my days.

I raise my spear.

"Today, we are not Springers. We are not humans. We are *all* from Omeyocan. We fight as one. Rely on each other, and kill as many of those bastards as you can!"

My warriors raise muskets, rifles and spears. A brief, unified bark of solidarity, then the crowd breaks up as they move to their assigned positions.

I jog toward my spider. Good old 05. The holes have been patched, the leg repaired, the shiny dents painted over. Victor and Bawden wait in the cockpit. Victor's hand is bandaged, as is his nose—there wasn't time to heal him correctly.

The three of us are a good team. I hope we all make it.

Next to the spider is Maria, sitting astride the furry, smelly bulk of Fenrir. She smiles the wicked smile of someone who is gifted at war and knows war is about to begin.

"Hail, Em," she says. "That was quite the fancy speech."

"Oh, come on, Maria—you don't use flowery words when your squad is going into battle?"

She shakes her head. "We don't talk. We just kill."

I wonder if Maria will survive the next four hours. I hope so. I hope so very much.

I hand my spear up to Victor, then climb aboard. I'm about to give the order to move out when Maria calls up to me.

"Em, one question?"

I nod.

"I like Bishop," she says. "If you die today, can I date him?"

I laugh. "Don't hold your breath, sugar. I'll be on the shuttle with him in a few hours."

"Or if Bishop dies," Victor says to me, "can I date *you*?"

I don't know if I should be angry or offended—his charming grin erases either possibility. I cut him up, yet still he smiles at me.

Bawden rolls her eyes.

"If we're done talking about our love lives, can we please go fight now?"

I push my spear into its bracket on the cockpit's rear wall, give the shaft a quick shake to make sure it's held firmly, then face forward.

"Take us out, half-speed," I say.

Number 05 crawls through the jungle.

Our careful strategy has already fallen apart.

Maria quietly led us toward the Wasp column, only to run headlong into three of their ticks. Our grand plan to attack instantly turned into running for our lives.

Bawden drives our spider full out, the armored hull bouncing off tree trunks as often as it goes around them. Two ticks scramble through the trees behind us, banking in and out of cover, their rapid-fire guns shredding wood and leaves. Bullets smack into our spider's armor, make the metal ring like a musical instrument.

I can't see Maria anywhere.

Victor pops up from the cover of our cockpit and fires his rifle over the spider's back, eight shots in three seconds, then drops down again. He reloads, hands a blur.

Ahead and to the right, I see a red flag waving from high in the branches—a Springer is up there, hidden among the vines and yellow leaves.

At least part of our plan is back on.

I grab Bawden's shoulder, point to the flag.

"I'm on it," she says, "hold tight!"

Victor and I both grip the armored ridge as Bawden turns the spider hard toward the wide space below the flag—between two thick tree trucks.

The lead tick is right behind us, guns pounding away at our armor.

The moment we pass below the flag, a Springer yells. I lean over the side to look back as hidden ropes are pulled tight— a net rises between the trees. The tick tries to turn, but it's too late. The eight-legged machine flies into the net. Anchoring ropes snap taut. The tick's nose slams hard into the jungle floor. The machine bounces once, spinning, smashes down in a cloud of dead leaves.

Springers hop out of the underbrush, rifles and muskets and hatchets ready to go to work.

I see two lightly armored Wasps slowly crawl from the ruined tick. Just before Bawden turns sharply and I lose sight, the Springers close in on them.

A hail of bullets rings off our spider, makes me drop down behind the cockpit's cover. Victor pops up, emptying the rifle in a blur.

"*There,*" Bawden shouts. "The tanks!"

Through the thick underbrush, I see one, a hulking block of camouflaged metal with that thick barrel jutting forth like a spear. In our mad, directionless escape from ticks, we found our target. Now for the real test—can we lure them away?

"Lighting the smoke," I say, then pull the pin on the thick canisters Borjigin mounted in the cockpit. With a *whuff* of compressed air, the skull-sized container inside shoots high, punching through the canopy before bursting in a cloud of purple smoke.

"Oh *shit-balls*," Bawden screams, and I'm almost thrown overboard as she turns our spider hard left. Out the right side, I see what she saw—hundreds of Wasp foot soldiers rushing through the underbrush toward us.

Bullets rake us from the left; the other pursuing tick. I lean forward, out in front of Bawden—the tick banks sharply just before I flick my fingers forward, and my beam vanishes harmlessly into the jungle.

Fire from the Wasp infantry pings madly off our spider, forcing Victor and me back down into the cockpit's cover.

"They're chasing us," he says.

Bawden throws him a fast glare. "Wow, Vic, I would have never known."

"Just *drive*, dammit," I say. "Get us to the target point."

We don't have many spiders—Bishop guessed the Wasps probably know that. In fact, we based our whole strategy around that guess. If the Wasps are smart, they know taking out our mechanized units will give them a permanent advantage. We can only hope they want that so bad we can use it against them.

Another musical burst of big bullets hammers into 05's rear. The tick is behind us again, firing away.

Our spider's smooth movement suddenly changes to a lurching shudder, as if someone is rocking it hard side to side.

"*Leg damage*," Bawden calls out. "I have to take that leg offline. Victor, help me!"

They flip switches, twist knobs, turn dials. While they work, I pop up and fire bracelet blasts over the spider's back, keeping the tick from closing in on us.

The lurching lessens.

"As good as it's going to get," Bawden says. "Hang on!"

As if I could do anything else.

Our spider rips through the jungle. We're hit with a hail of gunfire so concentrated that even Victor won't pop up to return fire. Bullets shred branches and trunks, tear the leaves around us, a swarm of invisible insects chewing the jungle to tiny bits.

Even over the unending gunfire, I hear the tank cannon's roar.

Ahead of us, a fireball erupts, showering us with dirt and mud. I feel a dozen piercing stings on my face and hands. We're moving too fast to avoid it—Bawden drives us straight through the blaze. It singes my skin, but we're through it almost instantly. I look at my hands: big splinters jut out of them, shreds of a tree blasted apart by the tank's powerful round. A glance at Bawden and Victor—their faces bleed from a dozen small cuts.

We're hurt, but the tank is following us . . . our plan is working.

Movement to the right: the tick, again trying to flank us. I flick my fingers forward—this time my beam connects, glances off the tick's armor. It banks away, working the trees and underbrush for cover.

Another tank round erupts near us, then another, and another, each detonation a hard kick to my ears. Concussion waves hammer my body. The air fills with dirt and dust and mud and smoke. Grit in my eyes, my mouth.

It's not just one tank following us . . . it's at least *three*.

The explosions smack our spider side to side, but somehow Bawden keeps the machine from tumbling.

"Trouble ahead," she shouts.

In front of us, the jungle flashes with a long line of rapid-fire bursts—camouflaged Wasp soldiers, dug in and ready.

We were so close to the target point, but now we're cut off from Barkah's troops and from Borjigin's surprise.

"Screw it," Bawden says. "Do or die, you sonsabitches!"

The crazy girl maxes out our speed.

I hit the deck. So does Victor. Bawden squats as low as she can. Bullets smack into the cockpit, ricochet around. A sting in my shoulder, a burn on my leg. Victor cries out.

The roar of gunfire gets closer, louder, then starts to fade— Bawden punched through their lines.

We slow slightly. Blue smoke up ahead; we've reached the target zone.

Gunfire continues to hammer the spider. No wonder these machines dominated the Springers for two centuries. The Wasp bullets damage it, but can't destroy it—simple musket balls would do almost nothing at all to this armor.

Something inside the spider clanks. The machine stumbles, slows to half-speed.

"Bawden," I scream, *"get us moving!"*

She kneels, pulls open a hatch and drops into the spider's guts. "Victor, drive! Em, keep them off us!"

Over the loud-as-hell tanks rumbling along in pursuit, I hear the roar of a tick engine. It's coming, but I can't tell from where.

A war cry of clicks and chirps—the Wasp infantry is advancing on us.

A tank round detonates just to our right, so close I feel the heat. Debris showers us.

And we're *still* slowing down.

"Where the hell is Borjigin?" Victor shouts. "He's supposed to be here!"

We did *our* job—Borjigin isn't here to do his. We're taking fire from all sides. If we get out of the slowing spider, we'll be dead before we hit the ground.

Is this how it ends?

I lie back on the cockpit deck. I look up into the jungle canopy. Yellow leaves, brown branches and tree trunks, blue vine stems. Through the foliage, the dappled late afternoon sky. A few clouds. Far above, Omeyocan's twin moons are just starting to show themselves.

This is a good place to die.

I hope we gave Gaston enough time.

Then, something massive blocks out the sky.

The tallest trees shudder. Long prongs of bright-blue metal push them aside. As easily as a child stepping through tall grass, Borjigin's giant machine steps through the trees, steps *over* us. Huge steel feet smash down, one after another, as it marches toward the oncoming tanks.

The constant hail of bullets switches from us to the giant.

I'm up in an instant, peeking over the back of the spider. The pursuing tick is still streaking toward us, but the sudden appearance of Borjigin's giant sends the Wasp infantry fleeing into the trees.

Our spider grinds to a halt.

"Victor," I say, taking aim at the oncoming tick, "signal to Barkah's troops to close in!"

As a disciplined unit, the Wasp foot soldiers seemed unbeatable—now they're scattered in the deep jungle, where Springers have fought for centuries.

The tick driver finally sees Borjigin's beast, slows and starts to turn away from the monstrosity. It's not shooting at our spider anymore—I finally have two seconds to line up a clean shot.

My bracelet beam blazes out, splashes off the tick's armored cockpit. I don't know if I hit anything inside, but the eight-legged machine stumbles awkwardly. It rights itself—just as a giant bright blue foot crushes through the branches and smashes down on the tick so hard the ground trembles.

A hail of bullets makes us duck down again. Victor pops up, firing fast. I join him, shooting bracelet blasts at a squad of Wasp infantry rushing toward us, led by a big one with copper-striped shoulders. The soldiers move from tree to tree, weaving in and out, firing all the way. This squad isn't like the ones that ran screaming into the jungle. These might be properly trained soldiers—the Wasps' version of circle-stars.

Victor's fire drops one Wasp, my beams drop a second.

I kneel low, look into the open hatch. Bawden is jammed in among the machinery, using her knife to chisel away at some cracked ceramic piece.

"Bawden, if you don't get this thing moving, we're *dead*!"

"Almost got it," she says, and keeps chipping.

"Here they come," Victor screams.

I hear something climbing up the side of the spider. I yank my spear from its bracket, lean out and drive the blade into a Wasp's armored face. The point punches through its helmet, knocking the soldier off the rungs.

Another Wasp leaps onto the spider's sloped front, one hand holding the armored ridge, the other aiming its heavy rifle at me. Victor kicks out hard, his boot smashes into the Wasp's chest—it fires as it falls back, but the bullets go wide.

A third Wasp lands in the middle of the cockpit, pistol in hand. Before it can fire, Victor tackles it, knocking it into me.

All three of us fall to the cockpit deck.

I can't reach my spear.

I draw my knife, wrap an arm around the Wasp's head and saw at the armor covering its throat.

The Wasp clicks and hisses, trying to bring its pistol to bear on Victor, who growls and grunts, holds the Wasp's wrist in a death grip.

We are animals fighting for life.

A flash of yellow whips in from above. Pincers snap shut. The alien is on top of me one moment, yanked high the next.

I scramble to my knees. Maria and Fenrir are next to us; she's firing her rifle, Fenrir is stuffing the Wasp into his mouth, chomping madly with his thick piranha teeth. Two more mounted hurukans rush out of the jungle. Pincers snap. Riders fire. Blood flies. The Wasps fight back, but Maria's huge beasts are too fast, too vicious—in moments, the enemy breaks and runs, scattering in all directions. Around us, a dozen Wasps lie dead, as do one of the hurukans and its Springer rider.

Maria and Fenrir stay beside our spider. The last hurukan, ridden by a howling Nedelka Holub, gives chase.

A tree falls, broken down by a tank that rolls over the stump and rumbles along the trunk, smashing flat the rattling branches and shaking leaves. Two tanks follow behind, a single-file column of destruction.

Borjigin's giant moves to attack.

The lead tank's cannon belches out a roaring cone of flame.

The shell detonates in the metal giant's right shoulder. The arm with the huge scoop comes free with a ringing *snap*, falls, smashes into the jungle floor.

I think everyone inside the giant must be dead, but the machine strides toward the tank.

Smoke billowing from the severed arm, the metal giant's massive pincer-hand reaches out, scoops up the lead tank. I watch, stunned to stillness, as the giant lifts the first tank high and smashes it down on the second.

There is the briefest pause, then both tanks erupt in a cloud of flame that engulfs the surrounding trees and sets them ablaze.

The flames also splash against the giant. Borjigin is driving. He has a crew of three. The fire is already spreading through the massive machine. If I don't do something, the four of them will be burned alive.

"Maria!" I meet her eyes, then point to the ladder that runs up the giant's spine to its hodgepodge head. "Can Fenrir climb up there?"

She leans back, holding the reins, looks up only for a moment before answering me.

"Let's find out." She whips the reins against the beast's back. "Fenrir, *climb*!"

The hurukan rushes at the giant and leaps, powerful legs launching the heavy beast high into the air. The fading sunlight piercing the jungle canopy plays against tawny fur, gleams off the pinkish blood marking a dozen small wounds.

Fenrir's front legs reach out—claws clutch the metal ladder, cling tight even as the snake neck wraps firmly around a broken bit of pipe jutting from the giant's back. Rear legs scramble against metal until they, too, lock on.

"God of Blood," Victor says, breathless. "Look at that."

Maria screams at her mount, urging it higher. One reaching claw after another, Fenrir climbs the burning giant like it is scaling a shaking, flaming tree.

Bawden hops up from the deck, slams the hatch shut behind her.

"We're back in business!"

I point my spear at Borjigin's great machine. "Get us there, now!"

Bawden steers our lurching, wounded Number 05 toward the giant.

The jungle erupts anew as a wave of routed Wasp soldiers rushes past, ignoring us as they flee for their lives. A horde of Springers descends upon them, tearing through the underbrush, dropping down from trees, even swinging in on vines. Guns and muskets fire briefly, then fighting shifts to hand-to-hand. A Wasp draws a long sword that crackles with energy and cleaves an attacking Springer in two. Both halves of the body are still twitching as three more Springers rush in and drag the Wasp down.

Hatchets and axes flash—as good as the color-shifting armor is, it can't stand up to the brutal savagery of these infuriated warriors.

I have never seen such destruction. Two species are fighting for the future of their kind. No one surrenders. No one offers respect to the wounded. There are no deals here, no yielding, only fighting until one side or the other is dead.

Despite the flames licking up the light blue giant, Borjigin moves his monster toward the final tank.

The tank's cannon roars. The shell detonates in the giant's left hip, a billowing explosion of orange flame and black smoke that rips the joint to pieces, sends forth a hail of metal shards that cut down vines, embed in tree trunks, punch through Springers and Wasps alike.

The metal giant sways to the left.

Maria's hurukan loses its grip—clawed feet slip free. High above the forest floor, the big beast swings out, held in place only by the snake neck that is stretched taut to the point of breaking. Maria grips tight to her saddle as the furred body slams into branches, snapping arm-thick wood like kindling. I wait for the beast and my friend both to spin through the jungle to their death. . . . somehow Fenrir hangs on.

Borjigin's giant stumbles, almost falls, but recovers—the machine stands straight.

Maria's mount swings back onto the ladder. Claws grip and *hold*.

Again, the hurukan scrambles higher.

A rectangular chunk of metal erupts from the back of the giant's head, spins through the air to vanish in the jungle. Borjigin climbs out, his coveralls dotted with sticky grease that burns with deep-orange flames. Only one kid, a girl, climbs out after him. They grip handholds, cling tight.

Fenrir reaches them. The long neck coils around the girl, lifts her free. Maria pulls the burning Borjigin onto the saddle behind her.

Fenrir scrambles down the ladder. Long tongues of flame shoot from the giant, making blue paint bubble, singeing Fenrir's bloody fur.

The tank is so close to the giant the long cannon barrel angles up at forty-five degrees. This time, the round erupts dead center in the machine's chest. The billowing fireball forces the hurukan to leap out into the air.

Fenrir slams into the ground—I hear bones break on impact.

The burning wreck of Borjigin's giant tips backward, then topples forward like a falling tree, crashes down on the tank in a whuffing storm of flame.

Something inside the smashed tank explodes, sends streamers of flame so high into the air they arc over the jungle canopy. There is no way the last two crew members of Borjigin's giant could have survived that.

I snatch up my spear. Victor and I are out of the spider, sprinting to our friends. Maria rolls on the ground, holding a shoulder that hangs at a strange angle. Borjigin's leg flops sickeningly. The girl—I recognize her, Sharyl Bohner—is half-trapped beneath Fenrir's bulk. The hurukan kicks, twitches and roars. With every lurch, Sharyl screams in agony.

The beast's death throes are going to kill the girl; I have to finish him.

Fenrir's snake neck finally lies limp. I raise my bracelet to the three black eyes that run down the side of his head and flick my fingers forward—nothing happens.

A shard of metal sticks out of my bracelet's white stone: a piece of shrapnel. Had it hit an inch higher or lower, it would have torn my arm apart.

Victor screams for me to kill the beast. He's got Sharyl's arms, is trying to pull her free.

I grab my spear with both hands. I time Fenrir's lurching, then thrust. The blade slides through an eye and into the head. Fenrir stiffens, spasms . . . falls still.

Bawden slides to a stop next to Victor. Victor's face screws tight with effort as he lifts Fenrir just enough for Bawden to pull Sharyl from beneath the dead animal.

I yank my spear free, grab Maria and drag her toward the spider. Borjigin crawls toward it as well, arm over arm, a look of utter determination etched on his bloody face.

All around us, Springers howl in a victorious battle cry. They've killed the last of the Wasps in this area.

Corpses, everywhere. Smoke rising. Flames crawling up massive tree trunks, twisting through vines. I smell burned flesh and scorched wood.

I smell *blood*.

This is what the Grub wanted.

Only the strong survive.

We load our wounded into the spider. It's a tight fit.

A thunderous blast, bigger than anything I've ever felt, showers us with dirt and broken splinters of wood. For a moment, I can't hear, then the sound of roaring flames comes rushing back. Someone grabs me, shakes me.

"Artillery," Victor says. "The Wasps are shelling us!"

Another explosion to our left makes the ground tremble like an earthquake.

I hear Springers screaming.

The Wasp artillery. We got three tanks, but we didn't get their cannons.

I hear the low sounds of Springer horns echoing across the jungle—three long blasts, all in a row.

The sun is setting: we did it.

"Bawden, get us home!"

Our spider jerks to life. Each halting step makes Maria and Borjigin cry out. We can't help them now; they'll have to bear the pain.

Victor shoves something against my chest—it's a Wasp rifle, long and heavy and wicked. He points to a button under the thick barrel.

"That's the trigger. When you press it, hold on *tight*, it's got a hell of a kick. You guard our back—I have to dress Sharyl's wounds or she'll bleed out!"

Bawden pushes the shuddering spider as fast as it will go, a painful pace that hurts us all.

Another explosion, then another, and another. The air fills with flying dirt and a deadly hail of shrapnel.

Over those deafening roars, I hear a familiar rocket-growl coming from the north—Wasp troopships.

They're bringing in their reserves.

FIFTY

The enemy is close behind.

The setting sun turns sparse clouds into long, ragged red slashes—today, even the sky bleeds.

My people are in full-on retreat, survivors all around us as we rush down the road from the abandoned Schechak toward Uchmal's North Gate. Some of us are barely able to walk; some carry wounded comrades; some stop every few feet to turn and fire back into the jungle ruins. A few don't bother to shoot, and I know why—their rifles are out of ammo, their bracelets are depleted of energy.

Just east of us, the one o'clock tower cannon fires volley after volley into the jungle, trying to take out our unseen pursuers.

Our lurching spider struggles through the tall metal doors. When Bawden finally brings us to a stop, leg joints blow in a burst of sparks. The machine's belly clangs down onto the paving stones.

"No fixing that," Bawden says. "Everyone out!"

Victor leaps to the ground. Bawden lowers Sharyl down to him.

I sling the Wasp rifle, grab my spear and scramble up onto the spider's back.

Big Pig is parked just inside the wall, throaty engine idling. Dozens of wounded lie in its wide bed. A pair of circles sprint to us. Bawden gently lowers Borjigin to their reaching hands.

A block down the street, Springers bustle around five wooden trebuchets. They used these weapons against us in the Battle of the Crescent-Shaped Clearing, but today they're loaded with barrels, not boulders. The launching arms—stripped down tree trunks—are cocked back, ready to fire.

No sign of Bishop or the people in his unit. He knew the plan. If he hasn't made it back by now . . .

So many lives at stake. We can't wait for him.

I face the one o'clock tower and wave both arms over my head, giving them the signal to abandon their position and head for the shuttle. The cannon fires one last burst, then falls quiet.

Victor carries Sharyl to Big Pig; people reach down from the bed, gently pull her in. The two circles load Borjigin in after her. Looks like he's passed out from the pain.

I help Bawden lower Maria to the ground.

Bawden slides under her good shoulder. I slip under her bad, my left hand around her waist, my right holding my spear. I can feel the broken bones grinding inside her.

We move toward Big Pig, but by some unspoken connection, the three of us stop and look back at the spider.

So many fresh bullet holes in the armor I think the machine might be more air than metal. Two legs stand normally, bent at that familiar sharp angle. Two legs are twisted and bent. One is missing altogether.

"Goodbye, Number Five," Bawden says, her voice hoarse from screaming, from smoke.

Maria nods. "And goodbye to you, Fenrir. You were a good boy."

Tears cut trails through the grime on her face. I don't know if she's crying from physical pain, for her hurukan, for leaving Omeyocan, or for the squad member she lost. Probably all of the above.

We help Maria to the truck. Hands reach down to help her up just as the air crackles with a round of rifle fire.

Victor shouts the alert: *"Here they come!"*

Bawden and I sprint for the gate. We slide to a stop, use the tall right-hand door for cover. I drop my spear and unsling the heavy Wasp rifle.

Victor and two circle-stars are at the left-hand door, firing rifles and bracelets.

A tick bursts from the jungle not even fifty meters away, twin guns blazing. It scrambles onto the road and scurries toward our gate. A dozen Wasp foot soldiers fan out behind it, led by a tall one with copper streaks on its shoulder armor.

Bullets spark off the paving stones at our feet, ping off the metal doors.

I aim at the tick, press the button. Recoil smashes the butt against my shoulder, a combination of punches so hard they make me stumble backward.

Our shots hit the armored tick, but they do nothing. It will be on us in seconds. I should have ordered the doors shut when I had the chance.

Then, behind the tick, the jungle erupts again as a spider tears into view. Kai Brown is driving . . . and Ramses Bishop mans the cannon. Behind the spider, a dozen circle-stars and a handful of Springers rush forward to fight.

Bishop's face is a bestial snarl: mouth open, teeth exposed in a primitive roar I can hear even over the gunfire. His face is covered in a mixture of blood, sweat, ash and mud.

He fires the spider cannon. The blast hits the tick in the rear. I see a muffled explosion inside the armored shell, then the machine tumbles, hits the ground and rolls, limp legs flopping.

The copper-striped Wasp commander shouts a click-clack-screech of orders to turn and fight, but his troops are caught in the open with enemy in front and behind.

Victor rises up and screams: *"Charge!"*

He rushes forward armed with only a spear—his rifle is out of ammo, his bracelet drained of power. The two circle-stars with him charge as well, one shooting a rifle on the run, the other armed with nothing but a knife.

I fire the Wasp weapon to give them cover—one round hammers my shoulder, then it does nothing. Empty.

I drop it, grab up my spear and sprint out of the gate, Bawden at my side.

Bishop's spider overruns the enemy. A pointed foot punches through a Wasp soldier, pinning the twitching alien to the dirt.

A burst of machine-gun fire rakes the spider cockpit. Bullets hit Kai Brown in the chest and face: he drops in a cloud of blood. The cannon sparks and starts to smoke—it's ruined.

Some of the Wasps toss their guns aside and draw knives or swords; we're not the only ones who have run out of ammo.

Bishop reaches back, yanks his red axe from its bracket. He roars and leaps from the cockpit, swinging the horrible weapon down—the axe-head drives through a Wasp helmet, splitting the skull within. The creature drops, as limp as if it had never been alive to begin with.

We reach the Wasps at the same time Bishop's circle-stars and Springers do, engulfing the enemy from all sides. Spears and hatchets and axes clash with swords and knives, but the Wasps have no chance. They fall one by one until only the copper-striped leader remains, sword blazing with energy.

It swings at Victor, who angles his body away and jabs his spear through its thin knee. The Wasp tries to swing again, but Bawden leaps and kicks it in the chest, knocking it flat on its back.

Before it can rise, I drive my spear through its neck.

The brave warrior dies on the soil of a foreign planet, far from a home it probably never saw.

My people sprint to the gate. Bishop grabs my waist, tosses me up into his spider. I land, almost slip on Kai Brown's blood. He lies face-up on the cockpit deck, as dead as the alien I just killed.

Bawden and Bishop scramble up the rungs. She takes the driver controls.

Two Springers leap into the cockpit—it's Barkah and Lahfah.

Are they evacuating with us?

The Springer king is badly cut, his blue blood mixing with the Wasp yellow that covers him head to toe.

"Hem," he says, then collapses onto the bloody deck. Lahfah kneels by his side.

I can't worry about them right now.

Bawden drives the spider through the gate: the huge doors start to swing shut behind us.

Victor is at the trebuchets with the Springers.

I wave my spear at him. *"Light them up!"*

With a heavy rattle of wood, the five trebuchets launch. The long tree trunks snap high into the air. Attached ropes yank taut, pulling harnesses that swing back, then up, then release their payloads—five barrels sail high over the wall, each trailing a thin line of black smoke.

We don't see them hit, but we hear them: *boom, boom-boom, boom-boom.*

Through the closing gates, I see a wall of fire rise up to engulf the jungle. The flames flare higher than the tallest tree. The intense, instant heat makes thousands of vines writhe in a dying dance.

"Good *gods*," Bawden says. "What was in those barrels?"

"Borjigin's accelerants," Bishop says. "Packed in with chemicals left over from Zubiri's fuel conversion process."

The chemical mix will burn hot enough to set everything around it ablaze, perhaps hot enough to turn the entire jungle into an inferno. Any Wasp foot soldiers—or ticks or tanks—caught in that instant slice of hell are already dying. Those that haven't reached it yet have to either go around or wait for the fire to die down.

That buys us a little more time.

The gate doors slam shut. The people who closed it rush to Big Pig and climb into the bed. Victor and the trebuchet Springers are the last ones in.

Big Pig's driver steers onto Latu Way and drives straight south, toward the Observatory.

Our spider falls in behind it.

Over the growl of Big Pig's engine, I hear a new sound. A high-pitched whistle, growing louder and louder. In the truck's bed, Victor screams at his fellow passengers.

"Artillery, *incoming!*"

The whistle sound grows to a deafening volume. Close behind us, a fireball blossoms from a three-layer ziggurat. Stones spin away, smash into other buildings. Rubble rains down on the streets.

The artillery we couldn't find has found us.

Big Pig picks up speed. The driver pushes the truck hard and fast.

Artillery shells rain down around us, turning our city into a foggy cloud of explosions, fire and smoke, sprays of deadly shrapnel. Buildings shatter. Streets erupt. Flames rise. Ziggurats crumble in upon themselves.

Uchmal has suffered two aerial bombardments so far, but neither compares to this assault. The city that has stood tall for two centuries is finally falling.

A Wasp fighter roars past overhead. A stream of red fire snakes out from the Observatory. The fighter angles up and races off, trailing flame.

If the Wasps only knew how little ammo we had left, they would have swarmed us with their fighters.

Three blocks from the plaza, we pull ahead of the artillery explosions. *The Grub* . . . the Wasps somehow know to not target the area above the Grub.

Big Pig screeches to a halt at the plaza's edge, next to the special cart used to move the Goff Spear rounds. I see the hexagonal rounds mounted under the shuttle's wings. It doesn't look like much is holding them on—I can only hope Zubiri and Gaston know what they're doing.

Bawden stops our spider next to the truck. The trebuchet Springers leap out of Big Pig and hop to us. They help Lahfah lower Barkah down from the spider, help her carry him to the Wasp troopships.

Dozens of people rush to Big Pig to unload the wounded. Bishop and Bawden jump out to help. I see Borjigin put on a stretcher, Okereke carrying Maria in his arms. Kenzie Smith shouts instructions as everyone scrambles up *Ximbal's* ramp.

A shimmering haze of heat makes the *Ximbal's* engines look

like they're masked by falling water. The engines of the two Wasp troopships glow red with the promise of power.

All around the plaza, artillery shells hammer down. Buildings that stood for centuries are gone in an instant. A wayward shot strikes the Observatory itself, fifteen layers up, breaking off huge blocks that tumble down the slope in an avalanche of stone.

Over the cries of our dying city, I hear people screaming my name. I look to the shuttle, see Spingate on the metal-grate deck, calling to me, more people around her doing the same.

I'm still standing in the spider's bloody cockpit—I'm the last one left.

I scramble down and sprint for the shuttle. One troop transport is already climbing into the air, slowly driven upward by a column of fire. The second is just starting to lift off.

And then, beneath my feet, the ground *shakes*. Not the hard-hitting thrum of a detonating artillery round . . . this is something more powerful, something much *bigger*.

To my right, a thick slab of plaza stone cracks, tilts upward. It sags back down for a moment, then angles high again. More stone shatters, pushed up from beneath, a miniature mountain growing right before my eyes. From the jagged tip of this new peak, something massive slithers out.

Something *copper*.

The Grub is rising.

My feet hit the *Ximbal's* ramp—I'm halfway up when the Grub bursts from the plaza. The ground trembles so hard the shuttle *slides*. Metal screeches, twists, warps. The ramp slides beneath me, snaps free and drops away. I manage a desperate leap for the deck. I reach and reach . . . I'm not going to make it—

—Spingate catches my wrist. My hand wraps around hers.

Ximbal slowly elevates, cones of flame pushing it straight up.

I hang in the air, my life in Spingate's hand. She lies on her side on the rattling metal deck, her left arm the only thing keeping me from falling to my death.

Ximbal's exterior door is still open. The deck twists and warps beneath Spingate—it's not supposed to be extended while *Ximbal* is flying. Her red hair tosses madly. Her arm is so straight, pulled tight by my weight.

"Spin! *Please* don't drop me!"

Her eyes are closed, her face split by a desperate grimace. Through clenched teeth, she growls out one word.

"*Never!*"

The shuttle continues to climb.

Dangling like a bug on a vine, I don't want to look down—but I can't help myself.

Below me, the undulating Grub squishes its way out, stone and concrete and dirt spilling off its glistening hide. It rears up, a writhing, twisting, wriggling thing still half in the ground—a copper eel, a metallic slug, a nightmare blob, a horrid demon billowing up from hell itself.

The head—if that's what it is—rises high. I see its horror of a mouth gape open: two long, thin jaws, one above the other, like the narrow beak of some nightmare insect.

It *roars,* a sound so concussive it injures the air.

We're far above the shattered plaza, high enough to see much of the city. From the west, Wasps pour down the streets, tanks and ticks and *thousands* of foot soldiers, a wave that would have instantly overwhelmed us.

To the north, Borjigin's fire sends up a thick column of dense black smoke.

To the south, just past the plaza, a pair of troopships set down on the street. Landing ramps lower. Hundreds of Wasp soldiers spill out, armor flashing with the colors of a dying city.

And all across Uchmal, flames rise high, engulfing buildings and ziggurats alike. I thought there was nothing left in the city that could catch fire—I was wrong.

Spingate's grip slips, ever so slightly.

I look up. She's in severe pain, her cheek mashed against the deck's metal grate.

She can't hold me.

The entire deck lurches, bends and suddenly tilts down.

Her grip loosens. I slide. Our fingers lock—it hurts, *so bad,* I'm sure my bones are breaking my muscles are tearing but if I let go I die I fall I die *I must hold on.*

My friend screams in agony, but she fights, she *will not* let me go.

A pair of muscular arms reach out of the open shuttle door, grab at Spingate's belt, at the back of her coveralls—it's Farrar and Bishop. They pull her up, and me along with her.

Wind whipping at my face and hair, I look down one last time.

Beneath us, the Grub crawls free from its huge hole. It wanted us to be worms? It is a worm itself, a thick, fat maggot with stubby legs that are nothing more than cones of wobbling flesh. Muscles ripple through the body, send waves across skin that is already hardening, turning a darker shade of copper.

Wasp soldiers swarm around the leviathan. They are tiny next to it, barely more than specks, but even from this far up I can see that they're dancing.

They're *worshiping* it.

Strong hands lock on my wrist; I'm pulled up like I weigh nothing at all.

Bishop hauls me into the shuttle.

Wind howls around us.

Farrar holds on to the door with both hands as his big boot

hammers down on the deck, once, twice, then with a third powerful kick and a squeal of metal the deck tumbles away.

Ximbal's exterior door slides shut.

The wind finally dies out.

Bishop holds me tight.

"Next time," he says, "try and move faster, all right?"

Kenzie is already with us, tending to Spingate—I think her shoulder is dislocated.

Gaston's voice booms throughout the shuttle, telling everyone things are going to get rough, to get into coffins as fast as possible.

I grab Bishop's face, kiss him so hard I hurt my mouth.

"Make sure everyone gets in and holds on tight," I say to him, then I scramble to my feet and rush into the pilothouse.

Gaston stands in the center, bathed in light. Peura is with him. The young gear must be handling the copilot duties that usually fall to Spingate.

The walls are transparent. I can see the city beneath us. The Springer troop transports are close by, the first slightly above and to our left, the second slightly below and behind us. I can see down into the cockpit of the lower one—Cathcart, the pilot, who suddenly looks far older than his thirteen years.

An alert sound screeches, high-pitched and insistent.

I feel the shuttle's rear thrusters kick in. We move forward, fast, the troopships move with us.

No . . . we're going *away* from Uchmal.

"Don't leave until you nuke that godsdamned Grub," I say to Gaston. "Do it now!"

He glances at me. "Em, get out of here and get in a coffin!"

"No way I miss you killing that thing. So *kill* it!"

He shakes his head.

"No can do. We're not high enough yet, and there's a pair of bogeys coming in fast. We have to take them on or we're dead. Peura, take the helm. *Ximbal*, give me targeting and pilothouse crew inertia support."

Around Gaston's head, a complex arrangement of floating icons flares to life.

Three spots in the ceiling suddenly bulge out, extend thin black tentacles. Before I can react, one snakes around my waist and expands, holding me firmly from armpits to upper thighs. The other two tentacles do the same to Gaston and Peura.

"That harness is for high-G maneuvering," Gaston says. "It will keep you from being splattered against the walls. Peura, do you have the damn helm or not?"

"Yessir, I have the helm." Peura's voice cracks on every other word. He's doing his best to stay calm, but he's clearly terrified.

A second piercing alarm makes me jump.

"Proximity alert," Peura says. "Incoming bogeys at six o'clock, twenty degrees down."

Gaston turns in place: the floating icons turn with him.

So much is happening at once. We're almost away, we can't get hit now, we *can't*.

Behind us, I see two flashes coming in fast—Wasp fighters.

"Just let us go," I say quietly. "You win, you can have this whole damn planet."

"Target acquired," Gaston says. "Launch missiles."

The shuttle shudders a familiar shudder, one I felt in the Battle of the Crescent-Shaped Clearing. Four smoke trails shoot toward the incoming fighters.

The fighters flare with staccato flashes—they're firing at us.

"Evasive," Peura says.

Ximbal banks so hard to the right that my head and arms flail left. The strange tentacle lifts me at the same time, shifts me a little to absorb some of the harsh move, then brings me right back to where I was.

Gaston was right: without this system, I'd have smashed against the pilothouse walls.

I regain my wits in time to see the smoke trails close in; one fighter erupts in a glorious cloud of fire and metal.

The other loses half a wing; it spins, trailing a corkscrew of smoke.

We did it. We *won*.

And then, fate shatters my moment of elation.

The Wasp fighter spins past us, below us, and slams into the Springer transport, punching into the flat black hull as one piece, ripping out the other side in a dozen. There is no fire, no explosion. The troopship seems to hover in place for a moment—I can see through the cockpit window, see Cathcart's horrified face—then it plummets straight down.

Just like that, in the time it takes to snap my fingers, a thousand refugees are gone.

"Godsdammit," Gaston says. "We were *out*. Gods*damn*it."

The cockpit is quiet for a few moments as we try to come to grips with what just happened.

We escaped the Wasps.

At the same time, we lost many of our own.

We lost Springers.

I don't know if Barkah and Lahfah were on that ship. We may have lost them as well.

Once again, we are victorious. Once again, the price of victory is far too high.

"They're gone," I say. "Now go back and drop our nuke. Kill that thing."

Gaston reaches out, takes my hand.

"We can't. I know how bad you want this, Em, but we burned too much fuel in that dogfight. We don't have enough to do the bomb run and still make it to the *Xolotl*. Remember when I said we needed a full tank?"

I start to weigh our options, to ask if we can kill the Grub and the Wasps and then set down somewhere else, but Gaston isn't giving me that option. He knows better than I what is and isn't possible at this point.

He takes control of the shuttle.

We tilt up, and we head for the stars.

PART IV

FLIGHT AND FIGHT

FIFTY-ONE

Below me, Uchmal gets smaller and smaller, until all details are gone, until it is nothing more than a brown spot with a river running into it, surrounded by jungle. It gets smaller still. Eventually, I can't see the river at all; the city itself vanishes into an ocean of yellow.

I see mountains. I see great plains. I see oceans.

It could have all been ours.

We're in space again.

The Springer troopship is on our right.

I don't want to think. I'm not sure I *can* think.

I feel gravity relax, weightlessness setting in although the mechanical arm keeps me fixed firmly to the pilothouse floor.

Eventually, Gaston brings me back to reality.

"Approaching the *Xolotl*," he says.

It's hard to finally turn my eyes away from what was supposed to be our home, the home of our children and grandchildren, the home of my people for all eternity.

I look forward, to our future, to the next battle we face.

I look upon the *Xolotl*.

Aside from a few variations in color, it looks exactly like the *Basilisk*.

Exactly like the *Goblin*.

Exactly like the *Dragon*.

I wonder at the powers of a being that made so many races abandon their homes. I had no choice in the matter. Nor did my friends. And as much as I hate to admit it, neither did Brewer, Bello, Matilda or any of our progenitors.

The Church of Mictlan existed before any of us were born. The church shaped our lives, controlled us, put us on a path that we could not avoid.

But is that what life is like for everyone? Can a person truly make a life of their own, or can they only continue the culture into which they are born?

"Where is the *Dragon*?" I ask.

"Too far away to stop us," Gaston says. "It appears to be holding its position, well outside Goff Spear range."

The *Xolotl* is a slowly spinning copper cylinder set against an endless black backdrop framed by bright stars. The closer we get, the bigger the ship seems.

Bishop floats into the pilothouse. He pushes off the door, grabs my strange harness and uses it to stand next to me.

"Opkick finished the head count," he says quietly. "Two hundred twenty-five on board."

Which means twenty-four of my people died in the fighting. Or were wounded and couldn't make it back. Or just got lost in the jungle during the battle and had to stand there, helplessly watching *Ximbal* rise in the sky.

I know there is fuel on the *Xolotl*. Matilda said so. But any survivors we may have left behind have no way of contacting us—we can't go back down and search a million square kilometers of jungle for them. The Wasps are waiting there, ready to hit us the instant we go back. The hard truth is that we still have to find a new home, and *Ximbal* is our only way of landing on new planets. I cannot risk this shuttle.

Reality is what it is whether we like it or not—anyone still on Omeyocan is gone forever.

Bishop puts his arm around my shoulders.

He lived up to his word. He gave his support. Now will he expect me to live up to my end of the bargain? Will he expect me to have a family with him?

Do I even *want* a family?

Anyone can make promises—*keeping* them is the hard part.

"The *Xolotl* is beautiful," he says.

He's right; the ship is stunning. Red sunlight plays off the copper hull. Copper, the same color as the Grub's hardened pincers . . . I wonder if there's a connection.

Gaston turns to face me. He's still covered in light, icons and symbols floating around his head.

"Shall I take us to the landing bay?"

I nod.

In minutes, the *Xolotl*'s true size becomes apparent. We are but a dot in comparison. As we get closer, we can't even see the entire ship, just the portion of it that's directly in front of us.

Gaston flies us silently along the endless, rotating hull. The surface is gouged and scratched. There are large craters, as if parts of the hull melted into liquid before cooling back to a solid.

"All that damage," Bishop says. "Gaston, do you think that's from a battle?"

Gaston nods. "Most of it, yes. Probably from when it fought the Springer ship."

We approach something I saw when I was in the Control

Room—a long, deepening groove that ends at massive, flat gray doors.

The landing bay.

Gaston puts the shuttle into a gentle barrel roll, stops the maneuver with the *Xolotl* now above us instead of below. I feel gravity return, a bit stronger than Omeyocan's, holding my feet to the pilothouse floor. The massive ship's rotation appears to slow, then stop. I realize that's because Gaston has the shuttle flying sideways as well as forward—we've matched the *Xolotl*'s rotation. The landing bay is now stationary in front of and above us. It's upside down . . . or is the shuttle upside down? Maybe in space there's no "up" or "down" at all.

"*Ximbal*," Gaston says, "tell the *Xolotl* to kindly open up for us."

Bishop whispers in my ear: "I'll get the circle-stars ready. We have a few rifle rounds left, and our bracelets are recharging."

I can tell by his tone he doesn't want a fight, but if one comes he'll be ready. The last time we were in the landing bay, the Grownups killed El-Saffani, the twins who followed Bishop no matter what he did or said. The twins died because we didn't have good weapons—now we do. If the Grownups bring violence, we'll bring more.

I kiss Bishop's cheek.

"I love you," I say. "Do what has to be done."

He smiles, then gently pushes off, floating toward the pilothouse door.

I wait. I stare at the huge gray doors. They don't open.

"Well, this is rather anticlimactic," Gaston says. "I assume someone on the *Xolotl* controls the doors. Hey, I wonder if I'll see the older me."

Gaston's progenitor flew Matilda back up here. He's still alive as far as we know.

We stare for a few more minutes.

Gaston sighs. "I'm bored. *Ximbal,* broadcast me on the *Xolotl*'s general frequency."

"Ready to transmit, Captain Xander."

Gaston squares his shoulders, gives his coveralls a quick tug. The little boy I knew is gone, has been for a long time. Gaston is a grown man. A husband. A father. A leader.

"Attention, *Xolotl*. This is Captain Xander Gaston, requesting permission to board. Open the damn landing bay doors already."

We wait.

A minute passes. Two minutes.

We start to wonder if the *Xolotl* can hear us at all, then the pilothouse's front wall fuzzes with static. The *Xolotl*'s copper hull vanishes from view. Multicolored sparkles appear, brighten, start to coalesce into a shape—a Grownup.

When the image finally crystallizes, it's not Gaston's progenitor we see.

It's mine.

"You've come back to me," Matilda says. "Good girl."

I stare at the image of the one-eyed, hateful creature who created me. To her, I'm nothing but a doll, a vehicle made so she can continue her pathetic life.

She had no right to be the leader of her people, yet that is what she became. I had no right to be the leader of mine, yet that is what *I* became. We are both ruthless and aggressive—no surprise there, since we are the same person.

But Matilda has grown old . . . *ancient*. She won't change her ways. She is a living fossil, stuck in that wrinkled black form forever, while I have matured and learned from my mistakes. I have become more than my creator could ever be.

"I'm no girl," I say. "Not anymore. Open the doors."

This grizzled, nasty *thing* shakes her head.

"And let your little army of uncivilized killers walk right in? I don't think so, darling-dear."

"We have nowhere to go," I say. "Because the *god* that supposedly called you here isn't a god at all. It's a *beast,* Matilda—an alien that has pitted all these races against each other. Did you know that?"

She doesn't answer right away, and in that instant I understand that she didn't know.

"You're a *liar,*" she says.

The intensity carried in that single word.

But I can't lie to her any more than she can lie to me. We both know that, and yet she doesn't believe me. At some level, she's *choosing* not to believe. Maybe this is a truth she can't allow herself to accept, as if accepting it might drive her insane.

Whatever her reason, it doesn't matter right now.

"Open the landing bay doors," I say.

Matilda ignores me. "Little Gaston, turn over control of the shuttle to me. My people will guide it remotely to an access hatch, where the shuttle will dock. Once there, Em, you will come across, alone and unarmed."

I start to refuse her demand outright, to scream at her, but I no longer react from pure emotion. There is information to be gathered first.

"If I comply, will you let the shuttle in?"

She nods. "Of course. I'm not a barbarian."

"And the Springers," I say. "They can come in as well?"

Matilda laughs.

"You think I would let vermin inside this ship? Vermin we almost wiped out when we built our city?"

She doesn't even bother lying to me about the Springers. I'll give her that much, at least.

"So what happens to them?" I ask. "They can't go back down to Omeyocan."

Matilda shrugs her narrow shoulders. "Not my concern. I only care about human lives."

I actually kind of admire her honesty. I can be honest, too.

"Open the doors, Matilda. *Or else.*"

More laughter.

"Such bravado from an infant, from a liar who would betray everything! That shuttle you're on is older than I am. It just went through a battle—it could break down at any moment. All those aboard could be seconds from death. Save your people, Em. Come aboard by yourself and I promise you everyone will be safe."

That agreeable tone of voice. When she wants something, Matilda sounds so reasonable, so nice. But I also hear the hunger within her words. Hunger, and deep concern. She's not lying about the *Ximbal*'s condition—she genuinely thinks it could have a critical malfunction at any moment. And if it does, she's trapped in that awful body forever.

"We have wounded," I say. "While you foam at the mouth, people are dying."

"Then *help* them, darling-dear. Come aboard. Up here, girl, you have no power. The choice is yours to make."

I've had enough.

I turn to Gaston. "How many missiles do you have left?"

"Six," he says, his eyes narrowing in suspicion. "Why?"

"Would that be enough to penetrate the landing bay doors?"

He stares at me like I am mad. By now, I probably am.

"Yes," he says. "But that would destroy the outer doors. We couldn't depressurize, the airlock would be ruined."

"But we *could* land? We would just have to figure out how to get everyone off the shuttle safely. Right?"

He thinks. His face suddenly scrunches, a telltale sign he's having a flashfire moment. His progenitor's knowledge is bubbling to the surface.

"There are emergency measures in the landing bay," he says. "It would take some time, but yes—we can get everyone off safely."

I wait. Matilda heard that exchange; I don't need to tell her what I'll do next.

"Don't threaten me," she says. "I control this ship. I control our *weapons*. If you think you're going to damage the *Xolotl*, you are mistaken. I will blow you out of the sky."

I smile at her.

"Do that, and this body you want so much dies. Which means I *do* have all the power. You can either open the doors or we will blow them open. Gaston, launch missiles in sixty seconds."

He shakes his head no, then his face scrunches again. He's remembering something else.

"*Ximbal,* break contact," he says.

Matilda vanishes.

"Gaston, what are you doing? I had her where I wanted her!"

He waves his hand dismissively.

"You always think you have people where you want them, and that usually ends with blood flying everywhere or something exploding. Listen to me—I think we can open the doors manually, but someone has to go extravehicular."

"Extravehicular?" I'm confused for a moment, then the word registers. "You mean go *outside* . . . in *space?*"

He grins that mischievous grin of his.

"Yeah. Outside. In space. And we better do it fast before *my* progenitor figures out what we're up to."

Through the pilothouse walls, Peura and I watch Xander Gaston float out into space.

He wears a thick pressure suit that covers him from head to toe. Tiny tongues of flame jut from his feet and waist, propelling him forward. He floats down the deepening groove.

"Approaching the emergency access panel."

His voice, coming through the pilothouse walls.

"All right," I answer, not knowing what else to say.

It looks like we're hovering above the ship's cratered surface, still as can be, although I know the cylinder—and the shuttle— continues to spin.

Peura glows with light. "I think I remember these lessons. The *Xolotl* has exterior landing bay controls in case anything goes wrong inside."

"What could go wrong inside?"

"Systems breakdown," he says. "Malfunctions, a fire, everyone dying from a gas leak. If no one can open the doors from the inside, you don't want your shuttle crew trapped in space. Emergency external access is a better solution than, say, using missiles to blow the doors apart."

Well well well . . . turns out chubby Noam Peura is a smartass. Who knew?

Gaston reaches the bottom right corner of the sprawling landing bay doors. He's so *small* out there.

Peura moves glowing icons. The wall display changes to a close-up of Gaston.

Gaston opens a copper-colored panel. Beneath it are a pair of parallel rings. No, not rings . . . *handles*. His gloved fingers wrap around them. He plants his booted feet on the copper hull.

"I hope this works," he says.

He pulls. There is a moment's hesitation, resistance, then he leans back—each handle is anchored to a steel cylinder. They slide out, then lock.

"*Oh, who am I kidding,*" Gaston says. "*This is* me *we're talking about—of course it will work.*"

He twists both hands inward. The handles and cylinders turn: what was parallel is now a line.

"I think that's it," Peura says. "There will be an emergency signal in the landing bay so anyone inside can get clear before it depressurizes."

We wait.

And then, the massive doors start to slide open.

FIFTY-TWO

Gaston pilots us into the landing bay, the Springers' troop-ship at our side. The huge hangar doors shut like jaws clamping tight just before food is swallowed. We opened those doors from the outside, but whoever controls the *Xolotl* closed them behind us.

"They're repressurizing," Gaston says.

Bishop enters the pilothouse, stands next to me. The walls show us the landing bay outside. This is where we escaped. This is where El-Saffani died.

How many more of us will die this day?

We smell of smoke, sweat and blood. We smell of the jungle. We're exhausted from fighting and lack of sleep. We're drained by so many deaths. But our work is not done. Before we can rest, we must take this ship.

We wait.

Equipment racks, machines and various tanks line the landing bay walls. Other than our shuttle and the Springer troopship, though, the large space is empty.

"Pressure equalized," Gaston says.

Which means people can now enter.

But no one does.

"I don't like this," Bishop says.

No movement. This feels wrong. Last time we were here, there were hundreds of Grownups, a shambling nightmarish mass of those who want to erase us.

So now that we've come back, where are they?

"My team is ready," Bishop says. "Farrar, Victor, Darzi and I will go out, with people just inside the *Ximbal*'s door for fire support. Em, I know you want to face danger first, but I insist you stay back. Our people need you now more than ever."

Bruises, splinters, cuts . . . I'm all beat up. Bishop is, too, but he was engineered for nonstop fighting. I wasn't. It isn't the pain so much—I've suffered worse—it's that my body is so depleted it isn't responding fast enough. Until I get some rest, I'm a liability, and we can't afford an iota of weakness.

"All right," I say. "But I'm with the second team giving you cover. And Victor stays with me—his progenitor is out there."

Bishop nods. "I'll take Bawden instead."

"I've finally reached the Springer troopship," Gaston says. He looks relieved. "Barkah and Lahfah are on it. Barkah needed some stitches, but he's all right. He's awake and in command."

My soul sags with relief. Yes, we lost a thousand Springers, but I didn't know them—my friends are still alive.

"Tell Barkah to make sure his people stay put," I say. "We don't need them complicating things."

Gaston nods. "Yes, ma'am."

I turn to Bishop.

"Please be careful."

I stand in the *Ximbal*'s exterior doorway, half-hidden by the bulkhead. I wear a freshly charged bracelet. I don't know whose it was. Several young circle-stars stand with me, including Nedelka Holub, also armed with a bracelet, and Victor, who holds a rifle. We all aim out into the landing bay, ready to shoot anything that threatens our people.

We especially watch the tall, wide doors that open into the rest of the ship. That's where the Grownups came from last time.

Ximbal's deck and ramp are gone. We're high enough above the landing bay floor that Bishop and his team had to hold on to the bottom of the door with their fingers before dropping down.

Bishop, Farrar, Darzi and Bawden spread out through the landing bay. They're still covered in jungle camouflage, skin and hair smeared with mud. Each of them is armed: a bracelet on one arm, white stone glowing. Farrar has his shovel, Bawden her pitchfork, little Darzi a long knife. Bishop, of course, has his red axe, still caked with Wasp blood and bits of yellow flesh.

A heavy clang of metal reverberates through the landing bay—the wide interior door starts to slide open.

Farrar and Darzi rush to different areas, taking cover behind machinery bolted to the walls.

Bawden and Bishop don't hide—they stand tall.

He waves at me to keep everyone where they are. The shuttle's hull is impervious to bracelet beams. If fighting breaks out, my spot is the best position from which to support him and the others.

I snap my wrist left, then right, feel my bracelet power up.

The big metal door rattles on its track. The space beyond is mostly dark, but I see movement.

I aim my bracelet. Victor and those around me take aim as well.

The huge doors open all the way. They stop with an echo of metal that slowly fades.

Finally, those that hide in the shadows step through the door. *Grownups.*

But only two. Behind them, *normal people,* a dozen, armed with knives or clubs. No guns or bracelets. They wear togas similar to what Marcus wore.

Wait . . . Marcus is one of them.

What's going on?

This strange welcoming committee approaches Bishop and Bawden. Old legs, withered bodies, gnarled skin. One of the Grownups can barely walk. He slides his left leg more than lifts it. Each step seems difficult, forced.

"I've got the limping one," I say quietly, and take aim.

"Got the one on the right," Victor says.

The circle-stars with us softly call out their targets.

The two Grownups stop in front of Bishop and Bawden. The taller one says something to Bishop.

Bishop calls to me, his voice echoing through the landing bay: "Em, they want you."

Victor whispers in my ear. "If they even *blink* funny, I'll take them all out."

Regardless of the way Victor vied for power, he believed in me before and he believes in me now.

The circle-stars take my hands and lower me down. Even with their help, it's a big drop—I land on the deck, pleased that I didn't stumble or fall.

I walk to the group, comforted by the bracelet's familiar thrum.

Bishop and Bawden step aside.

I stand face-to-face with the two Grownups.

When you first see Grownups, they all look the same. If you

pay close attention, though, you can tell them apart. The taller of the two, the one that was limping . . . he has white scars all over him, and a white circle-star carved into his black forehead.

"Victor Muller?"

"Correct," he says. His voice is raspy, breathy, *old*. "Welcome aboard."

This could still be a trick. I must be careful.

"Last time we were in this landing bay, we had to fight our way out," I say. "Now you conveniently control it?"

Marcus leans out from behind the Grownups. He's holding a metal pipe in a white-knuckle grip.

"Em, it's all right, Victor is on our side."

"I don't trust him," I say. "And I don't trust *you*, either. So if you're not in charge, keep your mouth shut."

His eyes widen. I think I hurt his feelings.

"Marcus, put the weapon down," Old Victor says. "All of you. If they wanted to fight, you'd be dead already."

Marcus drops the pipe. It clangs against the metal deck. The other normal people with him do the same.

"Yes, we control the landing bay," Old Victor says. "And now most of the ship. We've fought against Matilda for hundreds of years. When she took her best warriors down to Omeyocan, we were finally able to gain territory."

Warriors like Old Bishop, Old Farrar, Coyotl and more. She brought her most loyal and most dangerous followers.

We killed them all.

If Old Victor is telling the truth, Matilda's trip to the planet cost her significantly. She not only lost her inner circle, she lost much of her control aboard this ship. She lost the landing bay? That explains why she wanted us to dock somewhere else.

Serves the bitch right.

"That other ship in orbit, the *Dragon,* it could be coming to attack us," I say. "We need to get the *Xolotl* away from the planet."

"We can't. Matilda and Gaston still control the engines, she . . ."

His voice trails off. He's distracted. He looks over my shoulder, to the shuttle . . . to our Victor.

"Is that . . . is that *me*?"

Longing in that voice. I snap my fingers in front of his red eyes, draw his attention back to me.

"You go near him, you *die*," I say. "Understand?"

The ancient creature nods his disgusting head. "I do. Unlike Matilda, I have no desire to live forever. Death is part of life."

So says the man that's lived for a thousand years.

I get back to the important issue. "How do we capture the bridge so we can leave?"

Old Victor glances at the other Grownup. This one is shorter than him, but a little taller than me.

"Hello, Em," he says. "Welcome aboard."

That voice . . .

My stomach drops. The horror of a moment I want to forget floods back . . . blood and dust and tears . . . a young man crying for his mother . . .

"Yong?"

The Grownup nods.

I killed his receptacle, forever ended this man's ability to overwrite, to live on. Right or wrong, my actions have condemned him to a long, slow death.

Does he know what I did?

The red eyes stare.

"I can guess what you're thinking," he says. "Yes, I know it was you."

My bracelet hand curls into a fist, fingers ready to flick forward. The fight is about to begin.

Old Yong raises his hands, gnarled palms facing out.

"I won't hurt you," he says. "So please, don't hurt me."

He has no weapon. Bishop and Bawden are with me. Victor can shoot out both red eyes before the Grownup can even move. We could slaughter these people if we wanted to. They know this, yet here they stand.

I snap my wrist right, then left. There is a small whine as the bracelet powers down.

Old Yong slowly places his right hand on my left shoulder.

"Hail, Em. We're on the same side."

I'm so confused. I killed the younger him, yet he hails me in the circle-star manner, one warrior to another? He hails me with *respect*?

"Matilda and Gaston hold the bridge and the Tactical Command Center," Yong says. "That means they control most of the ship's systems—engines, navigation, weaponry and all external doors, which is why we couldn't open the landing bay for you."

"So let's take the bridge," Bishop says. "And kill her while we're at it."

"We've been trying to do both for hundreds of years." Yong sounds so much like the boy I killed, it's disturbing. "Matilda reset the navigation control codes. We think she's the only one who knows them, so we need her alive. And you have to be on the bridge to use those codes. That place is locked up tight. Not even Brewer could access it. Is he with you?"

I think of the sad old man in the white coffin.

"Dead," I say. "Buried on Omeyocan."

Yong and Old Victor exchange a glance.

"Then he is at peace," Old Victor says. "We haven't seen him in centuries, not since the early days of Matilda's rebellion. His death is irrelevant to our needs—the bridge is untouchable."

Bishop is getting agitated. "Then we'll talk to Matilda, convince her that we need to leave."

Yong shakes his head. His strange mouth-flaps wiggle in time.

"She will *never* leave. Matilda is obsessed—with Em *and* with Omeyocan. She would rather die than leave this place."

There has to be a way. There is always a way.

"We *must* take the bridge," I say. "Just because you haven't been able to do it doesn't mean it can't be done. We bring new eyes to the problem, new ways of thinking."

Yong shrugs. "Fair enough. Our war room is the best place to show you what we're up against."

Marcus finally musters enough courage to step out from behind the Grownups.

"Em, come meet your people," he says. "We've been waiting so long. See the ship, see how we live."

I shake my head. "There's no time for that."

Bishop leans close to me. "A word in private?"

He and I walk closer to the shuttle, out of earshot.

"You should go with Marcus," he says.

"Are you crazy? I don't trust these people."

"Neither do I. That's why you should go. See as much of this ship as possible, figure out if they're telling the truth. If we're going to take *Xolotl,* we need to know if Matilda has allies or if she's as isolated as they say. Farrar and I will work on the attack plan with Old Victor, you learn what you can."

His idea makes sense. Still, I hesitate.

"I don't like splitting up," I say. "It's a risk."

Bishop tilts his head toward the shuttle. "Take our Victor. He'll protect you with his life. Take Barkah and Lahfah as well. The Grownups probably don't know she's an exceptional fighter.

If all of you have charged bracelets, I'm sure you can defend yourselves."

Maybe the *Dragon* won't attack us. Maybe the Wasps are happy with taking Omeyocan. If they do come for us, though, we don't have time to play it safe.

I trust Bishop to come up with the best plan to take the bridge.

I'll do as he asks—maybe I'll find another way.

FIFTY-THREE

There is so much to see. Barkah, Lahfah, Victor and I walk with Marcus and Old Yong.

I also brought Spingate.

She was with me when we first talked to the Springers. I want her with me now. Her arm is in a sling. She winces with every step, but she gladly bears the pain for a chance to see this new wonder. For now, at least, I don't care what Theresa did—she is my friend and I want to share this with her.

Lahfah still looks like she just stepped off the battlefield. Barkah, however, is wearing his emerald-green coat and the necklace, his symbol of office. I wonder how many outfits he packed.

He tries to maintain his regal aura, but he's slowed by his wounds, and he's having a hard time processing what he sees. For him, a ship like this is the stuff of legends. No one he knows has ever seen anything like it. Only in the past year have his people stopped living underground—this must be overwhelming for him.

Lahfah is amazed and doesn't bother to hide it. She makes little noises at each new thing we see—the Springer equivalent of *ooh* and *aah*, I think.

The hallways are similar to what Spin and I saw when we first woke up. *Stone.* Only now does it strike me as odd there's so much stone on a starship.

If I live through this, maybe I'll research the *Xolotl*'s construction when I write the history of our people.

Marcus shows us an orchard. The huge room is identical in size to the Garden where we first ate fruit, where I killed the pig, where Bello was taken. That place was overgrown and wild: bushy trees with dead branches galore; walled pool choked with thick plants and surrounded by waist-high grass; forests so dense you couldn't walk through the underbrush without getting scratched; ceiling lights peppered with dark spots; water spraying out of a broken fountain.

In this orchard, trees grow in regimented rows, not mad tangles. Nothing blocks my view of the massive room's stone walls. Branches are pruned. The fruit looks healthy. The pool is bordered by a long rectangular brick wall, the grass around it is freshly mowed. There are chips and cracks here and there, sure, but those have been neatly patched with concrete or some other substance. The fountain consists of three stacked marble bowls, water spilling from top to middle to bottom. The sound it makes is lovely. And the *light*—the entire ceiling glows soft white. Our Garden was quite dim in comparison.

Perhaps twenty people of all ages are working in the orchard. They wear togas similar to Marcus's, in various colors and patterns. They pick fruit, prune trees, sweep the stone walkway surrounding the pool. When they see me and the others, they stop working.

They stare.

Spin, Victor and I are likely the first outsiders they've ever seen, and it's a safe guess they've never laid eyes on a Springer.

I learn that the orchard's ceiling lights are specifically made for these fruit trees, and that all other crops are grown in a place called "the Flatland." I remember Brewer mentioning that word. I ask Marcus what it is. He says I have to see it to understand it, that we'll finish our tour there.

Marcus and Old Yong show us more.

The "Coop" is lined with racks and racks of cages, each cage holding a black chicken. *Totally* black: beak, feet, eyes, crest . . . even the feathers, which gleam with a purple iridescence.

Thousands of chickens.

Barkah looks at one up close, asks me if Springers can eat them. I tell him I think so, but we'll check with Kalle. Lahfah hops up and down with excitement—I think her word for the chickens loosely translates to "fat midnight blurds."

The pigs that killed Latu were black, too. And when we were here before, Brewer showed us a display of all-black cows that are supposedly somewhere on the *Xolotl*.

"Why are all the animals black?" I ask.

"Per the Founder's scriptures," Yong says. "Animals were to have no color."

Spingate and I trade a glance.

"Why no color?" she says. "What's the purpose of that?"

Yong shrugs. "I think I knew, once. It doesn't matter. Hasn't mattered for hundreds of years—these are the animals we have."

The tour continues. This ship is twelve *centuries* old, and it looks it. Neat and clean, mostly, but stone walls are cracked, doors are worn down by the touch of thousands of hands. There are ruts in the stone floors, made over the centuries by countless footsteps. Some rooms are dim, some completely dark.

As we walk, Marcus tells me of the complicated system used

to keep everything alive. Grain grown in the Flatland feeds people, chicken, cattle and pigs. Animal waste—including *human* waste—is used to fertilize the grain fields. Crop leavings and any spoiled food are taken to one of a hundred compost rooms, where worms and insects break the matter down into fertilized soil. There are still huge chambers full of ice frozen even before the *Xolotl* left Solomon, yet all water is recycled.

In centuries past, he tells us, computers and robots managed the recycling of food and water. But after the rebellion, most of those machines eventually broke down. For centuries, these "New People" have dedicated themselves to mastering the system. It's become a religion unto itself, with strict "scriptures" dictating what must be done, when, and how.

This, at least, is a religion I can understand—if the system fails, everyone dies.

As we walk, it hits me that for most of this tour, I don't have that ever-so-slight sensation of going uphill or downhill. Occasionally we turn, and I feel it, but for the most part I don't—that means we're mostly walking along the cylinder's length, traveling deeper into the ship.

Some rooms are massive, full of strange machinery that either doesn't work or hasn't been used for generations. Yong tells us that much of the equipment is only needed when the *Xolotl* is traveling from star to star.

This ship was designed to last a thousand years—a thousand years came and went two centuries ago. Spingate whispers to me that it's no surprise things have broken down. She's shocked the *Xolotl* is still in one piece at all.

That doesn't exactly fill me with confidence, but it does speak to the technical prowess of the Grub species. And, I suppose, to the willpower of the Founder. The ship designs came from the signal, but this marvel was built by people.

Marcus takes us through long corridors: cracked stone walls, worn floors, glowing ceilings, doors made of sliding stone.

We see rooms full of people working on low-tech machines cobbled together from parts of far more complex devices. I'm reminded of the simple Springer factories. People spin yarn, dye fabric, saw lumber, manufacture tools and furniture, process meat and chicken for long-term storage.

In some rooms, we see Grownups side by side with normal people. They, too, are working on simple machines, doing simple tasks.

In every room, though, Grownups and New People alike stop what they're doing and stare at us. Victor stares back, hard, letting the universe know we are not to be messed with. He refuses to sling his rifle, choosing instead to keep it at the ready.

As we walk, we see hundreds of people, yet the ship is so massive it feels like a ghost town.

Spingate seems to sense the same thing.

"You told Em there were over five thousand of you," she says to Marcus. "So where is everyone?"

"In the Flatland." He's obviously proud of that place, says the name with reverence. "We're heading there next."

As we continue down the main corridor, I start to see marks from ancient battles. Chips and gouges in the stone walls, maybe from bullets. Blackened streaks from old fires or explosions. Some doors are cracked so badly that the slabs aren't worth fixing.

Below a particularly evil-looking scorch mark, I see three names engraved into the stone wall.

Jasmine Givens 3461–3484
Steve Wren 3470–3483
Claude Zacanna 3465–3483

"Marcus, who were these people?"

"They died in the rebellion," he says.

Yong runs his black fingers along Steve Wren's name.

"The fighting was awful," he says. "It got so bad there was no time for proper funerals. Where people fell, we chiseled their names, then we ejected their bodies into space."

"What about where we woke up?" Spin asks. "There were bodies all over our area. You didn't eject those."

Yong nods. "Brewer sealed that section off, to protect you. He didn't let anyone in. Not Matilda, not us, not anyone. He was alone for over four hundred years."

All that time. He was more of a hero than I knew.

Yes, Brewer—your life mattered.

We keep walking. The names grow more frequent.

One of them stops me cold: *Halim Horn 3445–3484.*

I think of the boy that died in the streets of Uchmal, who wanted to become more than he was. The person who died in this hallway, was it one of Halim's ancestors? Or perhaps even Halim's progenitor? If so, both versions of him are gone forever.

It makes things feel so futile. We fight to survive, we protect our own, we struggle on, and in the end every single one of us will die.

The Grownups wanted immortality. There is no such thing.

"These numbers," I say, gently touching the *3445–3484* next to Halim's name, "what are they?"

Marcus gives me a funny look.

"Are you serious? They're dates. Birth year and the year of death."

Dates . . . *calendars* . . . I realize, yet again, that my lack of a past leaves me missing something important, something basic.

"What year is it now?"

Marcus starts to answer, then stops. He looks off, thinking.

"You know, I'm not sure. Years don't really matter here any-more."

"For you it could be year zero," Yong says. "Start history over if you like. Leave all of this hatred and violence behind."

That's what we've always wanted, really—to start *anew*. But if I am to write about the history of our people, I can't do that without knowing how much time has passed.

"It matters to *us*," Spingate says, reading my mind as always. "What year is it now?"

"It is the year thirty-eight eighty-eight," Yong says.

Halim died on this spot *four centuries* ago. Two hundred years or so before the *Xolotl* even reached Omeyocan, before Uchmal was built.

Marcus seems annoyed at himself that he didn't know what year it was.

"You wanted to make this tour quick," he says. "Shall we continue to the Flatland?"

"No," Yong says. "There is something they must see first."

Another corridor, a short walk "uphill," then a rattling eleva-tor takes us higher. The farther we go, the heavier we feel. When the elevator stops, my legs are already aching with the effort of just standing. We felt this same effect in the Crystal Ball.

Yong leads us into a dusty, wide room made of metal, not stone. A window runs the room's width. Waving cracks in the glass, or whatever the material is, show that the window is easily thicker than I am tall.

Through the window, the grandeur of Omeyocan, surrounded by the void.

Barkah and Lahfah huddle close together. I don't know if they had any external views from inside the troopship—this might be the first time they've seen the blackness of space, or seen their planet from such a distance.

Below our position, the *Xolotl*'s copper cylinder arcs down to either side. There are craters all over it. Directly below us is a long, thick tube, twisted and warped in several places.

"That tube was our primary weapon," Yong says. "A Goff Spear, similar to the one in the Observatory. It was destroyed when the vermin . . ." he glances at Barkah and Lahfah, then back at me. ". . . excuse me, the *Springers,* as you call them, detonated a nuke close by."

Spingate breathes in sharply. "This ship survived a nuclear explosion?"

"Two of them, in fact," Yong says. "Weakened the hull some, destroyed most of our external weaponry. Pretty much all we have left is point defense and some long-range missiles. That's why Gaston wouldn't engage the other ships—with the punishment the *Xolotl* has already taken, he doesn't think we'd last long in a fight."

Gaston—*their* Gaston.

"But the Goff rounds are nukes," I say. "The *Basilisk* and the *Goblin* look just like the *Xolotl*—why were we able to destroy those ships?"

"I'm a soldier, not a scientist." Yong sounds like he's asked the same question himself, many times, and never got an answer he was happy with. "All I know is that the Founder suspected other ships would answer the call. She had a weapon designed to destroy ships built just like the *Xolotl*. The Goff rounds penetrate the thick hull, then explode from the inside."

Zubiri said something similar, that the bombs are nukes but have to go *through* the armor to work.

"Not that it matters," Yong says, tilting his head toward the warped tube. "That was our Goff cannon. It's destroyed. Even if it wasn't, we used up all our rounds against the Springer ship."

Marcus sighs heavily, as if all of this is unimportant.

"Enough with the dead parts of the ship," he says to Yong. "Can I show them the Flatland now?"

There's a whining tone in his voice I don't like very much.

Yong gestures out of the room. "Lead the way, Marcus."

I'm grateful to take the elevator down—maybe *in* is a better word—and give my legs a break. Back in the main corridor, we only walk for a few minutes until, far down the hall, I see a pair of huge stone doors, the biggest I've seen yet.

The closer we get to them, the more engraved names I see. The names become so dense they cover the wall from floor to ceiling, all the way down the corridor.

The slaughter here must have been unimaginable.

We reach the door.

Marcus is all smiles. "Welcome to the Flatland."

The huge stone doors slowly slide apart.

What I see beyond overwhelms me.

My head spins. I must be imagining things. This isn't possible, we're *inside a ship*.

"The cylinder," Spingate says, in utter awe. "It's even bigger than I thought."

Not that long ago, she used her fingertip to draw a picture in the dust, trying to explain how we walked in a straight line yet wound up where we started. I kind of understood, but also kind of didn't.

Now I do.

A vast, sprawling land spreads out before me. In front of us, it looks as flat as flat can be, but the farther out I look, the more I see the *curve*.

I feel like a tiny insect standing inside a hollowed-out log of the largest tree to ever grow on Omeyocan.

Winding roads and paths stretch down the cylinder's length, curve up and away to either side.

Large fenced spaces full of black cows, so far away they are little moving dots.

People riding horses.

Rectangular fields of crops: wheat, corn, tomatoes.

Spin nudges me, points to a nearby field of green plants.

"Those are turnips," she says. "Kalle is going to think she died and went to heaven."

Forest, too, rectangular swaths where the trees are *green,* not yellow.

Sprawling blue lakes.

Clusters of houses—*villages.*

Off to the left, a wooden silo painted red, and next to it, red with white trim, a barn. Around the barn, fenced-in black pigs.

A farm . . . something about a farm, something important . . .

Above me, a bright line of energy stretches down the length of this bizarre place. I feel its heat on my face. This line must act as the sun, spreading light across this curved landscape. The line is bright enough that I can't see past it, to where the cylinder's curves meet high above.

Yong laughs at our amazement. His laugh isn't like Brewer's, like the sound of broken bones scraping together, or harsh and evil like Matilda's—Yong's laugh is rich and full of life.

"Welcome home," he says.

Marcus takes a few steps ahead of me, turns, spreads his arms out wide.

"Look at it," he says. "For twelve centuries, the Flatland has sustained our people. The gods provide."

Yes, a "god" provided this. I wonder what Marcus would think if he knew what that god looked like.

If what Brewer says is true, the *Xolotl* once supported over forty thousand. With the New People, the Springers and us, we are at most sixty-five hundred—there is no reason we can't survive here, *flourish* here.

Barkah hops past Marcus. The Springer king gawks at the expansive space. I wonder what's going through his head.

Finally, he turns to look at me.

"*Hem . . . your home?*"

"*Our* home," I say. "For all of us, together."

He goes back to gawking. Lahfah hops out to join him. Their tails intertwine. Together, they stand there, trying to see everything all at once.

Victor puts an arm around me, shakes me out of pure excitement.

"Just *look* at this place! Em, you did it."

He jogs to Barkah and Lahfah. The three of them start dancing together.

Dancing.

Spingate takes my hand. Her smile is warm, loving, apologetic.

"Victor is right," she says. "You found a way."

She sounds different. She *looks* different. We are only a few hours separated from our ordeal on the planet, yet the hate, animosity and fear she's carried for weeks has finally drained away.

We may never know why some of us were more susceptible to the Grub's influence than others. All I know is that, finally, I am looking at the girl I knew. The *real* her.

I am looking at Theresa Spingate—my best friend.

"I still have to pay for what I did," she says quietly. "I'll never forgive myself."

I think of how Aramovsky stopped me. Spingate killed Bello—I would have killed Spingate and her baby.

"We'll figure it out," I say. "We can't take back the things we've done. All we can do is move forward and make the best life we can."

I hug her. She hugs me back. I smell like smoke and blood and war. Spin, somehow, still smells clean. We've been through everything together. Maybe she's not her full self, not yet, but once we leave this planet far behind, I know she will be.

I see a horse ride out from a village and gallop fast toward us. On it is a teenage boy wearing a robe like Marcus's, but in black.

Barkah and Lahfah flick their wrists left, then right. White stones glow. Victor takes aim with his rifle.

Yong holds up a hand. "Don't shoot. He's not attacking, he's a runner from Victor. *Our* Victor, I mean. *Old* Victor. Damn, this stuff gets confusing."

"You can say that again," Young Victor says.

The boy reins the horse to a stop before us.

"Victor needs you all at the war room," he says. "The other ship, it's changed course . . . it's coming toward us."

FIFTY-FOUR

We ride black horses through the corridors. *Horses,* on a starship. It reminds me of being on Fenrir. I feel a pang of loss for that brave animal.

The horses gallop down the hallways, hooves clacking on stone. When people on the *Xolotl* need to get somewhere fast, this is how they do it. Yong quickly explained the ship used to be full of small vehicles and something he called a "tram," but even the replacement parts for those things wore out centuries ago.

Such a strange place the *Xolotl* is.

We ride through a stone door into a larger room. Flags hang above the door. We saw a similar room a year ago, but it was dark and the floor was covered in grease.

Golden pedestals are set up all over the room. There are more Grownups here, as well as people wearing black togas. Teenagers run to us, take the horses' reins, help us down, then lead the animals away.

Three of the pedestals are close together in the center of the room, their displays combined to make an image almost as big as that above the red well.

Old Victor, Bishop, Farrar and Gaston stand around those pedestals, staring up at a glowing Omeyocan, the familiar red dot of the *Xolotl,* and the dreaded green dot that is the *Dragon.* A blue line arcs between the two ships. In the middle of that line, a counter that reads *0:17:34:22.* The last two digits are seconds, ticking down as we watch.

"*Dragon* is on an intercept trajectory with us," Gaston says. "It's coming fast."

"What's the countdown represent?" I ask.

Old Victor adjusts pedestal icons. The image above zooms in on the *Dragon.* It's fuzzy from this distance, but I can make out a long tube mounted on top of the massive copper cylinder.

"They have a Goff Spear," I say.

Gaston nods. "Not exactly like ours, and it's mounted on a different spot on their hull. That means the Grub probably didn't provide that weapon design. Humans came up with it on their own. So did the Wasps. There's no doubt, though—it serves exactly the same purpose ours did. It's a ship-killer."

"The timer represents how long it will take the Wasp ship to reach that weapon's can't-miss range," Old Victor says. "When the timer hits zero, if they fire their Goff Spear, we have no chance of stopping the round from connecting."

Seventeen hours, thirty-four minutes and counting.

I've hated Matilda since I first learned of her existence, but never so much as right now.

"We have to take the bridge," I say.

Bishop slowly shakes his head.

"Her area is sealed off by meter-thick blast doors which are guarded by beam-cannons in armored turrets," he says. "When Old Victor said they'd been trying to get in there for centuries, he wasn't kidding—we couldn't get to Matilda in seventeen *days,* let alone seventeen hours."

He rubs his fingers into his forehead. He's slouching. Bishop is not the kind to easily admit defeat. If he says we don't have enough time to get to Matilda, we don't.

I refuse to accept that. "There has to be another way."

Yong shakes his head. "There isn't. I told you that when you came aboard. Bishop now sees the same thing. You will not get what you want by force. She wants one thing, and one thing only."

Me. She wants *me.*

"No way," Gaston says. "That monster will not get my friend."

I look around the room, desperately hoping someone has an idea, even a bad one. No one does. Not Bishop, not Spingate, not Gaston, not the Grownups. I see rage and frustration, but no answers.

My chest feels tight. It can't end like this. There has to be a way. There *has* to be.

"Then we talk to Matilda again." I point to the green dot. "We need to make her understand what's coming for us."

Yong speaks softly, patiently. "She understands just fine. She's forcing us to decide right now—she gets Em, or everyone dies."

He doesn't sound surprised, or even concerned. Yong is ready for death. Life is just a show to him. No matter how the plot varies, he already knows how the story will end.

"But Matilda will die, too," Spingate says, desperation bleeding from her every pore. "The witch has to know that!"

Old Victor nods. "She knows. Her power base is gone. She only has about thirty people still with her. We control most of the ship. This is the only chance she will ever have to get Em. She's willing to risk death to take it."

I look at the countdown clock: *0:17:32:26.*

"Will the Wasps try to board us?" I ask no one in particular. "Like they did with the *Goblin*?"

Gaston throws up his hands. "Why would they? The *Goblin* was used as a sacrificial lamb so they could launch landing craft. There's no purpose to capturing the *Xolotl*—they'll just blow us out of the sky."

"It doesn't make sense," Spingate says. "Wasps control Omeyocan now. Why even bother with us?"

Someone answers her, but I don't really hear it. As the others talk, I close my eyes, try to get my head around the pieces of this new puzzle. Maybe the Wasps destroy anything they find, no matter where it is. Or maybe the Grub is making them come after us, driving them into a frenzy to satisfy its bloodlust.

The Grub . . .

It can't defend itself against all attacks, my false father said.

The Goff Spear cart on the plaza . . .

Several puzzle pieces form in my thoughts, and just as quickly, they snap together, fitting perfectly.

"They know. The Wasps *know* we have nukes."

Conversation stops.

It was my decision that doomed us.

"The Wasps saw what the Goff Spear could do," I say. "The first thing they would have done was search the Observatory for it, see if they could use our weapon against us to take out the *Xolotl*. The cannon is huge, it's not hard to find. They got the hatch open, they saw the hexagonal shape of the barrel. They realized it's the same size and shape as the cart on the plaza. The *empty* cart. It doesn't take a gear to figure out we took Goff Spear rounds with us."

Gaston hangs his head, covers his eyes with his hands.

"It might not even be that complicated," he says. "We had the damn things hanging under our wings. The Wasps on the ground probably saw them. Em is right—it doesn't take much intelligence to figure out what we've got."

Bishop looks confused. "But why does it matter? Why are they coming after us instead of just letting us go?"

"Because the Wasps will do anything to protect the Grub," I say. "If they think we have nukes that could kill the Grub, they'll destroy us to make sure we can't launch them. And they won't let us leave, because we might come back someday. They need to kill us. Right now."

The words sink in. Maybe the Wasps haven't figured out we have nukes and are coming for us anyway, or maybe they are coming *because* of the nukes. There is no way to know.

"Why they're coming doesn't really matter," our Victor says. "We can't outrun them, so we fight. Our ship against theirs."

His progenitor looks at him, red eyes swirling. "The *Xolotl* has been in a battle and taken heavy damage. Their ship has not. That probably gives them a significant firepower advantage. They'll chew us up from a distance, or sit back and launch boarding craft after they take out our point defense."

Brewer's words flare to life: *Destroy them with what? The six decrepit Macanas that Vick Tick Tick wastes his time with?*

Vick Tick Tick . . . *Vic* Tick Tick . . . *Victor.*

"The Macanas," I say. "Can they defend us against attack?"

Old Victor shakes his head, making his mouth-folds flap.

"We have six ancient interceptors left that *might* still fly. We think the Wasps, as you call them, still have eight of their combined atmospheric/exospheric fighters. Any one of their craft is easily a match for three of ours."

I close my eyes. The cold void is reaching out for me, digging in with invisible claws. Our chance is slipping away. We've come through so much . . . *I've* come through so much. This isn't fair.

"We have to repair the *Xolotl*'s Goff Spear," Gaston says. "Borjigin and Zubiri can help."

"We're old, not stupid," Yong says. "Our halves and gears spent decades trying to repair it. Too much of the barrel is warped. The cannon *cannot* be fixed. I'm sorry, but this isn't a movie or a play—there is no convenient third-act rescue that gives us an easy solution. This is real life."

I feel like I'm sinking.

This isn't fair . . . it isn't fair . . .

If we fight, we lose.

We can't run, because Matilda controls the ship.

I told her she didn't have any power.

I was wrong—she has *all* the power.

And just like that, I understand that it's over.

I look at Bishop. He looks at me. My question to him is unspoken, yet crystal clear. Some of my friends will understand that what comes next is the only way. Some, like Gaston and Spingate, I imagine, will fight it. But before I commit, I need to know Bishop is with me. I need to know he understands.

I need to know he will be by my side.

As the others talk, I silently wait for Bishop's answer.

He shakes his head, ever so slightly. Then, he closes his eyes. He lowers his head.

He nods.

I turn to Yong. "Can you contact Matilda?"

His red eyes bore into me. "I can."

If my people are to survive, there is only one choice left.

"Then call her," I say. "I'm ready to talk."

FIFTY-FIVE

I stand in a small, dusty room with Xander Gaston and Theresa Spingate. She holds baby Kevin like the universe might come alive at any moment and try to rip him away from her. She ran to get the child, I think, because even if she doesn't accept reality yet a part of her knows this will be the last time he sees me.

There is no furniture in this room. It happened to be close to the room with the pedestals. I absently wonder what this space was once used for. I know what it is used for now—to say good-bye.

I spoke with Matilda. Afterward, I gave everyone specific orders about what would happen next. Bishop didn't argue, even though it was easy to see this is killing him. Gaston threw a fit, insisted that I talk alone with him and Spin. I've never seen him act like this, so angry and frightened at the same time. He all but dragged me here.

He doesn't want to lose his friend.

"It's the only way," I say. "If I don't do this, we don't get the control codes. The Wasps will destroy us."

Gaston burns with fury. If his rage could be channeled into a weapon, we could destroy all who stand against us.

"I won't allow it." He's speaking with the voice he uses in combat, the voice of the *captain,* the voice of a leader who won't be questioned. "Tell her, Theresa."

Spingate is crying. She isn't even bothering to hold it back. Tears line her face, each wet streak tracing where her nose meets her cheek, then flowing to the outside corners of her full lips.

"You can't let Matilda overwrite you," she says. "We've seen what happens. It will be the end of you."

I nod.

"I know. There's no time for debate. It comes down to one person's life against the lives of sixty-five hundred."

Gaston and Spin are canvases painted in anguish. It hurts so much to see their pain. I wish there was something I could say to make them feel better. How strange: I'm the one sacrificing my life, yet I feel the need to console them.

"I forbid it," Gaston says.

I put my hand on his shoulder.

"It's not your choice to make. It's mine."

Spin shakes her head. Her lower lip quivers. Tears drip from her chin, land on little Kevin's nose. She wants to talk me out of it, but she knows me better than anyone ever has—she knows I won't waver from this decision.

"Godsdamned *bullshit!*" Gaston's tears come now, sudden and intense, half-strangling his words. "There's *thousands* of us, and only a handful of them! We have weapons. You said we had to conquer the Grownups and take the ship, so let's do that, *now!*"

I pull him close. I hold him tight.

"I love you," I say to him.

Sobs shake his body. This man can command starships, can

stand firm and orchestrate death on a grand scale, but here he has no power.

"Total *bullshit*," he says. "I don't want you to go."

I pull away. His tears cool on my cheeks.

"Goodbye, Xander. You're a good man. My life is better for having known you."

I move to Theresa. She's slowly shaking her head.

"How did this happen?" she says. "If you want us to fight, Em, we will fight. You are my friend—I would rather die than let you go."

There is steel in Theresa Spingate. I have seen her face down horrors, both alien and human alike. I have seen her stand up for what is right while everyone around her screams at her to shut up, to cave in, to go along with the wrong decision because that's what the crowd wants.

I hold her tight. I feel little Kevin between us, sleeping soundly.

"You are my friend," I say. "You were the first person I saw. I love you more than words can say. You need to let me go, let me do this. For you. For us. For Kevin. For everyone."

I feel like someone is dragging a jagged blade across my heart. I fear the end. I will never see these people again.

Spin reaches up with one hand, cups the back of my head. She pulls me closer.

"We never asked for any of this," she whispers. "Why can't they just leave us alone?"

The *they* she refers to . . . Grownups? Springers? Wasps? All of the above, probably.

"I don't know." Which is the truth. There is so much I don't know, and now I will never get the chance to learn.

I grip Spin's shoulders, hold her firm as I step back. She's shaking. I lean in, kiss her forehead.

"Thank you for everything," I say. "Who knows? Maybe I'll still be in here when it's done."

My hope is a false one. We all know it.

"Goodbye, Em."

Spin steps to Gaston, who is trying his hardest to stand up straight, to not collapse with heartbreak. She puts her arm around his shoulders.

Together, they stand there. A family. Father, mother, son. They represent the future of my kind. *They* are why I am doing this.

I turn my back on my friends and head toward my fate.

FIFTY-SIX

We meet in the Garden.

Not an "orchard," but rather *the* Garden. It's just as overgrown as when we were last here. The same thick woods where Bello was taken. The same tangled brambles we crawled through to escape. The same sickly-sweet smell of rotting fruit. The glowing ceiling arcing high above seems to have a few more black spots, but maybe that's just my imagination.

This is where we fought the Grownups.

I could have killed Matilda then. I did not. I wanted to be a better person than her.

That decision is about to cost me my life.

She stands near the broken fountain that is nothing more than water burbling up through tall reeds. She's with three wrinkled, coal-black Grownups. Old Gaston is one of them, a bit shorter than she is. I don't recognize the other two.

Bulbous red eyes, whirling with a soft internal light. The nasty mouth-folds, quivering slightly.

All four Grownups wear silver bracelets, white stones already flickering with power.

Her people are armed.

Mine are not. We weren't allowed to bring weapons.

I have brought three people with me as well, all of whom can fight. Bishop, because there is no Grownup waiting for him. Young Victor, because his Grownup is on our side. And Barkah, because as the leader of his people he needs to understand what's happening.

Bishop seems calm, a stone statue covered in skin, but I can see the turmoil in his soul. Victor is more outwardly upset—hands clench into fists, unclench, clench again. Two boys, both covered with dried mud, blood of different colors, both smelling of sweat and smoke and death. The rivalry between them is forgotten. Neither of them wants me to do this, yet both of them obey the orders I have given to not interfere.

Barkah seems to be taking it all in. I'm not sure what he's thinking.

We walk toward Matilda and her people.

The Grownups level their bracelets at us.

"Far enough," Matilda says.

My friends and I stop. El-Saffani tried rushing the Grownups; the Grownups killed them. Even Bishop has to see the futility of attacking. At least I hope he does.

"Let's not waste time talking," Matilda says. "We all know how this ends."

I can't help myself—I have to try one last time.

"You know I'm not lying about the God of Blood," I say. "You *know* we can't lie to each other. Omeyocan isn't the paradise you were promised. It never was."

I can taste the hate pouring off her.

"To think I was such a coward," she says. "To think that I might quit at the first sign of danger. Are you a sad special snowflake because the God of Blood put obstacles in your path? If you want something and you don't have to fight for it, darling-dear, then it was never worth having in the first place."

I was wrong. She *does* believe me about the Grub. She just doesn't care. Matilda is single-minded, a dauntless force of will.

"At least get the *Xolotl* out of here," I say. "Every second you wait is a second that brings us closer to a fight we can't win."

"You're telling me that as if I didn't already know. Tick-tock, darling-dear—time's a-wasting."

She is regal. Triumphant.

My heart sinks. "You're *horrible*. How can you put your life above the lives of so many others?"

Her one eye swirls.

"Am I putting my life above so many others, or are *you*? Every moment you waste is another moment that barbarian ship comes closer. And why is your non-life so important, anyway? Hundreds of thousands of people dedicated their existence, their fortunes, their *families*, to bring the human race to Omeyocan. It was a struggle, but great struggle is the price of great achievements. I outlasted my enemies. I outlasted Brewer. I outlasted *you*. You have something I want, Em. I have something you want. It's as simple as that."

Victor shakes a fist at her. "You selfish *bitch*. You're going to get us all killed!"

"*Silence*," Bishop snaps, turning his head slightly toward the younger circle-star. "Obey your orders!"

Old Gaston glances at Matilda, just for a moment, his red eyes briefly betraying emotion. Is there animosity between them?

If I had time, maybe I could exploit that, but time is something I don't have.

"Children, *please,*" Matilda says. "Young man, you're hardly the first to call me that name. But by all means, keep running your little mouths. Take as long as you like."

I stare at Matilda. She stares at me.

"Tick-tock," she says.

We are impossibly different. We are exactly the same. Maybe something happened to her that made her this evil. Or maybe something happened to *me* to make me less so.

We'll never know.

To get what she wants, Matilda Savage is willing to let everyone she knows die.

Em Savage is not.

And that is why, in the end, she wins.

"All right," I say. "I'll do it."

Bishop breaks ranks, steps forward. Grownup arms snap up, aim bracelets—I step between the weapons and my man, put a hand on his chest.

He stops. His face is a mask of calculating savagery.

"I'll kill her." His voice is quiet, controlled, which makes it all the more terrifying. "I'll kill them all."

"You promised me you wouldn't try to stop this."

He looks past me, to the Grownups.

"I lied," he says. "I can't lose you. I *won't.*"

Victor nods madly, a crazy grin splitting his face. "I'm with you, Bishop. Let's get them."

Barkah stamps a big foot down hard.

"*Stop,*" he says. "*Orders!*"

Just the one word, yet it seems to rattle Bishop and Victor both. The two are torn between their hardwired duty to obey their leader and a deep desire to protect me.

I step past Bishop, stand before Victor.

"It's me or it's everyone," I say. "If you want to protect your people, let me go."

He tries to look into my eyes, but he can't. His head drops.

"I'll go with you," he says. "I said I would follow you any-where. That includes following you into death itself. Please, let me."

I thought his feelings for me were just a crush. Yet one more thing I was wrong about, because I finally understand—Victor Muller is truly in love with me.

"Permission denied." I stand on my tiptoes and kiss his cheek. "You are so brave, Victor. Be brave now. Our people need you."

I stand in front of Bishop. I reach up, put my right hand on his left shoulder. Inside, he's crumbling. He's *shattering*.

"There has to be another way," he says.

The waver in his voice is almost enough to make *me* turn and rush the Grownups. My throat is dry. It hurts to know I will leave him so brokenhearted.

Ramses Bishop is a soldier. He would sacrifice anything for his people. He is a fighter, one who acts through violence, but this time, his violence would solve nothing.

"My decision," I say. "I do this for all of us."

He looks down. He nods. He puts his right hand on my left shoulder.

"Hail, Em. May the gods welcome you home."

I glance at Barkah. We have been foes. We have been friends. In some ways, this alien understands me better than anyone else, Bishop and Spingate included. Barkah knows exactly what is happening. He doesn't try to talk me out of it. He simply nods.

"Hem. Peace."

He gets that this isn't just about me. He gets the bigger picture—the lives of his people depend upon my actions.

I throw my arms around Bishop's neck and kiss him one last time, a deep kiss, a *real* kiss. A kiss that I will take with me into oblivion.

As soon as I let go of Bishop, Barkah hops forward and hugs me. I hug him back, smell the strange odor of his skin, the stench of battle that clings to him still.

I push away. I turn to face my killer.

"I have one condition," I say.

Matilda laughs, a hateful sound that makes me want to tear out her other eye and blind her forever.

"*Now* you have a condition? A tad late for that."

"Just one demand, Matilda. If you don't meet it, you'll find out you're not the only Savage who is willing to die to get what she wants."

For the first time, her aura of confidence wavers. There is the briefest moment where she examines me, trying to decide if my will is as strong as I say.

But she knows it is, because my will is her will.

"What's the condition?"

"When we're connected for the overwrite, *before* it begins, you give the navigation command codes to my Gaston."

"Ri*dic*ulous," she says. "You think I would give away my only bargaining chip?"

I shrug. "You don't have a choice. If you want this body, you give me your word. You're old, Matilda. You're frail. If you die in the process, I have to know my sacrifice is worth it."

She stares at me.

"Tick-tock," I say. "Wouldn't it be a shame to get what you want only to have the *Dragon* destroy us anyway? *Tick-tock*."

It feels good to throw those two words back in her face.

"I accept your condition," she says. "Let's go. We're wasting time."

She turns, gestures for me to walk with her.

I take a step, then look back at Bishop one last time. I was never sure if I loved him completely, the way I loved O'Malley. Only now, when I realize I will never see Bishop again, do I realize I love him just as much.

Maybe more.

Why do I only discover my true feelings for people when it is too late to do anything about them?

"Farewell, my love," I say. "I hope you find happiness."

He says nothing. A single tear rolls down his cheek, cutting a wet line through dirt, smoke stains and blood.

Three steps take me to Matilda. Side by side, I let her lead me toward our fate.

FIFTY-SEVEN

Bars slide from ancient white fabric, lock around my waist, my ankles and my wrists.

My heart kicks. It's hard to breathe.

For some reason, I expected the room where I die to be white, shiny and clean.

I was wrong.

It's no different from the room in which I first awoke. Dingy. Mostly dark due to lights that probably burned out centuries ago. There's dust here. This place smells of mold and death.

Matilda led me out of the Garden, past the spot where I first fought her, where she lost her eye, where Bishop killed Old Aramovsky. Through the darkness, the only light coming from thin lines of color embedded in the floor.

Through stone doors cracked and cratered by ancient explosions.

Past armored turrets with silver barrels that tracked our every step.

Through doors made of steel, not stone.

And finally, to this room, decorated with only two things: a golden coffin and a black X.

The coffin gleams. The white fabric inside is rippled with age, even torn in a few places.

This is where they overwrote Bello. I don't have to be told this to know my friend ended here.

Old Gaston and the others shackle Matilda to the X, locking down her wrists and ankles. They place the black crown on her head.

This is how Kevin O'Malley died.

I stabbed him, yes, but it's time to let that go. I had no way of knowing the boy I loved was still in there. It wasn't my fault. Finally, I accept that.

I hope that I'm wrong about religion. I hope there's an afterlife. I hope Kevin is there, waiting for me.

Golden coffin lids rise up on either side, slide shut and block out all light.

My life will end the same way it began: in darkness.

I am about to be *erased*.

My body will live on. Maybe some shred of my mind, too—O'Malley was still in there; Bello remembered things she couldn't possibly know. Perhaps a tiny piece of Em will exist within Matilda.

A part of me holds on to the hope that this will fail, but only a small part. I have no illusions: the person that I am will cease to exist. Of all the things that make me who I am—a friend, a killer, a leader, a manipulator, a lover—I am also a realist.

And reality is what it is whether we like it or not.

"Em, can you hear me?"

Matilda's voice.

Even though it's pitch-black in here, I shut my eyes tight. Do

I really have to listen to her now? Do I have to hear the voice of that horrible bitch?

There must be speakers in this coffin somewhere, hidden in the old white fabric.

"I know you're listening, darling-dear. Speak with me in your last moments."

Her words drip with smug satisfaction.

"Go to hell. You disgust me."

"How rude. We're the same person. You should be happy."

I want to jam my fingers into my ears but my wrists are locked down. The coffin is old; these bars are new—I can't break them like I did when I first awoke. I want Matilda to shut up, just *shut up,* but I know she will not, not until the gas drags us both down to blackness.

"I should have killed you when I had the chance."

"Yes, you should have. Compassion is for the weak. Because of your weakness, you end. Because of my strength, I live anew."

My eyes sting. What . . . *now?* For all the times I couldn't dredge up a single tear, I spend my last few moments crying?

"You were spectacular, darling-dear. So vicious. It's odd, but you made me proud. It seems fitting that the greatest foe I have ever faced is actually me.*"*

If that smug, preening, selfish monstrosity is what I could have become, then maybe it's for the best that I end now.

"Time to keep your promise. Release the navigation command codes."

She laughs. *"Don't be silly, foolish girl. You knew I wouldn't give you the codes. Down in your infant heart, you* wanted *to join with me. Your pathetic little demand was just for show."*

Rage consumes me, but it's hollow, there and gone in an instant. I gambled. I lost. My existence will end to the bitter sound of her self-satisfied cackle.

"Goodbye, Em. Gaston, I am ready. Begin the process."

Old Gaston's gravelly voice comes through the hidden speakers: *"No, Matilda—you made a deal."*

I stop breathing. I stare into the darkness.

Matilda isn't laughing anymore.

"Always the comedian, Admiral. Begin the process. Don't make me angry."

"You gave your word," he says.

"Since when does my word matter? We're at war."

Her voice cracks on the words. She's afraid.

"It matters now," Old Gaston says. *"I've listened to your lies for centuries. Not anymore. Your selfishness has put my descendants at risk."*

"Your descendants?" Matilda shrieks her words. *"You mean the bastard child from that whorish version of Theresa and your receptacle? Those aren't your children, Gaston!"*

"I'll never have children of my own, because I followed you. Give me the code."

"You godsdamned, backstabbing cockroach! Start the process or I'll have you skinned alive!"

"You gave your word," he says. *"Honor it or suffer the slow demise of dying where you are."*

He's calm, methodical, but he's also enjoying this.

"Fine," Matilda says.

She rattles off a string of letters and numbers that is so long I lose track of them by the tenth or eleventh digit.

"One moment while I verify," Old Gaston says.

The codes . . . if they're correct, will he release me? Maybe I won't end after all.

My heart thunders with hope.

I can't think, I dare not think at all. . . .

A few moments later, Old Gaston says, *"Codes confirmed."*

"Let me out of here! Please! We can fly away, we can escape, we can—"

"I'm sorry," he says. *"Matilda gave her word. So did you."*

With that, I know it's over. He's right. I did give my word.

I smell something. The gas . . .

"Ah, it begins," Matilda says. *"You did well, Em. You did what needed to be done."*

The creature I hate more than anything in the universe pays me a compliment. I should be repulsed. I'm not. She won, and she is gracious in victory.

I chose this end, but I did it so that others would continue on.

I only lived a single, short year, but—like Brewer—I made a difference.

So groggy . . . I don't know if my eyes are open or if I'm not able to open them at all. . . .

My constant anger, it's gone.

I feel at peace—my existence *mattered*.

As sleep claims me, I smile.

FIFTY-EIGHT

Ribbons of memory flutter and fly.

I am six years old.

A smell, stinky but welcome . . . old fish.

I am in a boat.

Not a boat, a canoe. It's red.

An old man is with me. He wears blue robes. He has a symbol on his forehead. Not a gear, not a half or a circle; this one is shaped different, like the number eight on its side.

No, wait, I know what that is . . . it's an infinity symbol. A tattoo, faded black on light brown skin.

I'm holding a fishing pole. We're on a lake. I don't see any other boats. Green trees grow on distant shores. The sun shines down, but it's cold. I'm warm enough, though, because I'm also wearing blue robes.

"Knock knock," the man says.

A surge of excitement. This is my grandfather. He loves to tell jokes.

"Who's there?"

"Boo," he says.

"Boo who?"

"Aw, Matilda, don't be sad!"

It takes me a moment to understand. Now I get it—*boohoo.*
I laugh a little, then harder. Grampa laughs. A wide smile carves
deep troughs in his stubbly face.

Suddenly I am outside the canoe, watching myself and my
grampa fishing.

My grampa . . . a man I trusted implicitly.

A man who was supposed to protect me.

"Matilda, can you keep a secret?"

I am looking at *myself,* at an excited face half-hidden by the
blue robe's hood. The little girl nods madly.

"Of *course,*" she says, almost shouting it. "Of course I can,
Grampa!"

Grampa frowns, across the water. "Oh, I don't know. . . ."

The little girl quickly reels in her line. The lure clacks against
the pole's last ring. Droplets on sharp hooks catch the sunlight,
sparkle like molten jewels.

"*Please,* Grampa. Tell me!"

His smile fades. There's a distant expression in his eyes.

Something bad is about to happen. The girl doesn't know it
yet. I want to shout *Get out of the boat* but I'm not really there.

"You can't tell your mother," Grampa says. "And you can't
tell your dad."

The little girl nods harder. So bright-eyed. So innocent. So
trusting.

Jump overboard and swim away!

"Do you love your dad?" Grampa asks the girl.

"Yes, I love Daddy so much."

Grampa doesn't love Daddy. Daddy is his son-in-law.

"Then this secret is *very* important," Grampa says. "Because if you don't keep it, your daddy will be hurt. Do you want your daddy to get hurt?"

The little girl's smile vanishes. She doesn't understand what's happening.

Jump in the water it doesn't matter if you drown because death would be better. . . .

"No, I don't want Daddy to get hurt."

I know what comes next.

I didn't want to remember this. Not ever.

Grampa smiles. Something about that smile makes the little girl lean away. Fear on her face now, fear of the unknown, of a grownup changing the rules.

"Good," he says. "Very good."

He rises, hands on the side of the canoe for balance. The canoe rocks slightly in the water as he moves toward the little girl, a smile on his face, a distant, *wrong* smile.

The scene vanishes. Coldness in my soul. *Deadness.* What he did . . . how could the girl ever recover from that?

It happened to Matilda.

It happened to *me.*

I'm in my bedroom. I'm scared and hurt. My world has shattered. I can't stop seeing Grampa moving toward me, that sick smile on his face.

My parents are in another room, arguing. Either they think I can't hear or they don't care. I came home . . . *after* . . . and told Mommy what happened. She called me a liar. She *slapped* me. Daddy heard and came rushing in. Mommy told me to be quiet, to not tell Daddy anything, but he picked me up, held me, petted my hair. I started crying so hard.

I told him what Grampa did.

My parents scream at each other. Mommy begs Daddy not to leave, says that he'll wind up in jail, or get shot. Daddy throws things, punches walls. Our house *shakes* with his rage.

Mommy believes me now. I can tell. She's crying so loud. I did something wrong—this is my fault. I made her sad. I made Daddy angry.

I hear the comm ring.

Mommy answers. I can't hear what she says.

I hear the chirp of her disconnecting the call.

"It was him," Daddy says. "Was it him?"

Mommy cries some more. "Yes. He . . . he said they had so much fun fishing."

I hear Daddy's fist punch through a wall.

"He was seeing if she told on him," he says. "That bastard, that fucking *bastard* . . . I'll send him straight to hell."

"There's more," Mommy says. Her voice is so soft I can barely hear it. "He said he's enrolling her in the convent. He's sending someone to pick her up tomorrow morning."

The pause is so long I wonder if they've both fallen asleep.

The convent . . . I know that place. We visited there once. It's part of the main church complex where Grampa lives.

My skin feels like ice. I start to shiver. Grampa wants me in the convent so he can be closer to me.

So he can do what he did in the canoe again.

And again.

And again.

Finally, Daddy speaks. He's not yelling anymore. His voice is just as thin and scared as Mommy's.

"We can't let him do that."

"There's no way to stop him," Mommy says. "He's a Mullah—he can do whatever he wants."

"Cardinals outrank him."

"We don't know any Cardinals," Mommy says. "My father runs the church here. You know that. You think some high-ranking church official is going to side with *us*?"

The awful tone in her voice. I'm only a little girl, but I know I'm smarter than most people my age. Smart enough to understand that tone—my mother sounds *helpless*.

But that can't be. My parents know everything. They are the best people in our city, on Solomon, in the entire Purist Nation. They can do anything.

"I'll kill him," my daddy says. "Swear to High One, I'll kill him."

"David, *please,* listen to me—you won't get near him. We have to think of something else. Can we leave tonight? Can we run?"

"And go where? We have no money. If we go to the forest, we'll die. If we go to another town, they'll find us. We'll never get clearance to leave the planet."

More silence.

"There is one place," my daddy says. "The Church of Mict-lan. Those are the only walls your father can't reach beyond."

"*Mictlan?* That crazy woman made the whole damn thing up! She cobbled it together from old Earth religions so she could trick people into building that ridiculous ark. Her religion is fake."

"More fake than ours?"

I start to cry. Somehow this has become the thing they always argue about—religion.

"Mictlan is a *cult,*" my mother screams. "Our faith is real! We know Stewart led the exodus from Earth! We made the pil-grimage, saw his landing site with our own eyes. High One led Stewart to leave that bed of sin and found the Purist Nation!"

"The same High One that put your father in power?"

Daddy's words are quiet and cold. They bring silence.

When Mommy finally speaks, she's no longer yelling.

"We might never see her again," she says. "We don't know anything about that place. And we can't afford the tuition."

"We can. If we pledge our labor."

"David . . . that's for *life*. We'd work until we die."

"Which is no different than our lives now," Daddy says, his voice rising. "We work every day. We suffer, and for what? For the promise of Heaven? For knowing that our child will lead the same life we did? Your father blocked me from entering the church. There's never been a way out for us. At least this way she'll be safe."

"We don't know that," Mommy says. "No one knows what goes on behind those walls."

"We know what went on in that canoe. We know what will go on if she's enrolled at the convent."

I pull my blankets tighter around me. Are they going to send me away? I shouldn't have said anything, I'm a bad girl, a *stupid* girl, and this is all my fault.

The ribbon of memory flutters. Another one waves in, soft curls sweeping me up, carrying me to a new place.

It's the middle of the night. I don't hear any grav-cars. During the day our town is noisy, but now it is quiet and still.

A metal gate set in walls of stone. I know, somehow, that when I'm older I will see another gate that looks like this one, only much, *much* larger. This is the place the kids at school talk about: the Mictlan compound. It is a church, but not *our* church. My friends' parents say the same things my mother says, that this place is blasphemous, that the lady who founded it can stand up to the Mullahs and Poseks and Cardinals only because she is richer than anyone in the Purist Nation.

I've seen the children of Mictlan around town. They have circular marks on their foreheads. Tooth-girls. Halves. Circle-stars. Most of them have empty circles, though.

Daddy is talking to a man dressed in black.

The gate opens.

The ribbon of existence flutters.

I'm on a bench. Mommy and Daddy are talking to a woman dressed in black. She's *old,* older than any person I have ever seen. She has so many metal parts on her I wonder if she's actually a robot. She frightens me.

Mommy is shaking. Daddy has his arm around her, holding her close. I've never seen them like this before. They've always been strong, the strongest anyone could ever be.

They are not strong now.

"Your contracts are for life," the woman says, a machine making her raspy voice just loud enough to hear. "You serve at my discretion. Your daughter will get an education. She will be safe behind our walls. If you do this, she belongs to us. Do you understand?"

Mommy asks: "Will we be able to see her?"

"Possibly," the machine-woman says. "But not for the first few years. Even then, we make no guarantees. What we're creating here is bigger than you, than her, than any family. The True God calls, and we all answer."

"The ark," my daddy says. "Will she be sent to the ship? Will we?"

The woman's machine voice is cold, uncaring. "That is not your concern. You are not the first parents to come here seeking safety for their sons and daughters. The Purist Church is corrupt beyond belief. They treat women like property. They turn a blind eye to unspeakable child abuse. If you enroll Matilda with us, she will be protected. She will serve a greater purpose. My only regret is that we didn't get her earlier. She's too old for advanced training. However, as she grows and matures, she may have children of her own. Your grandchildren could be doctors, engineers, scientists . . . all things are possible."

My parents look at each other.

"*Too old,*" Mommy says to Daddy, wiping at her tears with the back of her hand. "That means our daughter will be a *servant.* I don't care what they call it, we've seen the people with circles on their heads in town, catering to the people with those other symbols. Our daughter will be a servant her whole life."

Daddy twists in his chair, looks at me. He looks for a long time. Then he turns back to Mommy.

"It will be dawn in a few hours," he says. "There are worse things than being a servant."

Mommy hides her face in her hands. Her shoulders shake.

She nods.

The machine-lady pushes a small black box across her desk. The box has a hole in it. My daddy slides his thumb into the hole.

A little light on top of the box turns green.

"It is done," the machine-lady says.

The ribbon flutters, but doesn't vanish. It shifts, slightly. I'm sitting on Daddy's lap. I don't know where Mommy is.

Daddy is crying. He's trying to hold it back, to hide it, but I see his tears. I hear the pain in his voice.

"Matilda, I have to send you away. I know you can't understand right now, but you will. The only way I can keep you safe is to hide you. There may come a time when the tooth-girls tell you to do something dangerous, or the double-rings try to hurt you because they know no one will punish them. If that happens, remember—do whatever it takes to survive."

I shake my head. They can't leave me. They are my *parents*.

"I don't want you to go," I say. "Please, Daddy . . . I want to stay with you."

He pets my hair. He smells like soap.

"You're going to be special," he says. "You're going to be one of the Cherished. Doesn't that sound nice?"

I don't know what that word means. If it means I can't be with him, then I hate the word.

"Daddy, *please.*"

My words make him wince. For the first time in my life, I realize that words have power. A hard lesson that I will carry with me forever.

He stands, lifting me like I weigh nothing at all, hugs me, then sets me down. A woman in black clothes enters the room. She has a circle mark on her forehead.

Daddy kneels, kisses my cheeks.

"I'll see you again, sweetheart. Do what you're told. This will be hard for you, but I know you can do it. I know you can."

He turns, walks away. I reach for his hand but he's too fast—he's already gone.

My grandfather hurt me. Because of that, I'm losing my mom and my dad.

I've lost everything.

The world wavers and twists, the ribbon of memory shifts into something new.

I am eleven. I smell animal shit. The world is bright, but it's dimmer than real sunlight.

Because I'm on a starship.

A ship that is shaped like a big tube.

There are kids here with me, kids from my *lacha*. Korrynn Bello, with her frizzy blond hair. Little Bashar Brewer, my best friend. He's always looking out for me. Tall Boris Aramovsky, who is so good at chess. Theresa Spingate, so *gorgeous*—I wish I looked like her. Jason Yong, the bully who always sneaks up on me and yanks my braid.

Kevin O'Malley, the boy who is so pretty it sometimes hurts to look at him. All skin and bones, nothing like the man he will become.

And a brown-haired girl with a snotty look on her face.

Nyree Okadigbo.

I *hate* her.

The girls wear white blouses and plaid skirts. The boys, white shirts and black pants. School uniforms. We're forced to wear these. I want to wear pants, but that's not allowed for girls.

"This is so boring," Theresa says. "Like I need to see any of this."

She twirls a finger in her perfect red hair. She's trying to get O'Malley's attention. He's not watching her. Aramovsky is, though.

The world seems to expand around me, the dream-memory taking on detail.

Up above, the long ribbon of light that runs through our world. In front of us, a red wooden building with white trim: a barn. Green grass. Mud and dirt. Black cows. A pen with black pigs. A few chickens—also black—running loose.

A man walks out of the barn. He wears a funny hat. He smiles, that stupid way adults smile at kids they don't know.

"You all are here to see where your food comes from."

Aramovsky lets out a heavy sigh.

"It comes from the cafeteria," he says. "This trip is preposterous."

He's trying hard to look bored. So is Theresa. They're both nervous, though. I've learned that I can tell how people really feel, sometimes when they don't even know themselves.

"We kill animals quickly, with as little pain as we can," the farmer says. "That's the humane way. But it's not a pleasant experience. For some things to live, other things have to die. You understand?"

O'Malley and Bello nod. Okadigbo pretends not to hear. Aramovsky is busy looking at his shoes.

"Today, you'll watch us harvest a pig," the man says. "These are tame animals, but we still have to be careful. A pig is a strong creature. Any animal will fight hard once they realize they're in danger."

Aramovsky sighs again. "Right. Sure. Our pork chops are dangerous. What a stupid blank."

At that last word, Bello shrinks in on herself. *Blank*. It's a bad word, like *empty*.

The farmer is a grown man, much bigger than we are. No symbol on his dirt-smeared forehead. His hands are callused. He's supposed to avert his eyes, defer to the Cherished, but he stares straight at Aramovsky.

"You brats think you know so much. Here's something you don't know. The pig you eat for dinner? If you're not careful, that pig can hurt you. It can *kill* you. A pig will eat anything— grass, dirt, bugs, crops, meat, cloth, wood . . . even *bone*."

Aramovsky doesn't look bored anymore. He's surprised, as am I, that a vassal would talk to us this way.

Okadigbo, though, finally perks up. She loves it when someone challenges her. Or her friends. She lives to put people in their place.

"I guess we don't have to worry about killer pigs," she says. "Since no one in my *lacha* will ever stoop so low as to work on a farm."

The farmer glares at her. Unlike Aramovsky, Okadigbo doesn't back down.

"I suppose not," the farmer says. "Come with me."

He takes us into the barn.

On the way in, Okadigbo stops, stares down at her shoe.

She stepped in shit.

Yong sees this, laughs a cutting laugh.

"Idiot," he says.

Okadigbo looks at me. She smiles.

"Clean off my shoe, Matilda."

My face grows hot. She's doing this in front of O'Malley?

The farmer steps closer. "No need for that nonsense, missies. Just come along."

Okadigbo turns on him, her eyes alive and eager.

"Shut your mouth, *blank*," she says. "Or I'll tell Cardinal Reyez how you were staring at my legs in a way that made me feel funny."

The farmer's eyes go wide.

"I'm sorry," he says. "Very sorry. My apologies, miss."

Okadigbo smiles at me. She lifts her foot.

"Well, empty? Before we watch the little piggy get slaughtered, clean this shit off my boot."

I'm so mad at her. I hate her. I want to see her die.

Brewer grabs a rag off a fence rail.

"I got it, Mattie," he says, smiling as always. "I'll take a sample and use it for my project on animal digestion."

Okadigbo slowly shakes her head.

"If my shoe isn't cleaned, *by Matilda,* then Matilda gets the rod."

Brewer stops in his tracks.

She's done things like this before. If I don't do what she says, she'll tattle. I'll be punished, because I have to do what she says—I *belong* to her.

Bello stares at the ground, hugging her shoulders. Aramovsky grins at me, happy the power structure is back to the way it was before the farmer yelled at him. Kevin O'Malley has no expression at all.

No one will help me.

I reach for Brewer's rag.

"You can use the rag after," Okadigbo says. "To wipe off your hands."

I didn't do anything to her. I didn't say anything to her. Why does she humiliate me like this?

I *hate* her.

I want to see her die.

I want to see *all* the tooth-girls die.

Someday, I will make that happen. I *swear* it. But if I don't do what she says, the priests will hurt me.

I kneel before Nyree Okadigbo. I reach for her boot.

FIFTY-NINE

A stinging pain jolts me awake.

I reach to slap it away, but my hands won't move. I'm bolted down.

Of course you're bolted down, stupid—how many times do you have to get "stung" in the neck before you realize it's just a needle?

It's not a snake biting me in the dark. I'm not trapped, waiting for a monster to come get me . . .

. . . because I *am* the monster.

Aren't I?

No, I'm still me. And I am her.

I am ancient.

I feel *young*.

It worked: all my sacrifices, my plotting and planning . . . I have another chance, a chance to live my *own* life and not what others planned for me.

It worked: I'm still *me*, I remember waking up trapped in a coffin, meeting Spingate and the others. I remember the walking and the fighting and the laughter.

So many years, so many *centuries*. My memories are frag-
ments of a shattered vase, pieces all over, pieces missing.

Was the human mind ever meant to exist this long? To soak
up a millennium's worth of faces, names, places, experiences,
feelings, sensations, emotions?

It *worked:* I beat that silly girl.   It *worked:* I beat that horrid
                                         old woman.

My mind . . . it's splitting in two.
Who am I?
I'm Matilda Savage.
No, I am not no you're not no we're not . . .
I'm Em.
That's not who you are Em is gone you're not her . . .
I am . . . I am no one.
My scream—desperate, piercing, born from a terrified, an-
cient mind, driven by powerful young lungs.
What is happening to me?
The sound of machinery. My restraints snap away. Light, so
bright it's *blinding*.
"Em, calm down."
The one voice I truly need to hear, Spingate, calling to me. I
feel her hands on my wrists, firm but comforting.
"It's all right," she says. "You're safe."
Safe. That word again. The word of nothing. The word that
doesn't exist.
Theresa says I'm safe . . . but . . . but Theresa is dead. I had
her killed because she betrayed me. How can she be talking to
me now? She is a revenant come to drag me to hell.
I try to fight her but I'm still weak from the process.
The process.

| It worked it worked it | It failed it failed it failed . . . |
| worked . . . | |

Hands stronger than Theresa's slide under my arms, lift me up, hold me.

"Em, relax, I have you now."

Ramses.

| One lover of many. | The only boy I've been |
| | intimate with. |

No . . . Ramses is dead. I saw him die . . . I saw *me* kill him, during the fire in the Observatory . . .

I killed Ramses. So how is he holding me now? And O'Malley . . .

I killed Kevin.

My soul is tearing to pieces, cracking like the plaza stone when the Grub rose.

That thing Em saw . . . the	I told you! I told you and you
God of Blood can't be that it	wouldn't listen!
can't be that.	

The God of Blood has me, *all parts of me,* he's going to punish me for killing O'Malley and Yong, for all the rebels that died, for the butchery I did to my own people to show everyone on the *Xolotl* that I was the only way into the future, the way to life itself, punish me for all the Springers I slaughtered, for the city I destroyed, for the Wasps I shot and burned, for the—

"Shhhhh," Ramses Bishop says. "I have you now. *Breathe.*"

I breathe.

My panic ebbs. I am not free of fear, but it no longer controls me. I open my eyes, I look upon the face of Ramses Bishop.

He looks *so young*. . . .

"I have you, my love," he says. His words are sweet like chocolate. "I won't let anyone hurt you."

No, he won't hurt me.

It is I who will hurt him.

A little bit at first, because he's young and the young have hope that life will turn out the way they *want* it rather than the way it actually does. Later, I know his hurt will be so much worse, so much more.

Eventually, he will accept things.

For now, though, I have to give him his first taste of pain, the first tiny tear in his big heart.

"I have you, Em," he says. "I'll never let you go again."

"I'm not Em."

His smile fades. Spingate steps into view. The fear that left me must have pounced on her. I see growing despair in her eyes.

"Yes, you are," she says. "Just focus."

I almost feel bad for these two young people, for these . . . *infants*. They are beholden to their emotions, as they will be for many years to come.

Behind them, another face steps into the light. A face that is black, wrinkled and withered.

"Hello, Matilda," Jason Yong says. "I'm so happy to see you again."

His voice drips with malice, but the two children seem oblivious to the threat. Yong wants to kill me. He always has. Ever since the revolt. He's always wanted to be the leader.

No . . . it's not *me* he wants to kill.

"I'm not Matilda," I say.

I assume Yong will think I am lying, because I've lied to him so many times before . . . but from the look on his gnarled face I know he believes me.

He's been my foe for centuries. He and that bastard Victor.

To think that Old Victor and I used to *date*? The Em part of me is aghast at the Matilda part.

"Whoever you are," Yong says, "you have to finish the ritual."

He offers me a ceremonial knife. It's black. The hilt is decorated with two rings of rubies, one inside the other.

O'Malley used a knife just like this to kill the older version of himself.

And I used a knife just like it to kill O'Malley.

He was still in there. . . .

Bishop snatches the blade away.

"I'll do it," he says. "Em has been through enough."

Yong reaches for the blade. "She has to do it herself, that's the ritual."

Bishop easily pushes the smaller Grownup away.

"I said *no*. Don't test me, Yong."

Past the foot of my coffin is the black X. A withered, sagging body—*my* body—hangs limply, head down, wrists held by shackles. She's moaning softly.

Not *she* . . . *me*. Is that what I look like?

No, what I *used* to look like. Now I am Em, I am Me. Matilda is gone.

Not gone, right there, still alive, I am still alive that evil bitch is *still alive* . . .

But not for long.

The ritual must be completed.

I hold out my hand toward Bishop, palm-up.

He stares at it. "Em, don't do this."

"She has to," Yong says.

Spingate grabs my wrist, tries to push it down.

"Em, Bishop is right! We'll vent her into space, you don't have to be the one."

I grab Theresa's wrist with my free hand, and I squeeze. She snarls, thinking she can hold on, thinking she can resist me, but I squeeze tighter until her snarl shifts to a look of surprise, then pain—she lets go with a gasp.

So much *strength* in this body. I haven't felt anything like it in a thousand years.

"The knife," I say to Bishop. "I will do what must be done."

My words sound as cold as the void itself. I want this over with.

Bishop glances at the knife, then at my palm, then he looks me in the eyes.

"It is my right," I say.

He slaps the handle into my palm. My fingers close around it. I feel the weight.

A small, weak voice calls out: *"Help me . . . please."*

Matilda. *Me.*

I walk toward her. My steps are slow and awkward, yet stronger than they have been in a millennium.

Matilda's head is still hung low. She's pulling at her shackles, weakly, making the chains rattle like a sad, small musical instrument.

"Didn't work," she says. "Gaston, dammit, you . . . you screwed it up."

I stop in front of her.

Matilda's pitiful efforts cease—she's looking at my boots.

"No," she says.

She slowly lifts her head. Even this slight motion seems to take everything she's got.

Her one good eye is pink.

I am looking at Matilda. I am looking at myself. I am looking at a monster. I *am* a monster.

"*No*," she says. "I want to live."

She is an old woman. Ancient and twisted. She did what she thought was right. I can't remember all of what happened to her—to us, to *me*—but I know she felt justified in every action.

But was it her, or was it the "God of Blood"? Was she corrupted, just like Aramovsky was? I was Matilda, once—maybe those memories will return someday, maybe I'll know the answer.

"It's not fair," she says. "I want to live."

But even if Matilda was corrupted, she is responsible for the horrible things she did. Aramovsky had to pay. So does she. I touch her cheek—gnarled skin that was mine a few moments ago feels wretched and vile to these young fingers.

What does a thousand years of agony sound like? It sounds like Matilda.

"It didn't work," she says. "Why didn't it work?"

I almost feel bad for her. "It worked well enough. You knew what would happen. You knew one version of you would be chained here, knew that version would end. And you didn't care. So selfish, right to the end."

She finds the last of her strength, shakes her head hard enough to rattle the chains.

"Let me go! If you kill me, you won't get the codes!"

This is beyond confusing. My head spins in a dozen directions. At my core, though, I know she and I can't both exist. I had a chance to kill Matilda once. I let her live—look at the price of that choice.

"You already gave Gaston the codes. Remember?"

Her one eye stares at me. It's redder now; she's slowly regaining her strength.

She should die with a blade in the belly, in agony, like O'Malley did, but I can't bear to cause unnecessary suffering.

It's time to do the humane thing.

I put the point of the blade on her sternum. I expect firm resistance, but the bone beneath the coal-black skin gives a little, as if her skeleton is spongy with rot.

"I want to live," she says.

I nod. "And I want you to die."

The fingers of my right hand curl tighter around the hilt. My left palm cups the pommel. My strong, young arms push the blade forward.

It sinks in slowly, steel vanishing into blackness, blade hissing against skin until the cross guard thumps into her chest.

There is no winner here. No loser. Em earned a chance for her people. Matilda got her young body.

Thick, red-gray blood drips down from Matilda's sternum, splatters onto the floor.

"I hate you," she says.

"I know."

With that, I pull the blade free.

I stand there and watch Matilda Savage bleed to death.

When she stops twitching, I walk back to the golden coffin. Ramses and Theresa stare at me as if I am an alien thing. Yong simply watches, his feelings indiscernible.

"You say you're not Matilda," he says. "And you're not Em, either?"

I shake my head. Bishop and Spingate exchange a glance. It's obvious they wish with all their tender hearts that I will suddenly wake up and declare, *I was wrong, I'm your little friend, I'm Em!*

But that will never happen.

Yong's red eyes swirl. How I hated looking through eyes just like those, the way they let me see so many things and yet made everything different. I hated that body, too—so *ugly*. In the first few centuries, we called our bodies "pain suits," a joke meant to help us cope with the constant state of agony.

But I don't hurt now. Not at all.

It has been so long since I was without pain that being without it, feeling *normal*, seems maddeningly strange.

My memories roil and clash. They combine to make me recall things that I know never happened. Tiny shards of reality, like small islands in an endless haze of gray.

"If you're not Matilda," Yong says, "and you're not Em, then who are you?"

Parts of me are a woman older than even this ship. A woman who has done unspeakable things, who lost friends, who lost lovers. A woman who can't remember the face of her father, because he's been dead a thousand years.

Parts of me are a girl, barely past the age of twelve, who was thrust into a position with demands far beyond her years. A violent girl who fought and clawed, who learned to be devious because that was the only way she and her friends could survive. A girl who would *not* stop, no matter what the odds.

Two identities. Two completely different people.

And yet, both identities are unified in one key area.

Because both did the things that had to be done.

And in that commonality, I coalesce, I unify as the myriad shards meld together, lock into place like the pieces of puzzles that I am so good at solving.

Brewer warned that the longer Em was awake, forming her own memories and mental connections, the less likely the overwrite process would work. O'Malley was still in there. Some of Bello was as well. But Em was her own person for far longer than those two, and her intellect was too well developed to destroy. Instead of being overwritten, she and Matilda *fused,* their identities and experiences amalgamating into one individual.

An altogether new person.

Brewer. My childhood friend. I called him by his first name back then, I called him *Bashar.* He had a name for me as well.

I am not Em.

I am not Matilda.

I am neither—I am both.

I am something new.

"Mattie," I say. "My name is *Mattie.*"

Ramses, Theresa and Jason stare at me. The kids are crushed— they think they've lost someone they love. Yong looks . . . not *elated,* exactly, but so *hopeful.* I'm sure he's wondering if I'll unite all the people and lead us against the Wasps.

The multiple parts of me are talking to each other, comparing notes, seeing the connections that everyone else missed, that we *both* missed.

I'm not Em, I'm not Matilda, but one thing has not changed— I will do what must be done.

"Ramses, darling-dear, do something with this knife," I say. "We don't have much time, and I need to plan."

SIXTY

stand alone in the Tactical Control Center, watching the clock
tick down.

12:15:26
12:15:25
12:15:24

There isn't time for expansive plans or multiple options. I've
invited just five people to help me decide what to do, the only
five people who really matter for what happens next—Bishop,
Borjigin, Zubiri and both Gastons.

Like the rest of the *Xolotl,* the TCC was built twelve centuries
ago. Much of the equipment is dark. Lifeless. I wonder how long
it's been each piece stopped working, wonder if—somewhere
back on the planet Solomon or elsewhere in the universe—entire
empires rose and fell during that time.

The room is round, wide enough to hold twenty people easily.
Curved wall panels are displays, like those in the shuttle. A
quarter of them are blank and black. Others are peppered with
dark spots of varying sizes, like the overhead lights in the Gar-

den. A few panels flicker maddeningly. Those that work correctly show images of Omeyocan, the green dot of the *Dragon* following the red dot of the *Xolotl* around the planet's curve, inexorably closing in.

The Wasp ship is faster than ours—it's too late to make a clean getaway. I felt the God of Blood's power. Even if we break orbit and head straight out into space, I know the Wasps will follow us. They will not let an enemy go, risk that enemy coming back sometime in the future.

The Wasps want to wipe us out.

12:14:59

12:14:58

12:14:57

Memories rush back at a breakneck pace. I'm having trouble understanding what happened when, and to whom. The memories of the farm: those were burned into Matilda's thoughts forever, were the spark against the kindling that lit the fires of revolution. The memories of my parents sending me away, though . . . those memories had been mostly lost. Matilda's brain had blocked out what happened in the canoe, and much of what came after.

My mother and father said the Church of Mictlan was a farce? I/Matilda had completely forgotten that. I/she was only six years old at the time. The merging with Em shook up my long-term memory, broke loose things I didn't even know were there.

The Em part of me wondered if something caused Matilda to wind up so "evil." The Em part had no real past, was able to form her personality off of Matilda's core essence without the contamination of the bad things Matilda experienced. If Em was still around, if she knew what I know now, I wonder if that knowledge would answer her question.

All of this—the church, the *Xolotl,* the symbols, the rituals—
was began by a coppery worm burrowed deep in the dirt of a
distant planet. I can't recall most of the journey from Solomon.
I can't even fully recall how the rebellion began. Those memories will return, I feel them surging, reincarnating, but what matters right now is the next twelve hours.

Old Gaston—the "Admiral," as he prefers to be called—was
betraying Matilda. Since the debacle on Omeyocan where Old
Bishop and the others died, he'd been feeding Yong and Old Victor information. After my overwrite, he opened the doors to let
in Spingate, Bishop and Yong.

There was no one left loyal to Matilda and her cause, because
Matilda's true cause was *Matilda.* Centuries of dictatorship have
worn down the Cherished. They are ready to do whatever they
can to keep the human race alive.

12:13:46

12:13:45

12:13:44

Each second is a knife driving through flesh to gouge bone.
Our lives, our very existence as a people, are in danger of being
snuffed out forever. This is more than just *survival*—for all we
know, we're the last of our kind anywhere in the universe.

The doors to the TCC open. Young Gaston comes in first, followed by Zubiri, Borjigin in a wheelchair, then Old Gaston with
Bishop right behind him.

I'm sure the Admiral wants to overwrite his younger self, but
Bishop will not let that happen. I need both Gastons right now.
The Admiral has immeasurable experience and knowledge of
the *Xolotl.* Young Gaston thinks faster and he's got firsthand
experience fighting the Wasps.

I sent Bishop to round up these people. There has been no
formal declaration of leadership, so I make it now.

"I led the Cherished. I led the Birthday Children. Now I lead everyone. There isn't time for debate. There are decisions to be made. I will make them."

Bishop simply nods once.

The Gastons exchange a glance, but say nothing.

Borjigin looks like hell. He's hurting. Not as much as I was every day for centuries, but his pain is no laughing matter. There is no argument left in him.

Zubiri, though, wrinkles her nose as if she just smelled something bad.

"So, you're Matilda in Em's body?"

Such a pretty girl. A shame she lost that arm.

"Call me *Mattie*," I say. "I am neither. I am both. But that doesn't matter right now—I'm in charge, understand?"

She nods, but that nose doesn't unwrinkle. She's less than convinced. I like her.

"We have to act," Young Gaston says. "They're coming for us."

"I agree," says his older version. "If it's going to take a blood-bath, let's get it over with."

It is difficult to see them next to each other. Part of me has known Old Gaston almost my entire existence. *Centuries* of working together, arguing, fighting side by side, killing, watching those we love die. He is the Admiral. He has seen us through countless technical difficulties and disasters that could have wiped us out. Another part of me has known Young Gaston almost my entire existence. The little boy who became a man. He's just as much a warrior as Bishop is, as Em was.

12:13:01

12:13:00

12:12:59

"Admiral," I say, "how long will it take to prep the five fighters for launch?"

"I started that process as soon as you went into the coffin," the gnarled old man says. "Arming, fueling and systems checks are already under way. The fighters have barely been touched in decades. Flight testing revealed multiple failed parts that must be replaced before launch. Some of them have to be fabricated from scratch. Crews need another six hours."

"And is the shuttle fueling as well?"

Young Gaston nods.

He is more perceptive than Bishop. Far more. Young Gaston has no illusions—he knows his dear friend Em is gone forever. Maybe he's already cried enough, or maybe he will cry later. For now, he's pushed his pain aside to focus solely on our problem.

"Well done," I say. "What is the flight time from the *Xolotl* to Uchmal?"

Young Gaston's eyes narrow. He starts to ask *why,* then checks himself.

"Approximately one hour, fifteen minutes," he says. "But remember, the fighters can't fly in atmosphere. Only *Ximbal* can make that trip."

I look at the wall display, take in the position of the *Xolotl,* Uchmal and the *Dragon.*

We have to try. "Borjigin, Zubiri, I need you to build a Goff Spear cannon in the shuttle, and I need it done in nine hours or less."

Borjigin gives his head a little shake. "A Goff Spear cannon. In the shuttle."

"Correct."

He blinks a few times. "I assume to shoot a nuke at the *Dragon*?"

"Correct again."

He blinks faster. "And you want that done in nine hours?"

"If you need me to repeat the whole thing, young man, I will."

"Ridiculous," Zubiri says. "Strapping bombs to the wings is one thing. Engineering a cannon that can fire a round with enough velocity to penetrate that kind of armor is another. *Ximbal* is ancient. You want us to, what . . . to *hack* a twelve-century-old spacecraft? Make it do something for which it was never intended?"

I nod. "If you can't do it, the *Xolotl* will be destroyed, everyone aboard will die, and the human race might go extinct."

They stare at me.

"Wow," Borjigin says. "Not like you're putting pressure on us or anything."

"I prefer reality over pep talks. And *Ximbal* will be going into combat, so make sure your cannon is well armored."

Zubiri holds up her hand palm-out, waves it in a *wait just a minute* gesture.

"The Observatory's Goff Spear cannon was *twice* as long as the entire shuttle. Barrel length determines velocity. If we can find a way to put a launcher in *Ximbal*—and that's a big *if*—the round won't be moving as fast. That means the Wasp mother ship will have more time to shoot it down. I won't explain the math, but it matters. To score a hit, we'd have to fire from very close range."

I was hoping for better news, but I'll take what I can get.

"You make it fire, I'll take care of the distance," I say. "We'll assign every Cherished gear and half not working on the fighters to help you, but *you two are in charge*—make it work or everyone dies. Go get it done."

They trade one more glance, then they hurry out of the TCC.

12:12:14
12:12:13
12:12:12

"Admiral, give me a list of those who have fighter-pilot training."

Through Matilda's memories, I recall how all symbols except circles received extensive training from ages four to ten. Neural programming combined with chemical memory coding and hands-on repetition resulted in hardwired skills. Just like Bishop knew how to perfectly throw a spear without being taught, Kenzie Smith knew how to heal and Borjigin knew how to fix machines, some of our people can fly the Macana fighters—even if they don't know they possess that ability.

Old Gaston calls up a list of seven names. Many of those names trigger partial impressions, snippets of a face or the color of hair, strands of moments we spent together. My head throbs— I can't tell the difference between Matilda's past and Em's.

Aramovsky, B.
Dibaba, Z.
Goldberg, M.
Kalle, C.
Kalle, C.
McWhite, C.
Walezak, B.

Matilda's memories roil like an angry ocean. No circle-stars were trained as pilots. The Founder wanted them ready to defend the *Xolotl* against boarders, or even board other vessels themselves.

Pilots were drawn from SPIRIT, MIND and STRUCTURES. None from HEALTH, because doctors are expected to tend the wounded, and none from SERVICE, because how could a lowly *empty* manage the intricate complexities of a starfighter?

Dibaba, Goldberg and McWhite . . . all Cherished. Matilda knew/knows them well.

Kalle is there twice, once as a Grownup, once as a Birthday Child.

Aramovsky and Walezak: our double-rings doing double duty.

Five fighter craft. Seven potential pilots.

"Young pilots are preferable," the Admiral says. "So much of combat is about reaction time."

I don't think Bernice Walezak can handle the pressure. Any mistake, no matter how small, could spell doom for all of us. I need people strong of mind. People like Kalle—both versions of her, I imagine. Neither will like this assignment, but they don't have any choice.

Is Aramovsky strong enough? He's spent a year in that cell and he didn't crack. He was willing to die to stop me from killing Spingate. This is what he's waited for, a chance to make good on what he did.

"Aramovsky, Kalle—old and young both—McWhite and Goldberg," I say. "Get them whatever refresher training you can come up with on short notice. Prepare Dibaba and Walezak as well. They'll be backups in case anyone washes out."

"Tell me your plan," the Admiral says. "Because if you're going to fly five decrepit Macanas and a hot-rodded shuttle against the *Dragon*'s exceptional fighter craft, we might as well take as many drugs as possible so we're stoned out of our gourds by the time the Wasps blast us to pieces."

Young Gaston nods. "You saw what happened to the *Goblin*'s interceptors. We can't attack the *Dragon* head on."

"We're not going to," I say. "We're flying *Ximbal* to Uchmal. We're going to destroy the Grub."

The Gastons fall silent.

Bishop smiles. "I was hoping you'd say that."

His eyes sparkle. He doesn't believe what's happened to me is permanent. He probably still thinks I'll "get better," that true love is patient, that someday we'll settle down and have a family. The poor kid.

"But that doesn't help us," Young Gaston says. "Even if you kill the thing, we don't know if that will stop the *Dragon* from attacking the *Xolotl*."

"It might stop them, so we're *going* to kill it, but that's not the main goal," I say. "The Grub doesn't fear small weapons, but it does fear big ones. Like nuclear bombs. The Grub makes the species around it *protect* it, like a parent protects a child. I'm convinced the Wasps know we took at least one nuke with us. When *Ximbal* heads toward Uchmal, I think they'll assume the worst-case scenario—that we're going to blow up their new god. I believe the Wasps will scramble all remaining fighters to stop that from happening."

"That's a lot of assumptions," Bishop says.

I nod. "Remember how you felt on the training ground when you attacked Victor from behind? You wanted to protect Em. Imagine feeling that way about the Grub, only a thousand times more powerful."

Bishop looks down. The memory of that moment still disturbs him.

"She's right," he says. "If the Wasps think we're attacking the Grub, they won't take any chances. They'll send everything they've got."

Young Gaston shakes his head. "So what? You just said the

mother ship will attack us regardless. Why risk the shuttle to kill the Grub?"

"We're going to nuke the Grub, because it *needs* to die, but that's not our main goal," I say. "That strike is a functional feint to draw their fighter cover away. Once we destroy the God of Blood, we go full-burn straight up—we'll use *Ximbal* to attack the *Dragon*."

The Admiral gives a slow, dramatic clap. "Well done, Empress. Only about a billion things that could go wrong, but if none of them do, we'll have one shot at taking out their mother ship."

I smile at him. "You have any better ideas, old friend?"

"If I did, I would have said so already. I'm in."

The younger of the Gastons is far from convinced.

"The shuttle has slightly superior thrust in atmosphere, but once the battle moves into space their fighters will tear *Ximbal* apart. And the fighters won't be the *Dragon*'s only defense. Just like the *Xolotl*, it will have onboard gunnery to combat any incoming threats."

I already know that, because the Matilda part of me remembers the battle against the Springer mother ship. The endless salvos of missile fire, both ships shooting down as many missiles as possible but some getting through. Both ships being hammered, over and over again.

"That's why the *Xolotl* will attack," I say. "As soon as the *Dragon*'s fighters engage the shuttle, we change the *Xolotl*'s course and go straight toward the Wasp mother ship. We launch every missile we have, force the *Dragon*'s point-defense batteries to counter that assault. That won't give our shuttle a free pass, but it might tie up their counter fire enough for the shuttle to get close enough for that single shot."

Bishop crosses his arms. "We don't even know if Borjigin can build the Goff Spear cannon in time. If he can, we're putting our faith in an untested weapon. If it fails, we need a boarding party on the shuttle. Maybe we can blast our way in, damage their engines, slow them down long enough for the *Xolotl* to escape."

Young Gaston sighs. "You know that's a suicide mission, right?"

"This whole thing is a suicide mission," I say. "Even if the plan works flawlessly, *Ximbal* probably won't make it back."

All three men nod.

Bishop squares his shoulders, juts out his chin. "I don't care. I'm going. I'd rather die on my feet than on my knees."

"Very dramatic," Old Gaston says. "But don't worry about your feet or your knees—you'll probably die sitting on your ass in a gunnery chair before you even get close."

Twelve centuries old and he still feels the need to make sarcastic comments.

"Bishop is going," I say. "And so am I."

The Matilda half of me screams inside: *Why did we go through all of this, why did I* WIN, *if you're just going to kill us anyway?*

Em wants to live, too.

I don't care about either of them. I am *Mattie*. Mattie will do what must be done.

Young Gaston sighs again, rubs the heels of his hands into his eyes.

"Well, you two aren't going to hog all the glory without me. I'll pilot *Ximbal*."

"No," the Admiral says, "I will."

There's no room for misguided heroics. I need the best person for the job.

"His reaction time is better," I say. "You just told us that mattered."

The Admiral nods. "It does. Experience matters more, as does anything that would cloud the pilot's thoughts at the moment of action."

The old Gaston turns to the young.

"I didn't have kids. I focused only on the mission." He gestures to his withered body. "Then I did this, putting off a family until I reached Omeyocan and got my new body. After seeing what happened to Matilda when she tried to overwrite Em, I know that even if you and I agreed to join, *both* of us would end. Someone new would take our place. I can't ask that of you. Your babies are the children I never had. If this plan succeeds, they need a father. I'll have ensured my line continues. My life will matter. After all this time, it will *finally* matter."

The Admiral's words echo Brewer's. I feel the same. We've spent centuries bound up in a grand lie. This is a chance to do something good, something for others instead of for ourselves. We've lived our lives—it's time for the next generation to live theirs.

Young Gaston stares, dumbfounded, at his creator.

"I thought you would try and kill me. Like Matilda did Em."

I start to remind him I'm still alive, but that's not what he means. He's right—Em Savage is gone forever.

"You thought wrong," the Admiral says. "And besides, I've been at Matilda's side for a millennium. She doesn't get to be the only one to die a glorious death worthy of song and legend. The two of us will go out in a blaze of glory."

"Hey," Bishop says, "what about me?"

Old Gaston glances at him. "I have bad news for you, son. I watched your progenitor grow from a boy into a man. No matter how old you get, you still won't be able to grow a beard worth a crap."

Bishop's eyes dart to Young Gaston, who grins and strokes his thick beard. Bishop's face turns red.

Men—we're all about to die and he still actually cares about who can grow thicker facial hair?

Young Gaston steps closer to the ancient version of himself, puts his right hand on the wrinkled old shoulder.

"Hail, Admiral," he says. "Thank you. I don't know what to say."

For the first time, perhaps the only time, Xander Gaston is humbled.

Old Gaston puts his hand on Young Gaston's shoulder.

"Say the truth, that we're really doing this because *I'm* the best pilot that's ever lived—you'll have to tell your children that you're the *second* best."

"Ah, I see," Young Gaston says. "I thought I might eventually grow out of being an asshole. Good to know that will never happen."

The Admiral actually laughs.

11:59:37

11:59:36

11:59:35

I tell them the rest of the plan.

SIXTY-ONE

Time waits for no man. Or woman. Or hybrid.

    2:26:14

2:26:13

2:26:12

Beautiful, streamlined *Ximbal* looks like huge children grabbed it, shook it, dented it, then glued on whatever parts they could find. Man-sized ball mounts are crudely embedded on both sides of the ship, just behind and below the cockpit, and also on both sides just in front of the rear engines. Silver cannon barrels stick out of each ball.

Nine hours ago, I put out a ship-wide call: *We will soon be under attack. I need volunteers for a preemptive strike—but know that those who join me will not be coming back.*

There's actually a small chance that we *will* be coming back, but I wanted people who were willing to give their lives for everyone else. I expected a handful of volunteers. I got hundreds.

No time for vetting, for interviews, to establish who would be the best crew. I looked at the amassed Birthday Children, Cherished, New People, Springers, and I trusted my instincts.

Circle-stars will man the new turret guns, and be ready to board the Wasp ship if that's needed. Yong begged me to be part of this. I think he wants to die in battle, as any proper circle-star would. Joining him are Bishop, Bawden and Young Victor. They are our best marksmen, our best fighters, and that means we must have them.

Old Victor asked if he could join. He begged, too, but his body has been failing him for a long time; there is no margin for error, so he stays here.

If boarding is necessary, we also have two Springers with us: one of Barkah's huge bodyguards—a male named Shumalk—and Lahfah.

Barkah tried to stop Lahfah from coming. He's too wounded to join, and even if he wasn't, I'm not sure he'd volunteer. He ordered Lahfah to stay. She refused his order. He then ordered me to not let her come. I ignored him. If Lahfah is willing to do for her people what I am willing to do for mine, then that is her choice to make. Not his. Barkah tried to drag Lahfah away. I had young circle-stars remove him from the landing bay.

On Omeyocan he was king. Here, I am *empress*.

I take orders from no one.

Lahfah and Shumalk will also be part of the damage control team, along with two Cherished, two New People, and me.

The two Cherished are halves who know *Ximbal*'s systems. They both lost their receptacles at the Battle of the Crescent-Shaped Clearing—Abrantes and Aeschelman. Their receptacles died because the Em part of me ordered Spingate to fire missiles at Borjigin's giant. Now the older selves volunteer to die by my side.

War makes strange bedfellows.

The two New People are my "grandson" Marcus and a woman named Benga Basuki. She is a mother of three. She's so committed to the lives of her children she's willing to die for them. I think Marcus volunteered out of some sense of obligation rather than a genuine desire to sacrifice himself for the greater good; he is the leader of the New People, after all. I'd rather not have either of them, but the New People will need their heroes just as will the Birthday Children, the Springers and the Cherished.

I made sure every group is represented. I can't have future generations point to one group and say, *You didn't do your part.* If we win, there will be a memorial to the heroes who undertook this mission—that memorial will show *all* of the *Xolotl*'s cultures.

I don't know a thing about the *Ximbal*'s systems. Neither do Marcus, Benga, Lahfah or Shumalk. We've quickly been taught how to use "weld wands," how to use sealant to fix punctured pressure suits, how to patch holes, how to mend split cables and a handful of other simple tasks.

I am ancient, so jaded I see even full lives as brief flickers of light that snuff out before they've truly begun to burn. Matilda watched thousands die, for her cause and simply from old age. Over and over and over again on the *Xolotl*'s journey, she saw children born, watched them grow, saw them wither, saw them die.

Because of that, I feel little for the people who are going with me. We serve the greater good. It is the smallest member of our crew, though, that draws a pang of sadness. The purpose of this mission is to fire the Goff Spear—for that, Zubiri must be aboard. She is our expert. Borjigin designed the cobbled-together Goff cannon, but he's too wounded to join us.

The final member of our crew is a circle-cross Cherished: Francine Yilmaz. Like the Admiral, she has no desire to overwrite her younger self. Like Brewer, she wants her life to matter. That gives us a doctor on board to patch up minor wounds and get people back into the fight.

Turned out Old Kalle's hands shake constantly. She couldn't work the Macana controls, so she's out. Walezak broke down and cried during the refresher course. She can't handle the pressure, so we can't use her. Fortunately for us, Zoe Dibaba is ready and eager to fill Old Kalle's seat.

Our five fighter pilots: McWhite, Goldberg and Dibaba, people I've known for centuries, as well as Aramovsky and young Kalle, people I've known—in a strange way—my entire life.

A few centuries ago, Chris McWhite and Matilda had an intimate relationship. It only lasted a few years, but we both enjoyed it and parted on good terms. Goldberg is a wonderful poker player. Dibaba was an ally of Brewer—I never liked her, but she's ready to do her part, and for that I accept her as my ally.

Young Kalle glares at me constantly. She doesn't want to risk her life. I'm not giving her a choice. Lucky for her, Gaston thinks the fighter pilots have the best chance of returning alive.

The Admiral will pilot the *Ximbal*. Noam Peura volunteered to be the copilot. He's as scared as ever, his voice cracking on every word, but he's going.

Our last chance at survival: Eight Cherished. Two New People. Seven Birthday Children. Two Springers.

And me.

I am the *only* overwritten person. I suppose I am my own culture, a "Hybrid." Yes, that name should work for my last three hours of life.

I think of a quote I once heard: *I will never be old. To me, old age is always fifteen years older than I am.* Perhaps that quote worked for a 60-year-old looking at 75-year-olds—I wonder if it still applies when you turn 1,208?

Ximbal's crew and the fighter pilots gather beneath the shuttle wing for final instructions. I stand there, my helmet under my arm. I should give a rousing speech, but that was Em's role. We either succeed or we die. If people need more motivation than that, I can't help them.

My spear. For the first time, I realize it's still on Omeyocan. I'm not sure where I lost it. It has been with me almost constantly for a year, and I didn't even realize it was gone. I suppose it served its purpose—we no longer need a symbol of leadership. The role is mine until I choose to give it up.

The Admiral quickly reviews the plan. When he tells us to get to our positions, most do.

Aramovsky lingers for a moment, then approaches me.

Like all of us, he wears a thick gray pressure suit. It makes his lanky frame look thicker, more solid. He holds a helmet under his right arm, visor reflecting the *Ximbal*'s lights. He cuts a dashing figure—the hero pilot off to save his race.

"Em, I just wanted to thank you."

Physically, he is on the edge of being a fully grown man. Yet to me, he is beyond young. I am a millennium older than he is.

"My name is *Mattie*. Em is gone."

He pauses, nods.

"You always talked of *gods*," I say. "Now we're going to kill one. You sure you're ready?"

The tiniest sneer curls his upper lip. His eyes sparkle with hunger, a desire for revenge.

"I'm ready. When someone dies, we say, *Let the gods welcome him home.* I wonder what gods say when *they* die."

I reach up and grip his right shoulder. "Kick some ass, Boris."

He smiles, then heads to his fighter.

The Macanas are black, long and sleek. They sit so low I could swing my leg over the side to get into the cockpit. The fighters all bear the scars of an old battle. No wings, just a tube with an engine on one end, a Gatling gun on the other. Six thick poles angle back from behind the cockpit, each ending in a small thruster. Those change the ship's orientation. A rear gunner is supposed to sit behind the pilots, but the rear guns were all cannibalized for parts, even the seats—those spaces now sit empty.

Someone spray-painted a white null-set symbol on the side of each fighter. Drips of paint stretch down like frozen white blood.

I look at *Ximbal*. Sure enough, someone painted the same symbol on the fat black missile mounted under the shuttle's right wing. The Goff round is inside that missile. The nuke has been modified with something called a "chemical timer." Now we can fire the missile in close to make sure it hits, and use the forty-five-second delay to get clear of the blast radius.

I board the shuttle, climbing a ladder that takes the place of the still-missing metal ramp. I walk left, into what was the coffin room. Now it is a mass of thick plates welded in for extra protection. The length of the room has been converted to an ugly-looking contraption made of metal, plastic and, in some places, even wood. The construct holds several fused sections of the *Xolotl*'s ruined Goff Spear. Halves and gears spent six hours in exosuits, cutting free every straight bit of that warped barrel. Borjigin's genius showed itself yet again—he combined several small pieces together to make this weapon.

The Grownup engineers hadn't thought of that possibility. Maybe they are too old to be creative. They were very impressed with Borjigin's ingenuity. They should be.

We haven't test-fired the new cannon, of course. We can't. We don't know if it will work. If it does not, there is no hope.

Past the cannon's rear end is a hastily built metal rack, also covered in patchwork armor. Inside the rack, I can just make out the hexagonal shape of a Goff round.

One round in a missile for the Grub, one in the cannon for the *Dragon*.

Zubiri is working away, busying herself with final adjustments. She wears a thick pressure suit. She doesn't have her helmet on yet—I see tears on her dark-brown cheeks.

I have lived a hundred lifetimes. She has barely begun to live just one.

Together, we will both die today.

Admiral Gaston's voice rings through the shuttle.

"*Gunners, perform final checks, then retract barrels and button up for reentry. Everyone, remember that no battle plan survives contact with the enemy, and contact them we will. Stay calm, solve problems. And may the gods have mercy upon our enemies, because we sure as hell will not.*"

His words move me. I'm shocked: as old as I am, I didn't think that was possible. Xander Gaston—the Admiral—has been my friend for twelve centuries. Of course he could find the words to motivate, to inspire, even in the face of death.

2:17:46

2:17:45

2:17:44

It's time to fight.

I head for the pilothouse.

SIXTY-TWO

Ximbal streaks toward Omeyocan.

The first time it came, it brought children desperate to stay alive.

This time, it brings death.

1:01:13

1:01:12

1:01:11

I stand in the pilothouse. My charged bracelet is held in a bracket on the bulkhead wall. On one thigh, strapped over my pressure suit, is the sheathed knife I used on Omeyocan. On the other, my weld wand in its holster. My external pockets are stuffed with small tools, tubes of sealant, sheets of patch material.

Abrantes is on my right. We're assigned to damage control here. He knows engineering. I do not. Which means I—the "empress" of my people—will function merely as his assistant, as an extra set of hands.

In front of us, bathed in light, are the Admiral and Noam Peura. We all wear thick gray pressure suits—unless you look through our clear helmet visors, Birthday Children and Cherished look exactly the same.

All four of us are held firmly by tentacle-arms that extrude from the ceiling.

The pilothouse walls appear transparent. Below us, night falls on the vast yellow, brown and blue spectacle of Omeyocan. One way or another, this will be the last time I set eyes upon the planet that our prophet promised to us thirteen centuries ago.

I've made a decision. If I survive this mission, I'm done being the leader. My memories are returning. Em's dream burns as bright to me as it did to her—I'll write the history of what brought our people here. I think I'll even use a paper and pen. Who knows? Perhaps I'll create a new kind of "holy book." My sins and mistakes can become a source of wisdom for future generations, a how-*not*-to guide of life, if you will.

That's *if* I survive. Which, most likely, I will not.

"*Attention, shuttle. This is the* Xolotl.*"*

The voice comes from the walls. It is Young Gaston.

"*Ximbal* here," the Admiral says. "Descending toward Uchmal to make our run."

"*Be aware,* Dragon *has launched sixteen small craft. Relaying tracking info to your systems now. You're about to hit that electrical interference, so I'll lose contact with you. Good luck.*"

Sixteen fighters. We thought they had only eight. They kept some in reserve. We can only hope those sixteen are all they have left.

Old Gaston glances back at me through the haze of glowing symbols that surround him.

"Looks like your plan worked," he says.

Well, aren't I the smart one?

The interference. From here on out, the *Xolotl* can't reach us, can't warn us of any further threats. That means the *Dragon,* similarly, can't warn the Wasp fighters. At least we hope that's the case, because our entire plan hinges on it.

"They'll close on us before we reach Uchmal," the Admiral says. "We'll have to go through them to hit the Grub. If we survive that dogfight, they should all be chasing us when we go full-burn for the *Dragon.* Do you want to proceed, Empress? This is your last chance to abort the mission."

In truth, I'd love to abort. This hacked-up, ancient bucket of bolts going head-on against sixteen advanced enemy fighters? That's not a positive equation. But we only have this one shot. And we need them behind us anyway for the plan to work.

"Continue as planned," I say.

Old Gaston pushes a floating icon.

"Attention, attention." His voice rings through the shuttle. "Sixteen bogeys incoming, estimated contact, two minutes. Gunners prepare to fire. Damage control crews, get ready."

There's no point in straying from our approach path. We *want* the Wasps to see where we're going. I take a deep breath, try to enjoy the last few minutes of smooth flying.

Abrantes turns to look at me. Red eyes stare at me through his clear visor. His mouth-flaps are wet.

"You know how people always said you were a bitch?"

People have said that. For a long, long time. *Bitch* is what they call you when you won't do what you're told.

I nod.

"You're different now," Abrantes says. "I like you better this way."

With that, he faces forward.

Well, well, well. In my final moments, I've made a new friend.

Past the Admiral, through the pilothouse walls, I can just

make out the city of Uchmal, a distant spot nestled in the blanket of yellow jungle.

"Here they come," Old Gaston says. "Ten o'clock and down."

I look left. Through the darkening sky, sixteen points of light streak toward us.

The Admiral's hands move quickly. He's not as fast as Young Gaston, true, but his movements are confident and sure.

The shuttle shudders. Em's memories tell me we've just fired missiles. Glowing flashes shoot away, trailing smoke tails that quickly fade into the growing blackness.

The Admiral barks last-minute orders.

"Bishop, ignore the lead ships, focus on third and beyond. Yong, I'm going to bank left and down when they pass, so they'll be above you when they come into your arc. Bawden, Victor, hit anything that comes at our rear."

If the circle-stars answer, I don't hear them.

Ximbal banks hard, throwing me against my restraints. Abrantes grunts from the strain. A glimpse of a flash as a missile detonates. A new vibration from the floor beneath me as turret guns open fire.

A shudder and a roar. A man's scream. Air rushes in, loud as the angry shout of a god. The transparent wall to the right of Abrantes turns black.

"Pilothouse damage," Peura says, his cracking voice spookily calm. "Savage, Abrantes, please patch holes and repair the display."

He said *please*. We're getting shot to hell, and the boy is polite?

"Hold on to your privates," the Admiral says, then the world whirls as he throws *Ximbal* into a tight, diving spin. The arm that holds me keeps me from flopping around, stops me from smashing into the pilothouse walls.

The shuttle stops spinning—my head does not. I blink, try to get my bearings. Ragged tears in the floor beneath Abrantes, in the wall to his right.

Then I see the hole in his left hand.

Wild winds catch the red-gray stream pouring from his palm, scatter his blood all over the place.

Abrantes pulls sealant from a pouch on his suit, squirts the entire tube into the hole. The expanding foam seals both the suit and the wound.

"Don't just watch, Savage," he says. "Get those holes in the floor!"

He moves to the wall and opens an access panel.

Ximbal banks hard left and climbs. The mechanical arm keeps me on my feet, letting my body move a little to diffuse the momentum, then bringing me back to where I just was.

"Today, Savage," Abrantes screams. "Patch those holes!"

I grab my weld wand from its holster. From a big pouch on my chest, I pull a sheet of patch material. The shuttle shudders and vibrates around me: missiles launching, cannons firing, bullets tearing into us. The bottom end of the weld gun is a vibro-blade. It buzzes so fast it looks like a ghost, goes through metal like butter. I slice away ragged shards sticking up from the hole. Bits of metal scatter, thrown in all directions by Old Gaston's mad maneuvers.

Through the hole, the nighttime jungle of Omeyocan streaks by beneath us.

I place the patch over the hole, then run the weld wand's glowing blue tip along the edges. In seconds, the roar of rushing air dies down a little bit.

"Display repaired," Abrantes calls out.

I patch another hole.

Ximbal spins violently. Blood rushes to my head. The arm

holds me in place. Something hits us, rattling so hard my arms and legs flop around like those of a rag doll. When I put my feet back down again, they slide in something wet.

In the wall Abrantes just fixed is a hole the size of my chest. Abrantes lies on the floor in two pieces—he's been torn in half. Red eyes stare out. The fingers of his right hand flex and twitch.

"Abrantes," Old Gaston calls out, "my rotational damper is sluggish, fix it."

"He's gone," I say.

The Admiral turns in place, glances at the ravaged body, then again looks out *Ximbal*'s clear front.

"Peura, disengage, repair the damper," he says. "Savage, don't just stand there like an idiot, patch the damn holes!"

"Disengaging," Peura says. The lights covering him blink out. He kneels, opens an access panel.

Abrantes's guts are all over the floor. I kneel, slide a pile of them toward a hole. Swirling wind sucks them out with a *thwooop* of air. I grab a patch and seal up the blood-smeared hole.

The floor display is still working; I can see below us. We're coming in shallow, just above the treetops.

We're rushing toward Uchmal's walls. Far beyond them, the man-made mountain that is the Observatory rises up from the city center.

Two wall towers lash out at us with tongues of stuttering orange—the Wasps have installed their own cannons.

Something explodes to our left, then to our right. *Ximbal* begins to wobble in a way that I know is not good.

We fly over the wall. Beneath us, buildings and streets are a blur. A Wasp fighter flies past, trailing a fluttering cape of red and orange flame. It arcs down, smashes into a ziggurat and erupts in a fireball that quickly fades behind us.

"Starting our run," the Admiral says. "Gunners, keep them busy!"

We're flying north, directly above Latu Way. I can see right up to the plaza and the Observatory beyond it. The Wasps have set bonfires all around the Grub, a spotted ring of flame that casts flickering light upon the cause of countless deaths.

The God of Blood is massive. Wriggling and vile, it's already grown bigger than when we left.

Among the fires, I see tanks, eight-legged ticks, and tiny things moving around—*Wasps*. They surround their god. Are they worshiping it? Waiting for their chance to "merge" with it?

"Zubiri," the Admiral says, "prepare to fire."

I'm close enough that I can hear her voice through his helmet.

"Armed and ready. Forty-five-second delay to let us get clear."

That creature destroyed millions of lives—now it will pay the price.

I stand next to Xander. I point my finger forward and down, toward the coppery God of Blood.

"Burn that bastard son of a bitch, Admiral. *Burn it.*"

The Observatory rushes toward us, massive beyond compare. On either side of us, the city shoots past as a haze of black and brown.

"*Ximbal,* upon detonation, set rear pilothouse display to five thousand pulses per second," the Admiral says. "Our Empress would like to watch. Zubiri, release payload, now, now, *now.*"

The shuttle trembles. Everything vibrates, everything *thunders*. The howling wind cranks higher, screams so loud I'm sure the entire ship is about to shatter into a billion shards.

A flash of gold shoots forward, covering a thousand meters in the blink of an eye. I see a cloud of stone powder-puff up from the base of the Observatory's south wall.

The Admiral raises his hands to the ceiling: we tilt up, start climbing.

The extruded arm holds me in place.

I turn to face the pilothouse's back wall, which shows everything behind us as if the rest of the shuttle wasn't even there.

Our main engines blaze full-out. *Ximbal* shudders under the strain.

Fighters angle up behind us, giving chase. Past them, I see the plaza, the Observatory, growing smaller by the second.

Smaller . . .

Smaller . . .

A flash. The pilothouse wall darkens, protecting us against the blinding light.

The explosion happens in the blink of an eye, but the pilothouse screens slow it down for me, play out every millisecond in glorious detail.

A ring of orange flame expands from the Observatory's base, cascades across the plaza, engulfing the Wasps. They pop like a thousand tiny fireworks. The hated tanks are sent flying, melting as they tumble and spin. The ticks become splashes of liquid steel.

The ring of fire swallows the Grub. The coppery monster actually resists the blast of pressure and heat, survives it for the briefest instant, then massive chunks of metallic flesh fly free. Whatever passes for its blood instantly boils into dark-blue jets of steam.

The God of Blood's long jaws tear off, spin away.

Finally, the monster *bursts* as it vanishes in a growing ball of fire.

For a moment, the Observatory actually *rises,* as if it has engines of its own, then the impossible mountain swells and cracks.

The expanding fireball rips it into a million pieces that are swallowed by flame and lost forever.

The bomb's shock wave radiates out, leveling everything around it. In a flash, a hundred buildings disintegrate, their broken remainders scattered outward in a roiling hail of gravel.

Uchmal disintegrates. A fireball soars into the sky, turning night to day.

A sensation of pure satisfaction envelops me.

The God of Blood is dead.

I'll never know if the blast also killed the last two eggs. I hope it did.

I turn to face forward, see nothing but stars ahead. Peura is lit up again, back at his copilot duties.

"Accelerating," he says. "Full escape velocity."

The restraining arm holds me in place, but the thrust is so great that I feel my body *flattening*.

The walls blare with a piercing alarm.

"Eight bogeys in pursuit," the Admiral says. "We have enough distance that they won't shoot for fear they'll have to fly through their own bullets. They'll wait to attack until we escape the atmosphere. Rear gunners, hold your fire until they get closer."

We killed half of them. Will that be enough?

The seconds roll by.

The Admiral twists a glowing icon. "Exiting the stratosphere."

The wounded *Ximbal*'s constant shudder starts to taper off. Less air resistance up here, I think.

"Exiting mesosphere," the Admiral says. "Rear gunners, here they come!"

I turn to look at the rear wall. Eight glowing streaks blaze toward us, closing fast. They are directly behind us.

I look forward once again: our trap is springing shut.

Five black blurs dive straight at us.

Just as we couldn't see the Wasp mother ship hiding behind the *Goblin,* our shuttle is directly between our pursuers and the Macanas—the Wasp pilots have no idea our fighters are about to pounce.

The Macanas rip past us so fast I hurt my neck turning to watch them attack. The five craft instantly close on the Wasp fighters, Gatling guns blazing. Our five pass by their eight, leaving behind explosions so rapid and bright I squint against the sudden light.

"Six enemy fighters destroyed," Old Gaston says. "We lost one of ours."

I don't ask who died.

The two remaining Wasp fighters turn and bank, moving into another exchange with our Macanas. The pilothouse wall magnifies action that would otherwise be nothing but tiny lights.

The enemy ships move like they were born and raised in space itself. Our Macanas seem clumsy and awkward in comparison. As the fighters pass by each other, a Macana sparks briefly, then slowly spins toward Omeyocan. I silently wish for it to pull up, to gain control—it does not. If that pilot is still alive, he or she has only minutes to live.

The loss is costly, but it lets our three remaining Macanas get behind a Wasp fighter. A flash of light; the enemy ship breaks up into a hundred pieces.

Now it's three against one.

Our fighters bank and twist, coming at the lone enemy from multiple directions. I hold my breath, watch the Wasp fighter's impossible maneuvering. Another of our fighters sparks, then breaks into tumbling pieces.

In the end, our numbers prove too great. Our last two fighters close in—the final enemy craft glows brightly for a split second before snapping in two, both halves spinning away.

"Enemy bogeys destroyed," the Admiral says.

The pilothouse walls crackle first with static, then the sound of a familiar voice.

"*Macana Four to Ximbal. We should be outside the interference range, do you read me?*"

It's Kalle.

"We read you," the Admiral says.

"*No damage,*" Kalle says. "*Ammo capacity down to sixty percent.*"

"*This is Macana Two, no damage, ammo at seventy percent.*"

Aramovsky's voice.

The Em part of me breathes a silent sigh of relief, while the Matilda part grieves a little more—McWhite, Dibaba and Goldberg are all dead.

Peura is panting so hard his breath steams up the inside of his visor. He's terrified.

"Multiple casualties in rear section," he says. "Zubiri reports the Goff launcher is damaged."

"*Dammit,*" Xander says. "Opening up all comms. Savage, get back there and see if you can help."

The metal tentacle-arm releases me, slithers back into the pilothouse ceiling.

I'm weightless. I'd forgotten about that. I turn and clumsily push for the rear wall, bumping into the floating top half of Abrantes as I do. I spin the wheel lock and open the pilothouse door. I kick off the frame, shooting through the corridor to the area that used to be our coffin room.

Benga Basuki has no head. The stump of her neck trails a bobbing stream of shivering red liquid. Old Yilmaz floats lifeless, her suit torn open, ripped red-gray-coated intestines dan-

gling behind her slowly spinning corpse. The air is clouded with
detritus: severed limbs, bits of metal, chunks of plastic, splinters
of wood, a Springer leg. A stab of panic and loss, wondering if
the leg belongs to Lahfah, but I see her trying to patch a head-
sized hole in the hull.

Zubiri, Lahfah, Marcus and Aeschelman are cutting and pulling on the twisted remains of the bomb rack. I'm not sure why
they bother—the front half of Borjigin's launcher is ripped to
shreds. A half-dozen gaping holes in the walls, ceiling and floor
reveal stars twinkling against the blackness of space.

Yong, Bishop, Bawden and Victor must still be manning their
guns.

Admiral Gaston's voice in my helmet: "We're closing in. The
Xolotl will be in missile range shortly. As soon as the *Xolotl*
engages the *Dragon,* we make our run."

We're so screwed.

"Admiral, this is Savage. The Goff launcher is ruined."

"Then *fix* it! The *Dragon*'s ship-killing cannon will be in
can't-miss range in . . . dammit, twenty-three minutes, eleven
seconds."

"This thing is *not* going to fire," I say. "Can we attack their
cannon? Can Kalle and Aramovsky attack with us?"

"Our weapons are too small to punch through its armor. And
we won't get anywhere near it—their point defense will focus on
protecting that cannon and their engines. Figure out another solution, fast."

I try to stay calm. All of my parts—Matilda, Em and Mattie—
struggle against the fist of stress and anxiety that squeezes tight
my soul.

I shoot across the coffin room, grab onto the twisted bomb
rack to stop myself. The rack is a mess, but the hexagonal gold
bomb itself . . . it looks undamaged.

"Zubiri, will that thing still detonate?"

She wedges herself into a space in the wreckage, leans close to the bomb. She's looking at a readout of some kind.

"Arming computer is fried," she says. "Twenty minutes to fix it. But what difference does it make? The launcher is destroyed."

"It's a *nuke*," I say. "Can't we just get the shuttle close and detonate it?"

"The *Xolotl* survived two proximal nuke strikes," she says. "Goff rounds work because they penetrate the ship's armor, explode from the *inside*. Without the launcher, we can't generate enough velocity to do that. Just setting off the bombs won't stop them."

There has to be a way. *Has* to.

Wait . . . maybe there is . . .

"Admiral, their ship has the same layout as ours, right?"

"From everything we've seen, the ship designs are almost identical."

"So you know where the *Dragon*'s landing bay would be?"

"If it's in the same place as ours, yes."

"The younger version of you opened the *Xolotl*'s landing bay doors from the outside," I say. "You know how the emergency access works?"

"Of *course* I know how that works!"

Even in this dire situation, Xander can be offended? Amazing.

"If it's the same, could one of us open the landing bay doors?"

There is a pause.

"You want to nuke their ship from the inside?"

"Yes. Can you open it or walk someone else through the process?"

He should be the one to do it, but I need him piloting *Ximbal*.

"Yes to both," he says. "That's assuming the access system is identical."

I glance at Zubiri. "Does the landing bay count as *inside* their armor?"

Wide-eyed, she nods.

"Admiral," I say, "as soon as the *Xolotl* engages with missiles, take us to the landing bay."

In a half-destroyed shuttle with the survival of our race on the line, Admiral Xander Gaston starts to laugh.

"You always were a bitch, Savage, which is why I always followed you. Aramovsky, Kalle, on my wings. Gunners, prepare to board—we're going in."

SIXTY-THREE

'm in the pilothouse, the extruded arm wrapped around my waist and chest.

0:8:57

0:8:56

0:8:55

The Admiral is piloting. Peura is getting ready for his exo-walk. It will be up to him to get us in.

I pull my bracelet from its bracket, slide it up my arm over my pressure suit.

Xander has put the countdown clock in the upper right corner of our helmet displays. When that timer hits zero, the *Dragon*'s version of the Goff Spear will fire—the *Xolotl* will die.

As *Ximbal* closed in on the *Dragon*, I used my remaining patches to pin Abrantes's body to the deck. *Both* pieces of it.

Out in the void of space, two massive starships launch missiles at each other, a crisscross of shooting stars.

The *Xolotl* is tiny, a flickering dot thousands of kilometers away.

The *Dragon* is close; its slowly rotating cylinder takes up most of our view. The smooth copper surface reflects Omeyocan's reddish sun in a burnished gleam. The *Dragon* looks almost new, completely unscarred by battle.

That's about to change.

A volley of *Xolotl* missiles closes in. Most are destroyed by the *Dragon*'s point-defense guns, but some get through, impact with frightening fury, kicking up massive fireballs that spray out expanding clouds of copper shards, leave liquid yellow craters cooling quickly in the void's freezing embrace.

"Landing bay in view," the Admiral says. "Mapping defensive batteries that can hit us when we're close. Aramovsky, Kalle, transferring locations to your targeting systems—take them out."

"*Roger that,*" Kalle calls, her voice tinny and full of static. "*Come on, Boris, let's cook 'em!*"

The two sleek Macanas zip ahead of us, one above, one to our right. I don't know who is in each one.

The *Dragon*'s big gray landing bay doors look *exactly* like ours—will the emergency access panel be in the same place as well?

Defensive batteries fire at us. The pilothouse walls flash as bright as the sun. *Ximbal* shudders, shakes.

"Damage to engine two," the Admiral says, calm as can be. "Shutting it down."

"What does that mean?" I ask. "Are we going to explode?"

"It means we've lost one-third of our thrust. We can still maneuver, but getting back to the *Xolotl* will be tough."

I almost laugh. He thinks we can go back? I assumed there was no chance of that. The thought that we might plant the bomb and leave—that I might actually *survive* in this young body . . .

Beneath us, the *Dragon*'s kilometers-long copper cylinder slowly rotates. Another *Xolotl* missile lands, creating another puddle of molten copper that quickly cools as it slowly rotates away from us.

Ximbal vibrates madly. The pilothouse walls start to flicker.

A defensive gun flashes one last time, then erupts in a gout of flame as one of our fighters takes it out.

"Great shooting, Kalle," Old Gaston says. "That was the last battery that can hit us. We're in the clear. Peura, you ready?"

"Ready," a thin voice calls back.

The Admiral maneuvers the shuttle into position, matching the *Dragon*'s rotation just like he did when we reached the *Xolotl*. My feet once again press against the floor—gravity has returned. It seems like we're perfectly still, a copper behemoth floating motionless above our heads.

Close by, a *Xolotl* missile hits and erupts, a here-then-gone flash of orange and spinning bits of metal. The crater's molten center briefly bubbles.

Peura's voice sounds in my helmet.

"Exiting airlock. Beginning exowalk. Wish me luck, guys."

A chorus of *good luck*s answers him.

The pilothouse walls flicker, giving me a staccato vision of a boy in a thick gray pressure suit floating through space. He is alone out there. The hopes of an entire race ride with him.

Peura was beyond brave to volunteer as copilot, but this? Exowalking on an alien ship while missiles explode around us? I wouldn't have thought he had it in him. Sometimes courage is carried by a roar—sometimes it is hidden within a wavering voice.

Ximbal trembles continuously now, the shake of a dying animal.

The approach to the landing bay: a deepening groove leading to flat gray doors. It looks exactly like the *Xolotl*'s. Exactly. Peura follows that groove, reaches the bottom corner of the massive doors. The flickering pilothouse display makes him look so close I could reach out and touch him.

Sure enough, there is a copper-colored access panel, right where Young Gaston found one on the *Xolotl*.

Can this uniformity of design be our savior?

Peura opens the panel. Beneath are parallel rings, just like on the *Xolotl*.

"Activating emergency access," he says.

He plants his feet on the copper hull. He pulls the handles back, dragging out their cylinders with them. He twists both handles.

I realize I'm holding my breath. I slowly let it out, and I wait.

The landing bay doors begin to open.

"I did it," Peura screams over the comm. *"It worked!"*

A flash of orange and yellow—a missile detonates between us and Peura. Copper shrapnel blasts outward, rips a dozen new holes in the pilothouse.

I don't move. I wait for the pain to announce that metal shards have punched holes through Em's young body.

"Peura, get your fat ass back in here," the Admiral says. His voice sounds strained, forced. "Engine three is out. We're down to one primary engine. Everyone, double-check your suit integrity—that shrapnel hit us hard."

My helmet would let out an alarm if my suit was breached, but I run my hands across my arms, legs, chest and head anyway, searching for punctures.

I find none.

The Admiral is not as lucky. His left arm hangs limply. I see air jetting from his shoulder, carrying droplets of blood with it.

"Xander, you're hit!"

I pull suit sealant from a pouch and squirt it into the hole.

"We need to see if you have internal bleeding."

He pushes my hands away.

"No time. Peura, are you in the airlock?"

There's no answer.

Through the flickering pilothouse wall, I see a gray-clad body floating out into space, frozen globs of blood trailing along, reflecting sunlight with jewel-like sparkles.

I turn to leave. "I'll bring him back."

"Stay *here*," the Admiral barks, his tone so commanding it stops me cold. "Peura is gone. We're going in."

He moves his hands, wincing at the pain. *Ximbal* heads down the trench.

Maybe dying a good death matters to someone who has lived a thousand years. Peura lived only *one* year. I wonder if he had a chance to kiss someone, or if he died not knowing what that felt like.

The shuttle slides over the still-bubbling crater and into the landing bay.

A rush of déjà vu. This hangar is so much like ours back on the *Xolotl*—arcing metal beams overhead, walls curving down to meet the metal floor. The same, yet different. Different tanks and racks of equipment, two of their lethal fighters half-disassembled. I see a troopship and for a moment hope we might use it to escape, but there is a huge hole melted in its side.

0:6:01

0:6:00

0:5:59

I turn my wrist left, then right, activating my bracelet. I wish I had my spear, but I don't. I draw my knife. My suit's thick gloves make holding it a little awkward.

Ximbal lowers. I feel the landing gear clank against the deck.

"We're down," Xander says, his strained words echoing through our ravaged ship. "Boarding party, go!"

SIXTY-FOUR

leave the pilothouse. Bishop and Victor are at the sliding external door. It looks like Swiss cheese. It won't open all the way. Each man has his gloved fingers hooked around an edge. They yank and lean away from each other, forcing the opening wider.

Not enough room for them to get out, but I'm smaller.

I slide through and jump down. I hear Bishop shout, *"Em, wait,"* then I land. I notice it right away—this gravity is lighter than the *Xolotl's*, than Omeyocan.

I sweep my bracelet arm before me, looking for targets.

There are none.

Any Wasps in here must had had time to get to interior airlocks before the outer doors opened.

The landing bay rattles.

"Wasps are shutting exterior doors," the Admiral says, his voice in my helmet. "We can't stop it. When they close, the bay will repressurize and they'll come pouring in. Zubiri, status?"

0:5:15

0:5:14

0:5:13

"Four minutes to arm," she says. "Then one minute to detonation."

"Cutting it close," the Admiral says. "Any longer and they'll
be able to fire their ship-killer at the *Xolotl.* Get it done."

We have five minutes to live. Five minutes to hold off the
Wasps. Five damn minutes to keep the *Xolotl* alive.

Bishop and Victor finally force the doors open enough to
drop down, drawing my attention to the shuttle, the vehicle that
has seen us through so much. It is *shredded.* In several places, I
can see right through it to the far side of the landing bay. One
wing dips at an angle. The rear is blackened, the metal slagged
by what must have been intense fire.

Ximbal let us escape Matilda. It kept us alive on Omeyocan.
Without it, we couldn't have killed the Grub. We wouldn't be on
the precipice of defeating our enemy. It is an inanimate object,
yet it hurts to see it so abused.

"Take cover," Bishop calls out. "We caught them by surprise,
but they're probably putting on exosuits now. We'll be under
attack even before they pressurize the hangar. Bawden, stay with
Zubiri and guard the bomb. Aeschelman, stay with the Admiral.
Everyone else, grab a weapon and get out here!"

I see an equipment rack packed with heavy metal boxes. I
sprint to it. Each step launches me farther than I expect. It's
all I can do to stop from falling—I'm moving too fast and
slam into the rack. I kneel and take cover as best I can. My
heart kicks like a mule. I feel my pulse in my eyes, hear it in my
ears.

This is where I will die.

Aramovsky's voice over the commlink, scratchy, hard to understand: *"What's the status? Kalle and I are ready to escort you back."*

"Negative, Aramovsky," the Admiral answers. "Too much damage for us to get back. We're staying here. Go home."

"Bullshit," Aramovsky says instantly. *"We're not leaving you."*

The huge doors clang shut, making the entire hangar reverberate.

"Landing bay repressurizing," the Admiral says. "About two minutes to completion, but some of the internal airlocks are already cycling—we'll have company in less than thirty seconds."

0:4:22

0:4:21

0:4:20

More of my crew drop down from the ravaged shuttle: Yong, Marcus and Lahfah. Lahfah holds a Springer rifle. Yong has a bracelet on his right arm, a sword in his left hand. Marcus is empty-handed; his pistol is still in its holster. Human, Grownup, Springer, yet our gray pressure suits make us look like soldiers in the same army—except for Lahfah's tail, of course.

She hops once, soars high. She lets out a squeak of surprise.

Yong bounds toward a bulkhead that will give him some cover.

"Low grav," he says. *"Fantastic!* What a final fight this will be!"

Marcus stands there, confused.

"Marcus, to me," I call, waving my arm. He sees me, comes running, the suit making his movements clumsy and awkward.

"Mattie, why aren't we leaving? We have to get out of here!"

Through his visor, his face is a wide-eyed, open-mouth visage of panic.

"We're not leaving," I say. I pull his pistol from his holster, shove it against his chest.

He takes it, looks at it like it might sting him. He's not cut out for this. He's going to die here, just like the rest of us. I hope he can take a few Wasps with him.

0:4:01

0:4:00

0:3:59

If the nuke doesn't blow, all of this effort is for nothing.

"Zubiri, we still on track?"

"Almost there," she calls back. "Countdown clock is accurate."

The comm line buzzes with multiple voices.

Yong: "Kill 'em all and let the gods sort 'em out. Let's get some!"

Xander: "Internal airlock doors about to open."

Bishop: "Copy that. *Ximbal*'s nose is twelve o'clock for all directional call-outs. We can . . . Airlock opening at ten o'clock! *Here they come!*"

Ten o'clock is to my front left, past the shuttle. I see airlock doors slide open—a half-dozen Wasps pour in, their pressure suits red, not gray, their black rifles raging on full automatic.

Bracelet beams slice into them from several angles. The first two Wasps burst apart before they make it two steps into the hangar. I level my arm and flick my fingers forward, drop another one.

The rational part of me knows these Wasps are descendants of those who built their ship. In that way, they are no different than we are—fighting to stay alive, to protect their own kind. The emotional side of me, though, understands it is us or them, that this race has slaughtered my friends; every time my bracelet beam rips one to wet pieces, delicious satisfaction sweeps through my soul.

"Airlock opening at two o'clock," Yong shouts. "Take them out!"

The hangar devolves into utter chaos. I aim, fire, watch my beams cut down one Wasp after another. Bullets pound into the metal boxes in front of me.

A small metal ball bounces past me, skids out of view, then an explosion rocks me against the rack. Marcus falls to his hands and knees. He's lost his pistol. I don't think he fired a single shot.

Xander's voice roars so loud it distorts my helmet speakers: *"Landing bay fully pressurized, all airlocks opening—here they come!"*

0:2:24

0:2:23

0:2:22

Even through my suit and helmet, I hear doors hiss open, hear the screech-click war cry of Wasps rushing in. Strange heads, stranger clothes, fuchsia bodies. They're not wearing pressure suits. Some have guns, but most hold wrenches, pipes, knives, one is swinging a chair . . . these aren't soldiers, they were just the closest to the landing bay.

I flick my fingers forward, turning one into meat.

Aim, *flick.* Aim, *flick.* Aim, *flick.*

They are an avalanche—too many to stop.

"Eat this, you shit-bug bastards!" The Admiral's voice.

Ximbal's front right cannon turret moves—the thick beam lashes out, slashes through the oncoming wave of Wasps. Body parts fly in all directions, splash yellow blood on the walls, the floor, even the ceiling high above.

Marcus stands, tears off his helmet. He looks around wildly, chest heaving.

"Mattie, get me out of here! *Please!*"

I realize he's beyond the cover of our rack a moment before a bullet punches through his left temple and blows his brains out the right side of his skull.

He drops. Three Wasps rush around the rack. I react instantly. Aim-*flick*: the first Wasp erupts, splashing my visor with gore, but I'm already thrusting with my knife, through the blood-mist, driving the blade deep into the Wasp right behind. The third Wasp wears a red pressure suit, raises a rifle to my face.

I twist as it fires—the bullet burst hammers the metal boxes that protected me. I dive at the Wasp's legs. We both go down, sliding across splattered blood and chunks of flesh.

The Wasp reaches behind its narrow back, pulls a long knife. I thrust, he counters and slashes. I grab the wrist of his knife hand just as he grabs mine.

We roll across the deck, a desperate, primitive fight for life made awkward by the bulky pressure suits.

A massive explosion throws us hard against the rack. Metal boxes fall out, hit my helmet, bang hard against my shoulder. I fight the pain that clouds my thoughts, threatens to drag me into darkness.

"Gaston's dead!" Aeschelman, shouting over the comm. "They hit his gun with a grenade! They're rushing the shuttle, I'm falling back to protect Zubiri!"

Zubiri: "Almost there! Keep them off of me!"

Bishop: "Victor's down!"

I struggle to my knees.

My body won't respond . . . everything is sluggish, half-speed.

In *Ximbal*'s exterior door, Bawden half-hides behind a bullet-riddled bulkhead, one hand jabbing her pitchfork down over and over, the other firing bracelet beams, both weapons tearing into a dozen Wasps trying to climb up and in. I hear her guttural screams of rage . . . she doesn't make words, she gives voice to pure violence.

Yong bounds across the floor toward her—a spray of bullets cuts the ancient circle-star down in mid-leap. He hits the deck, skids to a stop against the landing gear.

He doesn't move.

The Wasp I was fighting rises, slashes at me. I twist away, but the blade slices through my pressure suit and cuts deep into my shoulder. I feel the edge glance off bone.

The pain is overwhelming.

I don't know where my knife is.

It slashes at me again. I fall to my back, barely avoiding a blade that trails a thin arc of my own blood.

The Wasp raises the knife high—a Springer hatchet arcs down, *thunks* through the red pressure suit and into the Wasp's back.

The Wasp twitches once, slumps to the side, hatchet handle sticking up at a strange angle.

Lahfah helps me up, then scoops up a loose Wasp rifle and starts firing away.

The hangar is filled with smoke. Raging flames cast strange shadows, making everything dance with light. Alarms scream. The dead are everywhere.

Movement—I look to the shuttle, see Bishop flying through the air, axe raised overhead, an impossible leap made possible by the lighter gravity. He roars as he comes down, kicking one Wasp away from *Ximbal*'s door, driving the blade down through the head of another. Somehow, he lands next to Bawden, who dies a split second later as bullets trace a tight line from her left hip to her right shoulder.

Aeschelman: "They found a way in!"

Zubiri: "They're coming! Help me, it's not ready yet!"

Bishop vanishes into the shuttle. Behind him, a handful of Wasps finally clamber through the door.

0:1:45

0:1:44

0:1:43

"Mattie, this is Aramovsky, what's going on?"

The idiot didn't leave?

"Get out of here, dammit! Get clear!"

"Screw that. Everyone, find something to hold on to, I'm coming in!"

My legs are knocked out from under me. The bloody metal floor smacks against my helmet. Spiderweb cracks spread across my visor, make it impossible to see. I grab at the helmet, tear it free. It rolls to the side, stops when it hits Lahfah.

She's lying next to me.

Through her visor, her three eyes are half-lidded, lifeless . . . she's dead.

Barkah will be heartbroken.

Three Wasps step over her body. Not wearing pressure suits. A wrench, an axe . . . only one carries what might be a gun, a small pistol.

Reality slows.

My final seconds stretch out. Time is thick syrup. I savor my last gasping breath, taste my own blood. Even the agony in my shoulder is delicious in its own way, for it is my body warning me of the damage, trying to keep me alive. *Life.* About to end.

A gun barrel presses against my temple.

It has been a good life—a *long* life.

A roar so loud the sound alone shakes me. Screeching metal, every atom in the hangar smashing together.

I'm still alive?

That roar . . . it wasn't the Wasp's gun.

Air moves around me. *All* of the air.

I'm coming in, Aramovsky said.

In an instant, time snaps back to normal and brings hell with it.

Wind screams, hits so hard it knocks the Wasps off their feet. A line of small explosions traces through the hangar door, slowly forming a wide circle.

Aramovsky is using his Macana's Gatling gun to cut a large hole in the thick metal—the landing bay is decompressing, *fast.*

Wind howls louder, pushes harder.

One of the Wasps tries to rise—the wind knocks it down, pulls it toward the ravaged door.

The heavy rack . . . its supports are bolted to the deck. I grab the support, hook the elbow of my wounded arm around it.

My helmet starts to roll—I snag it just before it's out of reach.

The second Wasp tumbles across the deck, the wind dragging it toward its death, dragging Lahfah's corpse as well.

A Wasp hand locks down on my ankle.

The ship trembles around me. I look to the landing bay doors just as the last Gatling gun rounds slice through it—the ragged-edged metal circle rips clear as explosive decompression hurls it out into space.

The wind blows so strong the Wasp is actually lifted into the air, its grip on my leg the only thing stopping it from being flung across the landing bay and out that hole.

The alien looks at me. The battle has been madness, a cacophony of sights and sounds and dangers, keeping me from focusing on any one thing. Until now—for the first time I see this race's *living* eyes. The eyes are magenta, with flecks of gold.

They *sparkle.*

Those eyes are perhaps the most beautiful things I have ever seen.

I recognize the emotion within them—the Wasp is terrified.

Not a soldier. A mechanic, perhaps? A craftsman? Is this intelligent being an artist? Does it make music? Have a family?

Its tight grip on my ankle is the only thing stopping it from being launched out into space. The wind batters me. The Wasp's weight adds to my own: the support digs into my elbow, makes my entire arm scream with agony.

I whip the helmet down on the hand that holds my ankle, once, twice, a third time.

Something in the alien's hand breaks.

The magenta eyes look into mine one last time, begging, *pleading* for life.

It wants to live.

So do I.

I bring the helmet down again, and the death grip finally loosens. The Wasp flies through the air. It hits the edge of the jagged hole, spins away, and is gone.

The wind dies out in an instant, easing the pressure on my arm. Internal airlock doors must have closed, cutting the landing bay off from the rest of the ship's air supply.

I can't breathe.

Fighting the pain in my arm, I put the helmet back on my head, lock it into place. Air pours in, oxygen fills my lungs.

The gunfire has stopped. The flames are all out. The smoke is gone. Warning lights continue to flash, but if there are alarms, I can't hear them, because there is no air in here to carry the sound.

0:1:06

0:1:05

0:1:04

The speakers in my helmet still work.

"This is Bishop. I've got Zubiri. Aeschelman's dead. Anyone else left?"

"I'm here," I croak, my voice barely audible even to me.

"Bomb armed," Zubiri says, her voice frail, dripping with pain. "One minute till detonation. Goodbye, everyone. I love you all."

Bishop saved her. Or, more accurately, he saved the bomb— she's going to die anyway.

As is he.

As am I.

And then, something flies through the blood-streaked hole in the hangar bay doors.

A Macana fighter . . .

Long and sleek and black and narrow, with a white null-set symbol spray-painted on the side. Reverse engines fire. It instantly slows to a stop, spins so the nose is pointed toward the hole. Landing gear hits the deck. The engines cut out.

The canopy slides back.

A helmeted pilot stands. A *tall* pilot.

Aramovsky.

I use the last of my strength, force myself to rise.

"Get out of here," I say. "You don't need to die."

He sees me. He leaps out of the cockpit and bounds toward me.

What is he doing? It's too late.

"Forty-five seconds," Zubiri says.

Aramovsky reaches me, throws me over his shoulder. I'm too spent to fight him. I'm cold all over.

He rushes back to the fighter, places me in the empty space where the gunner's chair once sat. I look back to *Ximbal*— Bishop is lowering Zubiri down to a waiting Victor. I thought

Victor was dead, but there he is, stumbling toward me with Zubiri in his arms.

Bishop drops to one knee—he's too weak to stand. He slowly tilts forward, then falls out of the open door and hits the deck headfirst. He rolls once, doesn't move. I see cracks in his visor.

Aramovsky sprints to him. Bishop is larger, but with the lighter gravity Aramovsky scoops him up and carries him with little more effort than he used to carry me.

"Victor," Aramovsky says, "put Zubiri in with Em."

Victor looks at me, at this tiny space.

Through his visor, I see his head shake. "There isn't room!"

"Then *make* room," Aramovsky says. "Just stuff her in there!"

I don't understand what's happening. This fighter is too small for all of us.

Victor dumps Zubiri on top of me. There are frozen bloodstains on his chest and shoulders, the holes filled with sealant foam. His every motion is pure agony.

The boy with the crush, the one who would do anything for me. Right to the bitter end, he is brave and loyal, willing to sacrifice himself for others. My heart swells with respect for what this boy—no, this *man*—has done for our people.

"Thirty," Zubiri says.

Victor grabs me, rolls me on my side. Then he grabs Zubiri, shoves her legs to her chest, puts her in front of me—I am the big spoon, she is the little.

Victor looks down at me; our eyes meet.

"I told you I'd follow you anywhere. It's too late to say it, but I'm in love with you."

He takes a step back.

"Twenty-five." Zubiri can barely speak the words.

Aramovsky is there, shoving Bishop into the pilot seat. There's blood all over Bishop's pressure suit. He isn't moving.

Aramovsky grabs Victor, lifts him and sets him in the pilot seat next to Bishop. The move is fast, definitive—I think Victor is in the cockpit before he realizes what just happened. The younger boy adjusts, tries to make two men fit into a space meant for one.

"Twenty," Zubiri says.

Aramovsky grabs Victor's hand, places it on a black joystick studded with controls.

"Move the stick which way you want to go," Aramovsky says. "Thumb button is thrust. Just get out of here, Kalle will help you the rest of the way."

"*Affirmative,*" comes Kalle's voice, tinny and scratchy from the distance.

"Fifteen seconds," Zubiri says.

Aramovsky reaches into the cockpit and presses a button. The canopy starts to slide forward. He steps back.

No . . . no, what is he doing?

"Get in," I say. "Get in here, *I'm ordering you!*"

He smiles at me. "No room."

The canopy closes.

In my helmet, I hear his last words.

"Find our people a home, Mattie. Victor . . . push the button."

The fighter shudders and shoots forward. The hangar doors rush toward us—we're going to shatter against them—and then we're through the ragged hole, swallowed up by the blackness of space.

Kalle's fighter banks in on our right.

"Seven seconds," Zubiri says.

"Full throttle," Kalle says. *"Now!"*

Zubiri and I are pulled backward as the Macana shoots forward.

"Three seconds," Zubiri says. And then, a last, energetic burst of hate: "I hope you burn in hell."

There is no fireball. There is no roar, no explosion that I can hear. A brief blast of static on the comm, then silence. For a moment, I see light reflected off parts of the fighter.

Then the light fades.

"Victor," Kalle says. *"Bank right. Just keep me at your ten o'clock and I'll get you home, okay?"*

Our fighter banks right.

I'm crammed tight in here, but there's just enough room for me to look out at the *Dragon.*

Or, more accurately, where the *Dragon* used to be.

Now that space is nothing but a cloud of debris, huge chunks and small bits alike spreading out in an ever-expanding, ever-thinning sphere. The massive cylinder is in a thousand pieces. Spinning copper shards the size of Uchmal's buildings reflect the red sun's light.

It is a horrid sight.

It is a spectacular sight.

We've done it.

We have killed our enemy. We are forever free.

"Victor," Kalle says, *"you still with me?"*

I feel cold, *so* cold.

Zubiri twists a little. My arm is over her. She pulls my hand to her chest, clutches it, needing any comfort I can give. I ignore the pain in my shoulder and I hold her tight.

"Yes," Victor grunts. "Still . . . here."

"Stick with me, kid," Kalle says. *"Stay conscious for fifteen minutes and we're home free."*

He says something else, but I don't really hear what it is.

Zubiri in my arms, I finally give in to the cold.

The darkness finally drags me down.

PART V

THE UNKNOWN

SIXTY-FIVE

I hear people talking.

The words lull me from a deep sleep.

"I think she's coming to."

Theresa's voice. She always seems to be there when I awake.

My eyes flutter open. I'm in a white coffin. I'm tired of waking up in these things. I'm in a small medical bay. It's warm in here. I feel soft blankets against my skin.

"Welcome back," Theresa says.

She sits by my side, her left hand resting on her round belly. Love in her eyes. A soft smile on her face. She looks tired.

In my mind, there are two Theresa Spingates. The beautiful girl I see before me now, the mother, the wife, the person who sacrificed so much for our people.

And the *other* Theresa.

The one who gave up her lovely face and perfect body to become a blackened, withered creature. The one who became selfish and bitter.

The one who betrayed me.

The one I ordered Bishop to kill.

No . . . *Matilda* gave that order, centuries ago. That wasn't *me*. I am something new.

I try to sit up. My body fails me.

"Take it easy," she says. "You lost a lot of blood. You were under for two days."

Maybe staying in the coffin a little while longer isn't so bad after all.

I nod toward her belly.

"How's the little one?"

Theresa's smile widens.

"Doing great. Kenzie tells me we're having a girl."

The baby . . .

Being pregnant . . .

Matilda had a child. I know only faint wisps of that moment. I wonder if those memories will return, or if they're gone forever.

My daughter . . . her name was Celeste. She had five kids of her own. Celeste didn't want to become Cherished. She wanted nothing to do with it, poisoned my grandchildren against it, against *me*. I watched her grow old. I watched her die. Then my grandchildren, all dying from old age while my wrinkled, transformed body carried on.

"We, um." Theresa looks down, uncomfortable. "We have a name for the baby. If you think it's acceptable."

I'm not sure why I would have any say in it, and . . .

Ah. I think I know.

"Korrynn. You want to name her Korrynn."

Theresa still can't look at me. She nods.

"That's beautiful," I say. "The name and the sentiment both."

Ramses Bishop steps into view. He looks horrible. Crutches

under his arms. Dark circles under his eyes. His skin, paler than normal. There are burns on his face and hands, only partially healed.

"You look like hell," I say.

He smiles. "Speak for yourself."

Even all that damage can't make him ugly. Ramses is a vision: strong, brave, loyal, dedicated. And yet I remember the *other* Bishop, the one Matilda knew. I remember the arguments. I remember the fighting. I remember love, then love dying, becoming hate, then even worse than hate—ambivalence.

Looking at his face, at his expression, I can see he doesn't understand yet. He's playing along, respecting me as Mattie, but he thinks that deep down, I'm still Em. He thinks he'll be patient, that he'll wait for me. He thinks I'll "get better."

He thinks we'll have a family.

I'll have to deal with that soon.

The pain is creeping in. My meds are wearing off. The bruises, the bumps, the stitches . . . I think a rib is broken. It's starting to feel like someone is pouring jagged gravel straight into my brain.

"Some bad news," Ramses says. "The incoming ship, the *Eel,* it has sped up. It will be here in six months. And we've detected two *new* ships heading to Omeyocan. The first will be here in about ten months, the second not long after that."

I close my eyes, rest my head on my pillow. *Three* ships are coming to this planet of endless war.

"Are we still in orbit?"

"The *Xolotl* took extensive missile damage," he says. "It barely survived. Gaston and Borjigin think we'll be ready to depart in another day or two, on your order."

Gaston. He means Young Gaston. *Old* Gaston—my friend of twelve centuries—is gone forever.

The first incoming ship is six months out. That gives us a little time, but we can't wait long. It could come after us just like the *Dragon* did. We need to be long gone before it arrives.

"Any word on the Wasps?"

Theresa nods. "Once you killed the Grub, that signal interference went away. Kalle and Opkick have been using the *Xolotl*'s instruments to observe the planet. Kalle thinks most of the Wasps were killed. Any that survived the explosion are likely dying of radiation poisoning. Uchmal—what's left of it—will be a no-man's-land for decades. Maybe centuries."

The interference is gone. The Grub produced it. Or maybe the Echo did. I don't think it makes a difference. One or the other or both wanted the races to fight up close and personal, where the hate could breed, where the rage could swell. I imagine in any war, you can launch bombs as long as you like, but sooner or later, if you want to take and hold territory, you have to put boots on the ground. Maybe the interference was meant to stop orbital ships from using high-tech targeting to take out small units, even single soldiers one at a time. Maybe it was meant to cause greater confusion, deprive armies of effective communication so chaos would rule and the strongest and most resourceful—not the most technologically developed—would win the day.

The interference persisted until we dropped that nuke.

I knew full well dropping the bomb meant I was poisoning the planet. Still, it's hard to hear that it actually occurred.

"And the Springers we left behind?"

"No sign of them," Ramses says. "Some small smoke trails from campfires far outside the ruins. Barkah thinks any survivors are long gone from the area, faded away into the jungle. He doesn't know where they went. Neither does Kalle or Opkick. Barkah is asking if we can go back for more, but Borjigin says he needs two weeks to synthesize enough fuel for a return trip to the surface."

Theresa leans closer. "Before you consider Barkah's request, I'll remind you the troopship is alien tech that we don't yet know how to maintain. If anything goes wrong, if anything malfunctions, whoever we send will be stuck on Omeyocan—we have no other ships to send. Borjigin and Gaston think it will take us at least a year to build another atmospheric-capable craft."

Two weeks for one trip back to the surface to rescue more Springers, and that's *if* we could even find them. Theresa makes the primary point painfully clear, though—if anything goes wrong, we lose the only ship we have that can take people from the *Xolotl* to the surface of any new planet we find.

I can't risk that. Not for the Springers, not for any of our people who might still be alive down there.

And we can't wait the time it takes to build another ship. The *Xolotl* is a wreck. Our missiles are depleted. We have no ship-killing cannon. All we have is a pair of Macanas, and those don't amount to much of a defense.

Which means if we're still in orbit when the *Eel* arrives, and it's hostile, we're dead.

The situation here is untenable.

Everything points in one direction—*away*.

"What about the Grub eggs? Did we destroy them?"

Theresa shrugs. "Kalle says there's no way of knowing, unless people start having nightmares."

"Or we start killing each other," Ramses adds.

I don't think we'll wait to find out.

Omeyocan has eaten up twelve centuries of my life, the lives of my friends, of our ancestors. Is it our job to make sure those eggs are destroyed?

No. It is not.

The Birthday Children have sacrificed enough. So have the Springers. And the Cherished, for that matter.

We've all known war. It's time to let something else run our lives.

"Tell Gaston to set a course for open space," I say. "Any direction that gives us the clearest path away from the three incoming ships. We are leaving, and we're never coming back."

Theresa glances at Ramses. He looks back at her. He nods. So does she.

It is done.

SIXTY-SIX

I ask Bishop to meet me in the Crystal Ball.

My body has healed. Mostly. The *Xolotl* has been repaired. Mostly. We are four days into our journey into the great unknown.

Our search for a new home has begun.

I will soon give up my leadership role, but not quite yet. Being the leader carries many burdens. It also carries a few privileges. One such privilege is taking the Crystal Ball as my own. This will be my personal space, my "office," if you will, for years to come.

When I was first here, there was a long-dead body on the metal grate floor, stabbed in the back by the spear that became our symbol of leadership. Quite fitting, when you think about it.

The spear is gone, of course. So is the body. People removed it, cleaned up the stains left by decomposition.

Most of the stains, anyway. In a few spots, the metal is permanently discolored. I think that's good—we should never forget the evil we've done to each other.

Em didn't know who that corpse was.

Matilda did—she set up that murder, watched it happen.

This place was where Bishop, Em, Gaston, Aramovsky and El-Saffani discovered we weren't in some endless dungeon, that we were in a starship, far above the land promised to us.

This was where Em first met Matilda.

Those two women are no more. I remain, a combination of them both.

I sit at a desk Borjigin crafted for me. It's made of gray stone, with the top polished flat as glass. He also found me a lovely chair.

My desktop is clean, uncluttered. The New People made me gifts: a glass inkwell, a quill made from a black chicken feather, and a thick, leather-bound book. The cover is branded with the null-set symbol. The pages are blank, save for the first one, where Barkah drew a beautiful image of Lahfah for me to remember her by.

The only other thing on my desk is a white porcelain cup sitting on a white saucer. Curls of steam slowly rise up from the tea inside.

I pick up the delicate cup and take a sip. I think of Korrynn Bello. She was right about one thing, at least—tea is *much* better than sholtag.

I wish she was here to have a cup with me. I lost her twice: once as Em's Bello, once as Matilda's Korrynn.

Losing friends once is hard enough. It's not fair I have to lose everyone a second time.

I stare out the Crystal Ball's clear walls at an endless sea of stars. In the direction of our current heading, there is nothing but empty space.

Behind us, a fist-sized crescent of yellow, brown and blue. Omeyocan, in shadow because we're heading away from it. I can also see tiny crescents of the planet's two moons, one bluish, one maroon.

Every minute we travel, Omeyocan appears smaller and smaller. Soon I won't see it as color, only as a point of light. Not long after that, I'm told, the *Xolotl*'s physics-altering engines—built from schematics provided by a five-hundred-million-year-old race of spacefaring aliens—will activate, and we will leave this area of the galaxy behind forever.

I hear feet on the ladder that leads down from our ship. I look up. The ladder seems to float there in space, connecting the Ball to a small hole in the *Xolotl*'s copper hull.

Bishop descends.

The hull looks a mess. The *Dragon*'s missile fire left huge craters, forever-frozen splashes in a metal pond. Some of the rings overlap each other.

I feel fortunate those strikes didn't take out the Crystal Ball.

I think of the people we lost on that desperate mission. Lahfah. The Admiral. Peura. Yong. Aeschelman and Abrantes. Yilmaz. Bawden. Marcus and Benga. Shumalk. McWhite, Goldberg and Dibaba.

Aramovsky.

He wanted redemption. He got it. I will make sure future generations know of him. Not just as a hero, but not just as a villain, either. My people need to understand that all of us are capable of change.

We don't have to be bad forever. We can fight our urges. We can *choose* to be good.

Zubiri has "retired" at the tender age of thirteen. She wants nothing to do with engineering or science, and *definitely* nothing to do with weapons and war. Maybe she'll change as she grows older. For now, she's chosen to raise pigs. The New People are teaching her their ways.

Victor is still in a med-chamber, kept unconscious by Kenzie. She says he should have died from his injuries. She's at a loss to explain how he was even conscious, let alone able to pilot that fighter back to the *Xolotl*. A bullet through his liver. Lacerated stomach. Punctured lung. And more. Kenzie tells me it could be months before he's out.

I've made sure Old Victor can't get anywhere near him.

Aside from myself, Zubiri, Victor and Kalle—who is as annoying as she ever was—there is only one other survivor of that mission: Ramses Bishop.

He reaches the bottom of the ladder. I stand to meet him. I take in his blond curls, his dark-yellow eyes. He is all smiles and scabs and scars.

"You look well, Mattie. Beautiful as ever."

I, too, am all scabs and scars, but I have no smile to offer. Even for a woman as old as I, this kind of thing never gets easier.

And yet, it must be done.

"Thank you for coming." I almost ask him what he thinks of the view, of leaving Omeyocan, but I realize that such pleasantries are procrastination, delaying the words that need to be said. Because I don't want to hurt him.

Perhaps there is still a bit of girl left in this ancient woman after all.

He's smiling, yes, but it's mostly empty. Hollow. He is happy to be alive, happy I'm alive, happy our people are safe. But, as I have, he's left a trail of dead friends in his wake. This huge, strong man is no brute. He feels deep loss. He knows great pain. His heart has been shattered over and over.

I am about to shatter it yet again.

"We can't be together," I say. "I am telling you, once and for all, that there is no *us*."

His smile fades. He blinks slowly.

"You . . . you're breaking up with me?"

That's not exactly right. I'm not the person he was with on Omeyocan—that was Em—but I nod anyway.

"I'm sorry," I say. "I don't want to lead you on in any way."

"But . . . *why*?"

"Because I'm over a thousand years old. I have a millennium's worth of memories and wisdom that give me perspective on life. You aren't even *twenty*. You are a man, yes, a great man who has sacrificed endlessly for our people and will continue to do so, but compared to my age you are barely even a child. It would not work. I am doing the right thing by letting you go now."

He stares at me for a few moments. He turns his head, gazes out at the blanket of bright stars.

"It's not fair," he says quietly.

I nod. "I know."

He wipes away a silent tear.

"I did everything I was supposed to do," he says. "I was a good person. A good man. I backed you every step of the way. Even when I knew I shouldn't. I changed who I was to be with you."

I reach out and take his big, scarred hand. I expect him to pull away. He does not. We lock fingers. Through his grip, I sense more of his pain—he desperately doesn't want to let me go. I remember how his hands felt against my skin. That part of me wants him still.

"You *are* a good person," I say. "Just not a good person for me. And I am not a good person for you, because the one you did those things for is gone. I'm not *me* anymore, Ramses."

He hangs his head. Another tear drips down. He sniffs once, then nods.

"I think I knew this was coming. I sensed you were different. I understand, Mattie . . . I just don't want it to be true."

I start to say *Reality is what it is whether we like it or not,* but I stop myself. He doesn't need a lecture. He doesn't need this explained. He is hurting enough without me adding to it by being a know-it-all asshole.

"You look just like her," he says. "I know your scars. I know how you got each and every one of them. Why do you have to look just like her?"

He lifts his head. Tears line his cheeks and he does not care. He is a warrior. He is a hero.

"We were *made* for each other," he says.

I nod. "We were. But we're mismatched in time. I know you'll find someone. You will make some lucky woman on this ship impossibly happy, and you will have your family."

He gives my hand a final squeeze.

Without another word, he climbs the ladder.

I watch him until he vanishes into the ship. Then I sit at my desk and gaze out at the stars.

Twelve centuries of wisdom, of watching people interact, of watching heartbreak and healing, it all tells me Ramses Bishop will be fine. That doesn't diminish his current pain, not in the least, but before he knows it he'll find love again.

Ramses Bishop will be happy.

Will I?

I am 1,208 years old. I have the body of a girl of eighteen. The Cherished are alien to me now, wrinkled black things that reek of a time of war and lies and blood and hatred. The Birthday Children are just that—*children.* The things they find important are mostly meaningless to me, things I left behind centuries ago. A few of the New People are a hundred years old or more, but even they seem like mere infants. Barkah and the Springers are another race entirely, friends but so *different* in the way they think and act.

My memories are coming back now. Although they are still a jumble, pieces are starting to fall into place. My final puzzle— that of my own past—is almost complete.

I open the book. I look at the picture of Lahfah, then flip to the first page.

It's blank.

I dip the quill into the inkwell, and I begin to write.

I made the sacrifices that needed to be made. For my people, I did what had to be done.

Because of that, I am the only one of my kind.

My name is Mattie Savage.

I am alone.

Epilogue

This is the life of Matilda Savage.
This is the life of Em Savage.
This is the story of our people, and our continuing journey.
And now, we approach a new planet. Will this be the place our next chapter begins? We can only hope.
If that happens—when it happens—I will create Volume Two of our history.
But for now, Volume One is complete.

> *July 14, 3892*
> *Signed,*
> *—Mattie Savage—*

I close the leather book.
I sit back in my chair, stare at the well-worn cover.
It's finished. I can't believe it.
I did it.

I finished my first book.

I've been alive for twelve centuries. I've accomplished so much. I didn't think I could feel this way again, reel from that rush of accomplishment. As I stare at the book—my constant companion of the last four years—I realize this is among the greatest things I have done.

Footsteps on the ladder. I'm not supposed to be bothered here, which means it can be only one person—the leader of our people.

The Crystal Ball is a disaster. There are food wrappers all over the metal grate floor. Scrolls, both tied up and loose, litter my stone desktop, as do crumbs and smears of meals past. I'm ever grateful we didn't bring ants with us into space, or they would live here for certain.

I've been wearing the same toga for days. For weeks, actually. I'm pretty sure I stink. *Bad.*

Some grand old matron of the human race I turned out to be.

I glance up: two people coming down, not just one.

I sweep as much of the garbage as I can off the desk and into the trash bin at its side, realizing too late the bin is already overflowing—I've made the mess worse.

The leader reaches the bottom of the ladder.

I straighten my toga as best I can.

"Hail, Maria."

Maria D'souza rolls her eyes at me.

"Do you *have* to do that crap, Mattie? We've been over this before—you can just say *hello.*"

She wears a green toga dotted with polished bits of steel. The Springers manufacture most of our clothes now, and usually decorate fabric with bits of polished glass, shaped copper, buttons of gold carved from old storage drives, anything that is colorful and fun. Not Maria, though—the only accent she allows is steel, which matches the polished rectangle hanging around her neck.

She chooses steel because that's what weapons are made from. She wants everyone to remember that war may come to us again, and if it does, we need to be ready.

Her forehead circle is gone. Kalle developed a way to surgically remove the symbols. No one has them anymore.

No one except me. I not only kept mine, I had it modified, added a line to it—my null-set symbol is part of who I am.

Maria didn't come alone. Little sandaled feet reach the last rung. The three-year-old boy turns, looks at me and smiles wide.

"Auntie!"

He runs to me and I pull him in for a glorious hug. I tousle his curly blond locks. With his mother's light brown skin and his father's hair and dark-yellow eyes, this boy will soon be a heartbreaker.

"Hello, Walter! Are you behaving?"

He kisses my cheek. When he does, his nose leaves a streak of snot on my skin. I don't even care.

"Ew, Auntie," he says, wrinkling his tiny nose. "Stinky."

I'm twelve centuries old and can still get embarrassed? Stunning how we continue to learn about ourselves.

"Sorry, Walt. I've been too busy to bathe."

He runs to his mother and hangs on her arm. She swings him lightly, absently, as if he's nothing more than a giggling handbag.

Maria nods to the desk. "You finished it?"

"How did you know?"

"I've never seen that book closed before. Well, did you?"

A warm feeling in my chest.

"Yes, I did."

Maria lets out a very unleaderlike squeal. With her free arm, she hugs me, kisses my cheek.

"Congratulations!"

My body stiffens. I can't help it.

"Oh, sorry," Maria says. She takes a step back. "I know you don't like to be touched. I just got so excited for you."

I nod. The moment isn't ruined, but it's become awkward.

Little kids can hold me, hug me, kiss me, but not adults. I don't feel comfortable around adults. The Birthday Children mostly leave me alone here. The Cherished have learned not to bother—I can't seem to exchange anything other than superficial pleasantries with them. The New People are the worst—they *bow* when they see me, treat me like I'm some kind of deity. I hate it.

"I'll make this fast," Maria says. "Three things."

That's her style. She communicates quickly and succinctly, then moves on.

When I stepped down as leader, Ramses didn't want the job. Neither did Theresa or Xander. Borjigin won our first election. He worked very hard and established several new policies that helped improve the ship, but in the end he wanted to focus on building machines and repairing long-broken parts of the *Xolotl*. After his one-year term as Yalani—that's what we call our overall leader—he didn't run for reelection.

Maria has won every election since.

She and Bishop are married. I have seen them together many times. They were happy before the birth of their son, and now are even more so. She is in her third one-year term as Yalani.

Maria visits me more often than anyone else. All decisions are hers to make, but she frequently asks for my counsel.

"Three things," I say. "Go ahead."

"First, Barkah is trying to set up a puppet government again, with him as king."

I'm reminded why I stay away from everyone: a ship full of children and their petty motivations.

"Is this the second time he's tried that?"

"Third," Maria says. "This time he's claiming that since the Springers are a minority, he should have a louder say in government, that their rights are being infringed upon."

"The Springers have *exactly* the same rights as everyone else." I tilt my head backward, indicating the turquoise-colored planet we've been approaching for months. "He's doing it because of that?"

"Of course," Maria says. "I think he's angling for a Springer-only homeland if the planet proves permanently habitable. Anyway, I need you in the next session of Congress to advise against any separationist movements. Will you help?"

I sigh, but I nod. While the Springers love Barkah, they realize Em is the main reason they're alive at all. The Springers don't really understand that I'm not her anymore, but since I look like her, I have significant sway over their general opinion.

"Second thing," Maria says. "You've insisted on keeping our history in that book alone. Now that it's complete, we need it properly recorded for future generations. I'm putting my foot down, Mattie—that book comes with me."

I glance at it. The leather-bound tome has been my only friend for the last four years. I don't want to let it go. But I'm not the leader, and it's not my choice to make.

I pick it up off the desk, feel its familiar weight.

Before I can change my mind, I hand it to Maria.

"Wonderful," she says. "Just one more debt the citizens of this ship owe you."

This is the most talking I've done in months. I feel my skin start to crawl. I just want to be by myself.

"And the third thing?"

"Someone is coming down right after I go up."

I sit in my desk chair.

"Please, Maria. I don't want to talk to anyone."

"Too bad, so sad," she says. "Four years of hiding here is enough, I don't give a damn how many lifetimes you've lived. Listen to me carefully—the person coming down made a choice. There was no coercion. None whatsoever. I conducted the interviews myself, repeatedly. So did Ramses and Theresa."

"What are you talking about?"

"You'll see." Maria kneels, holds the book in front of Walter. "This book is *very* important, honey. Can you hold it tight and not let go?"

A wide-eyed Walter nods solemnly, impressed with this new responsibility. He clutches the book tight to his chest.

Maria scoops the toddler up with one arm.

"Remember, this was a *choice*," she says to me, and she climbs the ladder.

I watch her go. Part of me wants her to stay, but it's useless. Conversation is always stilted, forced. I just have nothing in common with these children.

Maria enters the ship.

Someone else starts down the ladder. A man wearing a black toga. He moves with a certain grace, a certain dignity.

When he reaches the bottom, he turns to face me.

It's Victor Muller.

"Hello, Mattie," he says. "A pleasure to see you again."

Other than a few passing words in Congress when I'm required to speak out against particularly stupid ideas, I haven't spoken with Victor in years. He's matured—I can *sense* it more than see it.

"I'm very tired," I say. "What can I do for you?"

He's become more handsome since we left. There is a scar on his cheek he didn't have repaired. He has the face and body of someone seventeen or eighteen, with well-defined muscles and young skin. I know he and the other soldiers train for combat every day, teaching hundreds of New People and Springers in the ways of war. Victor, clearly, is in excellent shape.

"I thought we might talk," he says.

I rub my eyes. "That's the last thing I want, Victor. Whatever would we talk about?"

"Do you remember when I volunteered to join Matilda's mutiny?"

I stare at him, feel my eyes narrow.

"I do remember. Who told you about it?"

"I didn't need anyone to tell me about it. I was there."

"Don't be ridiculous. That was four hundred years ago, you weren't even . . ."

He can't remember that. He wasn't there . . . his progenitor was.

The young man before me smiles.

"Please, call me *Vic* from now on. *Victor* was someone else. We merged. We are one."

For the first time in years, I wish I had my spear. I stand up, so suddenly filled with rage I'm shaking.

"How could you do that to him? He was just a boy!"

"A boy who *chose* it," he says. "Didn't Maria tell you?"

She did. Her "interviews" . . . those were with Young Victor and Old Victor both.

"You . . . I mean . . . *he* . . . he *wanted* to be overwritten?"

"Such a harsh term," Victor says. "But yes, that part of me wanted it, perhaps even more than the old part did."

I feel a burst of excitement, of *hope*—someone I can talk to, someone who has been through what I've been through.

"But *why?*"

He reaches out slowly, takes my hand. I let him. For once, my skin does not crawl at the touch of someone else.

"Because Young Victor was in love with you," he says. "And while he never told you, so was Old Victor. And now, we both are."

I pull my hand away. I can't believe this is happening.

"You go through that process and you assume you can just come here and, what, that I'm *yours?*"

Victor—*Vic*—laughs.

"As if anyone could make Mattie Savage do anything she didn't want to do. I don't *assume* anything. I'm just a centuries-old man asking a centuries-old woman if she'd like to chat for a bit."

The way he and Em fought together on Omeyocan. The way he and Matilda fought together in the rebellion. Brave. Selfless.

Both versions of him.

I remember plunging the knife into Matilda's heart, her fury, her terror. But she was evil incarnate—she deserved it. Vic, the Vic I knew for centuries, did not.

"Old Victor helped us," I say. "He shouldn't have had to die that way."

Vic's smile widens.

"He didn't die. He's still alive."

It takes me a moment to process that.

"But the ritual," I say.

Vic shrugs. "The former young me and the former old me agreed there was no need for it. Everyone saw what happened to you, Mattie. When I . . . sorry, when *he* went to the X, he knew he would live on, as long as his body will allow. We have dinner together every night. We even started a book club."

We're all one people now—there's no need for barbaric executions. So obvious and such a simple decision to make, yet it never occurred to me this was possible.

It's nice to know that as old as I am, there can still be surprises.

Vic walks around the desk. He adjusts his black toga, sits on the desk's front left corner, and stares out at the blue planet.

"Speaking of books, Maria told me you just finished yours. Maybe that means you'd like to take a break. If you want me to leave, I will. But if you'd like to sit with me and talk, I'd like that."

The overwrite—perhaps now more accurately described as *fusing,* I suppose—carried risks. Young Victor knew the person he was would die in the process, cease to exist just as Em ceased to exist. He knew that. He did it anyway.

He did it . . . for *me.*

I shuffle more than walk around the desk. I sit on the front right corner.

"Yes, I'd like to talk," I say. "I'd like that very much."

ACKNOWLEDGMENTS

Scott would like to thank the following people for their research expertise:

- Dr. Joseph A. Albietz III, M.D.
- Chris Grall, MSG, U.S. Army Special Forces (Ret.)
- J.P. Harvey, Colonel, U.S. Air Force (Ret.)
- Dr. Nicole Gugliucci, Ph.D.
- A Kovacs
- Dr. Phil Plait, Ph.D.
- John Vizcarra

ABOUT THE AUTHOR

New York Times bestselling author SCOTT SIGLER is the author of sixteen novels, six novellas, and dozens of short stories. He is also the co-founder of Empty Set Entertainment, which publishes his YA Galactic Football League series. He lives in San Diego.

@scottsigler

scottsigler.com

Facebook.com/scottsigler

ABOUT THE TYPE

This book was set in Sabon, a typeface designed by the well-known German typographer Jan Tschichold (1902–74). Sabon's design is based upon the original letter forms of sixteenth-century French type designer Claude Garamond and was created specifically to be used for three sources: foundry type for hand composition, Linotype, and Monotype. Tschichold named his typeface for the famous Frankfurt typefounder Jacques Sabon (c. 1520–80).